Sideways

Sideways

Rex Pickett

LARGE PRINT

This large print edition published in 2005 by
RB Large Print
A division of Recorded Books
A Haights Cross Communications Company
270 Skipjack Road
Prince Frederick, MD 20678

Published by arrangement with St. Martin's Press

This book is a work of fiction. Names, characters, places, and incidents either are
products of the author's imagination or are used fictitiously. Any resemblance to
actual events or locales or persons, living or dead, is entirely coincidental.

Publisher's Cataloging In Publication Data
(Prepared by Donohue Group, Inc.)

Pickett, Rex.
  Sideways / Rex Pickett.

    p. (large print) ; cm.

  ISBN: 1-4193-5014-5

1. Automobile travel—Fiction. 2. Man-woman relationships—Fiction. 3. Male
friendship—Fiction. 4. Divorced men—Fiction. 5. Large type books.
6. California—Fiction. 7. Psychological fiction. 8. Adventure fiction.
9. Humorous fiction. I. Title.

PS3566.I316 S55 2005
813/.6

Printed in the United States of America

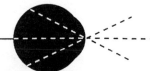

**This Large Print Book carries the
Seal of Approval of N.A.V.H.**

To Roy and Julian,
partners in wine

"We've gone on holiday by mistake."
—WITHNAIL, FROM *WITHNAIL AND I*

FRIDAY: UNCORKED

The sun poured bright parallelograms of mote-swirling light through the venetian blinds of my rundown, rent-controlled house in Santa Monica. I was moving frenetically from bedroom to living room packing for a road trip with my best friend, Jack Cole. We were headed for the Santa Ynez Valley and a week of wine tasting before he was to be married the following Sunday. Though I couldn't afford this impromptu excursion, I desperately needed to get out of L.A. The place was suffocating me, fueling paralyzing panic attacks that had been a chronic affliction of mine over the years.

The phone rang, but the number that materialized on my caller ID didn't register so I stood frozen over the answering machine, waiting.

"Miles, is Roman," my landlord began in his Transylvanian-sounding drawl. "It is the fifteenth of September and I still not receive rent. Every month we go through this. If I don't get check by tomorrow I have no choice but to begin eviction. I don't like this. You are my friend. I know you are starving writer. . . ."

1

I levered the volume on the answering machine to 0, the hair on my forearms tingling. The rest of Roman's exhortation I could recite from memory. He would warm up with how lenient he had been, then he would launch into a foaming-at-the-mouth diatribe about how my financial shortcomings were the cause of his elevated blood pressure and a host of other onuses that daily racked him on the property owner's cross. His jeremiads were worthy of Job and their intent was to make me feel guilty and scrape together the $850 in question.

I resumed packing, the call pecking away at the edges of my already frayed psyche. Into my travel-scarred suitcase I threw a couple of bleak-themed novels I knew I would never crack. For good measure I added *The Oxford Companion to Wine,* Jancis Robinson's brilliant and exhaustive tome on everything you ever wanted to know about the universe of wine. It was the perfect book to calm the nerves at three in the morning when you wake in an unfamiliar motel room in a cold sweat, trembling from excess. After all, Jack and I were journeying to wine country, and I wanted to have the one book that had supplied me with all the basics of my one undying passion—besides, of course, the unrepentant penning of two unpublished novels and scores of unproduced screenplays.

As I was about to shutter the house the phone rang a second time, jangling my nerves. I raced over to the caller ID, expecting it to be my disgruntled landlord again, amplifying on his first message with another warning salvo. But the number that came up on the display was a 212 area code so I lunged for the phone. "Hello," I answered breathlessly.

"Miles," sang a cheery woman's voice. "It's Evelyn, your favorite agent." She was the sixth in a long line of backstabbing sharks, but so far she seemed to be the rare exception: an agent who believed in me.

"Evelyn, what's up? You sound upbeat for a change." In fact, she had that uncharacteristic lilt in her voice that promised argosies, ships of fortune that would diminish the pain of the thirty-five rejection letters from the who's who of major publishing houses that I had arrayed on my living room walls: a festoon of failure, I proudly told everyone.

"Some *potentially* good news," Evelyn said. "Richard Davis at Conundrum liked your book."

My jaw dropped. The novel she was referring to had been shopped around New York for nearly a year now with no takers. There had been the first tier of submissions to the cream of the crop, when excitement was high and optimism exaggerated. Then there was the second tier: less prestigious houses, which meant less advance money, and considerably less budget for promotion once I got published, which I still assumed I would. The slow morphine drip continued as more rejection letters sluiced through Evelyn's New York office and were shunted to me in L.A. Bringing up the rear was the third tier: boutique houses on the periphery seeking a home run and a move into the second tier. Short of vanity presses and the Internet self-publishing venues, this was where Evelyn disembarked and moved on to the BBD—bigger and better deal. We were clinging to tattered ribbons and we both knew it.

"Great," I replied, almost not wanting to hear the qualifications for fear they would put a damper on my excitement.

"He's passing it to the other senior editors to read over the weekend. I'm expecting a decision toward the end of next week. Of course, he recommended some revisions."

"Of course," I replied. "A publishing deal would certainly have that galvanic effect on me."

Evelyn laughed heartily, the gallows laugh of a hard-working agent who wasn't getting any younger. "So, we're in pretty good shape," she said. "I've got my fingers crossed."

"Terrific," I replied, glancing at my watch. "I'm getting ready to take off for a little trip."

"Oh? Where?"

"Santa Ynez Valley. An hour north of Santa Barbara. The poor man's Napa/Sonoma. My friend Jack is getting married and we're going to go out in style. It's research for my next book," I added.

"Sounds like a blast," she said. "Are you writing anything new, Miles?"

"Well, um," I began haltingly. I glanced around at the rejection letters thumbtacked to my walls, their stinging words glaring reminders of why I had been unproductive recently. Of course, there

4

was also the divorce, the dwindling bank account, the renewed wave of panic attacks, the loss of my film agent to the St. Vitus's dance, and the sudden departure of a short-lived girlfriend who couldn't put up with my occupational moodiness. "I've got something brewing," I said finally. "Something epic."

"Well, keep writing," she encouraged. "And I'll call you when I hear something."

We signed off and I stood still for a moment, a hundred thoughts crisscrossing in my head. I had almost given up the book for dead—two years down the toilet and all the bad debts that backed up with it—but I was thrilled Evelyn had not. I made a mental note not to give up all hope in humankind.

I locked up my house, threw my suitcase into the back of my Toyota 4Runner, and headed off to the weekly Friday afternoon wine tasting at Epicurus, where I was to rendezvous with the incorrigibly late Jack.

Epicurus was a long railcar-shaped wine emporium wedged in between a mattress store and a spa that specialized in high colonics. Wine bottles were racked halfway up both walls and down the middle of the long rectangular space, arranged according to varietal and country of origin.

The familiar crowd was packed into the small cordoned-off tasting area, affectionately dubbed The Bullpen, in the rear of the shop. In recent years The Bullpen had been witness to many wild

Fridays after the owner had gone home, leaving the store entrusted to James, his English wine guru. Usually James would uncork bottle after bottle, recklessly cherry-picking the store's inventory in retaliation for what he referred to as his *insulting* salary. It was the place to be on Friday for the Westside wine cognoscenti.

This afternoon they were pouring Gary Farrell, a high-end vintner whose winery is smack in the middle of the Russian River Valley. Pinot Noir country. *My* grape. The one varietal that truly enchants me, both stills and steals my heart with its elusive loveliness and false promises of transcendence. I loved her, and I would continue to follow her siren call until my wallet—or liver, whichever came first—gave out.

There was a buzz in The Bullpen when I arrived. A few people called out hellos and waved as I squeezed into the small space and found a clean glass. Most of the regulars were already holding court in their customary positions, arms crooked with wineglasses held below their noses. They included: Carl, an electrician at Warner Brothers, a small roly-poly man with a thirst for Bordeaux and a private cellar stocked with some of France's finest (and the burst capillaries in his face to prove it); Jerry, a reptilian-faced, paunchy man in his forties, dentist by trade, oenophile by avocation, who used the Friday tastings as a way to meet prospective new paramours even though we all knew he was married; Eekoo, a wealthy Korean real

6

estate entrepreneur who boasted a temperature-controlled bedroom stacked floor to ceiling with the finest California Cabernets, Chardonnays, and Pinots, the highly allocated ones, the mythical bottles you don't find in wine stores. Eekoo's trademark was the varietal-specific Riedel stemware he lugged around in a wooden case from tasting to tasting. Then there was Malibu Jim, a slender, sallow-faced man in his fifties who sampled the wines, then typed in tasting notes on a laptop, research for a book he probably would never get around to writing. Recent newcomers, I noticed, were a pair of pleasantly plump office assistants who had discovered the best $5 party in the city and were fast becoming regulars. They didn't know much about wine, and they came reeking of perfume—a wine tasting no-no—but they were a load of laughs once they got a few tastes under their belts. And then there were the walk-ins, the one-timers, the curiosity seekers who heard the convivial banter in the back of the store, noticed wine being sampled, and thought it would be fun to join in. Sizing up the fresh dramatis personae, I became aware of three attractive women in their early thirties, huddled together, demarcating a proprietary space, conscious of the leering stares but determined to enjoy their afternoon outing.

"Miles," Carl called out, raising his glass, already flush in the face. He tended to arrive early and get a head start on the festivities. "Didn't think you were going to make it."

"Gary Farrell, are you kidding?" I said as I elbowed my way over to the lineup. Manning the bottles was a matronly woman with a pie-shaped face and a friendly but strained smile. As disembodied arms snaked in between jostling bodies she tried to monitor the amounts that were being poured. It usually began politely, then slowly deteriorated into a help-yourself-to-all-you-can-drink line of attack. We were still in the polite phase of the afternoon when I held out my glass to her.

"Would you like to begin with the Chardonnay?" she asked over the din of voices.

"Absolutely," I said.

She picked up an open bottle of the Farrell Sonoma and poured me a splash. I put my nose in the glass, inhaled deeply, and got a whiff of honeydew and underripe pears. On the palate the wine was indelicate, slightly oaky, very tropical-fruity, a little on the flabby side: a fairly typical California Chard for the Chard-swilling masses. I compared notes with Carl and he readily agreed.

As I waited for Jack, I edged my way nearer the three women who were making their first appearance. They were deep into the reds and I sensed they were getting ready to head for the hills.

"What do you think of the Farrells?" I asked the one in the middle, a pretty, dark-haired slip of a girl.

"Mm." She wrinkled her forehead. "I guess I

8

like the Merlot the best." Her pals concurred with her assessment, nodding and *mmm*-ing.

I grimaced. Merlot, a quintessential blending grape, when left to its own devices almost always—Pétrus notwithstanding—results in a bland, characterless wine. "What about the Pinots?" I asked, smiling what I hoped was a charming and knowing smile.

"I didn't like 'em." She formed her mouth into a tight little O trying to describe her displeasure with my favorite grape.

Disenchanted, I backed my way toward the lineup of bottles, sensing I had struck out. As the crowd shifted and reshifted in the cramped space, I quickly sampled the second Chard, a single-vineyard wine with a better balance of fruit and acidity and subtler oak overtones that imparted a slightly smoky, almost nutty taste.

"Excellent," I said to the wine rep, when she asked if I liked it. I rinsed my glass and held it back out. "Let's get serious."

She reached for the first Pinot and poured me a splash. It was Farrell's Sonoma standard, blended from a selection of vineyards. It gave off that unmistakable Pinot nose of cassis and black-berry, but it wasn't distinguished, drifting in the mouth like a rudderless boat. The second Pinot was a single-vineyard from the nearby storied Rochioli property. It had notes of cardamom and exotic berries, and it pinwheeled around on my palate, deliciously lingering. *Mm,* I thought to myself, rolling the wine around in my mouth, *this is more like it.*

I shuffled my way through the crush of bodies back to where the three neophytes were winding up with the Cabs, hoping for one last shot. I was beginning to feel a little high and it emboldened me to re-approach them.

"You don't like this Rochioli Pinot?" I asked.

The dark-headed one shook her head again.

"Really?" I sipped and took another spin around the block. "I think it's close to dazzling."

Jerry the dentist, face florid from having already traipsed through the lineup several times, butted in. "I don't think it's that dazzling," he contended, hoping to curry favor with women I didn't think would give him the time of day. They all smiled at him and I drifted away for a second and final time. Ten minutes later he had the dark-headed one buttonholed against the wall and—more appallingly—she seemed fascinated by his ineloquent winespeak.

Dispirited, I kept returning to the Rochioli as if to a trusted friend. As the rep poured me more, Carl sidled over to solicit my opinion. I barraged him with hyperbolic hosannas, reaching deep for the metaphors and the polysyllabics, which always made him chuckle.

"You're right," he said, after I had finished reeling off my lyrical account, the wine liberating my tongue to new heights of glibness. "Absolutely first-rate Pinot."

"How was Spain?" I asked.

"Excellent," he said. "Had a great time."

"Drink any good Riojas and Riberas?"

"Yeah, some really tasty ones." He winked, then filled me in about a big feast at a winery where they roasted lambs over flaming vine cuttings.

While listening to Carl's chronicle of his Spain trip, I bypassed the Merlot and reached for the Zin, not wanting the rep to think I was hogging the Pinot. I refilled Carl with a scandalously healthy splash that drew an admonitory stare from the rep. We clinked glasses and laughed, delighting in our naughtiness.

Then Carl bent close to my ear and whispered, "Woman in the black shirt and blond hair is checking you out."

I shot a furtive glance in the direction Carl was indicating. One of the dark-headed one's friends was not just looking at me, but smiling. I didn't know if she was flirting or had simply discovered the slippery pleasures of Pinot at my urging.

"They don't like the Rochioli," I told Carl. "I can't date a woman who doesn't like Pinot. That's like getting involved with someone who's disgusted by oral sex."

Carl laughed. "How long's it been since you've had a girlfriend?"

"I can't remember. A while." I sipped the Zin. It was spicy and full-bodied, but it didn't transport me. "But it's been a welcome break. I can feel the creative juices starting to flow again."

Carl screwed his face up in disbelief. Suffering months without sex was unimaginable to him. Indiscriminate in his own tastes, he often came to the Friday tastings accompanied by the lees of womankind. "Maybe it's time to reevaluate the pleasures of Merlot," Carl suggested, tipping his head toward our three novices.

"I'm not going to journey from the sublime to the pedestrian for a phone number," I said, shaking my head. "What's the deal with Jerry?" I noticed that the dentist was still locked in conversation with the dark-headed one.

"Flatters them, doesn't put them down for not liking Pinot," Carl affectionately criticized me.

"Imagine getting a root canal from that guy." I affectedly staggered in place, imitating a drunk. "He's probably one of those drill-and-fillers who anesthetizes his patients and then feels them up in the chair."

Carl laughed, goading me on. We loved the mordant humor that the combination of wine and gossip evoked in both of us.

Eekoo edged into our cabal, his Riedel Sommeliers glass cradled in his hand like the Hope Diamond. "What do you think of the Farrells?" he said, his speech hobbled by the series of tasting events he had strung together beginning early in the day.

"Rochioli is nice," I said.

He sipped the wine from his bulbous stemware and worked it professionally around in his mouth. "Not as good as the '99 Kistler."

Carl and I rolled our eyes at the same time. Of course, nobody but Eekoo could find—let alone, afford—the '99 Kistler, so the reference was a no-win one-upmanship, but we humorously tolerated his elitism all the same.

"Heard you were taking a little trip," Eekoo said to me, blinking like a gargoyle through the thick lenses of his glasses.

"My friend Jack's getting married a week from Sunday. We're going to do a little Santa Ynez wine tour."

"Ah," Eekoo said, smiling benignly as if recalling fond memories of just such a trip.

"Where *is* Jack?" Carl suddenly wondered.

I glanced at my watch. "Should be here pretty soon. You know Jack, he's always late."

"I miss that guy. Haven't seen him here in quite a while."

"His fiancée is holding him to the straight and narrow. That's what happens when you get into a *real* relationship."

Carl tilted his head back and laughed. Eekoo shot his arm between us in pursuit of one of the bottles, but his aim was off and he sent the Sonoma Pinot crashing to the cement floor. The explosion of glass produced a collective hush for a moment, but the silence was quickly swamped by a chorus of amiable catcalls. The party was in full swing now and the wine rep looked anxious, her eyes darting warily about the swelling, unmanageable crowd.

13

At the sound of shattering glass, Graham, the balding, barrel-chested proprietor, broke away from the cash register and strode toward us. "You animals," he boomed, squatting down to help the rep clean up the mess. It wasn't the first time and he was armed and ready with dustpan and brush.

"We've almost killed the Rochioli Pinot," I said. "Open another bottle."

Graham rose on the other side of the partition. He had a large, bowling-ball-shaped face created exclusively to intimidate. "This is a tasting, Miles, not a public service."

"Without us, you'd be in Chapter 11."

"If you didn't get so sideways on Fridays you might be on the last chapter of that novel of yours."

I smiled and pointed my finger at him. Touché. He returned the gesture.

"Come on. Open another bottle," I urged.

"Yeah," Carl said. "More people are coming."

Graham shook his head in mock disgust. He didn't like the Friday tastings, but he tolerated them because they were good for business. At their conclusion, the oenophiles, their wallets liberated in direct proportion to the amount of wine they had consumed, were usually in the mood to carry on elsewhere and would ring up extravagant purchases, sometimes solely to impress one another.

As Graham finished sweeping up the broken glass, arms reached indiscriminately for the remaining bottles. The Farrell rep, realizing that she had lost control, quickly filled a glass of the

Rochioli for herself and hoarded it in her corner. Graham, aspiring to be the wine mensch of Santa Monica, waved the dustpan theatrically and said in defeat, "Open another Rochioli, Carol."

The rep looked stricken for a moment, but she reluctantly reached down and unzipped her wine satchel and emerged with a second bottle. Raucous, but genial, cheers welcomed the sound of its uncorking. Glasses were refreshed all around and the *ooh*-ing and *aah*-ing started all over again.

Soon, I felt a warm glow spread through me. Voices overlapped and muddled into one another. As evening crept up on us, the light grew soft and the faces shadowed. Then, as if entering through the backdoor of a dream, Dani, a statuesque Aussie with a runner's physique—graphic designer by profession—came bounding down the back stairs, her braless breasts rising and falling inside a tight, midriff-revealing T-shirt. She circled into The Bullpen, a smile on her ruddy, sunburned face, eager to sample.

"Dani," I called out, happy to see my favorite regular.

"Miles!" She shoehorned her way through the throng and greeted me with a tight hug. With so much woman pressed against me, I nearly fainted. When she finally released me I had the presence of mind to right a clean glass and fill it half full of the second Chardonnay from a new, cold bottle the rep had also uncorked.

"I'm taking you right to the Allen Vineyard. None of this mediocre wine for you," I said.

"Oh, you are, are you?" she said, cocking her head coquettishly. She accepted the glass, took a sip, closed her eyes gently for a moment, and savored the wine. "Thanks, Miles. I needed that."

"My pleasure."

Carl, inebriated enough now to test the waters, had drifted over and was making small talk with the blond friend of the dark-headed one who was, judging by her expression, apparently in the process of getting the pants charmed off her by Jerry. Occasionally she even *laughed* at what the dentist was saying. I turned away. A wobbly Eekoo was staring bleary-eyed over Malibu Jim's shoulder at his laptop, critiquing his wine-tasting notes, stabbing a finger—which Jim kept shooing away—at his screen. The Farrell rep, having long since worn out her function as a pourer and explicator of Gary's winemaking methodologies, retreated deeper into her corner with a second—full (!)—glass of the Rochioli, resigned now to the pleasurable fact that she might as well get looped with the rest of us. The Bullpen had, in its inimitable way, collectively reduced our zeitgeist to a tribal low common denominator.

I leaned into Dani's apple red face. "Do you think it's unreasonable not to want to date anyone who doesn't like Pinot? It's the burning question for me this afternoon."

"Who's that?" Dani asked, her antennae tuned

16

now to the horde in The Bullpen. She grabbed a fistful of my shirt and maneuvered me over to the bottles so we wouldn't have to keep reaching through the crowd to refresh our glasses.

"Dark-haired one over there talking to Jerry," I said, nodding in their direction.

Dani squinted and glanced over my shoulder. She shrugged. "You're too critical, Miles."

"Someone's got to have standards around here."

She laughed and we touched glasses. "Where's Jack?"

"Should be here any minute." I reflexively checked my watch. An hour had disappeared like the flare of a match. *Have to slow down*, I cautioned myself.

"Are you leaving from here?" Dani asked. Her voice sounded a little like it was trying to reach me from underwater.

"Yeah. I'm getting an early start." I raised my glass to the impending trip, the promising news from my agent, and the feeling of warmth that had by now blanketed me. "I'm taking a week off and doing nothing but tasting wines and breathing fresh air."

"Sounds like fun. Wish I could come."

"When are you and Roger getting married?" I asked, referring to her handsome investment banker fiancé.

"This December."

"Really? That's great." I tried to offer my congratulations with conviction, but even I could

17

faintly make out a tinge of disappointment in my voice. Maybe I was infatuated with Dani because the only times I ever interacted with her were when I had a wine buzz going, but even on paper she was something special: wine lover, athlete, gourmet cook; what more could a guy want?

"Yeah," she was saying, her words coming back into my consciousness, "we're going to take the plunge." Without looking, she reached around for more of the Rochioli and topped both of us off, eliciting a snort of disdain from the beleaguered rep. We ignored her and carried on.

"Like this Pinot, Dani?"

"Mm hm." Dani made a face that underscored her pleasure. Her attention was drawn over my shoulder again. "Some woman keeps looking over here."

"Really?" I didn't bother to look. "Probably because she thinks I'm with you, her interest has rekindled." I stole a quick glance at the blonde Carl was chatting up. "Carl'll try to seduce her with his '97 Caymus Special Selection. If that doesn't get her excited, he'll go deep and offer to pop one of his *premiers crus* Bordeaux."

Dani threw back her head of short auburn hair and laughed hard. "So, what's happening with your novel?"

"Thirty-five rejections and counting. They just keep pouring in."

"No," Dani empathized.

"But thirty-six might be the charm. Just spoke

to my agent. Editor at some small publishing house expressed serious interest. He's passing it upstairs to the button-pushers as we drink."

"I want to read it," Dani insisted, a weekly refrain she never followed up on.

"She's got a good feeling this time," I said.

Dani bent closer to me until our faces were almost touching. Her breath smelled piquantly of wine and stinky French cheeses. I misinterpreted her gesture and turned my mouth toward hers for the kiss that I delusively thought she was offering.

"He's going for the kill," she whispered instead, thwarting me mid-kiss.

I threw a backward glance and glimpsed Jerry the dentist brushing the dark-headed woman's hair back off her forehead and gazing into her eyes in a way that could only be described as adoringly. Next to them, roly-poly Carl appeared to be making headway with her blond cohort. I flashed to a vision of a frolicking foursome, whisked off to Carl's nearby condo to partake of his small, but well-stocked, cellar. As if it hadn't been clear already, now it was a fait accompli that I was out of the picture. No doubt Jerry had already informed his mark that I was a chronically unemployed writer, which was usually about all it took to get desirable women to steer clear of me at all costs. That was one of the liabilities of getting hammered every Friday and unburdening yourself on people you thought were your friends. The personal revelations always came back to haunt you.

I turned back to Dani, shaking my head scornfully. "Amount of wine those guys have been drinking, I doubt either of them could get an erection."

Dani poured off more of the Rochioli, filling our small tasting glasses to the rim, before the others could get their mitts on it. As the tastings drew to a close, and the bottles grew depleted, selfishness became the common mantra of the afternoon.

"I'm happy for you and Roger," I heard myself say. "But if it doesn't work out, I want you to call me, okay?"

Dani dipped her head to one side and smiled.

"I'm serious," I blundered on, aware that I was spewing drunken nonsense, feeling that cavernous loneliness welling up in me again but oblivious of the consequences and determined to hurtle forward with abandon.

Dani placed a sympathetic hand on my shoulder. Then, unexpectedly, she planted her lips on mine and held them there for what seemed like an eternity. I felt her tongue hot and moist inside my mouth. It wasn't an affectionate kiss, but rather a showy display to flout propriety and draw attention.

From behind me, a chorus of rowdy, counterfeit hoorays erupted. On cue, Dani unstuck herself and chased the kiss with the last of her Rochioli. In one movement, she reached indiscriminately into the field of dead bottles to grab one that had anything sloshing around on the bottom. She fished out the Allen Chard, veering recklessly backward in the order—my girl! I held out my glass and she topped me off. I was light-headed from the wine, the unexpected kiss, and the clamor of laughter and indistinct voices. Our eyes sank into each other for a brief moment. I had a fantasy of Dani dragging me across the street to her apartment and granting me a sympathy pop while her fiancé, leaving her unattended on yet another lonely weekend, jetted around the globe. But looking into each other's bloodshot eyes, I knew it was a rotten idea, and I could tell she knew it, too, and we quickly dispelled it with a pair of awkward laughs.

I was eager for Jack to arrive and call it a tasting when, out of nowhere, Jerry the cavity filler directed something at me he probably intended as a harmless joke. I didn't exactly catch all of it, what with the riot of competing voices and my diminishing auditory faculties, but I was in a mood just askew enough, inspired by the swell of laughter that followed his remark, to whirl around and retort: "Where's your wife this week, Jerry? We miss her."

His goofy, mirthful face instantly imploded into a bilious scowl. The dark-haired woman, whose head he'd been filling with more than porcelain, broke into an aghast hand-to-the-mouth-oh-my-God! expression. She mouthed something to the dentist while simultaneously starting to back away.

21

Out of earshot one could reasonably assume it was a follow-up to my derogatory comment. Gesticulating a little wildly and visibly flustered, Jerry was clearly trying to explain away my remark. He held up his left hand to show her he didn't wear a wedding ring, but that was hardly convincing to a smart woman at a wine tasting where lies flowed freer than Chardonnay.

A few moments later, the three newcomers regrouped and fled The Bullpen, vowing no doubt never to return. Carl held up two empty arms to me as if he had fumbled a pass in the end zone, an innocent victim of collateral damage. Next to me, Dani, who maintained a proprietary death grip on the Chard—one of the only bottles with any wine remaining—was bent double, poleaxed with laughter.

Jerry the dentist, ditched and publicly humiliated, stormed out of The Bullpen into the main part of the store where he paced the Italian section and glowered at the Brunellos. Our eyes locked for a quick, spiteful moment. He straightened his middle finger and shook it in and out in front of his scowling face. That ignited me.

"Hey, Jerry," I called out, cupping my free hand around the corner of my mouth. "Get a bottle of the Muscadet, it'll pair perfectly with your wife's pussy!"

The Bullpen exploded into laughter. The mood was once again giddy and arms crisscrossed the ledge to check for dregs in the few remaining bottles. The Farrell rep quailed in her corner and sipped her wine, resigned to the carnage. The two tittering office assistants, totally liquored up, bumped hips to a tune only they heard.

I turned away to refresh myself with more wine when the dentist charged into The Bullpen and shoved me backward. I lost my balance and a half glass (damn!) of the Chard went flying.

"Hey, hey," I heard Dani soothe as though she were calling from another room. I was semiafraid for the dentist that Dani was going to physically come to my assistance. She owned a brown belt in martial arts and would have kicked his ass, only adding to Jerry's humiliation.

"That wasn't funny," Jerry screamed, his face malignantly red with bile and tannin.

"It's because of lecherous jerks like you that more single women don't come to these tastings," I shot back.

Jerry was the type in whom alcohol raises the level of violence. He rushed at me and wrapped his arms around my waist like some junior varsity wrestler and attempted to take me to the floor. The office assistants scrambled for their purses. Malibu Jim swiftly folded up his laptop and skulked off like a garter snake. Eekoo, in full panic mode, retrieved his wooden case of handblown Riedels and clutched it protectively to his chest. Carl darted over to save the precious few bottles, now teetering on the narrow ledge where they had once stood pristinely unopened. Graham angrily disengaged himself from a customer and rumbled into view.

As I grappled with the hysterical dentist, Dani, in an inspired move I don't think Gary Farrell had in mind when he vinified his '99 bottling, hoisted the silver spit bucket aloft—full from a long afternoon of tasting—and upended it on Jerry's head.

A fetid mixture of wine and cheese-infused saliva splattered everywhere. Jerking erect, Jerry flailed at his face, his arms scissoring back and forth like windshield wipers gone berserk.

"Try the Meritage, Jerry," I said, getting to my feet. "Fruit forward and drinkable now!"

Graham elbowed his way into The Bullpen. "All right, everybody, the tasting's over."

A scowling Jerry, his polo shirt stained with wine, started to advance on me again, but the heftier Graham stepped in between us. "Come on, Jerry," Graham warned. "I don't want to have to ban you from coming here."

Jerry brandished his middle finger at me again as Graham coaxed him out of the tasting area.

The buzz in The Bullpen gradually quieted. Dani, Carl, and I made small talk as the Farrell rep started to gather up her brochures and tote bags. A moment later, as if on cue, Jack materialized at the top of the back stairs, haloed by the late-afternoon sun. He was a tall, ursine man with movie-star good looks, fashionably unshaven, with a mop of sandy brown hair that shot in all directions on his large head. He was attired in his trademark black bowler's shirt with JACK embroidered in white lettering over the pocket, a pair of colorful Hawaiian shorts, and matching flip-flops.

"Miles," he declared.

"Jack! You made it!"

Jack was outsized in every way. When he broke into laughter, it rattled the shackles of your unconscious and demanded that you join in. When he walked into a movie theater he swallowed the entire aisle. He was the guy who got hired on the spot because of his infectious charisma, the guy who didn't have to work to get the girl. Unlike me, any weaknesses he had were secreted and any negativity painted over with broad strokes of optimism. Truth for Jack was what he could touch and smell and taste at any given moment. Self-reflection was generally too deep for him. He was a meat eater, a problem solver, a spirit lifter after a tough day, the guy everyone would want to rub shoulders with in a foxhole while mortars rained down. He seemed an unlikely candidate for marriage. Given his personality and looks, opportunities for long nights with the opposite sex were limitless, and another man not so endowed would wonder why Jack wouldn't want to live the Casanova life until his privates gave out. But Jack had a sentimental side, too, and I could—if I tried hard enough—envision him with a brood of children, sprawled in a La-Z-Boy with a six-pack on ice, spinning anecdotes about his colorful past.

Jack came down the stairs and wheeled into The Bullpen with his familiar swagger, which always lightened the mood instantly. He greeted Dani with a devouring hug, slapped Carl heartily on the shoulder, then slung an arm around me and poured himself what was left of the Zin, indiscriminate as always about his choice of quaff as long as it was red as blood and potently alcoholic.

A few minutes later everyone was laughing again. Graham returned, having successfully shooed Jerry out of his store.

Jack was getting up to speed on the melee. "The guy's married," I was explaining, "and he knew I was hitting on her."

Jack looked at me dismissively. "You overreacted, Miles."

"I made a little joke and the fucker got physical," I said.

"So what's the problem between you and Jerry?" Graham asked.

"I'll tell you my problem. A couple of weeks ago I brought a date here. He chats her up. That's cool—I know she's not going to go for him. Middle of the week he tracks her down on the set of a film she's working on, flatters her with a load of poppycock, then asks her out."

"What's wrong with that?" Graham said.

"What's *wrong* with *that?*" I echoed. "The guy tried to do an end run around. The woman thinks I hang out with creeps. You ought to ban him from these tastings."

Graham just screwed up his face in response.

Jack, bored with the argument, picked up one of the remaining bottles, but only managed a few dribbles of wine when he upended it. "Hey, Graham. How about opening another bottle? I need a glass for the road. Miles and I are officially on vacation."

"Where're you going?"

"Santa Ynez Valley," I answered. "Do the winery tour, then stuff Jack in the monkey suit and get him hitched a week from Sunday."

"It's a little bachelor week blowout," Jack elaborated. "Miles is going to educate me on wines and I'm going to educate him on life."

"Someone should call the cops," Graham said. Everyone laughed. "All right," he said. "What're you guys in the mood for?"

"Let's sample some champagne," I said. "Get in the matrimonial mode."

Graham beetled his brow and thought for a moment. Then he slapped his thigh. "I've got an idea." He strode upstairs, where he kept his private stash, and reappeared a minute later with a cold bottle of '92 Byron sparkling wine.

I set four clean glasses on the terrazzo ledge. Graham expertly uncorked the bottle and poured them foaming half full. We all toasted and sampled. It had the beautiful gold color of an aged champagne, appropriately yeasty and rich on the palate.

"What do you think?" Graham asked.

"Luscious," I remarked, taking another sip. "I didn't know Byron made a sparkling wine."

"Hundred percent Pinot Noir," Graham said. "I figured since you guys are doing Santa Ynez and Miles is a Pinot freak, this would be right up your alley."

"Why do you call it a sparkling wine and not champagne?" Jack asked.

"The term 'champagne' is trademarked by the French, and if it's not from the Champagne region of France, then it can't be called champagne—at least not on the label," I explained. "But because I'm sick of the French and their proprietary ways, Spumanti, Cava, California sparkling, they're all champagne to me. Right, Graham?"

"Whatever you say, Miles."

Jack nodded thoughtfully. "I'll remember that."

"I've only got one case left," Graham said. "They don't make it anymore. Two forty a case."

I looked at Jack with widened eyes and nodded vigorous approval.

"All right, we'll take it," Jack said.

Dani drained her glass. "I've got to be going. Roger's supposed to call."

"No, come with us," I said. "Roger won't mind. Take a week off."

Dani wagged a finger at us. "You two guys in the wine country for a week. Sounds like a hen's night out. Bye." She waved as she made her way out of The Bullpen. "Thanks for the champers." And then she was gone, leaving a rectangle of harsh orange sunlight in her wake.

Jack shook his head in an exaggerated manner. "Man, that chick's got it going on. Would I ever love to strap her on."

"Hey, don't talk about Dani like that. She's a good girl," I said.

"Yeah, right," Jack said, laughing. "Good to the *bone*."

"Hey, I saw your ex in here the other day," Graham said, referring to Victoria, the woman I had been married to for eight years. I hadn't seen or talked to her in some months.

"Oh, yeah?" I said, my mood changing abruptly. "What was she doing on the West Side?"

"Came over to fuck me," Graham replied, deadpan.

"Yeah, right. She'd remarry *me* before she'd mount you. Fucking goat."

Graham and Jack both laughed.

"Was she with anyone?" I probed.

"Yeah, some guy I've never seen before. Tall, good-looking, well dressed. Pretty much your opposite."

"Hah, hah. What was she buying?"

"Case of Krug."

"Oh, yeah?" I said, eyes widening. "What was the occasion?"

Graham started to respond, but abruptly halted midsentence, his eyes darting furtively over my shoulder in the vicinity of Jack.

I turned quickly and snatched a brief glimpse

of Jack raking his hand through his mop of hair as if he had just short-circuited a gesture to Graham behind my back.

Getting the message, I said, "Okay, okay, I'm over it, all right? I'm a very happily single man. A glass of wine, a crusty piece of baguette, a good book, and I'm fine."

Jack and Graham exchanged smirks, and refrained from digging the needle in any deeper. It had been over a year since the divorce, and I had to admit I missed the little things that marriage provided, the routines that kept my life in check and prevented me from going off the deep end.

"All right," Jack said, sensing the seismic pitch in my mood. "This place is dead. Let's get on the road."

We dispatched Graham upstairs to fetch the case of Byron. For good measure, we augmented the purchase with a case of Veuve Clicquot. We said our good-byes to Graham and Carl and then headed out to the parking lot, each with a case weighing down our arms. We piled them into the back of my 4Runner, the vehicle we had designated for the trip. I started automatically for the driver's side, but Jack grabbed hold of my shirt collar and yanked me around.

"Whoa, whoa, whoa, where're you going? I'm driving, Homes."

"What?"

"I don't want to spend the first night bailing you out of the tank."

"Give me a break. I've hardly wet my whistle."

Jack exploded into laughter. "You're sideways, brother. Scuffling with Jerry, asking Dani to come with us. Goodness gracious."

"What's wrong with asking Dani to come with us?"

"Give me the keys, Miles." Jack extended his hand and cocked his head to the side. Chastened, I surrendered the keys, then circled around to the passenger side and climbed in.

Jack fired up my 4Runner, turned onto Seventh Street and headed north. I rolled down my window, poked out my head, and let it loll on my arm. It was an unseasonably warm evening. The sky was an uncursed expanse of deepening blue and the air was pungent with the smell of the ocean. We cruised through ritzy Brentwood, whose sprawling, tree-shaded homes depressingly reminded me of my station in life, then turned on to San Vicente Boulevard. My gaze followed the wide grass median, where entertainment people jogged back and forth to maintain their ageless physiques and vent their frustrations with the movie business. It fled past me in a blissful wine-hazy blur.

On Sunset Boulevard, we forded the overpass and looped onto the 405 North. The freeway was thick with weekenders heading off to B&B's in Santa Barbara and other exclusive sybaritic hideaways north. We stayed in the slow-moving river of vehicles until we splintered off onto the 101 cloverleaf and made our way west. The sun was lowering in the sky, obscured by mist and smog. Its waning rays cast a harsh reflection on the mirrored and tinted fenestration of the city without end and beat mercilessly through our windshield with an angry, crimson ferocity. The mention of Victoria at Epicurus had dampened my usual post-tasting loquaciousness.

"You've got to wash this windshield," Jack said.

"I haven't had time. I've got other things on my mind."

Jack turned on the wipers and squirted cleaner fluid on the windshield. For a moment we were blinded by the water-smeared dirt and the blazing low-horizon sun. In those few blinding seconds, the traffic in front of us had slowed and Jack, recovering his field of vision, slammed on the brakes and angled sharply into the emergency lane to avoid a pileup.

"Jesus, Jack," I said, rattled. "Jesus."

"Relax," he said, starting up again. "I got it under control. Think if *you'd* been driving."

I shot him a reproving look, still upset about the scuffle with the dentist, the dark-headed woman's apparent lack of interest in me, the mention of Victoria being sighted at Epicurus by foul-mouthed Graham, my landlord's threatening words, and the beautiful buzz that was now diminishing.

"So, did you talk to your agent?" Jack asked, trying to kindle a conversation.

"Yeah. Evidently, there's a flicker of interest from a publisher I've never heard of. Well, maybe more than a flicker. In fact, you'd be shocked to learn that I'm vaguely hopeful for once."

Jack's face relaxed and he broke into a smile. "Good. When will you know?"

"End of next week. You get married, I get a publishing deal. Life is sweet," I said sarcastically.

"Well, you deserve something good to happen."

I smiled and squinted through the sun at the road ahead. Jack and I had collaborated on an independent film more than five years ago. I had written it and he had starred in it and directed it. It played the festival circuit but didn't get a distribution deal. We lost our own and our backers' investment. Jack, a successful character actor, had parlayed the effort into a succession of acting and directing jobs for various TV shows—artistically unfulfilling, but comfortingly income-producing. He had met Barbara—or Babs, as he called her—a costumer, on one of those gigs and fallen for her. Their relationship evolved in fits and starts, marred by infidelities and recriminations and reconciliations on both of their parts. But, eventually, they arrived at the conclusion that living apart was more painful than the prospect of being married, so they decided to give it a shot. Given their contentious history, I didn't exactly understand their wanting to tie the knot. But they were, and now we were on the road to the wedding, the soon-to-be tamed groom and I, his dissolute, novelist manqué, best man.

The traffic thinned as we continued up the 101

bound for Santa Barbara, the highway ribboning out in front of us with the promise of fun and adventure. The sun had dipped below the edge of the horizon and the sky was growing violet. Headlights started to snap on and the surrounding landscape broke out in a burning neon-lit iridescence, bringing to life a traveling city of light.

"Hold the wheel a sec," Jack said. I grabbed the wheel with my left hand and kept us on course as Jack reached behind the seat and rummaged around in his duffel bag. A moment later he produced a bottle of wine. He handed it to me proudly as he reclaimed control of the wheel.

I held the bottle up and my eyes widened when I saw the label: Chateau Latour—1982. "Where'd you steal this?"

"It was a gift from the lead on the show I'm directing. She gave one each to the entire staff. Is it any good?"

"Is it any *good*? It's a fucking '82 Latour. One of the great vintages of the last fifty years, from one of only six *grands crus* chateaus in Bordeaux, is it any *good*? The *Wine Advocate* rates it a hundred points. And it's drinking beautifully right now, I understand—of course how would I know, right?"

"Open it up," Jack said, unimpressed.

I turned to him with an openmouthed expression of shock. "Are you joking? This wine will get angry if you don't open it in a dark, quiet room, decant it and pour it into proper stemware, and pair it with a slab of very rare prime rib. It might spit in your face at such inadvertent contempt of its greatness. Andrea Immer would burst an aneurysm."

"Who's Andrea Immer?"

"Wine guru I'm besotted with. Of course I've only met her on TV."

"You and a million other wine geeks, probably," Jack jested.

"When my book gets published I'll be able to afford the rare Burgundies to romance her."

Jack laughed. "Well, then open up a bottle of that Byron bubbly. I've got a mighty thirst that needs slaking."

"On the freeway?"

"Fuck yes on the freeway."

I clambered into the back and slipped a bottle out of one of the cases.

"There should be a couple of glasses back there," Jack said.

I found two flutes, uncorked the Byron, filled them to overflowing and handed one to Jack. "It's warm."

"Who cares?" He held his glass back to me and we clinked. "Here's to a great week."

"I hope so," I said.

"It will be," Jack promised.

I stretched out in the back and sipped the Byron. "What do you think of this?" I asked.

"I like it," Jack said. "If it's a hundred percent Pinot, how come it's not a rosé?"

"Jesus, Jackson, don't ask questions like that up

in the wine country. They're going to think you're a fucking philistine."

"Just tell me, wiseass."

"The juice is free run. Color comes from the skin. There's no skin contact in the fermentation, i.e., no color."

"I'll try to remember that," Jack said. "Damn, it's delicious, though." He drained his glass and reached it around for a refill. I obliged.

"We've got to make a quick stop in Montecito," I announced.

"Montecito? What the fuck for?"

"My mother's."

"Your mother's? I didn't know you had a mother," he cracked.

"It's her birthday today."

"It's your mother's birthday today?"

"Yeah. That's what I just said. It's her birthday, and it would be remiss of me to drive right past her house, she being recently widowed and all and probably all alone on this special occasion, and not wish her a happy birthday."

Jack softened. "Did you get her a present at least?"

"I'll give her a bottle of the Veuve. She likes champagne."

"That's not a birthday present for your mother. Jesus, Miles. Didn't your parents teach you any manners?"

"I can't afford a real gift, okay? So don't rub it in."

36

"It's going to be late when we get to Santa Ynez."

"I know. I know."

We continued west on 101, as the sky darkened to night. On our left, the Pacific glittered like crumpled tin foil under a waxing pale yellow moon. Approaching the eastern end of Santa Barbara, I directed Jack to an off-ramp that took us up into the hills of Montecito, an affluent bedroom community. In the commercial district, Jack searched around for a florist, grousing that it wasn't right to show up for my mother's birthday without flowers. He finally found a small corner shop, its entrance overflowing with flowers, parked the car in a loading zone, and marched in without me. Inside the brightly lit shop I watched Jack asking advice of a middle-aged man with a bushy moustache. My thoughts drifted desultorily to mostly unpleasant topics.

A moment later, Jack returned carrying a dozen long-stemmed yellow roses swaddled in green wax paper. He thrust them at me. "Here," he said. "Tell her you love her." He started up the car and slipped it into drive. "After all, she gave birth to you."

"I'm supposed to thank her for that?" I deadpanned.

Jack merged back into traffic. "You're dyed-in-the-wool, brother. If you met Mr. Happiness he'd fold his tent and pack it in."

"Mr. Happiness is an illusion created by pharmaceutical companies."

Jack laughed, nearly losing it on a hairpin turn.

My mother lived a comfortable life in a small two-bedroom house on a terraced street that commanded a panoramic view of the ocean. The beautiful vista didn't much matter to her anymore: after my father died of a stroke she hardly ventured outside at all. She no longer drove and I suspected that some weeks her only human contact was with various delivery boys who brought her food and booze and medications. She was financially comfortable—my father had done well leasing laundry equipment to apartment complexes and saved like a miser—but it didn't seem like she had a whole lot to live for except for her dog and her martinis.

I was clutching the dozen roses and Jack had a bottle each of the Veuve and the Byron bubblies when my mother answered the door dressed in a nightie. She had once been a beautiful woman, vaguely reminiscent of Ingrid Bergman, but age and drink and loneliness had conspired to make her appearance a little frightening with her Bride of Frankenstein hairdo, pallid complexion, and rheumy eyes that didn't move in tandem. It was only 7:30 when we showed up at her doorstep, but she was already a little sloppy, tottering in her nightgown and furry mules, and it took her a couple of seconds to recognize her only son.

"Mom. Happy Birthday!" I handed over the roses.

The flowers were almost too cumbersome for

her and she pressed them clumsily to her chest. "Oh, they're so beautiful, Miles," she sang in a lilting voice. "Thank you." She looked over and focused on Jack. "And champagne."

"Veuve Clicquot," I said. "Your favorite."

"Oh, this is such a nice surprise. I didn't think you were going to come."

"I told you I was, Mom."

"And I can't remember you ever giving me flowers before."

Jack sneaked one of his disapproving looks at me and shook his head in a tight motion. The excitement of new voices—any voices—startled my mother's Yorkie into a yapping frenzy.

"Snapper, you be quiet," my mother scolded her rambunctious pet, having long ago fully anthropomorphized the little devil. He was thrilled to have company and was jumping up and down and turning in manic little circles. He probably hadn't seen other people in weeks and was going crazy enduring my mother's boozy soliloquies.

"Mom, this is Jack. He's the one I told you was getting married."

"How do you do, Mrs. Raymond?" Jack came forward and greeted her. "And Happy Birthday." He gave her a peck on the cheek.

"Oh, call me Phyllis, please, you make me sound so darn old." She pushed the door open and stepped aside. "Come on in." Snapper tilted his head up and barked once. She looked down and shook a finger at him. "Now, you be quiet. Go get your *comida*." Snapper scampered away, barking up a storm.

We followed my mother inside. She moved dreamily as if she were a somnambulist, gliding along on her slippered feet. I hadn't been to visit in a while, but her house had remained unchanged. The living room was sparsely furnished and impeccably neat. Her hardwood floors were so heavily waxed that her dog slid five feet every time he tried to apply the brakes. Along the darkened hallway leading into the kitchen I found the same pictures and mementos, representing a kind of loose chronology of the Raymond family, crowding the pastel-colored walls.

As my mother disappeared around the corner into the kitchen, Jack and I lingered over some of the family photos. Jack was particularly interested in a color-faded one of me, circa age twelve, posing in a blue and green Little League uniform and cradling a Louisville Slugger at an angle, buck teeth protruding forward in an unabashed wide-mouth smile.

"Is that you, Homes?" He liked to call me *Homes*. I could never quite pinpoint its origin, since I was white as a Swede, but no doubt it had sprung up one night when we'd had a few too many.

"Don't laugh. I hit .450 that season and led the league with eleven home runs and made the All Stars."

"You were still a scrawny punk. Thank God your

parents had the presence of mind to fix those pearlies. Jesus, man, you look like a walrus."

Eager for a drink, we caught up with my mother in the kitchen. She had rooted out three dusty Marie Antoinette glasses and said gaily, "Oh, let's go out on the patio. It's such a nice night." The tone of her voice gave the impression that going out on the patio was an adventure for her.

I found a mop bucket, filled it with ice and water, and brought it outside where Jack and my mother were already seated around a glass-topped table, talking animatedly. I eased into a plastic chair that was hard on my ass, and I took in the scenery. My mother's backyard featured a small, kidney-shaped swimming pool that glowed turquoise and emitted a miasma of steam, hot water that never really required heating since nobody ever swam in the forlorn thing. Bougainvillea crawled riotously helter-skelter up a high fence, hermetically sealing my mother off from the outside world. Cloistered in this little garden paradise, without my father around, she was quietly going insane, and I felt an overwhelming sense of sadness every time I visited her.

We let the champagne chill in the ice bath and made small talk. My mother wanted to know all about Jack's upcoming wedding and he gave her an earful of maudlin rot.

When the bottles were decently cold I pulled out the Byron and removed the wire capsule. "The secret to opening champagne," I said as I anchored the bottle in my lap, "is, once the cork's released, to keep the pressure against it as it starts to rise." I pushed down on the cork as I continued to slowly twist it. "Then, when it begins to come out, bend it ninety degrees to one side." I demonstrated. "The goal is to hear the slightest little sound, like a very prim and proper lady disguising a fart." Exactly on cue, a quiet *Thfft* emitted, as the cork came free.

"Oh, Miles," my mother said. "Don't be so crude."

"Yeah," Jack chimed in, laughing.

"Some French champagne expert once calculated the number of bubbles in a bottle and determined that the way most people open champagne they lose half of them in the uncorking alone."

"Pour us a glass, Dom Pérignon, before you lose the bubbles," Jack said, picking up a glass and extending it.

I filled the ghastly Marie Antoinette glasses right to the rim and we raised them in a toast, clinking them all around, wishing my mother more *Happy Birthday*s.

"What's for dinner, Phyllis?" Jack asked.

"I've got a beeeuuutiful roast chicken," my mother crooned, the champagne already starting to go to her head.

"Fantastic," Jack said. "Are you expecting other company?"

"No," my mother replied. "Just Snapper."

Snapper heard his name and barked acknowledgment. A short back-and-forth ensued between him and my mother until he finally sat on his haunches and quieted.

"Well, I'm glad we could make it," Jack said. "You shouldn't be alone on your birthday."

"So, you're really getting married?" she said to Jack, slurping her champagne none too daintily to ward off the emotion I could sense behind her eyes.

"Yep," Jack replied. He leaned toward me and hooked an arm around my neck to yank me nearer to him. "And your Miles is going to be my best man."

My mother raised her glass, losing about half her champagne in the process. Jack planted a wet kiss on my cheek. I recoiled and he released me. We sipped the Byron and refreshed our glasses as needed. Crickets chirred in the bougainvillea while shadows of palm fronds towering overhead swayed slowly across the brightly lighted pool. The sky had been sapped of its final spectrum of blue and had silently surrendered to a faint scintillation of stars that appeared like the eyes of nocturnal wildlife watching us from the dark.

My mother, susceptible to even the tiniest amounts of alcohol, began to grow animated. "I was down in San José del Cabo with my girl-friends," she was saying. She stopped, put a finger to her lips, looked all around, then whispered conspiratorially, "Now, don't tell your father this, Miles."

"Dad's dead, Mom," I said solemnly, hoping to hoist her back to reality.

She gazed heavenward. "Oh, he hears what we're saying." She crooked a finger at his hovering spirit. "I know. Doesn't he, Snapper?"

Jack and I exchanged raised eyebrows, then Jack silently mouthed: *let it go.* When I looked down I noticed that Snapper, who had come out to rejoin the party, was also looking up at the sky, rapt in my mother's dottiness.

"Tell us the story, Mom," I prodded, "before ghosts start materializing out of the bougainvillea."

"Oh, you be quiet. It's my birthday. I'm having fun." She pointed her champagne glass at me and glared over it. Snapper barked, echoing her reproach.

Jack and I shared a laugh at my mother's expense, but she didn't seem to mind. "Tell us the story, Phyllis," Jack said.

I filled our glasses. My mother fortified herself with another sip, then revved up her risqué little anecdote again. "We were staying at the Palmilla. Beeeuuutiful old hotel. Oh my gosh! We met this gorgeous Mexican man. I think he was some kind of movie star."

"Excuse me a minute." I was growing queasy at the prospect of hearing my mother's Dionysian revelation of an amorous tryst in Mexico too many margaritas ago. I drained my champagne and rose from my chair. "I've heard this one, Mom. Tell Jack. He's fascinated by all things R-rated."

44

I left Jack with my mother and escaped into the house. Jack's voice, urging my mother to continue, grew fainter and finally faded out as I made my way down the dimly lit hallway toward the study and the true, pathetic purpose of my visit.

In the study I switched on a green-shaded desk lamp. I knelt down on all fours and crawled under the desk. With both hands I felt around for the edges of a detachable flap of carpeting about the size of a book. I peeled it back, revealing a floor safe with a combination lock. Drawing from memory, I rotated the dial to the first number, turned it left to the second, then the gears in my head seized up. The third number wouldn't come. *Shit! Shitshitshit! Why did I drink so much at the damn tasting, this is a number I should know by heart, for God's sake, it was my own mother's date of birth. Maybe Jack was right, I didn't think about her enough.*

I replaced the carpet patch and padded back down the hallway and into the kitchen. At the sliding glass door that led out to the patio I paused. My mother was throwing an arm around in arabesques to highlight her story and Jack was politely laughing. I waved both hands over my head to attract Jack's attention. He finally noticed me, telescoped his head in my direction, and shot me a perplexed look. I motioned him over with a now furious windmilling of my arms and a clown-faced expression of urgency. Jack placed a hand on my mother's shoulder and said something to excuse himself, then straightened in his chair and rushed over. My mother gave a backward glance toward me and I ducked behind the curtain.

"What's up?" Jack asked through the crack in the sliding glass door.

"Ask my mother when she was born."

He jutted his large head forward. "Huh?"

"I need to know. And I can't ask her for reasons I don't want to go into," I said quickly and urgently.

"I thought her birthday was today."

"I need to know the year."

"What the fuck for? What are you doing in there? I'm getting hungry. Let's get on the road already."

"There isn't going to be any getting on the road if you don't get me the year. I've got to get some money to pay the rent and pull my weight on this trip. She's got a safe teeming with cash and the combination is her birthday, but I forgot the fucking year. Okay?"

"Jesus, Miles," Jack said.

"It's a short-term loan against my inheritance—which, as you can probably guess, is in the offing."

Jack glanced at my poor mother, lost in the mesmeric light of the pool and talking to a yelping Snapper. "Fuck, man, I don't know."

"Just do it for Christ's sake."

Jack's head went slack in disgust. He turned, walked back onto the patio, and sat down next to my mother, who was refilling her Marie Antoinette with the rest of the Byron.

While Jack worked his magic, I drifted into the hallway and stopped in front of a posed wedding photo of Victoria and me. I looked young and handsome in a black tuxedo, and she was stunningly beautiful in a veil and classic white gown. We both wore radiant smiles on our faces, flush with the promise that married life supposedly had to offer. It struck me just then how photos mock the present by staring back at us with their immutable luster of our youthful past. I studied Victoria's face more closely; if only I had known what she was thinking at that moment, what was going on behind those large, sparkling eyes, maybe I would have tried harder to avert the eventual dissolution.

The sliding glass door opened, jarring me out of my reverie. I broke away from the photo gallery and hurried into the kitchen where I found Jack shaking himself all over like a wet seal, as if to say: *This is too crazy for me.* He grudgingly relayed my mother's birth year—'33—chided me for not remembering such an easy number, then urged me to hurry up, that my mother was starting to ask about me.

"Open the Veuve. It's on me," I said.

Jack smirked, turned and walked back outside.

I retraced my steps back to the study. The

tumblers on the lock slid effortlessly into their grooves and the lid of the safe popped open, revealing the unreported Raymond family lucre inside: gold Krugerrands (my father was a lay eschatologist who was convinced that gold would be the currency standard in the coming apocalypse and stockpiled plenty), packets of bills, various trust and will documents, and a bit of jewelry that my mother felt uncomfortable having in the open. I went right for the stack of bills, removing the rubber band on one packet and counting out twenty one-hundred-dollar notes. Suddenly, I heard a low growl. I glanced over my shoulder and found Snapper at eye level, teeth bared, ears erect, tensed for a fight.

"Snapper, shut up," I said sharply. Not only didn't he shut up, but he inched aggressively forward and nipped at one of my pant legs, growling ferociously. I shook him off with a vicious kick. He leapt back, but retaliated by barking even louder, certain to draw my mother's concern. I pointed my finger at him. "Snapper, go get your *comida.*"

My words worked like *open sesame* to him, and he turned and raced out of the room.

I quickly finished counting out the two grand, rewrapped the rubber band around the packet, then dropped it back into the safe and sealed it up.

Snapper rejoined me in the kitchen and trailed me out to the patio, barking and nipping at my heels.

"Miles, where have you been?" my mother asked.

"Had to make a phone call, Mom. Long distance. Important."

Jack glared at me and shook his head slowly.

My mother sloshed back another glass of champagne, rose wobblingly to a standing position, and announced, "Well, shall we eat?"

Jack leapt to his feet and steadied her. "Are you okay, Phyllis?"

"Woo, that champagne went to my head. I'm flying with the angels." Jack and I both laughed hard. The transfusion of money had instantly lightened my mood and made me almost giddy. The immediate future looked rosy and laughter came tumbling out of me now.

We trooped inside, Jack chivalrously escorting my zigzagging mother by the arm. I trailed with the champagne and the Marie Antoinettes.

In the kitchen my mother hummed while she plated the meal. Jack dispatched me out to the car to get a red—"Fucking champagne's going to give me the runs"—and I slipped outside and dipped into my Ace Case: a wooden box containing six bottles that I was saving for special occasions. Heisting the two grand was reason enough, I rationalized, to liberate one. I selected a '95 Williams Selyem Olivet Lane and took it inside along with two Riedel Burgundy glasses that I had brought along for the week.

Inside, my mother carried out a roast chicken garlanded with carrots and green beans and baby

49

new potatoes on a silver platter. It smelled delicious; my mother always was a good cook. I uncorked the Williams Selyem, poured two glasses, and handed one to a smiling Jack. I held up the bottle to my mother. "Would you like to try some Pinot Noir, Mom?"

She scrunched up her face. "I'll stick with my champagne."

Jack imitated me swirling the wine around in my glass, then poured some into his mouth. We both tasted. His eyes squinted and he smacked his lips approvingly.

"It's a '95 Williams Selyem. Two guys working out of a shed up in Sonoma, sourcing grapes from the best vineyards, vinifying with ancient basket presses and traditional Burgundian methods. They sold out recently for more than nine million."

"Where did you learn so much about wine, Miles?" my mother asked as she served us each a plate. "I thought you were too broke to buy expensive wine."

Jack broke out laughing and I even chuckled. "I have friends in high places, Mom."

"I'll say," Jack wisecracked.

We tucked into my mother's succulent roast chicken, which paired nicely with the velvety Pinot. Life was spoiling us once again.

In the middle of the meal, my mother suddenly turned to me and asked: "Miles, when are you going to get remarried?"

"I just got divorced. Once I figure out where I

went wrong I might be able to give the idea some renewed consideration."

"If he can find someone," Jack needled.

"Why do you ask, Mom?"

"Well," she said, setting her champagne glass down, "I was reading this article and it said that people who live alone and don't believe in God have higher risk factors for all kinds of diseases and don't live as long."

I held up my glass of Williams Selyem. "I believe in God."

Jack laughed, but my mother didn't. "But you don't go to church anymore, do you?" she persisted.

"Every Friday, from five to seven. The Church of Epicurus. We worship Bacchus and sing hymns in the nude."

"Oh, stop joshing me," my mother said. "I'm worried about you, that's all. You should go to church and pray."

"Pray? For what?"

"That you can get a good job and find a nice woman."

I pretended to weigh her words thoughtfully for a moment. "A regular-paying job and a nice woman," I intoned. "What a novel concept!" I smiled warmly at my mother and toasted her across the table. Jack seemed to concur with my mother's words of wisdom, punctuating his agreement with a short raise of his Burgundy glass. He glanced from my mother to me and back to my mother.

I took another quaff of the Williams Selyem and closed my eyes to concentrate on what I was tasting. There were other Pinots, transcendent red Burgundies I couldn't afford, but this was silky and layered and eloquent in expression and it spoke to me with the voice of a siren in a dream.

I surfaced from my reverie and excused myself to go to the bathroom.

As I stood over the toilet with one hand planted against the wall to steady myself, I could overhear them talking about me.

"Do they see each other anymore?" My mother was asking Jack about me and Victoria.

"I think they're trying to get back together, Phyllis," Jack lied.

"Do you think she'd take him?" my mother asked. "He's got so many problems."

"Miles's got some good qualities. He's damn funny when he's not down."

"But he's always down, isn't he?" I heard my mother say.

"Last year's been kind of rough on him. He's a creative artist. They get bummed out a lot."

"I don't understand why he just doesn't go and get a normal job. That damn writing of his is what caused his marriage to fail."

Hmm, maybe, I thought. The toilet flushing mercifully masked the rest of their critique.

I let a few minutes pass, then returned to the kitchen, sank into my seat, and reached for my wine. I was prepared to launch into a defense of my impugned character, but decided as I gazed into my mother's rosy face—the countenance of a birthday girl sloshed on her favorite champagne—that she was entitled to her opinion of me, especially given that she had unsuspectingly paid $2,000 for the privilege.

After dinner we went back outside and sat in the dark. At one point I noticed my mother staring up at the night sky as if it had just been unveiled for the first time since its creation. It made me sad to hear her tipsily reminisce about my father almost as though he were still alive. Her sorrowful recounting of old times spent with him, times that she so dearly missed—the bottle of wine at five, the Sunday mimosa brunches, the steak-and-martini socials with other couples who had moved on—caused me to long for a life less alone.

"Do you need any money, Miles?" my mother charitably asked as the evening wound to a close. "Because I could loan you some if you do."

"No, I'm fine, Mom."

I shot a look at Jack. He had his fist supporting his chin and was staring off into the darkness with a puzzled look.

Snapper trotted over and looked up at me expectantly. Then he rolled over on his back and dog-paddled his forepaws in the air and smiled at me with his fangs, panting moronically. I mistakenly believed we had overcome our earlier lack of rapport, so I reached down to pet him. The little fiend seized the opportunity and nipped at my hand, drawing a trickle of blood. I went for more wine.

SATURDAY: TWO GUYS ON WINE

The morning dawned bright blue, sunlight slanting harshly through my mother's diaphanous drapery, rousing me early. I found myself on the living room floor in a twisted pile of sweaty sheets and a musty comforter. I shook Jack, who had somehow finagled the couch.

He propped himself up on his elbows, his hair a tumbleweed on his head, a crooked grin smeared on his face. "Huh? Where are we?"

"My mother's."

"We're not in Santa Ynez?"

"No."

Jack yawned in my face. "What time is it?"

"Time to get out of here," I said, "before she wakes up and corrals us into one of her home-on-the-range breakfasts. I don't think either of our stomachs is up for the challenge."

"I hear you, brother."

We pulled ourselves together as quickly as our hangovers would allow. I scribbled a hurried note to my mother, thanking her for the dinner, then briefly debated a second raid on the safe, but decided karma already had one demerit hanging over my head and I shouldn't tempt the invisible tentacles of fate.

We decamped the Montecito mausoleum and barreled out the front door, sans sunglasses, to meet a fierce early morning sun that had us squinting our way to the car.

Inside the 4Runner, we groped immediately for our sunglasses, now a vital necessity. They quickly restored the surroundings, torched by the glaring light, to some semblance of normalcy. I turned the engine over and gunned it to life.

"Man, I don't even get a shower. Jesus." Jack scratched himself all over in imitation of a zoo chimp.

"Tonight you'll be sitting in a Jacuzzi with a glass of wine and you'll be worshipping me for this early departure," I replied as the car lurched out of my mother's driveway and set off down the hill.

"Got to get something in my stomach," Jack moaned, jackknifing forward. "Man, you're right about champagne hangovers. I feel like someone pounded a railroad spike into my head."

We pulled into a coffee shop just before the on-ramp to the 101, close to a Union Bank where I needed to conduct some emergency business. Jack tried to focus on the sports page of the *L.A. Times*, moving the paper in and out in front of his haggard face.

"Do we really have to wait for this bank to open?" he asked.

"Yeah," I said. "Got to get a money order in the mail or I'm going to be evicted."

A moment later, our order of toasted bagels, sides of cream cheese, and coffees was carried over on a tray by a pretty brunette who couldn't have been more than twenty. She had youthful skin and a refreshingly subtle scent of flowers and the lithe figure that would inspire lust in many and attract her to few, especially Jack and me, two unshaved, unshowered, hungover denizens of a birthday bash. But that didn't prevent my pal from tracking her return to the kitchen with a lupine leer.

"Fuck, man," he shuddered affectedly. "That's just too early in the morning, you know what I mean?"

"I don't look at women like that anymore," I said.

"Oh, bullshit."

"Not that age."

"Bullshit."

"Okay, the girl's pretty, so what? It's just a visual thing, it has nothing to do with reality."

"What's the reality?"

"You wouldn't have anything in common."

"Want to bet?"

"It's purely an illusory thing."

"Don't do your Kierkegaard on me this early. I've got to get a couple of cups in me first."

"I'm serious, like that excites you?" I asked.

The waitress now was moving with a tray to

another table where a threesome of construction workers was ogling her.

"Yeah, like I'm not normal," Jack said, nodding his head in the direction of the construction workers.

"And besides, you're getting married."

Jack raised the newspaper in response, blocking his face from view.

At 10:00, the doors of Union Bank finally opened. I dragged myself inside as Jack drove off to find a gas station. I requested a money order made out to my landlord for the $850 due on the rent. The teller held each one of my hundred-dollar bills up to the overhead fluorescent lights and scrutinized it for the appropriate anticounterfeiting symbols, my scruffy appearance no doubt suggesting forgery was not an impossibility.

I let Jack take the wheel out of Montecito. We were both working our go-cups of steaming Kenya and were starting to come to life. We coasted down to the 101 where the traffic was light. The sky through the windshield was an intense, unmarred shade of blue. The steeply rising hills of Santa Barbara glittered where the sun reflected off the windows of the beautiful houses scattered among them.

"Where's your cell?" I asked Jack.

Jack produced his Nokia and handed it to me. I dialed Roman back in L.A. His gruff voice, forged from years of tenant harassment, answered on the third ring. "Yah?"

"Roman. This is Miles. I've got the rent."

"Who?"

I spoke more slowly. "Miles. Your tenant on twelfth. The writer. I've got the rent."

"You got rent for me?"

"I had a money order made and I'm putting it in the mail."

"The check's in the mail?"

"No, the money order's in the mail. That's better than the check's in the mail."

"Okay," my landlord was saying. "If it don't come by. . . ."

"It's coming, Roman," I chopped him off. "It's coming. All right? Don't evict me. I'm about to be famous."

"All right. I try to believe you this time." And the phone rudely went dead in my ear.

I punched the cell off, flung both arms in the air in mock exasperation, and commanded, "Get thee to a winery."

Jack laughed. "Amen, brother."

I leaned back and stared at the highway unfurling in front of us. Jack slipped the new Flaming Lips CD into the dash and raised the volume.

We settled into the rhythm of the road. North of Santa Barbara the terrain grew increasingly rural. The hillside homes gradually disappeared, giving way to gentle slopes covered with swaying grasses. The confluence of broad colors resembled a constantly changing impressionist painting.

Midway to the Santa Ynez Valley Jack picked up his cell and punched a single autodial number. There was obviously no answer on the other end because Jack adopted the affected tone one uses when leaving a message: "Hey, Michelle, it's Jack. How are you? I'm heading up to the wine country with my friend, Miles. I don't know if you and Stacy were still thinking about rendezvousing with us, but give me a call, we'd love to see you." He recited his cell number and then signed off.

I was staring at him when he turned to look at me.

"What?" he said.

"Who's Michelle?"

"Set P.A. I met."

"Does she know you're getting married?"

"Vaguely."

"Vaguely? Is there a looser version of *married* that I'm unfamiliar with?"

"I don't want to talk about it," he said.

We listened to the engine hum in the silence for a few moments.

"Nervous about the wedding?" I probed.

"Nope," he said, shaking his head confidently.

"Nervous about the bonds of holy matrimony?"

Jack cocked his head a quarter turn and shot me a suspicious look. "No."

"Get along with the in-laws?"

"In-laws are cool. No complaints there. Why?"

"Nothing," I said.

"You think I'm making a mistake?"

"No."

"You're jealous?"

I snorted a laugh.

"You wish you were still married to Victoria."

A sudden feeling of nostalgia welled up in me. His words unintentionally stung me and I didn't answer. The ocean colored into view on our left, a cold expanse of cobalt blue. From the immediate north, the Santa Ynez Mountains approached, looming like leviathans. We flew by slow-moving RVs, piling up the miles between us and L.A.

An hour into the drive, we labored up a curving pass through the mountains, battling an early afternoon wind that had started to kick up and was buffeting the car. As we crested the pass, a breathtaking view of the Santa Ynez Valley yawned before us and a pure feeling of elation washed over me. Once I was over this hill and down into the valley, where I had vacationed so many times before, I would feel as though I had completely shed the alienating concrete sprawl of L.A. I was entering a new pastoral realm of wine and tranquility, where insomnia and Xanax were a thing of the past.

"As far as the eye can see," I said, fanning my arm across the length of the windshield, "there are wineries. Some good ones, too."

"Excellent," Jack said. "Excellent. Let's wet our whistles."

"You don't want to get a motel first? Shower and clean up?"

"I need a bevie. Take the edge off."

I fished out my Santa Barbara County winery map from the glove compartment and studied it briefly. "Hmm . . . let's take the Santa Rosa turnoff and hit Sanford."

"What's their specialty?"

"Burgundian. Pinot and Chardonnay. One of the best producers in Santa Barbara County. And, more importantly, they're the closest one."

"I thought you didn't like Chardonnay?" Jack asked.

"I like Chardonnay. I like all varietals. I just don't like the way they manipulate it, especially in California. Too much time in oak, too much secondary malolactic fermentation."

"What's that?"

"After the first fermentation, many vintners will introduce lactic bacteria into the wine to stimulate the growth of lactic acid. It converts the tarter malic acid—think green apple—and produces lactic acid: caramel, banana, dairy, not sweet, but a cloying appearance of sucrosity."

Jack turned very slowly and raised his eyebrows. "Sucrosity?"

"Sweetness," I said. "The French don't use ML—as it's known in the trade—as much in Burgundy, which is why I like Sanford's Chards. They're trying to emulate that Burgundian style and not trying to create some treacly concoction to sell to undemanding palates."

Jack was staring straight ahead, shaking his head.

"You should get a job in a wine store. Solve your money crisis."

"Yeah, like that would be smart."

Jack laughed as we floated down into the Santa Ynez Valley. "I want you to teach me all about wines on this trip, okay?" he shouted over the wind rushing in through the open windows.

"You're ineducable," I needled.

"Don't start on me."

Just south of Buellton, we angled off at the Santa Rosa exit and turned west onto a narrow, one-lane shoulderless road. Vineyards bloomed into view, leafed out and dappled in autumn hues of yellow, ochre, and rust. On closer inspection, we could make out grape bunches drooping from the trellised, gnarled vines, the harvest imminent.

I gestured to a tiny sign that indicated the turnoff to Sanford and Jack hung a hard left. We rode slowly on an even narrower gravel road through an arbor of overhanging oaks. More vineyards bounded the road, row after perfect row of Santa Ynez's finest. We forded a mere trickle of a stream and then dead-ended at a small, ramshackle, wood-framed structure with a corrugated aluminum roof set in a clearing.

The sun felt warm as we climbed out of the car and stretched our limbs and drank in the unspoiled view. We were at the foot of the Santa Ynez Mountains, imposing hills carpeted in native grasses and dotted with gnarled oaks. After L.A., with its incessant automotive noise, putrid air, and constant congestion, the vista was positively invigorating.

"God, it's so gorgeous here," Jack said.

"Always love coming back," I said, feeling a smile break out on my face. I turned to Jack, clenched two fists, shook them in the air, and said, "Let's get into some wines, shall we?"

"Yeah!"

We marched over to the quaint tasting room. The inside smelled of wood and wine. A gentle breeze wafted through the open windows and acted as a natural air conditioner. A tall, middle-aged hippie with long hair tied in a ponytail was conducting the pouring duties. He wore a white Stetson adorned with a beaded Indian band. His weathered face evidenced equal exposure to sun and wine and was barely disguised by a wispy beard. We were clearly on the early side because the only other people in the room were an elderly couple who had already advanced to the reds.

Jack and I bellied up to the bar where a chorus line of uncorked bottles gleamed at the ready. After we each paid a five-dollar fee, the pourer set down tasting glasses in front of us and reached automatically for the first bottle. "Would you like to begin with the Sauvignon Blanc?" he asked.

"Absolutely," Jack said.

The pourer poured tiny amounts into our tasting glasses and recorked the bottle.

"Look at the wine in your glass up against the light," I instructed Jack as I held up mine and examined it. He did the same. "Now, set it back down on the counter and introduce some air into it." We both swirled the wine around. "Now, stick your nose in it and take a whiff." Jack imitated me bending over and putting my nose in the glass. Then, I upended the entire tasting amount into my mouth and sloshed it around as if it were mouthwash, then swallowed. Jack followed suit. "That's what I want to see you do with every one."

Jack smiled, happy to have such a rigorous tasting regimen imposed on him. "Okay."

We went down the line. The Sauvignon was steely: mineral and gunmetal on the palate, but bright and citrusy. The Chards were pleasant enough, not too buttery or oaky, but not thrilling either. I couldn't find any depth in them, only a vestige of what might have been. The Pinots dramatically improved, and I started to get interested.

"Do you have any of the '99 La Rinconada?" I asked, referring to Sanford's maiden bottling of a new single-vineyard Pinot that had been getting glowing reviews.

"Yeah, but we're not tasting it," the pourer said.

"How much is it a bottle?"

"Fifty-five," he replied.

I turned to Jack and said, "It's supposed to be monster."

"Get it," Jack said cavalierly. He turned to the pourer. "Can we drink it here?"

"Sure can," he said.

While I paid for the La Rinconada, Jack went out to the car to retrieve some chicken sandwiches he had picked up at the gas station in Montecito. The pourer uncorked the wine, stuck the cork halfway back in the bottle, and set it on the bar in front of me. I gathered it up with the two tasting glasses and walked outside, where I found Jack sitting at a weathered picnic bench under a spreading oak that dappled him with oblong splotches of shade. He was munching on a sandwich and looked pretty content sitting there all alone. I wanted to take a picture of him, but I didn't have a camera. Then he saw me and shot his arm into the air. I hurried over with the wine.

I poured two ample glasses of the La Rinconada and handed one to Jack. The wine was a deep, almost opaque purple in the glass. Against the sunlight it turned carmine, but you still couldn't see through it. On the nose it was full-throttle blackberry and leather and spice with hints of raspberry candy. The mouthfeel was explosive of highly extracted, but still young, Pinot Noir grapes draped in tannins. I suspected that another year or two would tame its exuberance, but it was fun to capture it now in its youthful promise.

"What do you think of it?" Jack asked, chewing the wine in his mouth.

"Lovely," I said, pouring us a little more. "Big and gamy, almost irreverent for a Pinot. I like it. A perfect beginning to this weeklong adventure."

We clinked glasses. Jack was relieved to see my spirits lifting. He handed me the other chicken sandwich and we ate them ravenously while continuing to revel in the La Rinconada. Over the vineyard, a turkey vulture wheeled in slow circles. Then, suddenly, as if it had been shot, it dive-bombed out of the sky and disappeared into the vines where it produced a violent struggle. Moments later, it ascended with a great clattering of furiously flapping wings, clutching a partially eviscerated rodent in its talons.

"I hope your marriage works, because that's what divorce is like," I observed, as the huge, black raptor winged away.

Jack laughed. Then, holding the glass to his mouth, asked: "What really happened to you at the tasting yesterday? It was way out of character for you."

I shrugged. "I don't know. I just kind of flipped. I get a little wine in me, spot an attractive woman, and it's all over. It's probably a product of being alone this last year."

"Dani's got it going on, doesn't she?"

"Yeah, Dani's great. But I don't know if we'd have a whole lot in common other than wine and sex."

Jack pointed his glass of Pinot at me and peered over the bridge of his sunglasses. "What else is there?"

"True. Though every now and then it's kind of nice to engage in an aesthetic discussion, debate whether the films of Bresson still hold up or not, I don't know."

"You're too picky, Miles."

"No, I'm not," I objected.

"Okay, tell me. What are you looking for?"

I thought for a moment. "Someone who can accept the reality of my life, who doesn't barrage me with recriminations for the path I've chosen. However potholed at times it might seem."

"Who's that? A Bedouin?" Jack chomped into his sandwich.

"You get enjoyment out of my suffering, don't you?"

"Actually, no. I want to see you succeed, meet someone, and get out of this rut—if that's possible."

I refilled our glasses. The wine smoothed the barbed edges of Jack's words. The warm sun felt good on my bare arms. The soothing quiet of our surroundings was broken only by the intermittent melodies of unseen birds, the far-off rise and fall of a dog's barking, and the wind rustling the leaves of the giant oaks. It all seemed to transport me to another realm, if only for a fleeting moment.

I held up my wineglass to Jack. "This is a good quaff."

He smiled amiably. "Think I should spring for a few bottles?"

"It's worth it. We may not drink a better wine all week."

Jack nodded. "Where do you think we should stay?"

"Three choices."

"Hit me with 'em."

I held up my index finger. "Windmill Inn. Actually, it's the Day's Inn Windmill now, but I refuse to acknowledge the corporate takeover. We call it the Windmill."

"What's it like?"

"Your basic no-frills square crib, pool, and Jacuzzi, but that's about it." I straightened my middle finger. "Marriott. Higher end. Nicer rooms, better pool." Then, my ring finger. "Ballard B&B. Quaint Victorian. Probably not the place to be stumbling into from an all-day wine-tasting spree."

Jack nodded in agreement. "Fuck the B&B. I'm not into rules and curfews and shit. What's the Marriott a night?"

"Probably two, unless you can sweet-talk your way into a corporate rate."

"Screw it. Let's do the Windmill. We're not going to be in the room much anyway."

"Fine with me." I refilled our glasses until the bottle was empty. The sun had started to arc down in the sky, creating elongated shadows through the trees. Jack and I kibitzed about some recent movies, agreeing that it had been a mostly uninspired year. We polished off the Pinot, hauled ourselves off the picnic bench, and bought two more bottles of the La Rinconada. Then we climbed back into the 4Runner, a little slaphappy, and motored off toward Buellton.

The sky had turned a deeper shade of blue,

streaked with wispy, scarf-shaped clouds of pale orange as we rolled into the Windmill Inn. It was a two-story, 100-odd-unit generic motel in Buellton, a highway pit-stop town of a few thousand inhabitants that was deafeningly bisected by the 101. The drive-up entrance to the motel was ruled over by a large, nonfunctioning windmill, a weather-eroded anomaly indicating the presence of nearby Solvang, an ersatz town founded in the early 1900s by Danish educators who sadly let it go to enterprising businessmen looking for a seine net to catch the Highway 1 RV crowd.

We were a little high when we reeled into the lobby, laughing about something silly.

"Cheryl!" I called out to the desk clerk, a pretty dishwater blonde in her late twenties who knew me from past trips and always greeted me warmly.

"Miles. Haven't seen you in a while." Cheryl smiled, revealing nicotine-stained teeth. "Up to play some golf?"

"Golf. Wine tasting. The whole nine yards." I swept my arm extravagantly toward Jack, both of us looking a little worse for wear after a day without showering and shaving. "This is my friend, Jack. It's his first time up here. He's getting married next week."

"Congratulations," Cheryl said.

"Jack, this is Cheryl."

"Cheryl! What's a beautiful woman like you doing working in a dead-end job like this? You should be in the movies."

Cheryl flushed in response.

I cringed and shook my head. "He says that to every woman," I said deliberately so she wouldn't fall for his fulsome flattery.

"So, where's the wedding?" Cheryl asked. "I want to come. I love weddings."

"Up in Paso Robles," I answered. "Week from Sunday. Why don't you join us? I need a date."

"Absolutely," Jack said, shambling forward and resting his forearms on the counter.

"Is it going to be a big wedding?" Cheryl asked.

"A gala event," I said. "Beaucoup bucks on both sides. No expense spared. Fabulous wines, sparkling and still, selected by yours truly." I glanced over at Jack. He was scratching his beard and suddenly looking a little gloomy. I could tell he didn't like my talking about his impending wedding, especially in front of a pretty young woman. I realized bringing it up drained the moment of adventure and made the future seem all too real.

"Oh, I love big weddings," Cheryl said. Then her face soured. "But I work weekends."

"Well, if you can get off, you're welcome to join us," I said. "Anyway, we need a room. Jack'll take care of it. His plastic still works. I've got to make a phone call."

I circled around a dividing wall to an annex off the lobby where the pay phones were located. Hunched on a stool, I dialed the calling card number and punched in a long PIN that I read off the back

71

of a business card. There were no messages. When I returned to the lobby, Jack had trespassed far over the counter and was now about a foot from Cheryl's face, blatantly flirting.

"Well," she was saying, "they've got masseuses over in Solvang who will come here, if *that*'s what you're looking for."

"Yeah," Jack said. "Something like that." He rotated his handsome head in an exaggerated circle. "Neck's killing me. Killing me."

Cheryl gestured to a nearby display rack. "There are brochures over there," she said.

"Thank you. You've been very helpful, Cheryl." Jack lumbered over to the rack and indiscriminately gorged himself on a raft of promotional materials.

"Let's go," I said sharply to Jack. "I need a shower."

"All right, all right," Jack replied. "See you, Cheryl. If you change your mind about dinner, give us a ring."

"Bye, guys." She waved enthusiastically. "Have fun."

We drove around to the back of the motel to find our room. Cheryl naturally assumed I wanted to be as far away as possible from the thunderous semis that roared back and forth all night on the 101.

The second-floor room itself was an uninspired space: two queens, wallpaper depicting seascapes patterned with drifting gulls and leaping dolphins, a noisy air conditioner that would desiccate my sinuses, a spitting shower nozzle designed by a sadistic product engineer to discourage theft, a blurry television with a Spartan channel selection—bolted to the dresser—the standard-issue abridged Bible with phone numbers scribbled inside the cover, some stationery, and a single Windmill Inn Bic pen. Not exactly the Four Seasons, but serviceable.

"They're not going to do what you think they're going to do," I pointed out, as we entered our room with the first load of luggage.

"You're telling me," Jack said, throwing his suitcase on the dresser, "that if I get a masseuse over here she's not going to suggest exploring other possibilities when I mention the almighty dollar? Bullshit, pardner, they're not going to come to the party."

Shaking my head, I shuffled back out to the 4Runner and collected the rest of my gear. High-flying jets from nearby Vandenberg Air Force Base discharged orange contrails against the twilit sky. It was dismaying to suddenly realize that Jack seemed hell-bent on the obvious, and I was beginning to grow uneasy that I wouldn't be able to corral him.

When I returned to the room, I found Jack sprawled on the bed, riffling through the brochures from the lobby. He found one that caused his eyes to widen. He thrust it out for me to see and jabbed a thick finger at it, grinning from ear to ear. "Massages. Day and night. Shiatsu. Oriental."

73

"It's not Vegas, Jack. It's Solvang. A picturesque little tourist trap with Danish shops selling kuchen and clogs. Mostly old people who have long ago lost interest in what's stirring below their belts." I brandished a finger back at him. "And I don't want to get nabbed in some local sting operation targeting goats like you."

Jack bulled ahead. "We get 'em over here, we take it a step at a time."

"No. No, not *we*. I'm not interested. I don't pay for sex. Never have, never will."

"Open a bottle, will you?" Jack requested, wanting to change the subject because I was wrecking the mood.

I rummaged around in one of the boxes and fished out a La Rinconada.

Jack produced a corkscrew and fired it under-handed at me. I grasped the air, but missed, and it smacked into the wall behind me.

"Bull*shit* you were an All-Star shortstop and hit .450." He laughed.

"I wasn't drinking back then."

Jack howled with laughter.

I opened the La Rinconada, poured us two glasses in my Burgundy stemware, and held out one to Jack.

He plucked it from my hand and raised it in a toast. "Here's to one last week of insanity."

I didn't say anything.

"And thanks for coming and all that other good shit," he added, taking a healthy quaff.

"No problem," I said.

We sipped the wine in silence for a few moments, that blackberry nose and hint of leather on the back palate causing me to close my eyes. I could always count on losing myself in wine.

"I'm starving," Jack said all of a sudden. "Where're we eating?"

We showered, shaved, and dressed, then went to the Hitching Post, a local institution on 246, a busy, accident-riddled, rural highway that crossed the 101, snaking west to Lompoc and east to Solvang. We prudently opted to walk the short distance there, fearing the local sheriffs who often parked outside the popular watering holes waiting for tottering prey. There was a fall chill in the air and the night sky, so sublimely different from L.A.'s, was littered with a jigsaw of stars. We jabbered about the Lakers and Tiger Woods while walking over.

The Hitching Post is a nut-brown, wood-framed, windowless building whose location is inconspicuously marked by a small yellow neon sign. As we approached, smoke from the wood-burning barbecue pierced our nostrils with enticing aromas of grilling steaks and other guilty pleasures.

At first glance, the Hitching Post resembles any other chophouse with its cheerless décor and typical fare. But on closer inspection one realizes that they've incorporated the local wine milieu into their operation, marrying all those slabs of beef with a variety of artisanal Pinot Noirs. The wines were overpriced for what they were—thin, lacking in strength—but where else could you get a decent glass of wine and a hamburger in a small town?

Inside, we strode past the hostess into the cocktail lounge, a low-ceilinged, wood-paneled room with a small L-shaped bar and a television mounted on the wall in the far corner over the kitchen entrance. Charlie, the Samoan bartender with his three inner tubes of a stomach barely hidden by an Hawaiian shirt, waddled over to serve us with a wide-mouth smile. He didn't so much man the bar area as fill it.

"Hey, Miles, how're you doing?" Charlie said, extending his hand across the bar. "Haven't seen you in a while."

I took his hand. It was a damp, bear-sized paw that you didn't really grasp so much as cower inside of. "Not bad," I replied. "Been busy."

"When's that book of yours coming out?" he asked, releasing my hand. "Everyone here's dying to read it."

"Soon, Charlie, soon," I answered, as a buried memory of a drunken night some months ago, when lies poured as abundantly as the Pinot, struggled to surface.

"How about a couple of glasses of Pinot?" Charlie asked.

"You read my mind, big fella," I said, brightening. "How's the '99 Bien Nacido?"

"Want a taste?"

"Yeah, give us a taste, would you?"

Charlie slid two Burgundy glasses out from the overhead rack and set them in front of Jack and me. He uncorked a fresh bottle of the '99 Bien Nacido on a commercial cork extractor with one powerful pistonlike action and poured a sizable, glad-to-see-you-again sample in each glass. "Tell me what you think."

I swirled the wine in the glass, sat back on my stool, sniffed the wine, then gestured to Jack. "Oh, this is my friend, Jack. He's getting married next week."

"Oh, yeah? Congratulations. Now, I guess the only thing you have to look forward to is divorce." Charlie laughed at his own remark.

"One step at a time," Jack said, sipping his wine.

Charlie pointed a chubby finger at my glass. "What do you think?"

Jack faced me with arched eyebrows, awaiting the verdict.

"Tighter than a nun's asshole, but decent concentration. Let's drink to its future. Pour us a couple."

"Mm," Jack said. "Nice. You're right, not as big as the La Rinconada, but delectable nonetheless."

"Actually, it's disappointing at ten dollars a glass," I whispered to Jack. "I just didn't want to offend him. We'll drink much better wines this week, I promise you."

Charlie filled the squat bottoms of our Burgundy glasses, emptying half the bottle in the process and endearing us to him for the evening.

"Thank you, Charlie," I said. "Guess we'll look at a couple of menus."

"Going to eat at the bar tonight?"

"Might as well be close to the source."

Charlie chuckled as he reached under the bar and produced two menus. Then he lumbered over to serve a middle-aged couple who had the appearance of golfers seeking solace from a bad day at the course.

As Jack and I studied our menus, I couldn't help stating the obvious: "God, it feels good to be out of that viper pit, L.A."

"Amen, brother," Jack concurred. "Amen."

Something caught his attention and he slowly lifted his head over the menu. I followed the angle of his straying eyes. At the far end of the bar, a tall, strikingly beautiful woman with brunette hair cascading over broad shoulders, in an eye-catching black cocktail dress, appeared with a drinks tray and recited an order to Charlie. She was the kind of lavishly built woman who had the magnetic pull to pry men's gazes away from their martinis and steaks.

"Check it out," Jack whispered to me, nodding in the waitress's direction.

"That's Maya," I said tonelessly.

Jack jerked his head in my direction, surprised. "You know her?"

"Yeah." To prove it, I held up my wineglass and toasted Maya. She responded with a half smile and a quick upward nod of her head.

Jack looked at me again, stunned. "You know that chick?"

"Yeah, I know her. I told you, I come up here all the time. This is the only place I eat. And sometimes I stay late. And the staff often drinks after hours here because there's no other better place to go."

"Why don't you go for her? She's dynamite."

"Don't get too excited. She's married. Check out the rock and the accompanying band."

Jack leaned forward and narrowed his eyes, telescoping in on her hand.

"Left hand, ring finger," I deadpanned.

"Fuck you."

"Get used to it."

"Yeah yeah yeah."

"Well?" I challenged.

Jack sipped his wine. "That don't mean shit. When Babs was maître d' at the Ivy a long time ago she wore a big ol' engagement ring just to prevent aggressive fucks from hitting on her. And do you think that stopped them? Hell no." Jack tipped his wineglass toward where Maya had left an empty space. "So, how do you know she's really married?"

I turned back to my glass of wine, cradled it with both hands, and stared into it reflectively. "It was right after my divorce. We kind of got down one night after hours here at the bar."

"And she told you about her husband?"

"Yeah. She followed some older lit professor out

here to UC Santa Barbara from Vermont or some-place and was going to get her MFA, but things weren't too cool between them. She admitted they were having problems but that they were working on them."

"What kind of problems?"

"I don't remember. Charismatic liberal arts professor. Nubile young students with stars in their eyes who think men their own age come too quickly. It doesn't take much of an imagination to figure out being married to one of those guys is rolling the dice. But they must've worked it out if she's still wearing her jewelry."

Jack bent toward me, intensely interested. "When was this that you got down with her?"

"I don't know. Year or so ago. Why?"

"If she's married to a UC professor, what's she doing working in a place like this?"

"Because she stands proud. She gets free Pinot. She doesn't want to sit at home. I don't know."

"She's probably divorced now just like you. A lot can happen in a year." Jack sat up on his stool and leaned across the bar. "I'm going to ask the bartender."

"No, don't do that, please," I pleaded, grabbing him by the shirt and yanking him back onto his stool.

"Why?"

"Why? Because. He'll tell her that we were asking, and I don't want her to know that."

"Well, how're you going to find out?"

"I don't *want* to find out! If she wants me to find out, she'll tell me. It's not like she's lacking for men. She's got a whole restaurant full of them drooling over her every night."

Jack sipped his Pinot some more and considered my words, shaking his head slowly in disbelief. He approached the prospect of making Maya's acquaintance from another angle: "So, what'd you get down about, besides her boring, philandering husband—probably now ex?"

"I don't remember. I was pretty framed."

"She probably was, too," Jack said with a glint in his eyes.

"Oh, that chick is crazy about wine, no argument there."

"So, come on. What'd you talk about?"

"She likes Pinot, and she knows quite a bit about wine. We probably talked a lot about the local wineries, I don't know."

"There you go," Jack said, throwing up his hands.

"She's a cocktail waitress in Buellton, Jack. She has a whole life up here that I'm not privy to."

"What are you? Some kind of fucking elitist?"

"That's not the issue. I'm a tourist. She's not moving to L.A. and I'm not moving to Buellton."

"Fuck, man, who said anything about moving?"

I sighed. I didn't want to go down this road with Jack and fan his flames. The bar was crowding up and I just wanted to melt into the scene, relax, and lose myself in wine and idle chatter. But Jack wouldn't give up.

"Given the opportunity," Jack said restlessly, "you wouldn't take a ride on that?"

"Why do you always couch everything in sexual terminology? Do I look like some kind of ibex who hasn't seen the opposite sex in months?"

"*Ibex*?" He frowned, hating it when I used a word he didn't know.

"Wild goat. Man beast. Satyr. Priapus. Take your pick."

When I looked up, Jack was gawking at me. Then, his eyes crinkled and he started laughing. "Miles, you crack me up."

Maya returned from the dining room to her station for another round of drinks. Jack was staring at her as if she were a moving monument to womanhood. Which, in fact, she was.

"She's a sweet girl, in a crumbling marriage, marooned in a small town she didn't grow up in, and I don't think she'd like it if she knew you were talking about her like this," I said.

"Oh, bullshit. I'm having a hormone meltdown just looking at her. Jesus. She's jammin'. And you *know* her?" He turned and regarded me in amazement. "Take advantage of the gift."

Just then Maya locked eyes with me and smiled warmly. Jack glanced excitedly back and forth at the two of us as if his head were mounted on ball bearings. Charlie set four glasses of wine on her tray. Maya kept looking at me the entire time, and for a moment I felt vaguely desired. She said something to Charlie, then, just before she turned to go, she winked at me. Jack caught the gesture and pounced on it.

"She fucking winked at you!" he said, rising up off his stool.

"She does that to everyone."

"Bullshit. There are winks and then there are *winks*," Jack said. He rested back onto his stool, confused and thunderstruck. He knitted his brow, outlining a plan of action. "I'm telling you, Miles, that rock is bogus. Fucking Zirc. Beard, beard, beard."

"What're you getting all worked up about?"

"What am I getting all worked up about?" he echoed snidely. "Oh, I don't know. She might have a friend. Two girls, two guys, small town, wine country. . . ." Jack knocked back his Pinot and motioned to Charlie to refresh our glasses.

"There's no way that woman is interested in me. No way."

Charlie heaved over with a full open bottle, poured us each a glass, and placed it on the bar between the two of us. "It's on Maya."

Jack turned to me and slapped a hand over his mouth in mock astonishment. "Oh, my God, she must hate your guts."

I sheepishly tossed Maya a schoolboy's wave. She smiled *You're welcome* back, and all Jack could do was slowly shake his head.

We ordered off the menu—Jack: filet mignon; me: duck breast; both ideal complements with the Pinot, which we drank with relish. I kept trying to coax the Bien Nacido out, but it never really opened up the way I had hoped, remaining budded and hidden from its full expression. Maya came and went, stoking Jack's libido with every appearance.

Jack wanted to hang around the bar after we had finished dinner, drink more wine, and wait until Maya got off her shift, but the congested room was already beginning to feel suffocating, and, more important, I feared a long intoxicated evening with a woman I barely knew and an about-to-be-married friend dying to get into her pants. After failing in his bid for us to stay, Jack paid up, we both waved good-bye to Maya, and left.

Outside, the night chill freshened our flushed faces and invigorated us for the half-mile-long walk back to the Windmill. It was a commercial district and many of the businesses had closed for the night. As we walked along the shoulder of 246, vehicles of all sizes hurtled by in both directions, the 18-wheelers buffeting us with the velocity of their passing. In between the roar of revving engines, the highway grew still for brief moments and we could hear the gentle hum of insects fill the void. We were a little tipsy from the two bottles of wine, but the universe was still comparatively in order.

Jack bumped my shoulder and I bumped him back. "I could take you," I said unconvincingly.

"Oh, right," Jack said, looming over me with hands on hips.

I adopted a boxer's pose. Jack did likewise, and we shadowboxed against the side of the road, feigning left jabs and right crosses, ducking and feinting, until both of us were laughing so hard tears sprang to our eyes. To passing motorists, we must have looked like some bad vaudeville duo who had been unceremoniously drummed out of town.

It was still relatively early and going back to the motel wasn't really in the cards for Jack. He kept trying to persuade me to go back to the Hitching Post, but I wasn't in the mood.

"So, what do you want to do?" he said. " 'Cause I ain't ready to call it a night."

"What about a movie?"

"A movie?" He smirked. "You mean like with a big box of popcorn and drinks with straws, stuck in the middle of a bunch of townies necking?"

"Okay, bad suggestion."

"I'm on vacation. I'm getting married a week from tomorrow. I want to party." He swept an arm grandiloquently across a desolate expanse of car dealerships, minimarts, and supermarkets. "Where's the action around here on a Saturday night?"

"All right," I said, "I'll take you to the happening place."

We headed back to the Windmill Inn and rolled into the Clubhouse, the motel bar. It was a spacious, tacky joint, with tiled mirrors serving as one wall behind a horseshoe-shaped bar that showcased a raft of available stools. In the center of the place, Naugahyde club chairs circled laminated wood tables that were grouped in front of a car-sized parquet dance floor. This was flanked by a barely elevated stage on which stood some kind of amplifier console and microphone stand.

Jack was underwhelmed. "This is it?"

"It'll pick up."

Jack looked skeptical. I pivoted onto a stool. Jack placed a hand on my shoulder and said, "Order me something, I've got to make a phone call." He unfolded his cell and strode outside, seeking privacy.

I surveyed the scene. The Clubhouse's customers were a mixed crew of locals, the early crowd made up of construction and service workers and other minimum wagers, shooting pool and quenching their thirst with pitchers of beer. The men wore jeans and T-shirts and grease-stained baseball caps, and the women were in tight jeans and halter tops. It had the feel of a place that could get downright rowdy given the right amount of excessive drinking.

The bartender came over to take my order. He was a quiet man with thinning red hair and a cadaverous face, courtesy of too many bartending jobs breathing other people's cigarettes, bending a tin ear to the incessant palaver of wrecked lives, and enduring countless soul-withering 2:00 A.M. close-ups.

"What's up tonight?" I said, nodding toward the dance floor.

"Karaoke," he replied.

"Oh, yeah?"

"Yeah. What can I get you?"

"Any Pinot?"

"What?"

"Pinot Noir. Red wine."

"No."

"Any red wine at all?"

"Cabernet and Merlot. That's it."

"Pour me two glasses of the Cab."

"Coming right up." He turned and crossed to the back of the bar, uncorked a bottle of already-opened Firestone—a mediocre local winery that valued quantity over quality—filled two generic wineglasses inappropriate for Cabernet, and put them down in front of me. I laid a hundred-dollar bill on the bar and he plucked it away, rang the order up on his register, then returned and fanned the change out on the bar as if I were going to contest the transaction. A nasty scar dividing one side of his face caused me to imagine that he once had to defend himself over just such a misunderstanding. He turned his attention back to a TV bolted into the wall, not interested in conversation.

I sipped the overly oaked Cab, puckering at its harshness and total absence of forward fruit. It was the kind of mass-produced wine where the crush probably included underripe grapes, leaves, bugs, rodents, and God only knows what else. Worse, it had probably been opened the day before and abandoned at room temperature to slowly putrefy. If I hadn't been with Jack I would have gone somewhere else where they took their wine seriously.

A shrill noise interrupted my reverie. I swiveled around on my stool for a view of the dance floor. A young woman, with long, ropy black hair tumbling over a Pea Soup Andersen's uniform, had mounted the stage and was turning on the karaoke apparatus, creating a few seconds of earsplitting amplifier feedback. Her cronies, who were dawdling around the pool table, whistled and hooted as she selected a song, wrapped a hand around the microphone, and waited for the music to kick in. A Fleetwood Mac song— "Landslide," for Christ's sake!—started and the girl came to life, imitating Stevie Nicks's familiar voice and stage movements, singing so ingloriously out of tune that I wondered why she would actually want to *pay* for the privilege of publicly humiliating herself.

As her performance droned on and her tone-deaf voice blared away in ever bolder flourishes, her contingent of supporters broke into wild howls of execration, shaking their fists and beating their cue sticks against the floor. It was as if her intent wasn't to prove whether she could sing, but to be the self-appointed object of her friends' derision. I reached the twin conclusions that she *did* have a purpose in life, and that Jack and I weren't exactly at the "in" spot.

Jack materialized out of the crowd and claimed a bar stool next to me. He reached for his glass and took an ample mouthful of wine in a show of anger.

"Local swill, sorry." I raised my chin toward the karaoke stage where "Stevie Nicks" was winding down her act.

"I heard." Jack shook his head. "Jesus. That's frightening."

I turned to him. He had a sour look on his face. I assumed the phone call had upset him. "Call Babs?"

"Yeah," he said unhappily.

"How is she?"

"Fine."

"How she holding up?"

"Okay, I guess."

"What's happening?"

He plunked his glass of wine down and it clinked loudly on the bar. "She's on my case," he said, his face hardening.

"What's her problem?"

"She thinks I'm up to no good."

An abrupt laugh shot from my mouth. "Well, at least we know you're marrying a smart, intuitive girl."

He looked at me mirthlessly. "It's not funny." He drained his drink, hefted himself off his stool, and said, "I've got to call her back and work this out."

"Why?"

"Because I hung up on her," he admitted.

"Hey, I have a radical idea."

"What?" he said, frozen midstride.

"Why don't you say something sweet to her so she can sleep peacefully tonight?"

Jack glared at me, then took off and threaded back through the jeering crowd as the Fleetwood Mac song broke off. The girl in the Pea Soup Andersen's uniform chugged a glass of beer down, then stepped off the tiny stage where she was swallowed up by her amiable persecutors. I turned back to my horrid wine. Jack wanting to torment Babs a week before their wedding caused me to wonder if there wasn't something else going on. We hadn't talked about it a lot, but I truly believed Jack loved her. Prior to this trip, I hadn't seen much of him because he was spending so much damn time with her.

"Do you believe that?" I heard a voice saying. I turned to find a young man with short, straw-colored hair crowning a doughy face stippled with bright red pimples. He was clad in the uniform of the place: white T-shirt, faded Levi's jacket, and matching jeans. On the bar in front of him rested a half-empty pitcher of beer that he guarded jealously, his face hanging expressionlessly over it.

"Pretty frightening," I agreed.

He nursed his beer slowly but continually, his arm moving back and forth from his mouth to the bar with the mechanical monotony of an oil derrick. "What do you do?" he asked, shifting his eyes toward me without moving his head.

"Me?" I said. "I'm a writer."

"No shit?" he asked, perking up.

"It's no big deal. I'm not famous or anything." Not that he would know.

"What do you write?"

"Books. Movies. Whatever pays the rent."

"Oh, yeah? Any I might have seen?"

"I once wrote a book that was made into a movie, but the book was never published, and then when the movie came out they hired some hack to do a novelization of it. Do you fucking believe that?"

My words had outraced his beer-fogged brain and he turned to me slowly as if allowing himself time to catch up. When it hit him, a smirk came to his face and he said, "Bummer."

I cleared my throat, not sure if he gleaned the full import of one of my past professional demoralizations.

"What was it called?" he asked.

"*Circling the Drain.*"

"Was it about plumbers?"

I laughed out loud and shook my head no.

"Then I probably didn't see it." He crossed his right arm over his left and extended his hand, palm downward, for a shake. "Name's Brad."

I took his hand and shook it. It was sticky from beer and bar pretzels and God knows what else.

"Miles," I said.

"What's your full name? In case you write another book."

"Miles Raymond. It's a nom de guerre," I quipped.

He did a double take, then threw me a look to let me know he knew I was fucking with him. "Funny," he said. He released my hand and took another guzzle of beer, sudsed it in his mouth and said, "How'd you like to go wild boar hunting with me?"

I straightened, caught off guard by the proposition. "What?"

"Wild boar hunting." He lowered his beer mug and forearmed foam off his upper lip.

"You're joking."

"Nope."

"You're a boar hunter?"

"In season," he replied.

"Hunt 'em at night?" I asked, puzzled but intrigued.

"Yep. That's when they like to come out. They sleep during the day."

"Why would you think I would want to go wild boar hunting?"

"I don't know." He shrugged. "You're a writer. Might be an idea for your next book. I'd read it."

"That's encouraging. Where do you hunt 'em?" I asked, pretending to be interested.

"On the cliffs over at Jalama Beach."

"And you'd like me to accompany you?"

"I don't like hunting alone," he confided.

"I don't know, Brad. Tonight's not good. I'm with a friend here. . . ."

"Have him come," he cut in.

"I'll take a rain check. But thanks for asking."

"That's cool," he said, disappointed. "Some other time, dude." He emptied the pitcher into his mug and drained it in one sustained quaff. Then he steadied himself with a hand planted on the bar and climbed down off his stool. "Later." He belched as he staggered past me and hauled his short, stocky frame out of the Clubhouse. I followed his unsteady retreat to the parking lot, picturing him hunkered down in a gully steadying a high-powered rifle as a hulking, snorting swine from hell charged at him. What madness!

A moment later an entirely different kind of madness manifested itself as Jack returned. A sinewy, snarly-looking guy in a blue work shirt hanging out over filthy jeans had stepped up to the karaoke stage and was belting out the Stones' "Jumping Jack Flash." He was gyrating around like some monstrous mechanized marionette, trying to imitate the Jagger strut and shouting instead of singing. It was so awful it was almost entertaining. Almost.

Jack reached for his wine and took a sip. "She didn't answer. Voice mail."

"Did you leave a message?"

"Yeah, but I didn't apologize. I told her I was getting drunk and was going to go have sex with the first woman I met."

"That's lovely."

"She's pissing me off."

"You did *not* say that, I hope."

"No, of course not. I told her I loved her and was looking forward to next week."

"So what'd she say that pissed you off so much you hung up on her?"

"She asked me to cut the trip short and join her up in Paso Robles with the relatives." He mimicked a woman's falsetto. "And sit around and watch women crochet and titter about weddings."

"What'd you say?"

"Fuck that. *No* is what I said," Jack spat. "And that's why she's all bent out of shape now and won't"—Jack broke into a high-pitched voice again—"answer the phone." Jack motioned to the bartender. "Hit us again, big guy."

The bartender refreshed our glasses. I took a sip, but realized I wasn't really tasting the wine anymore. The colored lights had begun to grow fuzzy, and with all the karaoke nonsense it was becoming increasingly difficult to distinguish what Jack was saying. I was sinking into myself and losing ground. I needed a pill or a bed or something.

I think Jack was complaining about Babs cramping his style when suddenly he chopped off his rant, jabbed me hard in the shoulder, and whispered: "Whoa, whoa, whoa, nine o'clock sharp."

I rotated my head in the direction he was staring

and there was Maya, changed into a black cashmere sweater and hip-hugging brown corduroys. She corkscrewed onto a stool in the end corner, bookending Jack between her and me. The bartender wasted no time in serving her. Maya pointed to the bottle of Cab and he poured her a glass.

"It's on us this time," Jack shouted over the epigone Mick Jagger now mangling "Satisfaction."

Maya raised her glass chest-high in a thank you.

"And thanks for the bottle of Pinot," Jack added.

"My pleasure," she said, taking a sip.

"My name's Jack. And you know Miles, right?"

Maya knitted her brow and narrowed her eyes and pretended not to remember me for a moment, suppressing a smile. "Yeah, I know Miles."

Jack folded his arms across his chest and leaned back on his stool to afford me a more luxurious view. I lifted a hand in a timid wave, but didn't say anything, fearful that I would slur my words.

Maya languorously lit an American Spirit cigarette and spewed smoke gently through pursed lips. She turned to us and recited: "The moment two people fall in love there is already sown the seed of tragedy." She flicked an ash off her cigarette. "Yeah, I remember Miles."

I dropped my head and stared down at the bar, vaguely recalling our wine-soaked philosophical exploration of love and relationships a year ago. When I looked up, Jack's face was etched in a disapproving frown. He shook his head reprovingly at me, then turned back to Maya. "He's got a whole new outlook on life," he reported.

"Oh, yeah," she replied, inhaling her cigarette. "Does he believe there's hope for men and women now?"

"I think he does," Jack said with mock sincerity.

Maya pushed her lips out and nodded thoughtfully.

The Jagger impersonator stumbled off the stage into the intoxicated crowd to the usual drill of good-natured booing and hissing.

The Clubhouse quieted briefly and the reception on Maya's voice came through a little clearer. She was saying, "Yeah, he must have been really drunk that night, because. . . ." when I impetuously rose from my bar stool and weaved crookedly in the direction of the stage. I could hear Jack expostulating until the noise of the crowd, primed for a fresh lamb to the slaughter, swallowed it whole.

I blinked at the song list on the monitor and selected the first one that came into focus, an oldie called "Crystal Blue Persuasion." I punched the START button, took the microphone in my hand, and brought it to my mouth. It hit my teeth with a shrill reverb. The crowd immediately started jeering, impatient to crucify me.

The music started and I sang the words as they scrolled down the monitor. I have a distinct memory of trying to inject some feeling into my phrasing, but I'm guessing I sounded more like an anguished parrot. There was something liberating in the spontaneity of the whole thing at the time—the colored lights raying off the rotating mirror ball on the ceiling, people I had never seen before contorting their faces in reaction to my performance—but, in time, it would become only an embarrassing memory.

When the song was over, I leapt jauntily off the stage, waved to the heckling locals, and returned to my bar stool, blood throbbing hot in my face. When I finally looked over to Jack and Maya for a reaction, Jack fixed me with an expression of disgust. Then he just started slowly shaking his head back and forth.

"I didn't know you could sing, Miles," Maya finally said.

"Me either." I drained my glass and signaled the bartender with an elaborate circling of my finger for an emergency refill. The bartender hurried over with the bottle and topped off my glass.

"So," Maya said, "your friend informs me you're getting published?"

My stomach lurched as if a trapdoor had just swung open beneath me. "What?" I looked to Jack for help.

Jack shot me one of his don't-fuck-it-up-brother glowers that he was fond of.

"Uh, yeah," I said, an excess of wine having unleashed the liar in me.

"That's great," Maya said. "Congratulations."

"And I'm optioning the film rights," Jack boasted.

Maya ignored his embellishing of the lie and directed her attention to me. "You're a big Pinot fan, aren't you, Miles?"

"Absolutely. Nectar of the gods."

"I hear you're going to the festival Friday?"

"That's the reason we're up here." I raised my glass in a toast to future intemperance. "Are you going to be there?"

"Wouldn't miss it." She inhaled her cigarette until the end burned bright orange. Her eyes reflected the hot light. "So, what are you two guys up to tonight?"

"We'll probably go back to our room and crash," I said without thinking.

"Oh." Maya frowned and stubbed out her cigarette in an apparent show of disappointment. I couldn't tell if she was insulted or not. She finished her drink and then got up from her stool. "Have a good one," she said, brushing by us. She vanished as quickly as she had appeared, as if she were an apparition.

Jack stared at the entrance with the defeated expression of an angler whose line had just gone slack. It hurts a man to see a woman like that disappear into the night; particularly a Saturday night, while on vacation, and away from the woman in his life. He turned to me and deliberately dropped his jaw. "We'll probably go back to our room and *crash*? What is up with that shit?" He tapped his finger against my head and I flicked it away.

"I'm tired, and that's probably what we *are* going to do, isn't it?" I said, bone weary.

"The girl was looking to have some fun, the two of you have a little history, and you tell her we're going to go back to our motel room on a Saturday night and *crash*. Jesus, Miles!" Jack slapped his forehead so hard it left a red imprint of his hand. "The woman digs you."

"Bullshit."

"She lit up like a pinball machine when I told her your book was getting published."

"Great! Now, I've got another fucking lie to live down. Thank you, Jack." I took a soul-searching slug of wine.

"Oh, bullshit. There are a million ways out of *that*. The point is, she wanted to party."

"What difference does it make? The woman's married."

"The woman's definitely *not* married!"

"What? You asked her?"

"Miles." Jack grabbed my shoulder and steadied me on my stool. "She wasn't wearing the rock."

"What?"

"She wasn't wearing the rock," he said, enunciating each word.

At this point in my memory, time breaks up into fragments. There was a segue that revealed itself as one of those inebriated ellipses where segments of the night's events mysteriously disappear. All I remember is the two of us zigzagging across the parking lot toward our room and Jack declaiming, "I'm telling you, she wasn't wearing the rock!"

"She wasn't wearing the rock?"

"She wasn't wearing the rock!" Jack yelled back.

Suddenly, a disembodied male voice erupted from one of the rooms. "Hey, would you two assholes shut up about that fucking rock so we can get some sleep!"

Jack and I bent toward each other and simultaneously put our index fingers to our lips, shushing each other until we were wheezing with laughter. Then we tiptoed back to our room, high-stepping like cat burglars in a dinner theater farce.

The red light was blinking on the phone when we clamored into our unit. Jack turned and pointed a finger at me, "Do not answer the phone under any circumstances, *comprende?*"

"*Sí, amigo.*"

As if on cue, the phone began ringing. Eight annoyingly loud rings later, I said to Jack, "Answer it, man. Talk to her. She's probably worried about you."

"Good."

"What is up with you two, anyway?" I said, turning toward the bathroom, not waiting for a reply.

I slumped onto the toilet, my head in my hands, too enervated and worried about my aim to pee standing up. I wanted the drama with Jack and Babs to be over so I could get some sleep.

When I hauled myself back into the main room,

Jack was holding his cell to one ear. He raised an index finger to his lips.

I struggled out of my clothes and climbed into my queen. The mattress felt firm and the springs moaned in response to my weight. The sheets were scratchy and stank of bleach, but I was glad to be down for the night. I rolled over and closed my eyes.

After a moment, I overheard Jack say, "It's me. I'm back in the room. Call me tomorrow. Love you."

I heard Jack undress and crawl into bed. Then, sweet darkness as he switched off the lights. The air conditioner hummed a monotone in the background. Outside, crickets revved up their chirring. "Voice mail," Jack said.

"Oh," I replied.

"She probably turned her ringer off."

"Maybe she's getting pounded by some guy she picked up in a bar in retaliation."

My words hung in the silence. Then, Jack finally said: "Just before I'm about to go to sleep, you perversely put that image in my imagination."

"You have no imagination; only a dick."

"You're a twisted fuck, Miles."

I pulled the covers over my head and laughed uncontrollably.

In the middle of the night I surfaced from a dreamless slumber, roused by the muffled sounds of someone talking. I propped myself up on my elbows and blinked the room into focus. A band of white light leaked from the space at the bottom of the bathroom door. I could make out Jack's voice saying something in low, earnest tones. My bladder was ballooned from all the wine and I leapt out of bed, practically hopping about in agony. In desperation, I found a plastic cup on the night-stand and urinated lustily into it. I replaced the cup on the dresser and quickly lapsed back into sleep.

Halfway to morning, I heard a banshee wail and bolted upright. The nightstand light illuminated Jack, hunched over in his underwear, sniffing the contents of the plastic cup. The upward glow of the light made him look ghoulishly like an earlier, primitive species of man. He heard me come awake and raged, "Jesus, Miles. What the fuck, man?"

"What?"

"That's not La Rinconada."

"I had to go. You were on the phone in the bathroom."

"You motherfucking clown," he bellowed, hurling the cup at the wall.

SUNDAY: BOYS MEET GIRLS

We woke midmorning. I felt ragged from lack of sleep. Jack had been sawing logs all night, and I had been besieged with doomful dreams that left me feeling empty.

We hauled ourselves out of bed and cleaned up in a grouchy silence. With wine-numbed brains and rubbery legs we trekked as if wading through hip-deep water to Ellen's Pancake House, a popular breakfast spot in the center of Buellton. We were both weighed down with man-sized hangovers and anorexics' appetites as we commandeered a red-checked table near the window. Around us, a grotesque diorama peopled by obese tourists and locals jackknifed over their eight-egg omelets, pork-chop-and-fried-egg combos, and tall stack drenched in imitation maple syrup assaulted our bleary, bloodshot eyes.

A smiling, pregnant waitress, whose otherwise pleasant face was disfigured by a cleft palate, appeared with a glass beaker of steaming coffee and a pair of laminated menus. Her compulsory cheerfulness sounded psycho-pharmacologically tuned to a constant even pitch. "Coffee?" she asked, upturning our cups.

"Please," Jack said in a downcast voice.

She filled our mugs, then minced her way to another table.

As I fumbled with a miniature plastic half-and-half container that stubbornly refused to open, Jack decided we were finally awake enough to do a postmortem on the night before. "I cannot believe you got up and sang 'Crystal Blue Persuasion.' "

"What was that?" I said, pretending not to remember.

"Karaoke, man. You don't remember?" Jack said, unconvinced.

"Vaguely. I'm not sure I want a recapitulation. I've got enough bad memories competing with one another this fine morning." I emptied two dairy creamers into my coffee and sipped the weak, flavorless brew.

Jack continued to shake his head in incomprehension while going over his menu. "What'd you do that for? In front of that girl?"

"I was trying to impress her."

"Why didn't you just jump up on the bar and take a dump?"

I made a face.

"And what'd you pick 'Crystal Blue Persuasion' for? That song's so fucking retro. Maya probably thinks we're older than we really are."

"What would you have suggested?"

Jack sat back in his chair. "Oh, I don't know. What about Merle Haggard's 'I Got So Drunk, The Gal Left Town'?" He stared at me in silent fury. "Jesus fucking Christ, Miles."

"All right, let's not rehash the evening." I lifted a hand in protest.

Playing the thespian, Jack projected the soul of a human into the bottle of ketchup sitting on the table and addressed it: "I guess Miles realizes the errors of his ways."

"Obviously, I'd had a little too much vino."

"Obviously." Jack picked up his menu and hid behind it.

I transfered my gaze out the window and took in the sun-drenched morning. "Beautiful day, isn't it?"

Jack lowered his menu to appraise me for sarcasm, then glanced out the window. "Beautiful," he concurred, not really caring.

The waitress approached with her bright manufactured smile. Jack ordered a Denver omelet and I, stomach still pitching about, decided on the oatmeal. Coffee cups were refreshed.

The food came quickly, as if it had been precooked. Jack ate ravenously while I toyed with my glop of instant oats.

Breakfasts pushed to the side, Jack lingered over the newspaper while I got out my Santa Barbara County wine guide and gave it my undivided attention. It was nearing eleven already: our stomachs were on the mend, the coffee was helping us make more sense of the world, and our frayed nerves were in need of a soothing libation.

"So, what's the plan, Shorthorn?" Jack asked, folding closed the sports section of his *USA Today*.

Tracing a squiggly line on the crude map in the guide, I said: "We'll head north, begin our grape tour there, then wend our way south. That way, the more we imbibe, the closer we'll be to the motel."

Jack tapped an index finger against his temple. "Fucking genius, Miles."

"Did you get hold of Babs?" I asked.

"Yeah."

"Where was she that you had to call her in the middle of the night to track her down?"

Jack eyed me suspiciously. "Out with the girls. Why?"

"Oh. Out with the girls."

Jack froze with his coffee cup halfway to his mouth and narrowed his eyes at me, awaiting the punch line.

"Don't worry," I said. "Women don't do that shit before their wedding."

"What shit?"

"You know, go fuck some random person just to exorcise the lust from their systems before they settle into routine marriage sex."

"They don't?"

"Traditionally, I think they maintain their virtue while the guy traipses through Slobberville to the blessed event. But," I threw up my arms in mock surrender, "I could be wrong. Babs has that reputation."

He ignored my jibe about his fiancée. "I'm going to get my nut on this trip, Miles," Jack confided, ramrod serious.

"I know you are, big guy. I've got a good feeling about your chances." I pumped my fist sarcastically.

He leaned across the table and dropped his voice to an undertone. "I am not shitting you. I have got to touch fresh pussy before I settle down. It's *essential.*"

"Well," I whispered back, "let's hope you have some success with the locals. I'd hate to see you go into the stockade of marriage a failure."

"Just so we're on page one." Jack reached around for his wallet while glancing at the check.

We left Ellen's, trudged back to the motel, piled into the 4Runner, and headed north on 101. Six miles later, we cut off on the 154, drove a few miles east, then steered a left at Foxen Canyon, a single-lane country road that stretched out sinuously in front of us. Vineyards fecund with fruit and shaggy with leafage fled past us in blurry grids.

"The reason this region's good for Pinot," I said over the music and the rushing air through our open windows, "is that the cold maritime air off the Pacific flows in at night through these transverse valleys and cools down the berries. Pinot doesn't like to be hot all the time. It needs temperature variances and a slow growing season to develop its acids. And it despises humidity because it's thin-skinned and susceptible to disease and rot. A finicky, elusive, but rewarding varietal."

"Similar to a high-maintenance woman?" Jack wondered.

"Exactly. Though with all the effort, the pleasure in the final product is ultimately more satisfying. Plus . . . plus, there's a different crop every year, so the experience is renewable. Sort of like teaching freshman English."

Jack leveled his eyes at me. I stared straight through the windshield and didn't meet his gaze. "You think I'm making a mistake, don't you?"

"I didn't say that. I was talking about wine, not marriage." I turned to him. "Man, you're touchy this morning. You need a bevie."

"What do you really think?"

"I don't."

"But if you were paid to have an opinion, what would it be?"

"I think you'll be happy having sex the same way with the same woman every day for the rest of your life."

It took Jack a moment, but he finally laughed. "You've got one dark aura, brother."

"Actually, I'm an incurable romantic."

More laughter exploded from Jack. "Uh-huh." Then he stopped and said, "You miss Victoria, don't you?"

"For a while after the divorce, I did," I said. "But now I don't. It would take a truly incandescent woman to move me to that kind of arrangement. Otherwise, what's the point? You're just marking time to the inevitable split."

"Good. Because I was starting to worry about you."

"Worry about me what?"

"Getting lost on me."

I snorted and looked away. Jack had a knack for getting under my skin and drawing me out. And he had an annoying habit of doing it at inopportune times, like this morning, when I wasn't feeling my most chipper and I wanted to forget about the real world of relationships, jobs, failed hopes and dreams, and the creeping inevitability of my mortality.

Our first stop was Byron, one of the northern-most wineries on the map. They had produced some good Pinots and Chardonnays in the late eighties and early nineties. But since having been acquired by the tentacular Mondavi empire in 1990 they had had some unimpressive years. I was curious to taste whether the new corporate umbrella had continued to handicap their vintner, or if they had returned to their artisanal risk-taking standards.

We turned right on Tepusquet and jostled east down a graded dirt road, a plume of dust billowing behind us. The morning view of the Santa Maria Valley was splendid, showcasing an infinitude of vineyards rollercoastering in all directions across the gently sloping hills.

We rolled into Byron around 11:30 and I nosed the 4Runner into a space in the uncrowded lot. We climbed out into the bright sunshine, spread our arms to the sky, and stretched. The air was flora-scented, warm and dry. I drew a deep, lung-expanding breath and exhaled slowly. Then I clapped my hands and held them together. "All right, let's get into some Pinots!"

"That's the Miles I want to hear."

When we set foot on the porch of the small, timbered tasting room we were greeted by a locked door and a cardboard sign hanging from a chain that read: CLOSED.

"I thought you said they opened at eleven?" Jack said, glancing at his monstrous TAG Heuer.

"Please excuse my failure of leadership."

"It's eleven thirty already. Where are these clowns?"

I was already poking around. Upon closer inspection, another, smaller sign informed us that the tasting room actually didn't open until twelve. "Sorry, Shakes, I was wrong. Noon."

"Fuck," Jack muttered.

We drifted over to a picnic bench that overlooked a dry wash. The brightening sun felt good on our faces. We sat side by side like that for a while, accompanied by the song of feeding birds. For a few minutes everything was blissfully perfect. Then:

"Guess I've got to tell you this," Jack began haltingly.

"What?"

Without turning to face me, Jack spit it out: "Babs doesn't think it's a good idea for you to be my best man."

My head turned in slow-motion toward Jack. He wouldn't meet my questioning gaze.

"Victoria's going to be there," he said matter-of-factly.

"I assumed that. Given that she and Babs are pretty tight."

"Yeah, but that's not the whole story."

I wasn't sure I wanted to hear the whole story. I fixed my eyes on a hawk slicing across the pristine sky and waited for the peripeteia.

"Victoria got remarried," Jack finally said.

The hawk caught an updraft and soared steeply vertical as if being reeled in by an unseen line, banked, and disappeared. When it was gone, I turned to Jack and said, "Pardon me?"

He squared around to face me. "She got re-married. Last week. She and her new husband will both be at the wedding. Babs doesn't think you can handle it." He punctuated the disclosure with a guilty, hangdog expression that he hoped would diminish its impact on me.

I hung my head dismally, trying to picture myself with this fresh agglomeration of dramatis personae. Nothing made sense. I clutched my head with both hands.

"That's the only reason Babs is against your coming."

"Well, why the fuck *am* I coming?"

"Because I want you there," Jack replied, his tone rising to match mine.

"Is this what all the drama with you and Babs has been about? Me being the best man?"

"Sort of. I'm working on it. It's going to work out."

I walked out to where the wooden patio ended and the deck dropped off precipitously. I hugged my arms to my chest and gazed out into the startlingly blue sky and the vineyards unfurling below me. There was suddenly a stark contrast between this outward beauty and my feeling of total disconnection from the world—and the people I knew. All at once, my thoughts were a jigsaw of ill-fitting pieces, and my delicate hold on sanity was beginning to buckle.

Jack shuffled up beside me. I heard him first, then I felt his breath on the back of my neck. He rested a hand on my shoulder for an extended moment, gave it an understanding little squeeze, then let it drop. I tilted my head skyward. High up, a fighter jet divided the sky in two with a zippered gash that bled white. I lowered my head and fixed my gaze on a pair of randy squirrels chasing each other in erratic circles.

As if to promote the start of a reaction, I began shaking my head back and forth. "You fucking drop this bombshell on me after you've already lured me out of L.A." I turned to him with a pained expression. "Jesus, Jack, have you no conscience?"

"It's not as if I don't have any conscience. It's because I don't have any other really close male friends." There was a pleading tone to his voice now. "I'm sorry."

"I don't know if I can go through with the wedding, Jack," I said. "Even if I am ultimately accepted."

"Come on, man. You've been divorced more than a year. Fuck, you had to figure this was going to happen sooner or later. People move on with their lives."

"Spare me the platitudes. That still doesn't mean I have to witness my ex-wife's post-matrimonial joyousness."

"I need you up there, man. It's not going to be easy for me, either."

I wheeled toward him, tensed for an argument. "Nobody *wants* me up there! I'm a common-variety gate crasher. Persona non grata. A fucking pariah."

"Babs is coming around. Everybody's cool." His voice sank to an undertone. "Even Victoria."

The last declaration was no doubt a blatant lie, but I let it slide. I ballooned one cheek out with my tongue and stared off, words failing me. The beautiful view was now a total blur as I journeyed inward.

"You've got to get back in the saddle again at some point," Jack added.

"Oh, fuck that."

"No, don't say *fuck that!*" He grabbed me by the shoulder and spun me a quarter turn to face

113

him. I refused to meet his eyes. "We're up here to have some fun and get a little nutty. You know as well as I do that nothing erases memories of a split better than a little pussy."

"Correction," I snapped. "For me, it's wine. Fuck pussy. It's the biggest waste of time."

"Oh, yeah, right." Jack laughed. "Like you don't wake up every morning hard as a hammer, wishing it would magically disappear."

I ignored this last remark. "I just can't believe you *waited* to tell me this."

"You wouldn't have come," Jack argued, throwing both arms wide open.

"Surprise, surprise!"

"So let's do the wine tour, then shine it, I don't give a shit whether you come or not! Peter's waiting in the wings to take your place." He pivoted and walked away.

The two mating squirrels posed on their hind legs, observing us. I didn't say anything. I didn't move. The sky loomed vast and interminable, a celestial ocean where I could get deliriously lost if only I had a gun. Before I could let that fatalistic fantasy run its course, we heard the squeaky hinges of a screen door pierce the silence. We turned at the same moment and found a large woman in her early thirties filling the doorframe of the tasting room. She had a head of long, straight black hair that flowed over her shoulders and onto her buxom chest. We followed her beckoning smile, both of us now desperate for a drink.

The tiny tasting room was cool and wood-scented. One side was devoted to the usual winery bric-a-brac: T-shirts, sweatshirts, corkscrews, postcards, hats, picnic baskets, and glasses.

We eased up to the bar where the bottles were newly uncorked and ready for exploration. The Fellini-esque pourer—quite sexy if you didn't imagine her on top—started us on the Sauvignon Blanc. It was an apple-ly, grassy rendition that served more as a palate starter than as something to get excited about. We sloshed our way through a pair of Chardonnays, one nutty, another buttery, neither thrilling.

Finally, we moved into some Pinots. Luckily, our wine server was pouring some of Byron's expensive single-vineyards. When we got to the Sierra Madre, I stopped and truly savored it. The wine was subtly elegant—silkier than the La Rinconada, less bombastic, but equally magnificent. I asked the pourer to revisit me with another taste. It just got better and more complex.

"What do you think?" Jack asked.

"Terrific."

"Wait till the 2000," the pourer tipped us off. "We barrel-sampled it the other day and it's out of this world."

I turned to Jack. "Let's get a bottle of this Sierra Madre."

"Whatever you want, Miles."

The pourer went into the back to get a bottle. Jack reached quickly for the one on the bar, filled us both half full, and we jacked them back at the same time like tequila shooters.

"I thought you could use a real one," Jack said.

"Yeah, I needed that," I said.

I loaded up some cheese and crackers in napkins from the snacks table while Jack paid for the Sierra Madre. We repaired to the picnic bench outside and laid out a spread. I went to the car to retrieve my Burgundy glasses. Jack had the bottle uncorked when I came back. I poured two glasses and extended one to him. We swirled and nosed and swished and luxuriated in the wine.

"This is delicious," Jack said.

"Wait until we get halfway through, it'll really start to pop," I said, briskly aerating the wine in my glass, forgetting for a moment all that I had just absorbed.

"Mm mm mm." Jack smacked his lips, holding his glass up to the sunlight, studying its color. "Comparable to a red Burgundy?"

"Low-end ones, maybe. Not the great ones, of course. But I'm not complaining."

We sat and sipped and snacked on the cheese and crackers. Soon, I could feel myself crossing that swaying footbridge from hangover to a numbed glow that I falsely associated with elation. The bitterness and depression that had been plaguing me since Jack's revelations about Victoria and the wedding dissolved in the embrace of the beverage I admired in my glass and worshipped with my senses. The Sierra Madre gradually sorted itself out as the midday sun warmed it to a more optimal temperature and the milky cheeses neutralized its bright acidity, elevating it to new heights.

"Mm, this *is* good," Jack said again.

"Lovely stuff," I agreed.

"Feeling better?" Jack asked gingerly, watching me out of the corner of his eye.

"Immeasurably." And I was. I didn't give a damn anymore. "I needed this," I added, holding up my glass.

Jack laughed. We corked the bottle at half mast—we had a lot of wineries left to visit—and called it a picnic.

Before we left Byron, Jack sprung for a case of the Sierra Madre and, feeling a little silly, we purchased a couple of sweatshirts with grape bunches embossed on them.

We drove the length of Tepusquet, turned back onto Foxen Canyon, and cruised south. All around us, open fields of resplendent heather pastured daydreaming livestock chewing their cuds in the lazy mid-afternoon sun.

Jack had hopscotched over my feelings about the wedding and had now shifted his concern to my money situation and was volunteering advice: "Why don't you write for television?"

I scowled. "You're already superannuated at thirty-five and I'm pushing forty."

"That's bullshit."

"It's not bullshit. Besides, I'm not a hack. I don't do formula."

"Oh, right, I forgot. You're an *artiste*. Truth and honesty and the baring of the soul."

"That's right. Don't make light of it."

Jack laughed. "Well, what about the panic attack experiments? That paid pretty well, didn't it?"

I shuddered. "I don't want to be a lab rat for some soulless research guy experimenting with re-uptake inhibitors." I tapped an index finger to my temple. "This is all I've got left, right here."

"Well, what're you going to do if the book doesn't sell?"

I shrugged.

A flare went off in Jack's head and he continued excitedly: "What about the Internet? There must be a way to make money there."

"The Internet is a dark road to infinity potholed with links," I opined. "For a writer, it's like shitting where you eat."

Jack clammed up, fresh out of ideas. "Okay. Sorry I brought it up."

"Apology accepted." I picked up my winery guide, relieved to move off the topic of my bleak future.

We detoured off Foxen Canyon and motored down a narrow road that dead-ended at Rancho Sisquoc Winery. Their wines were so uniformly wretched that we left without finishing the lineup. After our initial success at Byron, I was starting to grow disappointed.

Next on the wine trail, according to the map, was Foxen Winery, a quality producer of Pinots,

Cabs, Cab Francs, Chards, Syrahs, and even Mourvedre and Grenache. They were a small operation but wildly ambitious, and I had enjoyed their wines immensely in the past.

Their tiny tasting room was a ramshackle roadside barn broken at both ends by enormous sliding doors kept open to allow the sunlight and air to pour in. It was a refreshing change from the sterility of most tasting rooms, and an unprepossessing rebuke to the tawdry excesses of Fess Parker's vulgar estate just down the trail.

Tipsy now, we swayed into the tasting room, joking, momentarily back on good terms, wine having mended the fences. Jack was laughing pretty boisterously, and when he laughed like that his whole body convulsed and his voice boomed so that you could hear it from a long way off. Just when his laughter appeared to be subsiding, it was my role to ad lib something so funny that he would lose control and start up all over again. It was an Ed-and-Johnny routine and the more we drank, the sillier our performance became.

As we bellied up to the tasting bar, our ears buzzing, Jack turned to me and brought a finger to his mouth to shush me. But I'm sure it was already obvious to the pourer that Jack and I were already a little on the other side of the vineyard.

She broke away from a discreetly sipping couple and approached us with a bouncy step and an alacritous smile. She was all of five feet five with short blond hair combed over in a left-center part, framing a pale, lightly freckled face. She had flashing gray-green eyes as alert as a bird's, suggesting that she might be a product of the East Coast rather than the West with its sunworshipping surfer girls, skin tanned to leather, all trancelike smiles and no ambition. When she spoke, her New York accent came through, and she was quick-witted and sarcastic, affirming my prediction. "Doing the wine tour?" she asked.

"We are doing the wine tour," Jack said, loud enough to be heard in Solvang. "And my wine snob friend, Miles"—Jack hooked an arm affectionately around my neck—"claims Foxen makes one hell of a Pinot."

"Excuse my friend. Yesterday, he didn't know Pinot Noir from film noir."

The pourer laughed.

"Give me a break, Homes." Jack turned to the pourer, all sparkling and flirty eyes and said, "But I'm learning."

"That's good, I guess," she said. I got the impression, even in that daze of modest inebriation, that she was drawn to big, good-natured, southern boys like Jack. I started to get a queasy feeling.

"In town for a while? Or just up for the day?" she asked, thumping the cork out of the maiden Chardonnay.

"We're en route to Paso Robles where my friend, Jack, here is. . . ." A foot stomped on mine, making me cry out a little.

". . . Getting an introduction to the wines of the

120

Central Coast," Jack finished for me. He turned sharply to me and dared me to contradict him.

"Ah," she replied, uncertain how to read us. "Well, Jack and Miles," she said, leaning forward and drawing out both our names teasingly. "How about some Chardonnay?"

We nodded. She slid a glass in front of each of us and poured flirtatious dollops.

Jack swirled the wine around in his glass with the practiced air of a sommelier. "Now, there's someone who knows how to pour. What's your name?"

"Terra," she said.

"Terra firma?" I joked, hoping to alienate her with my silliness so she would turn a cold shoulder to Jack's charms.

"No, just Terra," she corrected.

Jack ignored our banter and leaned in closer to his new mark. I turned to the Chard. It was another undistinguished, generic rendition of the most corrupted varietal in the world, and I was eager to delve deeper into the lineup.

"Cab Franc?" Terra asked, moving right along, raising her eyebrows as she held up the next bottle. There's something about a beautiful woman holding up a bottle of wine that damages my soul. I was starting to soften to the possibilities that the day was offering.

"Fill 'er up," I urged. "Pour with your heart."

Terra laughed. No company miser her, she uninhibitedly poured both of us half glasses.

I took a mouthful, swished it around, then swallowed.

"What do you think?" Terra asked. She planted an elbow on the bar—as if wanting to afford us a closer look—and propped her chin on her hand.

"Quaffable. For a blending varietal. I don't expect greatness from Cab Franc."

"I like it," Jack said, his brow beetled as if trying to fertilize the seed of a description.

"You like all blending varietals," I needled.

Jack brushed me off with a laugh, then turned his attention back to Terra—glowing ever more beautiful through our winey haze—and asked, "Do you live around here?"

"Uh-huh. Just outside Buellton." She corked the Cab Franc and set it aside.

"Oh, yeah," Jack said, "that's where we're staying."

"Yeah, where?"

"Windmill Inn."

"Slumming it, huh?" Terra said.

"We like tacky," Jack said.

She laughed again. Then she pursed her lips to suppress a smile. Her eyes locked with Jack's in coquettish combat for a few moments, an electric current arcing in the intimate space they had mutually created.

"Hey," Jack said, emerging from his trance, "do you know a woman named Maya? Works at the Hitching Post?"

Terra brightened, revealing a mouth of brilliantly white teeth. "Yeah, I know Maya. Real well."

"No shit?" Jack said, excited now. "We had a drink with her last night."

Terra frowned, then burst into a sardonic laugh. "Don't tell me, were you the guys making fools out of yourselves singing karaoke at the Clubhouse?"

Jack jerked a thumb my way. "He's Caruso. Not me."

Terra shimmied forward on her elbows closer to Jack and practically whispered: "Oh, you don't sing?"

Jack bent his big head toward her smaller one. "Only in the shower and after you know what."

Their eyes pulled each other closer to actual physical contact. I suddenly had an image of Babs in a changing room fussing over the fitting of her wedding gown, and decided it was time to intrude. "Could we move on to that Pinot, please?"

"Sure," Terra said without unlocking her eyes from Jack's. After a few pointed seconds, she broke out of her dreamy state and uncorked the bottle of Pinot.

Jack turned and winked at me. I made a sour face and shook my head in disapproval.

Terra free-poured us each a quarter glass, continuing to defy tasting room protocol.

"Oh, you're a naughty, naughty girl, Terra," Jack teased, holding up his glass.

"I know. At the end of the day, I might need to be spanked," she bantered back. "Excuse me a second." She straightened up from the bar and

123

moved over to the only other people in the tasting room, a gay couple who had become visibly annoyed that we were monopolizing the pourer.

When I looked at Jack he was turned in my direction, away from Terra, his mouth frozen wide open in imitation of a man pantomiming a scream. He relaxed his countenance, elbowed me sharply, and whispered, "Cute, huh?"

"Yeah," I reluctantly admitted. I watched Terra work with a portraitist's eye. She was wearing a pale pink cashmere sweater decorated with delicate pearl white buttons. She down-dressed it with a white T-shirt underneath and a pair of nicely faded and frayed Levis. She glanced over at us frequently while she poured for the other visitors. In her eyes I sensed a feeding look that exposed her as the kind of woman, recently jilted, who hunted for men like Jack to quell her insatiable need for romance. If she flashed one more smile at us I thought I would scream. Worse, Jack signaled back every time by toasting her with his glass.

"I'm going to get this whole thing lined up," Jack announced sotto voce.

"What whole thing?"

Jack gave me a look as if I were as slow as one of those brainless bovines we had just passed on Foxen Canyon. "You. Me. Terra. Maya."

"Oh, yeah, right," I said unenthusiastically.

"What are you talking about, 'Oh, yeah, right'?" He snorted. "Miles, the-glass-half-empty."

"Do you know how many guys hit on these pourers? Especially ones as adorable as her?" I tried to discourage him because, for a weak moment, I thought of Babs, of men everywhere cheating on women, the whole male matrix of swinish deceit, and how, as it was salaciously shaping up, I didn't want any part of it. But then Terra returned, bearing a new bottle and a sexy smile, obviously as interested as Jack was in pursuing a connection, and something in my wine-weakened brain surrendered whatever shred of moral resolve I'd clung to.

"Like that Pinot?" Terra asked me.

"Not bad. Smooth." I took another sip. "Sort of gutless for the price."

Jack shot me a dark look and Terra picked up on it. "No, he's right," she said. "It's *not* a great Pinot." She plucked my glass away from me and upended it into the spit bucket. "Here, try this." She reached under the counter and poured me a healthy taste from an unlabeled bottle. "This is a barrel sample from our 2000 Pinot." She glanced at the couple at the other end of the bar and dropped her voice to a whisper. "It's not released yet."

The wine was dark and unfiltered, but it had a kind of feral richness that called to me. "Very nice. Can't wait until it comes out of hiding."

Terra smiled and poured Jack a sample. "Maya's a big Pinot fan, did she tell you that?"

"Yeah, I know."

125

"Are you going to the festival at Fess Parker's?"

"Got our tickets right here." I slapped my back pocket where my wallet was.

"Should be fun."

"We're excited," Jack said. "And I *love* this Pinot."

"I'm glad," Terra said.

"Where's the bathroom?" I asked, desperate to extricate myself from the growing flirtation.

Terra pointed and I shuffled off in the direction she indicated. Inside the tiny bathroom, I plopped wearily on the toilet and held my head in my hands. Negative thoughts swarmed in: What if the novel didn't sell? What did Victoria's new husband look like? Was he some virile, successful thirty-year-old? or my age? or some short roly-poly hairy Hollywood director type? For some reason I didn't want to know. Sitting on the toilet, I realized I'd already decided to play out the trip with Jack, humor him, then bail on him at the last moment, citing irreconcilable differences with the two newly married couples and their extended families.

I must have been camped out in the bathroom longer than I'd thought, because when I reemerged Terra was assembling a mixed case of Foxen's finest in a cardboard box for Jack, who was up on his tiptoes leaning over the bar. His sunburned face and tousled hair were inches from Terra's face, and he was making her laugh while closing the deal. He scribbled his cell number on the back of a business card and said: "So, call Maya and feel her out."

"I will," Terra said. She closed the case, gave it a slap, and shoved it across the bar toward Jack.

Jack hefted the case into his arms and called out to Terra at the register, "So, give me a call."

"It's a promise," she said.

Jack jerked his head toward the open door. "Let's move it, Homes."

"Bye, Terra," I said.

"Bye. See you tonight, maybe."

Jack shot me a glance, silencing me. I almost didn't believe it was happening, but I've witnessed Jack having this magnetic pull on women many times before, and this was just another example of how effective, when he was in full attack mode, he could be.

"That chick's got it going on," Jack said excitedly, as we stumbled our way out into the blinding sunlight back to the 4Runner.

"She's pretty good-looking."

"*Pretty* good-looking? She's fucking dynamite." I opened up the back of the 4Runner so Jack could stow the case. "And you fucking go and almost tell her I'm about to get married. What is *wrong* with you?"

We started back down Foxen Canyon. Jack was still on my case. "Do not tell these women I'm getting hitched."

"So, what's supposedly happening tonight?" I asked.

"She's going to call Maya and see if she wants

to get together and make it a foursome tonight for dinner."

I bit my upper lip and watched the pastoral landscape blur in my vision.

Jack kept crowing about his good fortune. "I told you I was going to get this whole thing lined up."

"What'd you have to do? Brag about being in the fucking movie business?"

"I'm hungry," Jack cut me off. "Let's get something to eat."

We drove into the tiny, quaint town of Los Olivos. The place had one major intersection and only a few blocks fanning out from there. It was both a stopping-off point for tourists on the Santa Ynez Valley wine tour and a place to hang out for the affluent residents who lived in splendor in the surrounding hills.

We found a good sandwich shop called Pannini's with outdoor tables shaded by large green umbrellas and ordered at the counter. While we waited, we cleansed our palates and cleared our heads with cold bottles of Pellegrino.

Jack kept staring at his cell phone, which was standing upright on the table as if it were a small animal in his clutches who might make a run for it. No sooner had our lunch been brought out by a teenaged girl with a pierced lower lip and streaked blue hair, than it rang. Jack glanced at the LCD. A grin of recognition spread from ear to ear. "The eagle has landed." He waited until the fourth ring, then answered, "Hello." He listened for a moment. "Hi, Terra," he said in a sexy voice. "What's the good news?" He listened some more, a smile broadening ever wider on his face. He was nodding at me all the time he was listening, in between: "Great"; "Fantastic"; "Seven o'clock, we'll be there"; and— Jesus fucking Christ!—"Bye, sweetness."

He folded his cell shut and said to me with a big grin plastered on his face, "We're on, brother."

"Come on," I said, incredulous.

"Turns out Maya's got the night off, so the four of us are rendezvousing at some place in Santa Ynez."

"Tonight?"

"Yes, tonight. Do you think I've got all week? Join the party, Homes."

"A date? With women?"

"Yes! Get with the fucking program, will you?"

"I need a drink."

Jack laughed. We finished up lunch and then strolled across the street to visit Andrew Murray's and Richard Longoria's neighboring tasting rooms. Both are excellent local vintners—Murray specializing in Rhône varietals and Longoria in Burgundian—but we were a little wined out from Terra's generous pourings so we mostly spat, which is not the way to really taste wine as far as I'm concerned.

By the time we left Los Olivos and headed back out 154 in the direction of the 101, the sun had started to bend off to the west, gilding the grassy hills. The wind had kicked up and a couple of raptors were soaring effortlessly on the swirling currents, rodent-hunting for their shrieking progeny. Jack was in an ebullient mood all the way back, drumming his hands on the steering wheel and singing out loud to a CD I wasn't familiar with.

We got back to the Windmill Inn as the sun was dipping over the Santa Ynez Mountains, silhouetting their serrated peaks in a blazing aureole of gold.

We raced each other up the Astroturf-treaded stairs and both bolted for the bathroom as we got back into the room. I won only by threatening not to accompany Jack for the evening.

After relieving ourselves, we took our places on our queens, enervated from the long day. I switched on the TV and surfed to a golf tournament. "I can't believe this guy's going for the green," I remarked.

My comment went unanswered by Jack. I looked over and saw him supine, breathing rhythmically in a light snore, dead asleep. I turned back to the television. The solemnity of the announcers' voices—"this is an important shot, Curtis"—was such a powerful soporific that I, too, quickly fell asleep.

When I woke several hours later, it was inky dark in the room, and for a few strange moments I was disoriented. I switched on the bedside light and blinked the room into focus. Jack was gone, but the soaring seagulls and leaping dolphins were still freeze-framed on the wall. I hauled myself off the bed, crossed the room into the bathroom, and shoehorned myself into the closet-sized shower. The needle spray spitting from the cheap shower-head seemed a harsh repudiation to the apparent fact that I was on vacation.

Jack was standing in the center of the room when I came out of the shower. He was spiffed up in a white cotton button-up shirt, faded jeans, and black penny loafers. His hair was shampooed and combed in a part, a level of grooming I hadn't seen on him since his twenties. He strutted and posed in place, a Marlboro Man without the Stetson, rugged and ready for action.

He fished a bottle of dripping-wet Byron bubbly out of the motel ice bucket and extended it across to me. "Open this, will you, Homes? I'll probably spray it all over, and you do it with just that right little je ne sais quoi that preserves all the bubbles."

"Fuck you." I knotted the towel around my waist and took the bottle from him, eager for a drink. Jack snaked a burly arm out, wrestled me into a headlock, and corkscrewed his fist into my hair.

"Get away from me," I said.

"Open the bottle," he said, releasing me with a laugh.

I did the honors. Jack found the little *thfft* sound when the cork was removed amusing. "You are good, Homes. You are good."

I poured two foaming, plastic motel cups and handed one to Jack. We toasted and sipped. Its years in the bottle had tamed the sparkling wine's mouth-puckering acids and given it an alluring smokiness and creaminess. It hit the spot. I've always felt that champagne is a perfect transition between more serious wines, perfect when I didn't want to sober up but didn't want to goose-step into the void either.

"Mm," I said. "Love this stuff."

"Delicious," Jack said. "Not too sweet."

"Did you go to the Jacuzzi?"

"Absolutely."

"How was it?"

"Excellent. I could have sworn this fucking chick was tickling me with her toes."

"Oh, come on!"

"I ain't lying. This place is fucking nuts up here. Chicks everywhere!"

"You've got pussy on the brain."

"Fuck, I know." He ran in place for a moment imitating a football player warming up on the sideline, then pounded a fist against the wall.

"You think these girls are hot to trot?"

"Fuck, man. What do *you* think, huh?"

I set my cup of champagne down. "What do I wear? Help me out here?"

"Just casual, man. They think you're an author. Exude confidence."

"Not exactly a characteristic of the profession."

Jack wagged a finger at me. "Now, that's the kind

of self-deprecation I hope to hear precious little of tonight."

"Good luck."

"Try." He clasped his hands together and beseeched, "For little ol' Jack who's getting the shackles put on him a week from today?"

I laughed. Jack hoisted up the bottle of Byron and I held up my glass for a refill. He refreshed me with a parsimonious splash.

"Hey," I protested, still thrusting my cup out. "Hey."

"I don't want you getting drunk. You know how it affects your stem."

I made a face, but before I could protest, the phone jangled. Jack looked disconcerted, then he whirled toward me and said, "Get in the bathroom and get dressed."

"What?"

The phone continued to importune us with its strident, drawn-out rings. Five, six . . . "I want to take this alone," he said, urgency in his tone.

"How do you know it's not for me?"

"I.R.S. know you're in Buellton? I don't think so, Homes. Just get out of here."

I dragged my suitcase off the luggage rack and hauled it into the bathroom. A moment later, the phone stopped ringing. As I got dressed I could overhear Jack saying, "Sweetheart," "I love you," "Don't worry," "Everything's fine," "I miss you, too, honey." Cringing, I switched on the overhead heating lamp, hoping the hum of the fan would drown out his specious endearments. When I could no longer hear Jack's voice, I emerged from the bathroom.

Jack was reclined on the bed, seemingly relieved that the phone call was behind him and another fire had been extinguished. He straightened to a standing position, looked me over, then said in a booming voice: "What—are—you—wearing—Liberace?"

"My tux," I said proudly, puffing out my chest. I had borrowed a purple velvet tuxedo from a friend of mine in an effort to save a little cash, and though it wasn't tailored to a perfect fit, I thought it would get me through. Besides, I reasoned, I was infamous for occasionally appearing sartorially outré at social functions, and rationalized it would be dismissed as a joke.

"You are *not* going out in that eyesore," Jack howled. "They're going to think we're a couple of wheelhousers."

"This is what I brought for the wedding."

Jack frowned. "We'll rectify that later this week. Now, get out of that silly monkey suit and into some manly jeans, would you? Fucking hurting my eyes." He checked his watch. "Let's get cracking. We're late."

Following his example, I quickly changed into jeans, ankle-high urban boots, and a long-sleeved black T-shirt: my signature look. Stroking his chin and looking down his nose at me, Jack finally approved.

Nervous about the double date, I had smuggled the Byron into the car and was hitting off the bottle at regular intervals to build up some courage, much to Jack's disapproval as he did the honors and chauffeured us to our destination.

The trace of a zephyr bearing the piney scent of nearby mountains caressed our faces as we rolled into the tiny town of Santa Ynez. The place cultivated a kind of faux Western motif with its timbered facades and replica red barns and other anachronistic Old West architectural flourishes.

We found a parking spot, tumbled out of the 4Runner, and walked along a planked sidewalk that creaked in protest with our heavy footfalls. As we neared the supposedly trendy restaurant with the supposedly unrivaled wine list, the murmurous voices from the diners inside increased in volume. Fifty paces from the entrance, Jack stopped me and said, "Are you weaving?"

"No, I'm not *weaving*."

"Let's have a look." Jack gave me a final once-over. He raked a hand through my hair and straightened up my shirt, then amiably slapped me on the cheek. "You're a mess."

"I'm an artist. Epigone though I may be."

"Let's hold off on the ten-dollar words, Webster, okay?" He jabbed a forefinger into my chest. "It's fucking ostentatious."

"Pretentious."

"Whatever. Okay?"

"We don't want to risk intimidating them, is that what you're implying?"

"Just put the pompous-asshole side of your personality away tonight."

"Be patronizing?"

"No," Jack said. "Just be yourself."

"This has been my contention all evening."

"The self you used to be."

"Who was that?"

"Before you went into the tailspin," Jack pointed out.

I slapped my forehead. "Oh . . . oh, the *tail*spin! You mean before the divorce and the failure of my first book and the reclaimed credit cards, *that* self. Oh, oh, okay."

He ignored the sarcasm. "It's a new Miles." Jack tried to bolster my ebbing spirits. "And, remember, your novel's coming out in the fall."

"What's it called?"

Jack looked stricken. "What do you mean what's it called? You've got a title, don't you?"

"*Confessions of an Onanist*," I cried out.

"Shh. Jesus. Are you just out to sabotage me?"

"I wouldn't dream of standing in the way of your cheating on your fiancée. Uh-uh. No, not me."

He brandished a finger at me. "Don't sabotage me. If you want to be a lightweight with Maya, that's your call. But don't sabotage *me*. Or this trip ends *mañana*."

I affected a similarly serious air and saluted him.

"Aye, aye, Captain. We're on a correct heading. Full speed ahead."

He gripped my shoulder and spun me around. "Let's go. Maintain. Don't weave."

"You're the one weaving, not me."

"I'm weaving because you're weaving."

"Weaves of grass."

"No references to esoteric poetry, either."

"Whitman? Esoteric? *Incroyable!*"

"Don't slip into French, Homes. Do *not* go into Frog. That's when I know you're really twisted."

We started back down the wooden sidewalk, Jack leading the campaign. The restaurant glowed yellow from inside large picture windows adorned with quaint white lace curtains. I was ambivalent, I knew I was ambivalent, and I knew I should have just turned around, but I felt too weak to protest any further. Not to mention that my reservations were compromised by the expectation of a gastronomic blowout funded by Jack's resolve to get laid.

As we approached the restaurant, Jack stopped me with a halfback's stiff arm from barging in. He peered through the window to case the scene. "Oh, my God!" he said. "Oh, my fucking God."

I attempted to push past his arm to take a look. But Jack clutched me by the shirt and held me slightly back to afford me a restricted view. I could make out Maya and Terra sitting next to each other at a horseshoe-shaped copper-top bar,

137

glasses of wine in front of them. Terra was wearing an unbuttoned charcoal gray sweater and a pair of tight low-rise blue jeans that offered a glimpse of her flat midriff—pierced bellybutton included. Maya wore a short black skirt and a tight-fitting red woolen shirt. From my perspective, she looked like a lioness secure in her preeminence on the food chain. Firelight from a wood-burning brick oven romanticized their features and made them seem all the more unapproachable.

"Oh, baby," Jack crooned, rubbing his hands together. "Come to papa. Come to papa."

"I thought they were going to blow us off," I said, feeling a tingle radiate up my spine.

Jack smirked. "Don't try to monopolize the wine selection. We're going with their palates. If they want to drink Merlot, we're drinking Merlot."

"They're not going to order Merlot. They're way too hip for that." I turned to Jack and threw open my arms. "And if they do, I'm splitting."

"Relax, Miles. Jesus. Calm down." Jack glanced back inside and luxuriated in a second look. "Man, they're beautiful." He turned to me, wrapped his arms around me in a bear hug and lifted me off the sidewalk. "Thank you for suggesting we come up here. I knew you were good for something." He let go of me and raised his arms dramatically. "How did I pull this off?"

"They can smell a man about to be married two vineyards away."

Jack giggled. "Shh. Shhshhshh!"

138

"Something musky emanating from him. Noble rot."

Jack clamped a hand over his mouth to suppress his laughter, then cautioned: "No marriage shit. No matter how much you have to drink, no mention of Babs. You understand?"

I held up my hands in surrender. "No mention of my ex either. Big downer."

"It could work in your favor. She might feel sorry for you."

"She'll conclude I'm a loser, but maybe vouch-safe me a mercy fuck, is that what you're implying?"

"Come on, what did we talk about?" Jack tried to rally me. "Act confident." He administered a playful wake-up slap. "Okay, here's the plan. We're going to walk in there like we're the shit. And you're going to swing around with a swagger in your step to the side that Maya's on, and I'm going to pitch my tent next to Terra firma."

"Hey, wait a second," I interrupted, pretending I didn't understand. "I thought Terra was mine."

"Homes! She thinks you're an arrogant wine snob jerk."

"Oh, and no doubt you confirmed that to her this afternoon while I was MIA in the bathroom."

Jack wrestled me away from the restaurant window and stuck his face close to mine. "Yeah, well, while you were MIA I was in that tasting room using all my charms so that tonight we wouldn't be DOA in that fucking morgue called the Clubhouse."

"QED."

"QED. Fuck you. Look, Miles, let me explain something to you. Terra is hot to trot. She's my type. We're not going to let our fucking brains interfere with the task at hand. You and Maya, on the other hand, have a history, you have Pinot in common. Intelligent conversation. Okay?" He leaned closer. "She's obviously the more beautiful of the two. I'm doing you a favor. I could get either one of them tonight. I could get both of them in fact!"

"Oh, give me a break. You are so fucking full of yourself."

"Miles. Miles." He placed both hands on my shoulders and spoke to me gently now. "This may come as a total shock to you but sometimes . . . chicks just want to get pounded."

I looked wordlessly into the artificial smile frozen on his big round face.

"Let's go," he said. "They're waiting."

"Wait a second."

"What now?"

"I feel a mild panic attack coming on."

"For crying out loud," Jack said, exasperated. "Did you bring your meds?"

I unpocketed a small vial of Xanax and rattled the pills around inside. I hadn't had to resort to any since my most recent hospitalization a few months before, but I carried them with me everywhere as a kind of security blanket.

"Good. Because, Lord only knows where 911's going to take us up here."

I chuckled anxiously.

140

"All right," Jack said. "Let's rock and roll."

We circled around to the entrance. Inside the loud, crowded restaurant we paraded right past the "Hey, can I help you?" maître d', and made a beeline to the bar. Jack, sporting his ear-to-ear convivial grin, spearheaded our offensive.

"Hey, girls," he said in a rising tone. "Sorry we're late."

They swiveled on their stools at the same moment and faced us with friendly smiles and a toast of their glasses.

"We got stuck in traffic," I said.

"Yeah, that 246 can get really jammed up this time of night," Terra joked.

Everyone laughed. As planned, Jack circled around and plopped down on a stool next to Terra and I mimicked his move on the north battlefield next to Maya. I noticed Jack touching a hand briefly to Terra's bare neck and massaging it casually. "How're you doing, beautiful?" he said in his sweetest voice.

"Good," she said, beaming at him. "How're you?"

"Great," Jack said. "You look smashing."

"Thank you. Not bad yourself, sexy."

I finally eased onto the stool next to Maya. Unlike Jack the actor I was clumsy at flummery. Besides, I didn't think Maya was really the type who would fall for it. "There's no karaoke here," I said. "Let's split."

There was laughter as Jack and Terra turned toward us.

141

"My apologies for last night," I said to Maya. "I really don't despise myself that much."

Maya looked at me. "That's good to hear. I found it amusing. In a kind of sad and pathetic way."

I laughed. "You must be bored here in Buellton."

"Homes!" Jack reproached me with arching eyebrows.

"Why does he call you Homes?" Maya asked in her throaty, low-register voice.

"Because if he uses my real name it'll sound too personal. We've depersonalized our relationship for the sake of its longevity."

"So, what's *his* nickname?"

"Oh, it varies. Lately I've been stuck on pecker-head, but I'm open to suggestions."

Maya cracked a smile and I looked away. Our shoulders were touching, and there was something electrifying in that glancing tactility that I couldn't wrap my brain around. Part of me wanted to close my eyes and lean all the way into her lap, but I knew that that indiscretion had the potential to capsize the whole evening, at least as Jack had it scripted out.

Jack and Terra were laughing hard on the starboard end of our foursome, and for a moment I fantasized what it would be like if Babs were watching us on a hidden camera, what conclusions she would draw. What gun shop she would patronize.

"So, what are you drinking here?" I asked Maya.

"Andrew Murray Viognier."

I brightened. "Oh, yeah, how is it?"

She slid the glass in front of me. "Here, try it."

I swirled the wine in the tulip-shaped glass and put my nose in it. It smelled of apricots and melons. I took a sip. It was massive, a viscous conflation of tropical fruit, butterscotch, and spritzes of limes. "Nice," I said. "Very nice."

"I thought you'd like it."

"I like it a lot." I helped myself to another mouthful. God, the wine tasted delicious on my palate. It was refreshing to be once again beyond the narrow simplicity of champagne and back into some serious grape. "Mm. Delish," I said, sliding the glass back to her.

The maître d' appeared behind us and said, "Your table's ready."

All four of us pivoted off our bar stools and were escorted to a corner table. We assumed strategic positions: boy, girl, boy, girl. Terra knew the maître d' and thanked him personally. After he passed out menus, he recited the roster of the evening's specials: seared ahi on a bed of mixed baby greens as an appetizer; medallions of pork with a light dusting of black truffles; a poulet with *pommes frites*; and Copper River salmon roasted on an alder wood plank. After he had concluded his recitation, he said, "Who would like to see the wine list?"

I raised my arm in the air with the zeal of an overachieving first grader, but Jack was zapping me with one of those withering looks of his, so I lowered my paw.

"Did you want to choose the wine?" Terra asked, laughing.

"No. No. Be my guest. Please." I held up my hands in surrender.

Across the table, Jack nodded at me with a Cheshire-cat smile. The wine list was handed to Terra. "So, what is everyone in the mood for?" Terra wondered.

"Whatever you girls are drinking, it's on me," Jack said magnanimously.

"What is everyone ordering?" Maya said. "Then we can sort out the wine."

I turned and looked at her. "*Exactement!*"

Jack wagged a finger at me. "No, Jean-Pierre, no."

Maya and Terra exchanged bemused looks, but pressed on reading their menus.

"I'm going to have the salmon," Maya decided.

"That's exactly what I'm going to have," I said, slamming my menu shut.

"Duck breast for me," Terra said. "Maybe the house salad to start."

"Excellent choice," Jack said, slapping his menu decisively on the table.

"So," Terra said, turning her attention back to the wine list again. "What—are—we—going—to—drink?" She pretended to be poring over the list for a few serious moments, then raised her head and rested her chin on the rim of the menu, peering over it with theatrically batting eyelashes. She looked coquettishly at Maya, then at me, then back and forth a few more times. "Sounds like Pinot Noir to me!"

"Pinot!" Jack and I both echoed simultaneously, raising fists into the air. Our rah-rah response caused our dates to titter. They were probably wondering if we were fun guys or full-blown lushes.

"The question is," Terra settled us down, "which Pinot?" She handed the list across the table to Maya. "Let's go to the expert, shall we?"

Maya scanned the list briefly.

"May I make a humble suggestion?" I offered, timidly holding up my hand.

"No," Maya snapped without looking at me. Then she smiled to mollify her curt response.

I leaned over, cupped a hand to shield my mouth from Jack, and whispered into Maya's ear, "Remember, Jack's paying, and he's *butt* rich." Maya touched my arm conspiratorially. "Don't be afraid to cross the Atlantic," I added.

I straightened back in my chair. Jack's eyes were narrowed at us, trying to decipher our little tête-à-tête.

"Why don't we go back in memory lane and revisit the '95 Whitcraft from our own Santa Ynez Valley?" Maya suggested.

"Sounds good," Terra said.

"We'll pay for the food," Maya said.

"Forget it," Jack said. "It's on us. We're celebrating Miles's book deal."

My head slouched forward and I shielded my embarrassment with a swiftly moving hand.

145

"So when does it come out?" Terra asked. "You must be excited."

"In the spring," I said softly. I hated to lie, but I had little choice.

"Isn't that awfully quick for a book just acquired?" Maya asked.

"It's a hot commodity." Jack came in to shore up the levee.

"Very little editing," I said.

Maya gave me the gimlet eye, then lifted her Viognier to her lips. Her mouth closed over the last sip, and I was suddenly desperate for a glass myself.

The maître d' returned—thank God!—erect and proper in his black pants and white shirt.

Maya looked up at him and said, "Greg, a bottle of the '95 Whitcraft."

"Excellent selection, as I would expect." He disappeared into the back to uncellar the bottle.

"Have you had the Whitcraft?" I asked Maya, wanting to steer her away from my bogus book deal.

"I've had the previous years, which were all pretty amazing." She turned to Terra. "You've had the '95, haven't you?"

"Yeah. It was great. Be interesting to see if it holds up." She raised her eyebrows in anticipation of its uncorking and smiled. Jack kneaded the back of her neck again and she gazed up at him with moony eyes.

Maya turned to me. "Ninety-five was a really

dry year and the taproots had to go deep for water. That produced a low yield but a highly concentrated fruit."

A giddy feeling washed over me. It was fun to be in the company of these two knowledgeable wine women, and I was beginning to feel slightly guilty for having agreed to the dinner on such false pretenses, in tow with my wickedly amoral friend.

The maître d' promptly returned with the bottle of Whitcraft, opened it, and placed the cork aside.

"Hey, aren't you supposed to smell the cork?" Jack blurted out.

Maya, Terra, the maître d', and I all exchanged raised eyebrows. I broke the silence: "Jack, that's like sniffing a woman's butt before you have sex with her."

Maya stifled a laugh with her hand. Tears of hilarity sprang to Terra's eyes and she bent to one side, losing it for a moment.

"Hey, I'm learning," Jack said. "I didn't know." And then he, too, laughed.

Maya turned serious as the maître d' poured her a small amount in a proper Burgundy glass. She swirled the wine, brought it to her nose, and breathed it in for a full three seconds. She set the glass back down and raised her eyes to the maître d'. "It's fine, Greg. You can pour the rest of us."

Greg poured us glasses all around.

I must have been staring at Maya for the longest

time because she finally turned to me and said, "What?"

"Nothing," I said, awestruck. I wanted to say: You're beautiful, and goddamn if you're not the first woman I've met who didn't need to taste the wine to know that it wasn't corked, which makes you even that much more extraordinary. Instead, I looked away and took hold of my glass and swirled the ruby-colored liquid around until little bubbles formed on the surface. I trickled some into my mouth and thrashed it around.

"Well?" Maya asked. "What's the verdict?"

"Very concentrated, like you said," I commented. I took another sip. "Jammy."

"Mm, I like this," Jack said. "Very fruity."

"What do you think, Terra?" Maya asked.

"Maybe starting to fade a tad, stewed plums on the nose," Terra replied after relishing a mouthful.

A second taste only affirmed the first and seemed to build on it. I turned to Maya. "This area's just ripe for Pinot to explode, isn't it?"

"Ten years and we're going to be right there with DRC."

"I don't know about that," I countered, "but these wines coming out of here are pretty fucking delicious."

"All right, all right," Jack interjected, arms folded across his chest, "what's DRC?"

"Don't Rain on our Company," I shot back, for a little more laughter at his expense.

"Domaine de la Romanée-Conti," Terra decoded

148

the famous initials. Judging by Jack's puzzled expression, that hadn't helped a whole lot.

"Famous Burgundian producer," I elucidated, remembering that he was paying for the wine and not wanting to bite the hand that intoxicated me.

"Ah," Jack replied. Then, in an effort to reenter the conversation, he let slip, "We've got a bottle of '82 Latour back at the motel."

"Oh, *yeah?*" Maya said, her eyes widening. "Why didn't you bring that?"

I closed my eyes and bowed my head for a protracted moment. One bottle of '82 Latour should be drunk alone or between two, tops, but among four its depth and richness would be reduced to little more than abbreviated foreplay.

"Miles claims it's one of the great years of the last half century," Jack added, sticking his foot deeper into his mouth.

"Miles is right," Terra said.

"I would *love* to taste that," Maya said, warming to me.

"We've decided to cellar it another few years."

"Oh, that's too bad," Maya said. "Because I'm of the impression that the '82 is on the decline, despite the ravings of Robert Parker."

Terra was the first to burst out laughing. Then, everybody else chimed in. It took me a moment to realize they were all laughing at me, and that my proprietary tone toward the coveted '82 was so blatant I might as well have screamed: *It's all mine, leave me alone, go away!*

"Homes, you crack me up," Jack said, having successfully rejoined the conversation. That broke Terra up again. Maya, sensitive to my chagrin, tried hard not to laugh. I hid behind my glass of Whitcraft, adrift in its mysteriousness. When I reached for the bottle for a refill, Jack clamped his hand on my wrist and said, "Slow down there, F. Scott. We've got a long evening ahead of us."

"Bungo," I said.

"So, who's publishing your book?" Maya asked, shifting the conversation to an ostensibly less touchy topic.

I quickly scrambled back to that false-hearted corner of my mind. "The truth is," I started haltingly—I noticed Jack's face start to blanch—"it's gone to auction with a floor bid of sixty-thousand from a very good house. I'm not sure who the ultimate publisher is going to be, just that it's a *fait accompli*. I'll know more middle of next week."

Jack closed his eyes for an almost imperceptible moment, as if an angel had alighted on his shoulder to whisper to him that it was all going to be okay. In that moment I snared the Whitcraft and replenished my glass. And Maya's. And, then, eventually, Jack's and Terra's. I had righted the ship, and we were back on course.

After we had put in our orders, Jack told the maître d', "Better bring us another bottle of the Whitcraft."

150

"Let's try something else," Maya said. "If that's all right with everybody."

"Excellent idea," I said. "Let's have an unofficial Pinot tasting."

The maître d' handed Maya the wine list. She cracked it open. I swayed toward her and read it with her over her shoulder. "Remember," I whispered, "Jack's got *serious* bank."

Maya's finger slipped lower under the Pinot category until she came to the three-figure section. She closed the list, turned to the maître d', and ordered with quiet confidence. "Bring us a bottle of the '99 Kistler Rochioli."

"With pleasure," the Maître d' said, beaming. He reached for the wine list, which Maya was holding out to him, but I intercepted it.

"Better leave it here," I said. "We're just getting started."

Maya turned to me. "You're the devil, aren't you?"

"Harmlessly so," I replied.

"So, how do you two guys know each other?" Terra asked.

"We met in prison," I cracked.

"Miles flashed me a crooked grin in the shower," Jack added, poker-faced. "I straightened him out and we've been friends ever since." Maya and Terra laughed politely. "No," Jack said, "we met on a film that I was acting in. Miles wrote the screenplay. Then, a couple of years later, we made a film that Miles wrote and I directed and starred in."

"Anything we might have seen?" Terra asked.

151

"Not unless you were at the Tierra del Fuego Film Festival in ninety-seven," I said.

The women exchanged puzzled looks.

"It didn't get a theatrical release," Jack clarified.

"He fucked up my script!" I said.

"Yeah, well, you depleted my trust fund with your dark vision."

I bent toward Maya and whispered, "Don't believe him. He's loaded." I turned to Jack and Terra. "You know the real problem? The film called for frontal nudity and Jack was the lead. We tried using wide-angle lenses, but to no avail."

Laughter exploded from everyone. Jack pointed his finger at me as if to say *touché*.

The maître d' returned with the '99 Kistler Pinot, a highly allocated wine made by Steve Kistler, one of the great Sonoma winemakers.

Maya approved the wine. Greg served the four of us in clean stemware brought to the table by a serious-looking young man. I looked into my glass. I was starting to get drunk now, and I was clinging with my fingertips to the last vestige of decorum. Soon, however, I knew there would come that moment when, without anyone's bidding, I would slip through a crack in the floorboards and find myself rowing across the River Styx with my demon entourage, and not until morning would I fully be able to assess the consequences.

"So, you're both in the movie business?" I heard Terra say.

"I am," Jack said. "Miles's on hiatus."

"Permanently," I added. Maya chuckled knowingly. I wondered for a moment if she had had a flirtation with Hollywood, but I decided not to probe.

"What did you think of the movies this year?" Terra asked.

"Fabulous year," I said, raising my glass of Kistler. "Outstanding product."

"I thought everything stank," Maya said.

"I haven't seen anything I liked," Terra concurred.

"Was not a great year," Jack, that pussy-on-the-brain Benedict Arnold, chorused.

"Jack instructed me specifically not to say anything negative tonight. Was afraid I would alienate you," I quickly explained so that they didn't think I was lacking in taste. "Cynicism is the hair of the dog!"

"What?" Jack said, screwing his face into a coil of wrinkles.

"Hair of the dog," I repeated, toasting the group with my glass and spilling a little on the white tablecloth in the process. "Whoops."

Jack turned to Terra and said something that made her nod and smile. It felt as if they had moved across the room and were huddled in a cabal, conspiring against me. I couldn't tell exactly what Jack was saying, but I assumed it was something to gain sympathy for my drunken antics—"He's recently divorced," "It's been a tough year." Good, I thought, at least my banter was helping them to bond.

I finally sampled the Kistler. My palate was

battle-fatigued, but the wine had a powerful nose of black cherries and burnt spices.

Maya leaned closer. "What do you think of the Kistler?"

"Exciting. Dancing on my tongue. A little closed." I sensed I was already slurring and my face had flushed beet red, as it usually did when I teetered on the abyss.

"I think it needs a few years," she said. "But it's built for potential greatness."

"I agree." I turned to Maya. In the soft, amber light she looked stunning. Her eyes were onyx black; as I stared into them I thought I was free-falling into a night ocean. There was nothing real about her, the wine, or the evening anymore. "I thought the Whitcraft, if you want to know the truth, was a little vegetal-ly," I managed, one hand barely on the rudder.

"A little rough around the edges and falling apart, I agree," Maya said, nodding.

"Positively primitive on the palate. But this Kis is delish."

Maya laughed, but when I glanced at her she wore a kind of bemused expression as if I had said something odd. I turned to Jack and his eyes were bulged out at me, unblinking and admonitory. Clearly, I had either missed something or had uttered something remiss.

"So, what do you girls do around here for fun, other than drink wine?" I asked. "I'm thinking of relocating."

"Do you think the chamber of commerce would let you move up here?" Terra joked.

"What do you mean 'not let me move up here'?" I volleyballed. "I am to the vineyard what the bee is to the flower." Everyone laughed. I glanced at Jack and he was nodding. In his mind, I'm sure, he was saying, *That's more like it, more of those, Miles, keep 'em coming, keep 'em laughing, that's how we move from point A to point F.*

Our entrées finally arrived, steaming fucking masterpieces, artisanal creations. (I can't recall if I actually said that or rehearsed it in my head and scrapped it at the last minute.) I admired mine with an exaggerated awe that was nine-tenths wine and one-tenth reality. "Beautiful," I said. "Gorgeous. Absolutely gorgeous." I looked up at everyone. "Should we get another bottle? Let's get out of this California rut and cross the Atlantic. Let's board the bullet train to the Côte d'Or!"

Amidst the laughter, I turned and caught Maya toggling her index finger at the maître d'. He hurried over, no doubt smelling a blowout and a monster gratuity.

"Bring us a bottle of the '96 Comte Armand Pommard," Maya told him.

"That's the spirit!" I said.

Greg strode back to the cellar.

We dug into our entrées. The Comte Armand was rushed to the table and uncorked. We were finally in Burgundy now. It was a whole new realm of sensations, different *terroir*, different *climat*, all

155

of it focused in that microcosmic world known as wine.

Owing to the price of the Comte Armand, Maya elected to taste the wine this time as the maître d' hovered over us with the bottle. She moved it around in her mouth thoughtfully, caressing it. Then, as if heroin had hit her bloodstream, her eyes closed for an extended moment and her mouth widened slightly. "Mm," she moaned. She opened her eyes and said to the maître d', "Very nice, Greg."

The serious-looking waiter set more new glistening stemware in front of us. We were refreshed all around with the Comte Armand. As the wine rose to our lips, we were vertiginously winched up to a more rarefied plateau. It was as if we had just left the harbor and entered the sea, as if the clouds had parted and the sky had colored lavender and wraith-like little sprites were dancing on the surface of the water.

"Now *this* is Pinot Noir," I said. "Thank you, Maya." I raised my glass and toasted her. We clinked crystal and exchanged smiles. I noticed that Jack had his arm slung around Terra's shoulder and he was nuzzling her ear, whispering unintelligible sweet nothings and making her giggle. Then, in a flash, she rushed her mouth to his and their faces closed together in a short but deeply sensual kiss. I grew instantly nauseated. The Comte Armand went to vinegar in my mouth.

The next thing I remember was threading

through the tables toward the bathroom as though I were straddling a small dinghy pitching about on stormy seas. When I got to the bathroom, the door was locked. I knocked vehemently to alert the occupant that someone was waiting. Spotting a pay phone, I turned to it and reached for the receiver. I dialed first my calling card number, then my PIN, then the only other number I knew by heart. It was astonishing that I could remember all those numbers after all the wine I'd consumed, and even more astonishing when I heard Victoria's familiar voice.

"Miles?" I heard her say as if she were speaking from a bathysphere.

"Victoria! How the hell are you? Heard you got remarried? Congratulations. Didn't think you had the stomach for another go-round after the disaster of our blessed union."

"Oh, Miles. You sound drunk."

"A little Whitcraft, north to the Russian River, then the SST all the way to Bourgogne," I said, finishing on a sound like a rocket whistling over an enemy target.

"Where are you?" she pried, concerned.

"En route to the wedding," I confessed. "I'm Jack's best man. That's supposed to be top secret. Shh shh shh. Don't tell anyone."

There was a dismaying silence. I knew if I hung up, the phone lines between L.A. and Paso Robles were going to heat up, so I leapt back in to allay her apprehensions. "Don't worry, Vicki," I started.

"I'm not coming. But don't tell Babs, because then she'll tell Jack and the shit will hit the fan. The truth is, I'm his monitor up here, keeping him out of mischief."

"Sounds like it," she said sardonically.

"No, seriously. I'm watching him like a hawk."

"Miles, I don't care if you come to the wedding or not."

"You don't? Because I just learned that you and your new husband will be there and I didn't want to be an unwelcome presence."

"I mean, if *you're* going to be uncomfortable, I don't want you to come."

"Don't worry," I said. "I'm not about to ruin anyone's special moment."

"Well, that's charitable of you."

"It's just that I found out about all this today and I was kind of taken aback. I guess I thought there was still hope for us somewhere down the road, dark and painful as its course has been."

She didn't say anything for an ominous few seconds. "Listen, Miles, it might be best if you *didn't* come."

"Whatever you say, Vicki, whatever you say. You're the boss." I replaced the receiver and turned to the bathroom and banged irately on the door. "What're you doing in there?" I yelled. "There are patrons soiling themselves out here!"

A few seconds later, the door opened and a middle-aged woman emerged, scowling as she pushed her way past me. I glanced up and noticed that the sign on the door read, FEMMES. Christ almighty! The adjoining door for HOMMES was locked, so I slipped into FEMMES.

Navigating on broken wings, I braved the gangplank back into the dining room, groping for handholds along the way. I reached our table and eased into my chair—or at least I thought I had—but a moment later Maya was helping me up from the floor.

"Are you all right, Miles?" she was saying.

"Fine. Just slipped. Oops!"

I clambered back into my chair. When I looked up from my half-eaten filet of salmon, everyone was wearing a concerned expression. Terra made a little head gesture to Maya and they excused themselves and retreated to the bathroom.

As soon as they were out of view, Jack bent forward across the table, an anxious look disorganizing his face. "What's up?"

"Nothing," I said, reaching for my Comte Armand.

"Pull yourself together, man," Jack scolded. "You're drinking too fast. You're getting The Voice."

I thrust my hands across the table pleadingly. "I'm fine." But a glass of water seemed to have spilled in the process. Jack quickly righted it and threw a napkin on the tablecloth.

"Fine, right. Where were you all this fucking time? What were you doing?"

"Making a phone call."

"Did you D-and-D Victoria?" he accused.

He was referring to drink-and-dial, and I didn't say anything, feeling ashamed, even in my benumbed state.

His tone turned conciliatory. "Why do you always do this, Miles? She's gone, man. Vapor. Poof. I'm helping you out here. Maya's smart, she's cool, she's funny as shit. What's this morose fucking come-down bullshit? We're up here to blow out. And these girls want to have fun."

"I'm feeling uncomfortable with the whole scenario," I admitted, shaking my head.

"What whole scenario? That I'm going to sleep with someone? Fuck, Miles, every guy I know hires a hooker before he gets married and gets his nut. So, I lucked out. But I *am* getting my nut. With or without you." He stabbed a finger toward me. "Don't go fucking Jerry Falwell on me. Not when it's all about to come to papa."

I brought the Comte Armand to my lips and took a sip. It was really taking off. Wheee! I was soaring now and I wanted the world to fade away and leave me alone.

Jack's voice was going in and out of my consciousness like a bad cell connection. "What's the matter? That girl digs you. You should see the way she looks at you, man. I mean, *I* don't get it." He leaned closer, clutched my wrist, and prevented me from moving. "Why do you always do this?"

"What?" I bristled.

"As soon as some woman shows interest in you, you start self-destructing. What's the point? And you're not *that* drunk." He let go of my wrist and sat back in his chair, defiant.

"I'm not?" I said, feigning shock.

"Fuck, Homes, I've had as much as you, if not more. And our friends here. . . ."—he threw an arm in the direction of the bathroom—". . . in case you haven't noticed, didn't exactly ride on over from the local rehab center."

I stayed silent. I was mortified that I had fallen out of my chair and I wanted to go back to the motel and crash, put a lid on the evening.

"Come on, let's ratchet this up a notch," Jack encouraged. "You know how to do it. Here." He pushed a glass of ice water across the table. "Drink some water. I don't want you doing a face-plant on me."

I looked at the water as though it were truth serum. I drained the glass, then set my wine aside.

Our dates came back to the table. Colloquies had taken place on opposite sides of the restaurant and we were now ready for the hoped-for rapprochement, the segue to higher zeniths of libidinousness.

"Should we get dessert?" I said in a manufactured cheery voice, hoping it would momentarily put to rest fears that I had somersaulted off the deep end.

"Why don't we go back to my place?" Terra proposed, smiling at Jack. "We've got wine, music, whatever you like." She looked back and forth between the two of us.

"Excellent idea," Jack said, raising both arms like a referee signaling a touchdown.

"Great," Terra said.

I was too tired to protest.

While Terra wrote directions to her house on the back of a napkin, Maya and I indulged ourselves in the last of the Comte Armand. I was willy-nilly in for the duration and I needed fortification.

Terra and Maya left together as Jack and I hung back to settle the bill. When the maître d' handed Jack the check his eyes popped out of his head like shooter's marbles.

"Jesus fucking Christ," he exploded. "$828.69!"

"I didn't want to mention that the Comte Armand was $300. Was afraid it might make you look cheap."

Jack scowled and fished his wallet from his back pocket as resignedly as someone about to write a check for a parking ticket. "This is one expensive fuck, I'll tell you that." He painfully counted out ten hundred-dollar bills and parted with them morosely. "Talk about sobering up, brother."

I was laughing hard as we left the restaurant. The maître d' was all handshakes and *thank you*s as we went out the swinging saloon-style door.

The drive to Terra's house was a Mr. Toad's Wild Ride along dark, tree-lined, curving mountain roads. Jack, with the tracking instincts of an Indian on the spoor of fresh game, skillfully negotiated the scrawled directions that I woozily recited to him as we careered and fishtailed to our next den of iniquity.

Sometime later we were idling on a dirt driveway in front of a wood-framed home in the hills of Santa Ynez. It was a miracle how we had found the place, what with the poorly-lit and unmarked streets, the numerous turnoffs, and all we'd had to drink. I rolled down the window to get some air. The night was warm and sexy and, as soon as Jack killed the engine, crickets chorused in. It was so quiet and peaceful I wanted to stay put and go to sleep in the back of my 4Runner.

"Give me the keys," I demanded.

"What?" Jack looked at me like I was crazy. "You're not driving anywhere. You fell off your chair in the restaurant."

"I'm not sleeping on some unfamiliar couch."

"No one is sleeping on the couch, Homes. Women do not invite you back to their place after three bottles of expensive wine. . . ."—he shook his head contemptuously at the memory of the bill—". . . then ask you to crash on their couch." He slapped his forehead. "I am mystified as to how you got out of high school."

"Leave the keys under the mat," I suggested as a compromise.

Jack looked thunderstruck. "There's no way you're driving out of here at three A.M., brother.

If we're going down, we're going down in tandem."
He pocketed the keys, then reached into his coat
pocket and produced a string of condoms. He tore
one off and handed it to me. "All right, here's one
for you and three for me."

"What?"

"In your condition, you'll be lucky to get this
halfway to the Promised Land."

"I don't know about this," I started.

"Miles. Miles. Listen to me. Let's just go in, sip
some of their Pinot, get to know these girls in a
little more comfortable setting. Just have a good
time. No pressure. All right?"

I refused to take the condom from him, so Jack
dropped it into my shirt pocket. He patted my
protection reassuringly. "These are extra-large, so
hold on to your hat, Shorthorn, you might lose it
in the saddle."

"Right, Jack."

I climbed reluctantly out of the car and trailed
Jack in a shambling walk up to the porch of Terra's
house. I spotted a comfy-looking two-seater swing
and plopped down in it, petulant. "I'll wait out
here," I mumbled.

Jack quickly hooked an arm under one of mine
and jerked me to my feet. "We're going inside,"
he ordered. "Come on. Act sociable."

He hauled me toward the front door and knocked
once, rattling the screen. Then, without waiting,
he opened it and shoved me in front of him. We
stumbled across the forbidden threshold.

A moment later, I found myself inside Terra's musty-smelling living room. The décor was an anachronistic bohemian motif, furnished with Oriental rugs, ornate wall tapestries, sloppily maintained bookcases, and antique velvet upholstered chairs and a sofa draped with knitted woolen throws. A brick fireplace stacked with freshly lit logs burned a warm orange, crackling noisily. The mantelpiece was decorated with wine bottles, which gleamed translucent green in the underlight of the fire. Candles of all colors and sizes flickered everywhere as though we had crashed a séance.

"What is this?" I laughed. "Am I going to commune with my former self?"

"Shh, they're being romantic."

"I thought candles went out with Timothy Leary."

"Shh, shh," Jack exhorted. "Terra?" he called out. "We're here!"

Terra bounced into the living room from what appeared to be the kitchen. "What happened to you guys? Didn't think you were going to make it."

"It was a bitch to find," Jack apologized. They came together and embraced and held it just long enough to suggest to each other that it wouldn't be the last embrace of the evening, then kissed briefly, but meaningfully, before disengaging. "Hi," Jack said.

"Hi," Terra sweetly said back. Then, in a louder voice meant to include me: "Would you guys like something to drink?"

"Most definitely," Jack said.

Terra turned to me with an amiable smile on her face. "Maya's in the kitchen. Why don't you go in and help her decide on something?"

I missed my cue. Jack elbowed me sharply in the ribs, prodding me along, and I shuffled off dutifully, now an accessory and little more. The pairing off was fully underway.

I didn't see anyone in the kitchen when I first walked in. Hearing some bottles clinking, I followed the sirenic sound until I came to a cozy pantry area. There, I found Maya squatting in front of a chest high, temperature-controlled wine cellar scrutinizing Terra's wine collection.

"Hi," I said.

She turned, showed her lovely face, and smiled. "Hey. Glad you could make it."

I bent down next to her, drawn to the racks of wine and her subtle, flowery smell. "Terra got any good stuff in there?"

"Oh, a lot of goodies. She likes Pinots, too." She pulled out a '99 Ponzi Reserve, an Oregonian Pinot from the Willamette Valley.

"Interesting," I said. "Probably should hold back on that for a few years. I heard it's pretty massive."

"I think you're right, Miles," she said, sliding the bottle back into the cellar. "It's got to be way too buttoned up." I loved hearing my name spoken in her throaty voice. It sounded so familiar somehow.

She removed another bottle from the racks and

166

handed it to me. It was a '98 Bien Nacido from Tantara, a tiny, local producer of purportedly good Pinots. "We could do that," I said. "I've never had their wines before."

"Or," she said, conveying another bottle and turning the label so I could see it. It was a '90 Henri Jayer Richebourg, one of the great Burgundian reds from a classic year.

My eyes widened. "Wow," I said. "Terra's got *some* collection."

"Actually, it's mine," Maya confided.

"Where'd you get this?" I asked, still stunned.

"My ex. Had quite the cellar, which I plundered in the settlement."

"Smart girl."

"I know."

"Do you want to get married? We could have quite a future together."

"No, thanks, I just got done with one."

"Yeah, me, too. Maybe we should celebrate with the Jayer," I suggested greedily.

"It's not the right moment," she said, carefully replacing the bottle. "Some other time," she added, smiling mischievously.

"Yeah, tempting as it is, I think our palates are a little shot for that tonight."

Maya decided on the Tantara and we started to move into the kitchen. But I was blocking her path. My reflexes dulled, I didn't step aside adroitly or quickly enough and we collided. I held her broad shoulders for a moment to regain my balance. When I glanced back at her, she was looking directly up into my eyes, gazing intently, and I wondered if what Jack had said was right. Maybe women sometimes just wanted sex and nothing more.

"Hey, don't drop that bottle," I said. We both laughed, and I let her squeeze past me.

I lingered in the pantry checking out the bottles in their cellar. It was impressive and pretty far-ranging for such a tiny collection. "How long have you been into wine, Maya?"

"All my adult life," she answered from the kitchen. I heard a cork pop, which I sensed was my signal to rejoin her.

As I approached her she turned to me and extended a half-filled glass of the Tantara Pinot. We took seats at a planked dining table. We didn't make a whole lot of fuss swirling the wine, but when I looked over at Maya she had her head held back and was working the Pinot around in her mouth. "Mm," she was quick to remark. "This is pretty good."

I sampled the wine. It wasn't coming through, but I didn't think the wine was the problem. I kept working it like crazy, but my palate was washed out. "It's a waste on me now," I said.

Maya smiled until the kitchen warmed. She poured two more glasses and rose. "Back in a sec," she said.

She carried the newly poured glasses out to the living room, while I hung back. I heard Jack's voice cheering, "All right! More wine." Partying laughter erupted from the three of them. A few seconds later, music blasted from the stereo system. I didn't know if they were waiting for me to join them or not, but I stayed in the kitchen anyway, holding my face with both hands as if trying to prop myself up.

Maya reappeared, thank God, rolling her eyes at the music and chuckling. It was a romantic ballad belted out by Tom Jones and my mind suddenly came alive with the image of Jack and Terra in the living room performing some kind of tribal, hip-grinding dance, rubbing their crotches together like crazed Vegas dancers.

"Your friend is a hoot," Maya said.

"Oh, yeah," I said sarcastically, hoping she would catch it. "He's a bundle of laughs."

"Terra seems pretty taken with him." From the timbre of her voice I could feel she was mildly concerned about her friend.

"Jack has that effect on women."

Maya sat back down at the table and refilled her glass. Jack was right about one thing: these girls could hold their own when it came to drinking. She sipped her wine and combed her fingers through her hair. "What happened back at the restaurant?" she asked with real feeling. "You were having so much fun, then you suddenly seemed depressed about something."

"Oh, it was stupid. I called somebody I shouldn't have, and, uh. . . ." I trailed off and reached instinctively for my glass.

"Girlfriend?" Maya probed.

"No, I don't have a girlfriend, Maya." I leveled my gaze at her. I was transfixed by her large, dark, liquid eyes and I just sank into them for a moment. "Ex-wife," I finally confessed.

"Oh." But the way she said it suggested she was confused about why exactly that would depress me.

"I just learned today that she got remarried," I continued.

"Ah," she said, this time with empathy. "Did that make you sad to hear it?"

"It was just weird, that's all." I tried to shrug it off, but I could feel the gesture probably seemed insincere to her.

"You must still be in love with her," she said.

"I honestly don't know. But it really doesn't matter *now*, does it?"

Her wide mouth broke into a strained smile, then quickly disappeared. I sensed that she had experienced her own share of sadness and disappointment in life and didn't find sharing mine all that comforting.

"What the *hell* are they listening to anyway?" I said, louder, in an effort to brighten the mood.

"Terra's going through a Tom Jones phase. Don't ask me why, but she's nuts about him. Especially when she has a man over."

"That a frequent occurrence?" I asked, refilling my glass.

"Mm," she said, swallowing a taste of wine. "She broke up with a guy recently, dyed her hair blond, got her belly button pierced, and has been, uh, well, let's just say, dating a lot."

"Why is it when women end a relationship they start dating like crazy, and when men break up they go into a protracted hibernation?"

"A somewhat sweeping generalization, don't you think? When I divorced I just wanted to be alone. And I was. For a long time."

A silence descended, which the music blaringly filled. We sipped our wine for a moment, having momentarily lost the thread of our conversation.

"Do you like Tom Jones?" Maya asked, her face twisted into a grimace.

"He's an acquired taste," I said. "Has to be the right occasion. Though I'm hard-pressed to conjure one at the moment. Maybe after a successful run at the blackjack table and five double Scotches."

She laughed. "I know what you mean." She traced a red-nailed finger along the rim of her wineglass and cast her eyes down. I kept oxygenating the wine in my glass out of habit, even though it had long since stopped needing it. We were both marking time until Jack and Terra withdrew somewhere more private. "So, what's your novel about?" she finally broke the silence.

"It's a mystery."

"What's the story, or the premise, or whatever?"

"It features a private eye who can only solve cases after he's had two bottles of the finest Bourgogne Rouge."

She laughed. "Lew Archer meets Robert Parker?"

171

I laughed.

"No," I elaborated, "it's about skullduggery in Hollywood."

"That's great you're getting it published."

I bit my upper lip and hoped it wasn't noticeable. "Yeah, I guess," I said weakly, pretending modesty.

"Is that what you want to be writing? Mysteries?"

I shrugged, eager to shift to another topic. "If this one takes off, yeah. I can write one a year and become Sue Grafton's dark side."

Maya laughed softly. She sipped her wine again and mercifully changed the subject. "What do you think of this Tantara?"

"I don't know if it's my palate or not, but it seems to be losing its fruit. I can't quite put my finger on it."

She held the glass up to appraising, narrowed eyes. "Too much alcohol. Overwhelms the fruit."

"Is that what it is?" I wondered.

"Sometimes they build them too powerfully," she said.

I stared at her until she blushed. I had momentarily forgotten about my debauched, betrothed friend and was losing myself in Maya's wiles and wines. "You really do know a lot about wine, don't you?"

"Why? Does that surprise you?" she said defensively.

I shook my head. "It's just refreshing. The wine world is so male dominated."

There was another silence. Tom Jones crooned

away. I didn't hear any other sounds from the living room, so I assumed Jack and Terra were pretty deeply entangled in each other. I must have looked downcast, because Maya said, "Are you uncomfortable here?"

I raised my head to look at her. She was a tall, full-figured woman, with high cheekbones and bold facial features. And yet they seemed under-scored by something paradoxical. Her eyes, though strikingly beautiful, also radiated a kind of sadness. And her mouth, though undeniably sexy, had the tendency to turn down at the corners when her face was relaxed, lending a slightly pensive aspect. "No," I answered finally. "It's just been a long day of wine tasting and I wasn't anticipating a night on the town."

She nodded. A few wordless minutes passed. Then the volume on the music dropped abruptly. Maya gestured with her head in the direction of the living room. "Want to go in the other room where it's more comfortable?"

"What's happening with them?" I said.

"Oh," Maya smiled slyly, "I think your friend and mine have moved on to bigger and better things."

"Oh, I see," I said, getting a sick feeling in my stomach. Then it occurred to me that it would all be over in a few hours. In the morning I would duti-fully listen to Jack's blow-by-blow of the best fuck of his life and that would be that. We would play some golf, do some more wine tasting, gorge ourselves at the local restaurants, and then I'd send him off to the altar. "Yeah, let's," I replied, convincing myself that this was a one-night anomaly.

We rose from the kitchen table, and Maya picked up the Tantara and led me into the main room. There were no lights on anymore. The room was lit solely by candles and the warm glow emanating from the embers in the fireplace. I settled down on the couch as Maya knelt in front of the stereo, which was positioned low on an entertainment console. Her sweater rose up out of the back of her skirt and I could make out the two firm lower back muscles that flanked her spine. My eyes followed them down to a dark hollow leading into her underwear. From a bedroom down the hall we could hear occasional shrieks of laughter interspersed with silences. I imagined half-clothed bodies in amorous clenches.

"Any preferences?" Maya asked, throwing me a backward glance and smiling.

I shook my head. "Whatever you feel like. I'm easy."

She selected a jazz compilation CD to cleanse the air of Tom Jones. Then she coiled to a standing position, stepped across the room, sat opposite me on the couch, and draped her arm on the backrest. She locked her eyes on mine, but I looked away and sipped the wine. Drunk as I was, I was keenly aware of the fact that if this woman knew the truth about my life she wouldn't be caught dead with me, even for one night.

"I take it you're no longer with the Lit professor?" I inquired.

She shook her head slowly several times, one for each reason she didn't feel like explaining. "Nope."

"What happened?"

"Like all men," she started haltingly, then corrected herself. "Like most men, the romance is short-lived, and then you settle into something mundane, then they take you for granted. And then," she puffed her cheek out with her tongue, "they cheat on you. Then they lie. . . ."

"Okay," I stopped her. "I get it. Men suck."

She laughed spontaneously. "Not all men. Or so I've heard rumors."

Her pessimistic outlook made me laugh; it was refreshingly similar to mine. There was something about her dark intensity that cut into me like a deep feeling. We sipped our wine for a minute in silence, sealing our unspoken bond. A spirited yelp from Terra escaped from the back bedroom. We both turned abruptly and exchanged embarrassed looks. Jack was a big man with a megawatt sexual appetite, and though he had consumed a fair amount of wine, I had the feeling that his impending marriage had him so pent up with doubt and anxiety that Terra was about to be the beneficiary of his bottled ardor.

Maya shrugged. "I guess they're getting along."

"I guess so," I said, sipping my wine.

"Have you been dating much since your divorce?" Maya wondered.

175

I cocked my head to one side, ransacking my memory bank for recollections of recent dates. "Here and there. Rarely goes past one. Almost never past two or three."

"Oh, yeah," she chuckled. "Why is that?"

I held up a finger. "Anorexia nervosa. Very common in L.A. And very unattractive." I straightened up a second finger. "High maintenance. Low yield. Also pandemic." Maya laughed in between sips of wine. "Wannabe writer, wannabe actress, wannabe something."

Maya shook her head.

"Born-again Christian."

"What?" Maya said.

"Went out with a woman who said she couldn't have premarital sex because God disapproved."

Maya gravitated closer to me on the couch. "What did you tell her?"

"I told her God was too busy to be interested in her sex life."

"You didn't!"

I laughed in response, letting her know that I'd made it up.

We sipped the Tantara and talked on for what seemed like hours about every topic imaginable: novels, movies, wine, relationships. At one point she let on that she'd been researching a nonfiction book about the history of the Santa Ynez Valley wine country that she hoped to write and my interest in her steepened. As I waited for Jack to emerge out of the back bedroom so we could get back on the road, I grew steadily drunker listening to Maya and trying to keep up with her incandescent mind, which ranged effortlessly and eloquently from subject to subject. She was widely read and it was more and more a mystery to me what she was doing in Podunk Buellton. The more I learned about her, the more I was drawn to her. My initial reservations about the evening diminished in the face of our mutual interests and lively conversation. But Jack didn't show.

Sometime in the wee hours, long after we had uncorked a second bottle, a sleepy-eyed, friendly golden retriever padded into the living room and curled up at the foot of the couch. Maya and I both reached down at the same moment to pet him. Unlike my mother's impertinent little devil, this dog accepted our affections happily, panting contentedly.

Noticing my way with Terra's dog, Maya remarked, "You must be an animal lover."

"That's what all the girls say," I quipped.

Maya threw back her head and laughed out loud. Then she shifted unexpectedly toward me—or fell toward me, I don't remember exactly—and suddenly her lips were on mine, encircling and overwhelming mine so passionately that I felt that we were about to go somewhere I didn't want to go. But I didn't resist. Something came unleashed deep inside me, and I found myself kissing and groping Maya back with equal abandon. Our make-out session went on for quite a while; two drunken mariners drifting out to sea. I remember at some point asking if I could see her breasts and her being surprisingly obliging. After I had slobbered over them for a bit, I raised my no doubt drugged-looking face to hers and slurringly lyricized, "Maya, Indian goddess of illusions. Siren of shipwrecked sailors. If only you lactated Pinot Noir, you'd be perfect." To which I remember her throaty laughter, and then nothing else as I slipped heavy as an anchor into a watery oblivion.

MONDAY: PLAYING BY THE RULES

Sunlight broke in colored prisms as if shafting through stained glass windows. I rolled over and my head felt like a circus elephant had one foot perched on it, preparing to launch himself through a flaming ring. I propped myself up on my elbows, insensible to the world, blinking against the harsh, midmorning light. What was I doing in the motel room? What was the other bed doing unmade? What was Maya's leather coat doing on it?

I hauled myself into the bathroom and plopped down heavily on the porcelain. I scratched two fingers in my pubic hair and brought them to my nose. Didn't smell like sex. Didn't smell like rose petals either. I urinated with the force of a farm animal, then rose leadenly to my feet, braced both hands on the sink, and leaned my grizzled mug into the mirror. My unshaved face looked back at me with the mottled redness of a pomegranate gone to seed. My mid-length hair was incongruously thatched, lending me a visage reminiscent of self-portraits of Van Gogh in his asylum period. My light blue eyes floated in microcosmic seas of red, the whites having been obliterated overnight by the

179

excess of wine. I rubbed my face. I was still a decent-looking guy at thirty-nine, not square-jawed and charismatically handsome like Jack, but still probably desirable to a discerning few, I decided. I turned on the faucet and splashed cold water on my face, but it didn't quite rouse me to full consciousness like I had hoped.

I managed a shower and a shave purely out of trace memory, but after I had dressed I was too worried about Jack, and aggravated by my sledge-hammer hangover, to do anything but lie back down on the bed and pray for redemption. Pray that I hadn't called an old girlfriend in the middle of the night, pray that my car was outside and still in one piece, pray to God that I hadn't acted inappropriately to Maya, a woman whose memory glowed warmly in the recesses of my wine-soaked brain. But when my thoughts turned to Jack, the unrepentant fiancé, in bed with her best friend, the unsettled feeling in my stomach turned into a raw nausea.

My eyes eventually closed and I dreamt that I was destitute, that I was being hounded by the IRS., that no woman would date me, and that I was turning suicidal. A soft, persistent knock at the door finally drew my attention and I realized I hadn't been dreaming. Before I could call out that I wasn't ready for maid service—or any other kind of interaction for that matter—the door cracked open and a woman's head peeped in, splitting the sunlight into twin spears.

"Are you decent?" I recognized Maya's throaty voice.

"Physically, but not psychologically," I slowly croaked.

She chuckled as she slipped into the room, closed the door quietly behind her, walked over, eased down onto the edge of the bed, and opened a white paper bag. Familiar aromas of hot coffee and pastry wafted out.

"Would you like some coffee?"

"Yeah, thanks," I managed, accepting a warm cup.

"Croissant?" she added, swinging a flaky crescent between thumb and forefinger so I could get an eyeful.

I shook my head.

"No?" She took a bite out of the crusty croissant. "Mm. Good. Sure you don't want one?" she offered again, extending it out to me.

"No thanks. I'm trying to cut down on my cholesterol." I sipped my coffee and smiled weakly. "Actually, I don't think my stomach could handle it."

"How're you feeling?" she asked solicitously.

"Like a chimp in a head trauma study."

She laughed. "You were pretty funny last night."

"Don't tell me, did I sing karaoke again?"

"No. No karaoke."

"Thank God." I met her eyes. "Look, if I did or said anything embarrassing, please forgive me. I was pretty sideways."

"Shh."

Feeling vulnerable still, I rambled on: "Finding out about my ex getting remarried kind of unsettled me."

"It's okay," she said. "I understand. You were fine. A perfect gentleman. Aside from a few stumbles and a couple of off-the-wall insights on the plight of humankind that I'm still pondering, I had a good time."

"I did, too. I think."

She took a languorous bite of her croissant.

"Did you sleep here last night?"

She nodded. Then she reached an arm over to the nightstand and picked up the unopened condom package and dangled it between us, tangible evidence of my failure.

"I have no comment," I said, shaking my head in embarrassment.

"You wanted to come back to the motel for some reason, and then you didn't want me to leave because you said you were afraid to be alone. I like you, Miles, but I didn't want to have sex with you last night."

"That's good. Because I would hate not to be able to remember it."

She rose from the bed. "Anyway, I've got to go. Got some errands to run."

"All right. I'd kiss you good-bye, but my breath is so rancid I'm afraid your lips would decompose."

She pulled on her coat. "Call me if you still want to go to the Pinot festival together."

I flung a hand to my head. "Pinot. Did you really utter that word?"

"I had fun," she said, standing in the middle of the room and towering over me. "Get some sleep. You'll feel better."

"What about our friends?" I asked queasily.

She shrugged, hooked a hand in the strap of her purse, and trilled theatrically, "I don't know. Could be trouble."

Maya was swallowed in a harsh rectangle of sunlight as she slipped out the door, shutting it quietly behind her. I lay back on the hard mattress, my head propped up on the pillow, and nursed the coffee. Her parting words—"could be trouble"—disconcerted me.

The phone jangled, startling me up onto my elbows. I reached over to answer it, but stopped short with my hand poised over the receiver. It might be Babs, and I didn't want to be babbling to Babs about where Jack wasn't.

I lugged myself to my feet and escaped the cramped confines of the room. The bright sunlight assaulted my eyes through my lightly tinted sunglasses, painfully blinding me. Naturally, my 4Runner wasn't where it would normally be, so I adventured off in the direction of Ellen's Pancake House for comestible fortification and human contact. It was yet another beautiful blue-sky day in the Santa Ynez Valley. The ascendant sun exploded on the white concrete sidewalk, reflecting back into my eyes and exacerbating my stabbing headache. I was a little shaky, and I was walking a tad lead-footed, heaving one leg in front of the other as stiff-gaited as a zombie.

It was Monday and Ellen's was uncrowded, the noise level tolerable. I corkscrewed into a chair at a window table and looked for the waitress. Outside, there wasn't much of a view except for the minimart across the street, but in the distance, low-rolling hills framed by an expanse of cloudless sky compensated for the depressing foreground.

The waitress with the cleft palate appeared, bearing a menu and the same cheerful mien as the day before.

"I'll just have the oatmeal and a cup of coffee," I said without taking the menu, my head still clutched in my hands.

"Okeydokey," she said. She poured me a cup of coffee, then turned around and went to serve another table.

I sipped my coffee. It wasn't as good as the cup Maya had brought me, but the place was quiet and allowed me some privacy to collect my thoughts. *All right, no more wine until the Pinot festival, have got to flush out the poisons. Play some golf, movie in the evening, a little TV, hit the sack early. Tomorrow, I call Evelyn and see if anything's happening with the book. Have to decide when to break the news to Jack that I'm not going to be his best man at the wedding so he can get a tux for Peter in time. A day before? No, maybe two, just so he doesn't totally freak.*

184

My oatmeal arrived. It looked inedible, lumpy and gray, but I wolfed it down anyway.

I shambled back to the motel, the coffee burning a hole in the glop of oatmeal weighing down my stomach.

Jack still wasn't back. Jesus! The red light on the phone was flashing insistently, so I called the front office for messages. Predictably, Babs had phoned several times, but that was it. I dialed my place for messages. There was one from Victoria rehashing the previous night's conversation. She speculated ominously about my behavior at the upcoming wedding and suggested alternatives, most of which included other travel destinations. If I wasn't going to be able to come to terms with her remarriage, she said adamantly, quite obviously I might as well not come. I considered calling her back and telling her that it was just this sort of trenchant critique that had been responsible for our demise, but my heart wasn't in it. Besides, it wasn't true.

Before I could adequately wallow in the shitty feeling Victoria had summoned up in me, the door blew open. Jack stood silhouetted in a trapezoid of bright sunlight, twirling a golf club, a sheepish grin on his unshaven face. His white cotton dress shirt was hanging half out of his jeans, wrinkled and grape-stained. The Marlboro Man back from the cattle drive, sore thighs and bedroom eyes.

He took a couple of little half-practice swings. "Ready to hit the links?"

"How'd it go?" I said, trying to disguise any sarcasm that might have crept into my voice.

"*Muy excellente*," he said, tin-eared to my mood as usual. "Fucking chick is unbelievable. Un-be-*lieve*-able."

"Get it out of your system?" I asked, hoping that his system was capable of readdressing the task at hand.

"Fuck." He shook his head with a smile. "You *never* get it out of your system, that's the problem. How'd you fare, Shorthorn?"

"Can't remember."

"Can't remember?"

"We slept here. In separate beds."

Jack came into the room and shut the door. "Oh, how Ozzie and Harriet of you."

I laughed, in spite of his derision.

"So, come on, let's tee it up."

"Call Babs. She left a couple of messages."

He craned his head forward. "I hope you didn't talk to her!"

"All I said was that you were making good on your promise, but by Sunday you'd be all fucked out and ready for marriage, so not to worry."

"You did not talk to her I hope?"

"Fuck no. What do you think, I'm crazy?"

"Good."

"Call her," I said sharply.

"I *will*. Give me a sec, will you."

"Now."

He gestured with the golf club for me to wait

186

outside. I got up from the bed and brushed past Jack on the way out. He hadn't showered yet and he smelled pungent, redolent of sweat and massage oils and incense and the faint christening of sex.

Outside, I sprawled on the hood of the 4Runner, pillowed my head with clasped hands, and gazed up at the Santa Ynez Mountains. An enormous feather of pearl gray fog drifted at the top of its westernmost ridge, a visible reminder of the ocean-borne air that streams through the area's east-west valleys and flows over the inland vineyards and cools the vines. Below the encroaching fog bank, the face of the mountain ran away in a waterfall of green grasses still sparklingly dewy from the moist night.

Moments later, Jack came outside. He looked unsettled.

"What's up?" I said.

"Let's boogie."

We climbed into the 4Runner and rode down 246 in the direction of La Purisima Golf Course. Jack had one untied tennis shoe propped up on the dash and seemed to be meditating on something. "What'd you tell Victoria last night when you moronically called her from the restaurant?" he asked without looking at me.

"I don't remember, to tell you the truth," I said, glancing over at him.

"Somehow everyone's got the impression that your coming to the wedding is a really big mistake now."

I focused on the road and didn't say anything in response.

"That could be the straw that broke the camel's back," Jack said.

I turned toward him. "What?"

He scratched his beard and nodded in a self-satisfied way. "Nothing," he said, staring forward at some fixed point in his mind. "God, that chick, Terra, is sweet," he reflected fondly, a picture of her naked loveliness clearly developing in his mind. He closed his eyes and shuddered exaggeratedly. "Goddamn, Miles. Nasty. Nasty nasty nasty."

I turned away, the oatmeal and coffee still locked in combat in my stomach. Bounding 246 were agricultural parcels, grassy ranchlands, and flower farms so dazzlingly colorful they were nearly blinding. Near the golf course, we came up on the turnoff to Babcock Winery, marked by a large wooden sign. When Jack saw it, he said excitedly, "Pull in!"

"I'm not drinking until tonight," I told him.

"Oh, bullshit," he said, knowing me better than that. "Turn in."

"They're not open on Monday."

"Oh, man," he groaned, slumping back in his seat. "I need a fluid change. Big time."

"Let's just play some golf and take it easy today. Relax, enjoy nature."

Jack swung his bearish head toward me, lowered his sunglasses to the tip of his nose, and reproved me with a dismissive look. Then he just shook his head back and forth as if my remark merited no comment.

La Purisima Golf Course is nestled in a humped valley, routed through canyons dense with scrub oak and bordered by grassy, pristine hillsides unsullied by any building or other manmade development. The nearest town is tiny, working-class Lompoc, a grueling two-and-a-half hour drive from L.A., so during the week the course is blissfully uncrowded.

I parked in the nearly empty lot and Jack and I hauled our clubs out and trudged to the pro shop to check in and pay our green fees. We argued about whether to rent a cart or walk, but Jack— bad back, hangover, rubbery legs from all-night fucking—won, and we elected to ride.

Standing on the first tee, we were buffeted by a strong, cool ocean wind that started early, developed to almost gale-force proportions in the afternoon, and didn't let up until the sun was sinking on the horizon. I was a better player than Jack, so I decided to give him six strokes a side, but only under one, stringent, condition.

"What's that?" he asked skeptically while taking vicious practice swipes at the air with his oversized driver.

"You play by the rules."

"I always play by the rules."

"No, you don't. You're a cheating motherfucker. The best wood in your bag is your pencil. You haven't recorded a legitimate score in your life."

189

"Oh, come on, what the *fuck* are you talking about, Miles?" he said, feet apart, challenging me.

"We're going to play strictly by USGA rules. The rules that all pros play by." Jack was notorious for bumping his lies, surreptitiously kicking his ball out of hazards and deep rough, conceding himself all putts within four feet whether he holed them or not, as well as other flagrant infractions. "Play it as it lies, and if you have a rules question, ask me and I'll set you straight."

"Six a side?" he said, disbelievingly.

"Six a side. Fifty-dollar Nassau. Fifty on the side if you break a hundred, gross, from the tips. No equitable stroke control. Think you can handle it?"

He rotated his shoulders, loosening them up. "Tee it up, Homes. USGA rules or not, I'll still kick your ass. But, you're paying this time. No IOUs." He pointed his driver at me. "Even if you have to go back and filch from poor ol' Mom again."

I pointed my finger back at him in response. "And don't touch your fucking Titleist from tee to green unless you're taking a legal drop or I'll call it on you."

"Shut your trap and golf your ball."

I didn't get off to a particularly good start and those six strokes were murdering me. Jack, brain-dead from wine and lack of sleep, was swinging loose as a goose, not a mechanical thought in his head, miraculously carding pars and steady bogeys while I was scrambling all over the course trying to find my once reliable low-handicap swing.

On the seventh hole—a difficult dogleg left par four—Jack lost his rhythm and hit a low snipe hook into the barranca on the left. He charged into the dense undergrowth and managed to find his ball and execute a nearly impossible recovery shot. He emerged all smiles, but his face fell when I informed him that I had to assess him a two-stroke penalty for soling his club.

"Oh, fuck!" he exclaimed. "You're joking!"

"I said we're playing by USGA rules. You can't touch the ground with your club in a hazard."

"I didn't even know it was a hazard," he protested.

"What do you think those red stakes are for? Decoration?"

Rattled, Jack carded an eight to my five and the game was back on. But his competitive fire returned and he managed to finish the front side with a four-stroke margin.

Jack went up to the snack bar at the turn to get some beers while I waited on the tenth tee box. The sun had advanced high in the sky and the wind was gusting through the valley with increased velocity, rattling dead leaves in the gnarled branches of the stately oaks. Hawks glided effortlessly on the thermals, their raptor heads angled downward, surveying the barrancas for rodents.

Jack came back from the snack bar with four

Firestone Ales and a pair of turkey sandwiches. "You want a beer?" he asked, holding one out to me.

I shook my head. "Don't drink when I'm playing. Interferes with my swing thoughts."

"Fuck your swing thoughts. Have a beer. Lighten up."

"All right."

He handed me a beer and I popped it open. It was cold and refreshing.

The beer seemed to take the edge off and I finally started to find my swing. Jack, however, played even better when he was drinking and was matching me par for par. It was beginning to look like I was going to lose this Nassau all the way around.

On the fourteenth hole—a very tight, tricky par four—Jack blocked a driver into the canyon on the right. He turned to me and said gloomily, "Is that gone?"

"Yep, I'm afraid so. Want to know your options under the rules?"

He shook his head petulantly. "I know my options. Throw me another fucking ball, will you?"

I squeezed another Titleist out of the ball holder and underhanded it to him. He teed it up and, with another beer-scorched swing, sliced it even deeper into the same canyon. Jack stared at its disappearing arc in disbelief, ragingly pissed. He held out his arm without looking at me. "Throw me another."

I tossed him a third ball. He stubbornly deposited that one into the canyon. A turkey buzzard, frightened by the errant projectile, shrieked madly and rose out of the undergrowth on anxiously flapping wings.

"Jesus, Jack, you're a fucking biohazard."

"Shut the fuck up and throw me another."

I tossed him a fourth and, astonishingly, he managed to compose himself and hit it into the fairway.

We carted out to where our balls lay and climbed out to survey our approach shots.

"So, what do I lie?" Jack asked.

"Seven," I said.

"Seven? How do you figure that?"

"Four swings, three penalty strokes for the three that didn't make the short grass. That's seven."

"Jesus fucking Christ!" he yelled, his voice echoing in the low of the canyon. He plucked out an iron and set up to his ball.

"However," I said, interrupting him, "that canyon is a lateral water hazard. You should have gone to the point of entry after your first one and taken a drop. You'd only be lying three."

Jack turned slowly to me. "Why the fuck didn't you tell me?"

"You said you knew your options."

"Fuck that. I'm lying three."

"No, you're not. You're lying seven. You stupidly elected to take your stroke-and-distance option and paid dearly."

Jack could tell I wasn't kidding, and he turned away. He was so infuriated he laid the sod over his 8-iron and chunked it into the front bunker. When the carnage was over he had carded a thirteen to my four.

When I was finished holing out I noticed that Jack had ditched me and taken the cart up to the next tee, which was out of view. I walked through the trees up to the fifteenth hole and found the cart, but no Jack. His bag was still strapped onto the back. I called out his name. There was no answer, so I hit my tee shot, then drove out into the fairway. He still was nowhere to be found and I assumed he had walked in.

After two more shots, I arrived at the green. When I circled around it, I found Jack reclining on his towel in the rear sand trap, his back propped up against the steep face. He had a bottle of Foxen Pinot open, a pair of tasting glasses planted in the sand, and was puffing morosely on a cigar. He refused to look at me or even acknowledge that I was there. I walked over to the green and two-putted for par, then returned to the sand trap where Jack was blithely blowing smoke rings and sipping wine. "What the hell," I said. "What the hell."

I unhooked the golf towel from my bag and climbed down into the hazard with him. Jack didn't say anything. He just mechanically poured a second glass of wine and handed it to me. I leaned my back up against the face of the bunker and lazed there with him, the trap serving as an oversized chaise longue. The fifteenth hole was at the easternmost edge, and highest vantage point, of La Purisima, elevated so that we had an untrammeled view of the entire course. In the distance, a fog bank was lowering on the horizon, slowly swallowing the mid-afternoon sun.

After a moment, Jack began laughing. Then I started laughing. We must have laughed together, in spiralingly convulsive waves, for five minutes until we actually had tears streaming down our sunburned cheeks.

"Homes, you crack me up," Jack said, his laughter subsiding.

Feeling magnanimous, I said, "Forget the bet. It's cool."

"Fuck it," he said. "I'll pay you. You won fair and square. Besides, you need the fucking money worse than me."

I didn't argue with him. We were silent for a moment, drinking in the fading warmth of the sun—and the Pinot.

"Tastes good right here, right now, doesn't it?" Jack observed. He held his glass up to the sun and watched the light dance around inside it.

"Excellent," I agreed. "Perfect. Golf course all to ourselves. A nice sunset, a decent if unremarkable quaff. I'm content."

"So, you didn't get your nut?" Jack asked, sincerely disappointed.

"I was too out of it, to tell you the truth."

"But you like her?" he persisted.

"Yeah. She's got a lot of feeling. Brought me coffee and croissants this morning."

Jack tipped his cigar at me and flicked off a meaningful ash. "I'm telling you. That woman digs you."

"Maybe."

"Maybe?" he said, astonished. "You almost do a face-plant and she shows in the morning with coffee and pastries. She digs you, man."

I didn't say anything. He had a point.

"I'm thinking we should all go out again to-night." Jack refilled his glass. I automatically held out mine and he topped if off.

"Let's give it a rest. Back-to-back night games, especially on the road, are debilitating."

"You're always crapping out on me," Jack whined.

"No, I'm not. I just don't want to reprise last evening."

I looked at Jack for a reaction. His face had a dark, faraway expression knitted into a focal point on the horizon that was really some debauched place in his mind. "I think I have to see her again," he said a little fearfully.

"What?" I said, that sick feeling in my stomach returning.

"It was wild last night," Jack confided. "I mean way more than just sex. We burrowed into each other like a couple of corn weevils."

"I'm sure it *was* wild, but let's not leap into the quagmire, shall we?"

"What quagmire?"

"Fuck, man, you know what I'm talking about." I was getting angry now.

He tried to reason with me. "Fuck, man, do you know how long it's been since I've had my tongue on a woman's clit?"

"I don't want to know," I said. And I didn't.

"God, it was pink and sweet as bubble gum." He turned to me. "Babs doesn't dig that kind of shit," he confessed.

I looked away and sighed, audible enough I hoped to discourage him.

But Jack wanted to spill his guts. "That girl last night had me throttled like I was back in college."

"So, re-enroll!" I said, in rising exasperation. "Teach acting and fuck all the sophomores you want."

"I might!" he threatened.

"Is that going to buy you happiness?"

"I don't know. I'm fucking confused." He quaffed a big gulp of Pinot in an effort to disentangle the knot of emotions warring inside him.

"You're going to the altar in six days with a beautiful, caring woman who loves you—God knows why!—and you don't need to have your gonads tweaked and be thrown into the maelstrom, Jackson. You got your mercy pop, my lips are sealed, time to move on."

"I'm not sure I'm cut out for marriage," Jack said a little wildly, ignoring my rebuke.

"A little late for that, isn't it?"

"It's never too late."

"Love is love and sex is sex and I hope to God you know the difference."

"What the fuck is that supposed to mean?"

I scrambled to my feet and exploded. "Fuck, man, take the gift and forget about it."

Jack kept shaking his head to himself, fixated on Terra's pussy and how wonderful his cock must have felt in its cavernous newness. "I went deep last night, brother. I mean, deep."

"And you're going to take her, and Babs, and me, down with you?"

"I guess he doesn't approve," Jack spoke sarcastically over his shoulder to a make-believe friend sitting on his other side in the trap.

"You got that right," I snapped to Jack and his imaginary ally. I didn't wait for a response. Men with fresh pussy experience are unreasonable and irrational creatures. I scrambled out of the bunker and walked back to the cart, unstrapped my golf bag, slung it over my shoulder, irons rattling, and stalked over to the sixteenth tee. The wine had robbed the starch from my legs, and I hit a snipe hook that bounced along the ground on a zigzag course. I was so angry—Jack, my golf game, hangover—that I tomahawked my driver a hundred yards down the fairway. Some minutes later, trudging toward the green, I finally caught sight of Jack approaching in the cart, moving through long shadows cast by tall trees that lined the fairway. He was hanging out one side, waving a white towel and flashing a smile. His disarming approach left me no choice but to forgive him.

Back at the Windmill Inn, Jack hit the phones while I meandered over to the Jacuzzi to soak my aching muscles. Slouched in the bubbling, foamy water, that reeked of chlorine, I gazed upward. The twilit sky was starting to break out with little pinpricks of starry light. I closed my eyes and grew lost in it for a drowsy moment. All I could hear was the peaceful hum of air-conditioning units droning away from the surrounding rooms.

I finally dragged myself out of the Jacuzzi and barefooted it back to the room. Jack was nowhere to be found. I switched on the TV out of habit and went into the bathroom for a shower to rinse off the chlorine smell. Taped to the mirror was a note handwritten in large block letters:

WE'RE AT THE HITCHING POST.
HOPE TO SEE YOUR FACE IN THE PLACE.

Fanned out on the Formica vanity were six fifty-dollar bills: payment on the golf debt. I ripped the note off the mirror angrily, crumpled it into a ball, and flushed it down the toilet.

Under the needle shower, weariness overcame me. I fantasized about heading back to L.A., leaving Jack a note of my own saying I didn't want any more to do with his newfound affair. He'd cheated on Babs many times before. One that almost wrecked their relationship had to be worked out over a stormy, tequila-soaked weekend in Acapulco—a contrite Jack no doubt on his knees blubbering *I love yous*— but if she found out this time there would be no reconciliation. I was paranoid that maybe Jack *wanted* her to find out and blow the whole wedding, a wedding that had been in the planning stages for months. He was that reckless.

In the main room, I lay on the bed and shuttled through the TV channels—all twelve of them— uncertain what to do. The news had the eerie familiarity of a déja vu: a philandering politician, a weather catastrophe that destroyed half an island country, heinous murders and global terrorism and medical marvels and something uplifting involving domesticated animals.

Unsettled, and wanting to avoid the Hitching Post at all costs, I drove to the local multiplex and took in a movie. The theater was crowded and stank of perspiration and cheap cologne. The seats were cramped and the soles of my shoes stuck to the soda-pop-coated floor. The movie was one of those cripplingly boring summer action flicks star-ring a smirking overpaid actor who seemed to be mouthing, amidst all the special effects, that we in the audience were all a bunch of idiots while he was laughing all the way to the bank. Walking up the aisle before the end credits, I felt like I'd been sucked off by a toothless hooker.

I loitered outside the theater, my ears still ringing from the aural assault, thinking about what to do next. Driving around seemed silly and returning to the motel depressing. Jack always had a plan, was never at a loss for the next stage in the evening's revelry, and I felt idiotically incomplete without him. I wasn't sure if I was seething because he was cheating on his fiancée or because he had abandoned me.

Stubbornly, I drove past the Hitching Post without stopping. I had a vivid image of Jack and Terra and Maya drinking Pinot and laughing and having a grand time. It took all my fortitude to keep from turning around and pulling in.

I headed in the direction of Solvang. Yellow streetlights illuminated Highway 246 on either side of me in a limpid light. Cruising past one of the many ostrich farms that had sprung up in the area, I could make out the surreal silhouettes of the tall birds standing motionless in the moonlight.

Passing slowly through sleepy Solvang, I glimpsed a woman hunched in the doorway of a shop, smoking a cigarette, her elbows chickenwinged into her stomach, warding off the cold night air. I projected my own loneliness onto her, picturing her closing up, then making the thirty-mile hump on a desolate 246 back to a cheerless apartment in Lompoc.

I shook off the image and hung a left on Alamo Pintado Road, heading aimlessly north. The streetlights disappeared, darkening the terrain.

The sky's ceiling was now brightly speckled with stars. A flare went off in my memory banks and I braked the car to a stop on the gravel shoulder and climbed out. I suddenly remembered that the night before, Maya had stopped on a similar dark stretch of road and coaxed me out of the car to look at the sky. According to her, a comet was streaking madly across the empyrean, leaving a static phosphorescent tail in its wake, even though it was hurtling through the cosmos at millions of miles per hour. I searched the sky until I found it, feeling a certain elation in my success. I wondered absurdly if my own dying would be that visually dramatic, if I, too, would cross the galaxy in a flaming instant and burn out in glory.

A truck hurtled past and broke my reverie. I got back in my car, drove a few more miles, and parked in front of the Café Chardonnay, situated on the first floor of the quaint Ballard Bed & Breakfast, a two-story Victorian house in the tiny, nondescript town of Ballard. Eight years ago, Victoria and I had honeymooned here. It was a good week, marked by lust and intense conversations about our glorious future together. I didn't really know what had gone wrong, and the thought of trying to analyze our relationship while eating by myself only intensified my feelings of emptiness and remorse. The thought of dinner by myself was too depressing, so I left without going in.

The roads were almost deserted when I drove back to the Windmill Inn. I poked my head out the window several times hunting for the comet. I found it finally, but was hard-pressed to tell if it had budged at all. Maybe a million miles per hour in a faraway galaxy is only an inch through my windshield. Reminded suddenly of my mother's advice to say a prayer every night—and my failure to do so—I wondered whether God was waiting for me to break down and invoke Him or had moved on to more important matters.

Evidently not, because Jack, as expected, wasn't at the motel when I got back. The message light on the phone was flashing obnoxiously, pulsing red onto the walls. I rummaged through the boxes stacked by the door and rooted out a bottle of the Byron Sierra Madre—to hell with Jack!—and meandered my way over to the lobby.

A balding man with a gray moustache and dark eyes hidden behind dark-framed glasses was manning the office when I came in, bottle and corkscrew in tow. Closer up, the harsh overhead lights revealed his alligator-dimpled complexion. I asked him about Cheryl—thinking I would share the bottle with her—but he said she was off for the night and went back to his crossword puzzle, buzzing switchboard, and forlorn graveyard shift.

Disappointed, I took the bottle back to the room, feeling fidgety, not wanting to drink it alone.

Restless, I left the room and crossed the parking lot to the Clubhouse. It had closed early and I was starting to feel like it was a conspiracy. I took a walk to clear my head. The night offered nothing but stillness and emptiness and I needed something else, but I didn't know what exactly.

Back in the motel room I wanted the red light on the phone to go away, so I called the desk for messages. There were six: Babs for Jack (twice), Jack for me, Babs for *me* (shit!), Jack for me (urgent!), and . . . Maya for me (phone number included).

The first call I returned was Maya's. A sleepy voice answered on the other end, "Hello."

"Hi, this is Miles," I said. "Karaoke specialist. You called?"

She chuckled hoarsely, then cleared her throat. "Yeah. We missed you tonight."

"I was a little under the weather, as you can well imagine."

"Oh," she said with a tinge of disappointment. "I was hoping we could continue that argument on whether true love is still feasible after divorce."

I had a fractured memory of the discussion. "It had nothing to do with you. I just needed to chill out tonight."

"I'm glad," she replied. Then, she lobbed a grenade: "I think Terra has it bad for your friend."

An imaginary spider skittered up my spine. "Apparently," I said, trying to disguise my disgust. "I haven't seen him since this afternoon. Must be quite a romance."

"You don't approve?" Maya asked, picking up on the edge in my voice.

I didn't say anything. We fell into silence. I had decided not to spill the beans and bring Jack's wrath down on me. What he did was his business, even if I disapproved. And, I was still confident that it would all end with the suddenness of a Midwest thunderstorm, just as abruptly as it had begun. If Terra got her heart broken, *c'est la vie.* At least she would learn in the future to give a wide berth to the Jacks of the world. "Oh, I don't know, Maya," I finally answered.

"Do you want some company?" she asked.

I did, desperately, which is why I had gone looking for Cheryl and visited old honeymoon haunts and gazed up at comets in an effort to summon up some sense of belonging to a world that wasn't solely stitched out of fading memories. But, as much as I liked talking to Maya, I didn't want to encourage Jack's fantasy of an orgiastic, wine-swilling foursome. "Not tonight, Maya," I said. "Thanks, but I'm wiped."

"Okay," she said.

"Hey, I saw the comet again tonight."

"You remembered?"

"Yeah, it just sort of struck me all of a sudden. It's weird the things you remember the night after getting sideways."

"How'd it look?"

"Still disintegrating, I guess. Sort of like life."

That last remark injected a chill into the phone

line and brought a formality back to her voice. "Well, call me when you feel like it." We exchanged good-byes and hung up.

I looked at the phone in my hand for a moment, and decided not to return any more calls.

I crawled into bed and turned the television on. Channel after channel insulted me with its inanity, deepening my melancholy, so I shut it off and lay wide awake in the dark. It was as if I had enwombed myself in a sensory deprivation chamber. My feeling of dread spiraled. Soon, I felt like I was floating, borne by some fickle wind, defenseless, sucking the marrow of my own brain. The beginning stirrings of a panic attack began to assail me. I felt like something was about to go horribly wrong: heart attack, stroke, asphyxiation. As my anxiety slowly tightened around me, I wheezed for air, pusillanimously invoked God—a god I didn't believe existed except when I needed him—and cursed my absence of a partner who might have consoled me in this troubled moment. I broke down and dissolved a Xanax under my tongue. It took maybe thirty minutes for the drug to kick in, but that half hour felt like a terrifying eternity. Storms raged in my head. At the height of the attack, a sentimental memory of Victoria caused tears to spring to my eyes, and the fortress of my cynicism started to crumble. In that vulnerable moment I thought pathetically of the Beatles song, "All You Need is Love," and for a few minutes the refrain wouldn't leave my head.

Eventually, as the Xanax worked its magic, the undersong of crickets lulled me over the precipice into a welcome sleep.

In the dead of night, I woke to the jangling of the cheap motel phone. I didn't answer it. A few minutes later, the message light began flashing, accompanied by an annoying little *ding ding* noise every few seconds, and the room was suddenly throbbing red all over again. I inserted a pair of earplugs and pulled the covers over my head. Maybe I should have taken Maya up on her offer.

TUESDAY: STALKING THE BOAR

Jack wasn't in the room when I returned from breakfast, so I climbed into my 4Runner and rode out to La Purisima. The sky was an opulent sea of blue, and the local flora was turned out in one of Nature's more resplendent displays, imparting a sense of peace to my anxious soul.

I played twenty-seven holes with a reticent Japanese kid whose wealthy parents, he told me, were bankrolling his unrealistic dream of making it on the PGA Tour.

Afterward, I sat up in the observation tower sipping a frosty bottle of Firestone Ale and watched the shadows lengthen over the fairways, the late-afternoon sun bewitching the course in a green-gold light.

At a pay phone mounted on the side of the clubhouse I called home for messages. My agent hadn't called and I was starting to worry about the response from the editor at Conundrum. Was this going to be yet another disappointment? When I hung up, my fears escalated. What the fuck was I going to do if it didn't sell? I had made money in the past as a screenwriter, but I had frittered most of it away on a succession of vacuous women and overpriced Pinots. Like so many writers, I gorged on success and never planned on failure. I was an accountant's nightmare and a creditor's bête noire.

I drove back to the motel in the faint light of dusk, lost in self-deprecations. In my rearview mirror, the sun was a red disc narrowing on the horizon. Momentarily distracted by my bleak reverie and blinded by the sun's intensity, I swerved at the last moment to prevent being flattened by a horn-blaring 18-wheeler.

It was almost night when I arrived in Buellton and swung into the Windmill Inn. As soon as I opened the door to our unit, I stopped dead in my tracks, assailed by the sounds of pleasurable moaning. In the dim light of the curtained room I could make out Jack on top of a splay-legged Terra, his hairy ass thrusting piston-like as he grunted like a rutting rhino. When they realized someone had broken in on their lovemaking, Jack leapt off Terra like the fornicator en flagrante he was, exposing her magnificently flourishing black bush. Terra started laughing uncontrollably, and her naked body seemed to be unintentionally rebuking me.

"Sorry, folks." I quickly backed out of the room, shutting the door behind me, as muffled laughter erupted from inside.

I strode over to the Clubhouse, desperately needing a libation or five. The only other person in the place was the sepulchral-faced bartender and he was so mesmerized by a baseball game squawking on the overhead TV that he didn't even see me at first. He finally turned when I called out "Hello," and came over, without apology. I ordered a glass of the wretched Firestone Cab and he poured me one. An attempt to make small talk about the game quickly broke down because my heart wasn't in it. I glanced over at the ghostly karaoke stage, trying to recall that first night when the place was jumping and I claimed the microphone to sing "Crystal Blue Persuasion," but the memory was too mortifying, so I shook it off.

Two glasses of Cab later, I had sandpapered the rough edges and momentarily shaken the image of my naked friend and his tittering small-town courtesan and her hot naked body. A body the likes of which I hadn't experienced in nearly a year.

I climbed off the stool, found a pay phone by the bathroom, and called Maya. She wasn't in and I didn't leave a message. Had she been at home, I had half-resolved to disclose what was going on with Jack and his impending marriage. But not on an answering machine.

I slipped back into the bar and returned to my stool. Locals punching out of work were beginning to trickle in and the noise of pool balls smacking one another and voices jawing and music on the jukebox started to rise and overtake the gloomy quiet.

An hour or so later, Jack finally rolled in with Terra hanging on his arm and tilting her head up into his sheepish smile. She was laughing at something he was saying with the air of a young girl in love. It was obvious from the bloom in their faces and their disheveled appearance that they had been drinking and fucking all night and into the next day: a debauch of Dionysian dimensions.

"Miles, where've you been, brother?" Jack boomed.

"Played some golf, hung out," I muttered, not bothering to conceal the disgruntlement in my voice.

"Hi, Miles," Terra cheerfully called out, insensitive to the fact she was wrecking our little vacation.

"Hi, Terra," I said, mustering a reserve of politeness.

"Maya missed you last night," she said.

"Yeah, I spoke to her briefly."

"You should have come with."

I forced a swift smile, then turned back to my glass, salvation and sanctuary viniferously bundled into one. When I looked up, Jack and Terra were clutching each other feverishly, their mouths crushed together like reunited lovers on a rain-swept tarmac. Jesus! For a moment I was afraid they were going to go at it right in the bar.

I heard Terra say, "Okay, baby, I'll see you later." She gave Jack one last throat-probing kiss, then turned jauntily to me and waved. "Bye, Miles."

I tossed Terra a halfhearted little wave. Jack wolfishly followed her sashaying exit with his bloodshot eyes.

Then he plopped down next to me, fatigue and exhilaration competing in his sagging frame. He signaled to the bartender, who automatically brought over the Firestone Cab and poured him a glass. I pointed to mine and he freshened it to almost overflowing, no doubt remembering Jack's generous tips and our inclination for multiple orders.

When he had drifted away, I turned to Jack and mimicked acidly, "*Baby*?" Jack shrugged and displayed a lopsided grin. "What the *fuck* are you doing, man?" I said.

"I don't know," Jack said, in between healthy sips, "She's just fucking hot."

I shook my head back and forth with my tongue pushed crossly against one cheek. "Are you going to blow off this wedding?"

Jack drank a third of his glass in one gulp, then clinked it down on the bar. "I might have to put it on hold," he replied.

I flushed with anger and squared around on my stool to face him. "You think in one month, when this torrid sex peaks, that you're going to want to drive up here, hang out in motel rooms, and bang this woman? Give me a break, Jack."

"This chick drives me crazy. She's all over me. Smells different. Tastes different. Fucks different. Screws like an animal." He was as animated and fervent as I had ever seen him, as though he had just witnessed the Second Coming. I stared at him until he met my gaze. He looked at me uncomprehendingly and asked, "What?"

"What? What do you mean, *What*?"

"Yeah, *what*?" Without waiting for the bartender, he reached for the bottle and refilled both our glasses. I didn't touch mine.

"Yeah, I'm saying *what*. As in, *what* the fuck do you think you're doing?"

"What is your problem, Homes?" he replied, without looking at me.

"I'll tell you my problem," I started, gathering my thoughts. "I'm shanghaied off to a wedding where I'm not wanted. I've got a rep as an impecunious writer who's prone to going off the deep end—a potential reception wrecker if ever there was one—and you're about ready to blow the whole deal sky-high and you don't think I'm going to be the guy everybody points the finger at?" I switched to a mocking tone: "Miles took Jack up to the wine country and got his brains fucked out and convinced him that getting married was tantamount to a stretch in Sing-Sing."

"Oh, bullshit."

"It's not bullshit, it's how they're going to interpret it," I pleaded, reaching for the moral support of my wine.

An uneasy silence fell between us. Maudlin classic rock from the '70s saccharined the emptiness with its plangent strains, further sickening me.

"So, what are you going to do?" I said, the edge in my voice gone. My whole being, with three nights of little sleep and emotional strain, surrendered to weariness. "Piss on it? Shock a nice, respectable family down to their pantaloons?"

Jack wheeled on me. "I need some understanding from you, brother. And I'm not getting it." He almost sounded like he was going to cry.

I stared at him in astonishment. This was no time for weak-kneed blubbering and male-bonding empathy. "What's there to understand?"

"Like I'm telling you I might be in love with another woman."

"Oh, man." I raked a hand through my hair. "Twenty-four hours and you're in *love*?" I scoffed. "Well, hot-diggity."

"Don't fucking condescend to me, Homes. You've been there."

"Yeah, I've been there. It's like being in a sewer main without a flashlight." I tapped my temple. "I was so fucking messed up in the head once over this woman I used to cruise past her apartment just to see if I could get a glimpse of her, while meanwhile I had a beautiful, loving wife pacing around in a fucking frenzy wondering where her sex-crazed, soon-to-be ex-husband was!" I waited until he leveled his eyes at me. "You don't think you're going to regret this?" He didn't say anything, but I could tell I wasn't getting through. "You're just playing out some propagate-the-species-the-grass-is-greener-genetic-imperative, and you have the temerity to call it *love*. You're fucking apeshit, man."

"What are you getting all worked up about? You don't even *like* Babs."

This was a curare dart designed to skewer my argument. I turned away. "That's horseshit."

"When I met her you told me she was a shallow, bubble-titted costume designer."

"I did not. Besides, I have long since reversed my opinion. And you know that. You're just lamely trying to get me to fall into the conga line. But, fuck that. The $64,000 question is: Are you willing to risk everything you're about to bring down on yourself over this Buellton wine pourer?"

"There you go again with your fucking elitism," he said, flinging an arm into the air.

I bobbed my head up and down. "Okay, fine. She's stimulating. Knows her wines. Points for that. In fact, knows a lot more about wine than you do, which is why *I* should be with her instead of you. But do you really think she's worth destroying a long-term relationship over? One that I promise you, from experience, you're going to rue until your cock shrivels into dust."

Jack stared intensely into his glass of wine. "I'm just seeing things in a different light right now."

"Duh. That's because you're getting hosed. But, after a while she's going to seem as commonplace as all the other pussy you've diddled, and you're not going to be able to serial monogamize the rest of your life. Look at me. Okay, George Clooney maybe, some others, but not you. Not me. We need to find an oasis of womanhood. Otherwise we will wither on the vine. You've found it. And now you're about to abandon it," I finished in a grave tone.

"I didn't realize you were so fucking puritanical," Jack responded.

"You made a commitment to Babs when you asked her to marry you!"

"The rest of my fucking life."

"Yeah, I think that's the definition, Jackson."

"It's not normal." He attacked his wine with a childish vengeance. We had both arrived at that moment I called The Switch. When it snapped on, we would soon find ourselves free-falling together into that rollercoastering void of alcohol's blissful nepenthe. I could already feel it lifting me out of my weariness.

"She's beautiful, isn't she?" he asked.

"Yeah, she's a doll," I conceded, having shot my wad on Babs's behalf.

"Kisses like you wouldn't believe."

"She recently got dumped by some guy. What do you expect? She's lonely. Hungry for affection."

"Whatever the reason," Jack said blithely, unable to shake the memory. "Feels awful damn sweet."

"And worse. She may have already fallen for you. And that's going to be a problem. You know why?" Jack turned and looked at me. "Because down the serpentine road of sex and more sex, of heavenly cock sucking and marathon pussy licking . . . she's going to want the same things Babs wants."

"Here's what I'm thinking," Jack interrupted. "We move up here, you and me, get a groove going with Terra and Maya, maybe buy a vineyard, establish a winery. . . ."

"Jack," I said, chopping him off, "you're fucking nuts. You've flipped. You have *got* to dry out and see this for what it really is."

"Raymond Cole Estate. We'll make awesome Pinot. Think about it," he said, as though I were calling out to him from deep underwater.

"I don't want to think about it. It depresses me." I turned away, scowling.

"There's just like, this thing. . . ." Jack balled up his fist and shook it to himself. "I can't describe it."

"Are you going to come to your senses?"

He was getting drunk now and his face took on the sad look of a basset hound. "I'm coming into a whole new realization of who I am."

"Oh, don't give me this sententious alcoholic hogwash," I shot back.

"What?"

I didn't feel like defining *sententious*. "Look, call Babs before she has a fucking cow."

"No," Jack said defiantly.

"She called *me*, for Christ's sake!"

"I don't think I'm ready for marriage," he said, petulant.

"Oh, fuck me with a hot poker." I drained my wine, pivoted off my stool, and blazed a trail to the bathroom.

When I returned, Jack had vanished. I reclaimed my stool, my brain throbbing indignantly. Across the sea of pool and lounge tables, near a pinball machine, I could make out Jack on his cell. I inhaled deeply and then let it all go in a weary sigh, wondering what my next move was going to be. I sipped my wine, casting for answers, but I kept drawing a blank.

On my right flank I heard a vaguely familiar voice and I turned to see who it was. It was the pimple-faced boar hunter from Saturday night, though with all that was happening, it seemed like ages ago. He had another big, frothy pitcher of straw-colored beer in front of him.

"Hey, what's happening?" he said when he caught my eye.

"Not much," I said, the understatement of the year. "No karaoke tonight?"

"Nope," he said.

"What was your name again?"

"Brad."

"Brad, right," I said.

"You're the writer?" he recalled.

"Miles. Yeah."

"Right," he said, his face vacant. He was one of those beer drunks who grew dully introspective as they got wasted.

"Going boar hunting tonight, Brad?"

He took a drink of his beer and turned to me. "Thinking about it. Want to come?"

I was intrigued. "Maybe. I have to see what my friend's up to when he gets off the phone."

He nodded once. "You'd dig it." He refilled his mug from the pitcher in a slow deliberate pour, as if measuring precious potions.

"What do you shoot em with?" I asked distractedly, the wine having sharpened my low-common-denominator conversation skills.

"Thirty-ought-six. Some guys I know hunt 'em with .45 magnums. Wait till they charge right up to them, and then, *POW*. Right between the eyes." He touched his index finger to the top of his nose.

"No shit?" I said, genuinely impressed, trying to picture a bearded pipe fitter standing in the dark undergrowth of a canyon in the middle of nowhere aiming a high-caliber handgun at a charging boar.

"They're insane," Brad said.

"I'll take your word for it."

"Yep," Brad repeated, as if speaking to a Doppelgänger. "They're insane."

"Now, do you haul 'em out, skin 'em, and eat 'em?" I asked, not really wanting to know.

The boar hunter turned his head slowly and stared at me for a moment with dark thumbtack eyes. "Yeah, I *fucking* eat 'em."

"How do they taste?"

"Like pig."

"Makes sense."

Jack returned and sat down on my left, sandwiching me between Brad and him. He was beaming.

"Did you call Babs?"

"Yeah."

"How is she?"

"Fine."

"What'd you tell her?"

"Nothing."

"Nothing. What do you mean *nothing*? What does she think's happening?"

"I don't know what she thinks. I don't care," Jack said defensively. "So, we're invited to dinner over at Terra's."

I turned away. "Not interested."

"Come on, Homes. They're going to bust open some high-end Pinots. You saw that cellar. Don't be a killjoy."

"I don't care. I'm not going to be a part of it."

"Part of what?" Jack asked, defying me to moralize.

"Your disaffection from Babs's family."

"*Disaffection*? Jesus. I'm trying to get you lined up here," he said.

"I don't need any help," I said.

"Bullshit. If it wasn't for me, you would never have gotten to know Maya."

I didn't say anything. He was right, of course. I wouldn't have gotten to know her, and though I had no idea if it would ever go anywhere, Jack deserved credit for planting the seed.

"So, what do you think?" Brad blared in my other ear.

I had forgotten all about him. "Think about what?"

"Goin' hunting."

I leaned back on my bar stool, opened my left hand, and gestured toward Jack. "This is my friend, Jack. Jack, meet Brad. He hunts wild boar. At night. They're nocturnal creatures, right, Brad?"

Brad nodded with the beer glass tipped to his mouth, then turned. From underneath a moustache of foam I heard a simple "Yep" emerge.

I turned to Jack. He was taking in an eyeful of Brad in his white T-shirt, faded jean jacket, stippled complexion, and half empty pitcher of Budweiser, and didn't like what he saw.

"So, do you want to go boar hunting?" I asked an incredulous Jack.

"What?"

"Into the wild," I replied, raising my glass, suddenly giddy.

"We're supposed to be over at Terra's at eight."

"Let's bring some boar to the barbecue!" I exclaimed.

"You've lost it, Homes." Jack raised his head to Brad and shouted over the racket, "Some other time there, Davy Crockett."

I slammed my fist histrionically on the bar. "I want to go boar hunting!"

"Oh, come on," Jack moaned. "What the fuck do you want to do that for?"

"Everything's fucking nutty. Might as well traipse off here with Brad. Make it a real bachelor's week."

"Just come with me," Jack said. He clutched my shoulder pleadingly. "I need you."

"I don't want to have dinner with those women," I said, raising my hands in a gesture of surrender.

"Oh, man, what is *up* with you?" Jack tilted his large frame toward me and whispered urgently, "This guy's a cracker. I'm not getting in a car with him. What do you want to go off with him for?"

I whispered back, "Imagine seeing a wild boar right now. How many chances do you get, huh?"

"How many chances do I *want* is what you mean. You're already sideways, man."

"I've had a few glasses."

"A *few* glasses?" Jack laughed, slapping me on the back. "A *few* glasses, my bar tab!"

I turned to the boar hunter. "Okay, Bradley, we're going to follow you out to wherever your hunting grounds are and watch you in action."

"All right," Brad said, perking up. He pounded his meaty fist on the bar. "Fucking A, let's get some pig."

I turned to Jack, laughing at Brad's gusto and the idea of doing something completely different. "It's going to be fun."

A dismayed Jack could see that I was dead serious. He dug his fingers into my shoulder, his face drained of mirth. "What?"

"You don't have to come."

"I need the car."

"*I'm* taking the car."

He scrunched up his face. "You're in no condition to operate light machinery, Homes."

"Oh, and you are?"

"Fuck," Jack said, acquiescing. "Fuck."

We settled up and went back to the room. Jack continued to attempt to talk me out of the boar hunt while we fumbled around for provisions.

"It ain't on the itinerary," Jack kept saying.

"Oh, and your Terra is?" I said, rummaging for my new Byron sweatshirt.

Outside in the parking lot, Brad blasted his horn a few times, urging us along.

"This is nuts," Jack said, turning circles in the room while I rooted around in the boxes for a couple of bottles of wine. Then the phone jangled, unnerving both of us, Jack visibly more than me.

"All right," Jack said, suddenly galvanized. "Let's get the fuck out of here. We'll go watch this cracker shoot a boar, then we'll go over to Terra's and party."

"That's the spirit."

We tumbled outside laden down with coats and wine. Brad's headlights were shining directly at us, momentarily blinding us. I waved, and Brad gunned his engine and turned around. We hopped into the 4Runner, Jack commandeering the wheel, groaning and complaining, and followed Brad out of the parking lot. We swung onto 246 trailing the boar hunter in his black Ford pickup.

"Do you have any idea where he's going?" Jack said.

"I think he mentioned something about Jalama Beach." I extracted the cork on the first Pinot, filled two plastic cups, and handed one to Jack.

"Is this my Byron?" Jack asked.

"What do you care? You can't tell the fucking difference."

He turned to me in the dim light of the cab. "Hey. I may not have your palate, but I can tell a good Pinot when I taste one." He turned his attention back to the road. "Fuck, this guy drives fast."

Out in front of us, Brad's taillights were shrinking in the distance. There were practically no cars on the road so it was pretty easy to keep a bead on his truck. Jack accelerated to keep pace with him. As we pulled up on his tail, we could make out a pair of rifles mounted horizontally in the rear cab window.

"Come on, let's blow this guy off," Jack urged.

"I want to see if he's for real," I protested.

"He's *obviously* for real. See those guns behind his head?"

"No, I mean when a boar comes charging, if he's going to be able to bring it down."

"Where are we going to be, huh?"

"We'll be parked on a hill, drinking our wine, spectating, like at a bullfight. Olé!" I raised my arm, but forgot that it was the one holding the wine, and splashed some Byron over my jeans. "Oops. There goes ten dollars' worth."

"Jesus, Miles, get a grip. Come on," Jack whined, as I refreshed my cup. "Let's turn back. This is ridiculous."

"No! I want to see this guy in action. He's a true original. A local legend."

"A local legend." Jack shook his head reproachfully but kept driving. He knew I got nutty like this from time to time and his response was always to ride it out, get me drunk enough, and then make sure I made it home.

Just before Lompoc, we hung a left on Highway 1 and headed south. The road wound through a gorge in the Santa Ynez Mountains, whose towering slopes closed off most of the star-riddled sky. I rolled down the window and inhaled the fragrant night air, invigorated by its cool freshness and the impending adventure.

The boar hunter angled off at Jalama Road and we followed. Soon we were on a tortuous, unlit, single-lane road headed oceanward. There were no other vehicles or lights burning along the roadside. We started to get the sense that we were really in the boar hunter's country now. Brad had obviously traveled this way many times before because he negotiated the hairpin turns in his bulky pickup with practiced ease.

"Fuck, man," Jack said, as he nearly lost it on a dipping ninety-degree curve. "This guy's a *fucking* maniac!"

"Yi *ha!*" I shouted, banging my fist on the dash in excitement. "Yi ha!"

"Give me that bottle," Jack demanded, now that we were off the main highway. I handed him the bottle. He tilted his head back and guzzled it. He passed it back and then bore down on Brad's retreating taillights in disgruntled pursuit, destination unknown.

Ten miles or so of careening on the relentlessly twisting road, we rounded yet another bend, but this time Brad's taillights were no longer visible.

"Where the fuck did he go?" Jack yelled, slowing the 4Runner and searching the road ahead of us. "This is nuts. Let's go back. I'm hungry. I want to hold that girl in my arms in front of a warm fire."

"There he is!" I pointed. Jack craned his neck in the direction I was indicating. Above us, as if scaling the sky, we saw the headlights of Brad's pickup coiling upward, perforating the darkness. "Take this turnoff," I insisted.

"What?" Jack said, stopping the car. We idled in the middle of the desolate road.

"Here. Turn off here." I gestured to an unpaved turnoff we could barely make out.

Jack looked skeptical, but he was eager to get this stupid adventure over with, so he fired off another execration and stomped on the accelerator. The tires squealed and I crashed against the door, my wine spilling, but I didn't care. We angled onto a dirt fire trail riotously overgrown with scrub oak that I'm sure Jack fatalistically envisioned was the *via regia* to Hell.

Branches whipped at the windows as we jostled along the rutted switchback. We had lost sight of Brad, but there was only one direction to move in and that's where we were bound, barreling along in a murky tunnel of flora. Jack was angry and I felt a little crazy; the combination did not bode well.

We climbed the mountain in the lower gears of the four-wheel drive and eventually arrived at a large clearing. Brad's truck was parked in full view of us, but there was no immediate sign of him. We clambered out of the 4Runner to figure out exactly where we were. I had the second bottle of Pinot out and was holding it between my legs to uncork it. The cork popped loudly in the silence and I chugged lustily. Jack—The Switch already flipped to the ON position in both of us—kept reaching for the bottle, and I kept pulling it away.

"Where the fuck is he?" Jack yelled. He swept his eyes over the terrain.

"He's out stalking the boar."

"Out stalking the boar," Jack mocked. "Give me that bottle."

I finally gave him the bottle and he took a healthy quaff. As our eyes adjusted to the moonlight it became clear that we were on a crown in the middle of a vast network of canyons. The air smelled of sage and rotting kelp and though we couldn't see the ocean, we could hear its sighing waves. Above us, the night sky chandeliered us with stars. Everything felt free and wild.

"Where—the—fuck—is—he?" Jack said, getting royally pissed off. "Hey, cracker!" Jack shouted. "Come out, come out, wherever you are!"

We wandered away from our car and scouted the knoll. Unseen animals migrated noisily about in the undergrowth, unnerving us. There was still no sign of Brad. Jack and I looked at each other and I shrugged and Jack made a face that displayed his utter disgust with our impromptu adventure.

He was about to say something about heading back to Buellton when, suddenly, the night echoed with a sharp report, like someone clapping his hands next to a live microphone. Almost simultaneously, the ground shuddered in front of our feet and a tiny cloud of dust puffed up in our faces. We were drunk and didn't figure out what had happened right away.

"What the fuck?" Jack shouted, crouching and tensing.

A few seconds later, a second shot cracked like lightning in the cold silence. This one crashed through the branches of a nearby oak.

"Jesus Christ, he's shooting at us!" Jack cried, a quavering fear in his voice.

"He's shooting boar!" I let out a war whoop.

A third shot rang out, splintering the canyon silence.

"Bullshit," Jack said, breaking into a trot. "He's shooting at us!"

We took off running. Nettles tore at our clothes

as we scrambled off the crown and fled tangle-footed down a narrow, twisting trail. A fourth shot sounded, echoing through the canyon, and we ran faster, hurtling headlong into the uncharted night.

"Over here," I heard Jack hiss a moment later. "*Over here!*"

I clambered awkwardly down a steep embankment and found Jack hunched behind a thick cluster of scrub oak, clinging to a branch and furiously motioning me toward him. We were both winded and gulping air to get our breath, and I could feel my heart thumping against my chest, as if trying to escape.

"He's a true original," Jack ridiculed me. "A true original serial killer, you fucking asshole."

"He probably mistook us for boar."

"Do we look like wild boar?" Jack fumed. "Jesus." He slapped his forehead so hard I thought he was going to knock himself over backward.

We both shifted anxiously in place, wondering what to do. This predicament was virgin territory. "Maybe I'll just go up there and have a kind word with him," I reasoned, still not a hundred percent convinced that Brad was shooting at us. I made a move to start back up the slope, but Jack yanked me back by my belt.

"What the fuck do you think you're doing?" he reproved me.

"Go figure this out. The guy isn't trying to kill us. That's absurd."

"How the fuck do you know?"

229

"He's not trying to shoot us," I insisted.

"Fuck, I could be sitting by a fire, eating a great meal right about now, and instead here I am, out with you, trapped in some fucking canyon with some cracker taking potshots at me," he spat.

"I'm going to figure this out. Give me that bottle." I grabbed the bottle from Jack, who surrendered it reluctantly, and took a swig to fortify myself. I passed the bottle back and started off.

"Where're you going?" Jack demanded, not budging from the shelter of the copse we had been hiding in.

"Have a talk with him," I said. Then, before Jack could restrain me, I scrambled on all fours up the slope. I thrashed my way through the undergrowth until I came to the rim of the clearing. I peered over but didn't see anyone. No movement, nothing, just our two cars. I leveraged myself onto the crown and straightened, wobbling, to my feet. The cricket-song silence was suddenly eerie, but I'd had enough to drink to quash most of my apprehensions. Later, Jack would claim I had had a death wish.

I cupped my hands around my mouth. "Hey, Brad," I shouted out in the direction of the cars. "What's happening? We heard some shots." I listened for a response. The chirring of crickets punctuated my entreaties. "Hey, Bradley! Yo, what's up, dude?"

A few seconds elapsed and then another shot like a bullwhip cracking shattered the silence. I broad-jumped back into the brush and scrabbled off the crown, sliding and tumbling on my ass back to where Jack was cowering in terror.

"Are you all right?" Jack asked solicitously. "Did he wing you?"

"I don't think so. But I probably wouldn't feel it if he did," I said, picking myself up off the dirt.

"Jesus," Jack said. "I don't think I've ever had anybody shoot at me before."

I brandished a finger in his face. "Stick with me and you'll experience things you've never experienced before."

"Stick with you and I'm going to be six feet under fertilizing daffodils is more like it."

I had a thought. "Did you bring your cell phone?"

"Why, do you want to call your agent?" Jack said, sticking his face into mine. "No, I don't have my fucking cell!"

"I thought you always carried it with you."

"I wasn't anticipating an extended stay in the *fucking bushes* while some creep you met at a bar used us for target practice." He stood threateningly over me like he was about to smack me.

"You never know when you're going to need it," I bantered, hoping to lessen the severity of the situation.

"Who're you going to call anyway?" Jack argued. "I couldn't even begin to direct the cops to where we are. Besides, they get one whiff of us and we're down for the count. So, don't get on my case for not having my cell."

"All right. All right. Let's figure this out."

Jack made an X with his arms across his chest and shivered, both because of the cold and the extent to which he feared for his life. "What've you got in mind? Suicide? The guy's got us pinned down here, for Christ's sake."

"We could hike to the ocean and wait him out till morning," I proposed.

"Brilliant. Which way is the ocean, Magellan?"

"I'm not sure. We'll follow the sound of the surf."

"Do I look like Hiawatha, Homes?"

"'By the shores of Gitche Gumee . . .'"

"Shut up," Jack hissed. "Shut up. The guy can hear us."

I giggled in spite of my fear, then clamped a hand over my mouth.

"Get a grip on your mug, man." Jack cuffed me on the side of the head, not hard enough to really hurt. "This is *serious* shit here."

"Do you think there's still time to make the eleven o'clock news?" I slapped my hand back over my mouth before I gave away our encampment.

"It ain't funny," Jack said. "We've got to figure something out."

"I've got it," I said, throwing both arms into the air triumphantly.

"What?" Jack barked.

"Let's go back up there, get down on all fours, start snorting like wild boars, and he'll mistake us for humans."

Jack sighed. "You're gone, brother. *Way* gone." He turned away.

232

"No, wait a minute. Wait a minute," I said, suddenly calm. "Let's just go up there and check this out. The guy's got to come out eventually."

Jack wheeled on me. "Let me explain something to you, Homes. He's armed. We're not. *Comprende*?"

"We're two against one, Jackson. Let's just go up together and see what the deal is."

Jack shook his head, too drained to really be angry anymore. His shoulders fell and he heaved another sigh. "All right. All right. I guess we don't have any other *fucking* choice."

Jack fell in behind me as I spearheaded the assault on the knoll. Painstakingly, mimicking infantrymen, we bellied our way through the brush up the face of the embankment. When we reached the crest, I ventured a glance over. The moon and starlight illuminated the barren crown in a soft, milky glow. From behind, Jack's warm breath ebbed and flowed against my cold neck. In the muted light, I glimpsed a form, but I couldn't quite make it out. It was an indistinct shadow of something moving. The shadow neared our vehicle, then stopped. Peering closer, I could make out the silhouette of Brad looking into my 4Runner, cradling his hunting rifle. I ducked down out of sight. Jack had parked himself with his back braced against the bank and was chugging from the bottle of wine.

"He's up there," I whispered. I eased down next to Jack, trying to stay completely quiet. "He's over by my car. Did you leave the keys in?"

Jack patted his pants pocket. "Yeah, I'm afraid so."

"Great." I tilted my head back and rested it against the dirt embankment. "He's probably looking for a trade-in."

"He lured us out here to *kill* us," Jack said, tense. "He's not interested in your fucking junker."

"Punk." I snatched the bottle from Jack, who didn't resist, and took a swig. "All right, here's what we're going to do."

Jack waited for the Miles plan, ready to deride it.

"I'm going to circle around and draw his attention. When you hear *Hey, Brad*, that's your cue to surprise him and whack him over the head with the bottle." I took another swig and handed our designated weapon back to Jack. "Let's lock and load."

Jack's eyes bulged. "Sounds like something you saw in a movie. Forget it." He wouldn't take the bottle.

"You got a better idea? I'm not going to hunker down here in the bushes all night because some local yokel thinks he can scare us. I'm not afraid of some fat little fucking pizza-face."

"Do I have to remind you? The fucker's *armed*."

"A rifle. They're awkward at close range. If we surprise him, we can easily take this guy."

Jack leveled his eyes at me and I held his gaze. I could see he was considering my plan. I thrust the empty wine bottle at him. He looked at it like it was a dead pet. Grudgingly, he finally accepted the makeshift weapon.

"All right, I'm off," I said. I started to move away.

"Wait wait *wait*," Jack hissed.

I stopped in a crouch and looked over my shoulder. "What? It's now or never, Jackson. Either shit or get off the porcelain."

"What's the cue?"

"I forget."

"Jesus, Homes."

"*Hey Brad*, whatever you hear me shout out, what the fuck difference does it make?"

"Fuck, if I get shot by a boar hunter, I swear to God, Homes, I am going to hurl bolts at you from heaven until Kingdom Come," Jack replied.

"You think that's where you're going?"

"It'd better be. Hell's going to be awfully crowded with you and your relatives there." He gripped the wine bottle by its neck, and held it upside down, ready for action.

"Okay, I'm off. On my cue, you come up like a bat out of hell and coldcock the fucker."

"Wait a sec," Jack said. "Let's go over this. . . ."

I tore my wrist free from his grip and broke away before he could hold me back with another barrage of doubts. If I hadn't been drinking, I'm sure I would have waited Brad out in the bushes all night until he gave up and drove off. But I *had* been drinking—and drinking heavily—since the Clubhouse, and I was lost in a maze where reason and prudence weren't illuminating the way out.

I edged along the crest of the knoll, scrabbling just below the rim, employing the scrub as handholds. Now and then I lost my grip and could hear twigs snapping and rocks and dirt avalanching out from under my feet. When that happened, I would pause for a few tense moments, my ears tuned to any fresh sound. Every time, the sound of crickets would rush in and reclaim the silence.

When I decided I had put enough distance between Jack and me and sandwiched Brad in between, I rose up out of the brush and poked my head over the rim. In the faint light, I spotted Brad snooping around inside my 4Runner, his rifle propped against the left wheel well. Angry that he was looking around for something to loot, and seizing the opportunity of his momentary disarmament, I vaulted up onto the crown and strode directly toward the boar hunter. "Hey, Brad, what's going on?" I called out loud enough for Jack to hear. My legs were shaking, but I thought I sounded authoritative and in control.

Brad leapt out of the car, spun around, and advanced on me without his rifle. I heard a scuffle of heavy footfalls and, moments later, glimpsed Jack hurtling up onto the crown, wine bottle raised aloft like a Sioux's tomahawk.

"Brad, buddy, what's going on?" I called out again, never once breaking stride, in an effort to distract him.

Jack, moving fast, discovering Brad weaponless, ditched the bottle, lowered his shoulder and collided with him on the dead run—like a linebacker taking out a tight end—and tackled him to the ground. Being bigger and stronger, Jack easily overpowered the boar hunter, quickly pinning his right arm behind his back and digging a knee into his lower spine. Brad squealed in pain.

"Get the gun," Jack commanded, now in charge. "Get the gun."

I hurried over to the 4Runner to claim the boar hunter's rifle. "I got the gun," I said, feeling a surge of excitement that my plan had succeeded. "I got the gun."

"What the fuck do you think you're doing, cracker?" Jack shouted at a helpless Brad, who was now moaning pathetically in the dirt.

"I was just spooking you, that's all," Brad whined. "Just some fun."

"Is this your idea of fun, huh, crackerman? Huh?" Jack wrenched Brad's arm higher up his back and he let out a yelp. "You think that's funny, huh?"

I stepped forward. "You little motherfucker," I screamed, joining in on the victory dance. "How would you like it if we took a couple of shots at you?"

Jack jerked his arm up even higher. "You scared now, you little critterman!" Jack taunted.

I pulled back the cocking lever on the thirty-ought-six, then tickled Brad's ear with the end of the barrel. "Should we just blow him away right here, Jack? What do you think? Then torch him in his truck and make it look like suicide?" I screwed the muzzle into the back of his head for emphasis. "Motherfucker."

"I wasn't going to shoot you, I wasn't, I was just trying to scare you," Brad blubbered. Jack and I both thought he was starting to bawl.

"You fucking wuss," Jack yelled at him so close it must have damaged his eardrums.

I shifted the gun away from his head and raised it in the air. Suddenly there was an enormous explosion, as if a grenade had gone off, and I momentarily lost my balance, staggering in place.

"Jesus, Homes!" Jack yelled. "Jesus!"

"I wasn't trying to shoot it."

"Don't kill me," Brad cried, "don't kill me. I'll do anything you want. I swear to God." There were real tears in his eyes now.

Jack looked up at me, still kneeling on Brad. "Don't point that bad boy over here, Homes, you've had a shitload to drink."

"I wasn't trying to shoot it. It just went off," I said lamely.

Jack turned back to the matter at hand. "Hey, crater face, have you ever seen the movie, *Deliverance?*"

"Don't kill me, please don't kill me," Brad repeated over and over, squirming helplessly under Jack's weight.

"Should we do a Ned Beatty on him, Homes?"

"That's your department, Jackson."

"Maybe we should just stick his gun up his ass and see if he likes it."

"Would give a whole new meaning to *hair trigger*, wouldn't it?"

Jack and I shared a cathartic laugh while Brad shot us a horrified backward glance, his eyes stricken with terror. The sociopath had met his match.

"What're we going to do with this punk?" Jack said, growing impatient.

"Don't kill me, don't kill me," Brad continued to plead.

"Shut up," Jack shouted back at him. "Shut the *fuck* up. We're not going to kill you. We'll turn you in to the cops before we kill you. We're upstanding citizens, unlike you!" Jack looked up at me. "What do you think, Homes? Call the fuzz on him? Turn him in?"

I shrugged and thought about it for a few seconds. In truth I was tired and was eager to get back to the warmth of the motel. "Bradley?" I addressed the boar hunter in a nonthreatening voice.

"Yes?" Brad peeped.

"What were you doing, man? Tell us the truth. It could help your cause."

"I was just going to scare you. I guess I get a little twisted sometimes."

"A *little* twisted?" Jack raged. "You should be *fucking* institutionalized!" Jack looked at me. "That's so fucking lame, Homes. Let's just take him to the cops, or take his keys and make him hoof it home."

"No, please don't take me to the cops. I've got a record."

"Surprise, surprise," Jack said. He pinched one of Brad's whey-colored cheeks. "Never would have figured *you* for a felon."

"It's not what you think," Brad protested weakly.

Jack grabbed a fistful of Brad's hair and bent his head back as if he were going to scalp him. "If I told you what I was thinking, critterman, you'd crap your pants." He let go of his hair and Brad's forehead thumped hollowly against the hard dirt.

"Jesus, Jackson," I said, feeling a sudden twinge of sympathy for Brad.

"Sorry, Brad. But it's a lot less painful than the hundred volts they're going to zap you with up at the state loony bin," Jack finished.

"What were you arrested for, Brad?" I asked.

"DUI—twice," Brad stammered.

"I'm impressed," Jack said. "You do the program?"

"What?" Brad asked, straining to look backward. "Yeah, I did the program."

"Didn't work, did it?"

"No," Brad replied, as if it were expected of him.

"That's because you're a *dumb* fuck!" Jack said. Brad didn't reply. "Say you're a dumb fuck, crater face."

"I'm a dumb fuck," Brad repeated meekly.

Jack cuffed him on the side of the head. "Louder!"

Brad raised his head and shouted, "I'M A DUMB FUCK. I'M A DUMB FUCK."

"That's better," Jack barked.

"All right, all right," I said. I squatted down next to Brad, rested the stock of the rifle on my knee, and pressed the muzzle flush to his temple. "Do you still have your driver's license, Bradley?"

He looked at me, bewildered. "Yeah, why?"

"Here's what we're going to do. Friday they're holding a big wine festival up at Fess Parker's. We need a chauffeur. Are you interested?"

"What?" Jack protested, alarmed. "I'm not going to let this cracker ferry us around. You're fucking nuts!"

I silenced Jack with an index finger to my lips, signaling him to let me continue the negotiations. "Bradley?"

"Yeah, I'm interested," Brad squeaked.

I moved the muzzle of the rifle away from his head and straightened to my feet. "All right. We're going to confiscate your gun and your wallet. If you're not at the Windmill Inn Friday bright and early—around noon—we're turning them into the police and telling them what happened out here and that you escaped and you're on the lam."

Brad didn't respond right away and Jack yanked his arm up, twisting it in its socket. "Answer my partner, critterman."

"Okay, okay," Brad said, clearly relieved, but just as clearly baffled. "I'll drive you. I'll drive you."

Jack fumbled roughly around in Brad's back pocket and removed his wallet. Then he released him and rose to his feet. Jack admonished him to remain on the ground until we had driven off, adding: "Otherwise, we're going to shoot your dick off and feed it to the boar."

We climbed back in the car with Brad's rifle, executed a swerving one eighty, and roared off the clearing. Through the back window I could see Brad still lying on the ground, obeying our orders. We bounced back down the rocky switchback and connected up with the main road.

The ride back to Buellton was longer than I thought it would be. We had disappeared farther into the hinterlands than I had imagined, or maybe sobriety had made the distance greater. Neither of us had much to say to each other on the way back. Jack was still furious with me, but because we had come through the ordeal relatively unscathed, he was inclined to keep his wrath to himself. I didn't think Brad's lenient sentence was much to Jack's liking either, but we were headed back to Buellton in one piece and that's all that really mattered.

Back at the motel I was dispatched to the Club-house while Jack made apologetic calls to the women in his life. I half-heartedly nursed a glass of wine in the deserted lounge and made small talk with the barkeep, never mentioning the incident with Brad. For an absurd moment, I fantasized that Maya might walk in from work, take a stool next to me, and start a conversation, but no doubt she and Terra were sitting at home with food for four and unhappy about being stood up.

I gave it an hour, then, unable to bear the solitude and alienating decor of the bar anymore, I trudged back to the room. I half expected Jack to be gone, off on another all-night tear with Terra, but instead I found him lying in bed, staring introspectively up at the ceiling.

I took off my coat and hung it up. "Talk to Terra?" I asked.

Jack nodded without looking at me.

"What's happening?" I asked, peeling off my new Byron sweatshirt.

"Didn't feel like going over," he said tonelessly. "Told her something came up."

I looked at him for elaboration, but he avoided my gaze.

"Talk to Babs?"

"Yeah."

"Did you tell her we went boar hunting tonight?"

Jack rolled his head slowly and looked at me and smirked. "We had a good talk."

I finished undressing and slipped into my queen. "She stop hassling you about cutting the trip short?"

"Yeah. We're over that."

"Good. Glad to hear it."

Jack switched the TV on and shuttled through the channels. He didn't find anything so he snapped it off, plunging the room into darkness. We shifted restlessly in our beds, still keyed up from the bizarre confrontation with the boar hunter. Against the wall I could make out the silhouette of the confiscated rifle, and it made it seem all that more real. With our cases of wine it made an impressive cache. I chuckled, wondering what the maid would think when she saw it in the morning.

"Fucker almost killed us tonight," Jack said, dead sober.

"I don't think he was ever going to kill us," I said.

"Yeah, now, maybe, in retrospect, but at the time, I thought the fucker was shooting at us. Lead us out, some dark road, blow us away, steal our money, that's what I was thinking."

"I wasn't thinking shit. I was pretty loaded."

"You were a little twisted, Homes." Jack chuckled. "I'll grant you that."

"But I held it together."

"You made the call."

"I stared him down, that little motherfucker."

"I did the dirty work," Jack boasted. "As usual."

I laughed. "Yeah, we make a pretty good team."

"Think he'll make the bell Friday?"

"If he doesn't come back tonight with more artillery and blow us away," I said.

"Why'd you say that? You really think that?" Jack asked.

"No. He was just goofing us like he said."

"With a fucking rifle. I mean, some of those shots were close."

"Yeah, well. He's got a twisted sense of humor."

The heater hummed as we fell silent. It felt weird all of a sudden to be lying in the dark in the same room with another man. Except for eight years of marriage, I'd lived alone all my adult life.

"When he was shooting at us, you know what I was thinking about?" Jack suddenly asked. "Aside from dying, that is?"

I waited.

"I thought about Babs."

"It took a near-death experience to bring her and the wedding back into focus, huh?"

"Don't make fun, Homes. I'm getting personal here. You undercut me every time I get serious."

"Can't be that often then," I said, shifting uncomfortably in bed.

There was a pause as Jack gathered his thoughts. "So, I'm thinking about this woman, Terra, and how I don't really know her, and how some of the things you were saying earlier started to make sense and that, I mean, what are we on this earth for?"

"I know what I'm here for," I said, making light of his confession.

"Yeah, but you made that decision a long time ago. Don't tell me you don't have regrets about all the shit that happened with Victoria?"

"Look," I cut him off. "I'm the wrong guy on

this subject, Jackson. I've come to the inescapable conclusion that individuals like me are unfit for cohabitation. I recognize this flaw—if, indeed, it is a flaw—and I operate accordingly. Others are different."

"But this is what I've been struggling with," Jack said sincerely.

"I understand. But you're not going to find your answer up here in Buellton. That's just what's so ridiculous about the whole thing."

His voice sharpened. "I know that."

"In a way, we've both got the wrong personalities in the wrong aesthetics."

"What the fuck are you talking about, Homes?"

"Well, I wish I had your gift to meet women. That way I could leapfrog unhappily from one to the next without fear of long lonely gaps in between. You, on the other hand, could use some of my introspection, my capacity for aloneness, so that you wouldn't feel the need to go traipsing from one woman to the next. Especially now that you're getting married."

"You don't really believe that, do you, about leapfrogging from one woman to the next?"

"For now it seems to be the only thing that works."

"So, you're saying because I'm outgoing I'm always at risk?"

"Exactly," I replied. "You comprise the ten percent that ninety percent of the single women date and ultimately hate. You give the rest of us a bad name."

Jack laughed. "And if I were a dark little misanthropic fucker like you, I'd be better suited to cohabitation?"

"Contradiction in terms, I guess."

Another silence fell. I could tell Jack wasn't asleep, and neither was I. The cricket song competed with our breathing. After a long few minutes, as if he had been cogitating on something all the time, Jack said out of the blue: "Do you believe in love? Love with one person until your dying days?"

I didn't answer right away. My eyes had adjusted to the room now, and I could make out Jack's hulking shape in my peripheral vision.

After a minute or so he rotated his large head toward my queen and said, "Huh?"

I started to snicker.

"I guess that's a no," Jack said, unamused.

The floodgates opened and I disintegrated into uncontrollable laughter.

Then, unable to restrain himself, Jack, too, burst into laughter. We laughed together until we couldn't have spoken if we'd wanted to. Then, suddenly, as if the gears had been thrown into reverse, he started yelping in pain. "Ow, ow, shit. Shit!"

"What?"

"Fuck." He switched on the end-table light, sat up in bed, and examined his rib cage. He fingered a sensitive area and winced. "Ow. Shit. I think I broke something out there, Homes. Jesus."

I sat up on my elbows and looked over at him. He was genuinely grimacing in pain. The upward light of the lamp caricatured his anguish. "Go see a doctor tomorrow," I suggested.

"Fuck," he said, sucking in his breath against the hurt. "This is all I need."

"Nothing you can do about it tonight. Unless you want me to take you to the emergency room."

"No." Jack snapped the light off and eased back down onto the mattress. "Oh, man, this hurts all of a sudden."

"There was this pro golfer who was out for six months because he cracked a couple of ribs. Know how he did it?"

"No, why would I?"

"Laughing."

"You think I just *now* cracked it?"

"Might have. Might have been weakened by that tackle."

Jack started to laugh again, but his laughter quickly broke up into grunts of discomfort.

In a bad imitation of a woman's voice I said, "Honey, how'd you crack your rib? Oh, tackling a boar hunter," I finished in a huskier man's voice.

Jack slapped a hand over his mouth and tried to stifle his laughter. In a muffled voice, he pleaded, "Stop it."

WEDNESDAY: THE PERILS OF SOBRIETY

The next morning I drove a somber-faced Jack to the emergency room at Lompoc Hospital, a sprawling, single-story, ranch-style complex at the southern end of town. Inside the ER, a young, bespectacled intern with an owlish face asked him to remove his shirt and climb up onto a paper-covered table in a curtained cubicle. I waited off to the side as he performed a cursory examination. After Jack flinched in pain in response to his exploratory touches, the intern ordered an X-ray.

As Jack was led into the bowels of the hospital to the radiology department, I retreated to the waiting room and flipped absently through a stack of dog-eared magazines. In a women's rag I scanned a Q&A on how to determine if your man is cheating on you: "Does he make excuses for withholding sex?" "Is his routine different from when you first started living together?" "Does he exhibit frequent mood swings, alternating from euphoria to depression?" What women don't understand, I sassed the magazine, is that for

249

most men adultery is the best sex they're ever going to experience. Its clandestineness in motel rooms, parked cars, and unfamiliar apartments with promiscuous and naughty love-starved tarts who delight in husband theft is just too much for the intervention of Freud's superego. It rocks men's worlds, reducing them to sex-crazed primitives, blithering idiots, and reckless drivers. Sure, they leave dumb paper and phone trails and are quickly found out, becoming blubbering fools contritely seeking forgiveness from their bruised wives, while their paramours weep over unfulfilled promises whispered in perfervid clenches. Contrite for the moment, that is, until the next whiff of torrid betrayal grips their groins. And marriage, with its imprisoning aspects to a man, often inspires the full flowering of its always hurtful, and destructive, recrudescence. Except for pockets of God-fearing Christians staring at hell through a crucifix, cheating is not going to stop. Spouses should probably encourage random sex with anonymous partners on an infrequent basis to halt the charade of fidelity. That way, relationships could actually prosper and grow deeper, I concluded cynically.

Bored, I folded the magazine shut and looked up. Two toddlers clung to their mother's legs, the three of them presenting a silent and grim-faced tableau. I wondered if Dad wasn't at that moment under the knife in some grim fluorescent-lit room having his heart resuscitated. To their left, a man with long, stringy hair was jackknifed forward, drumming a hand rhythmically on his knee as if warding off some appalling image that kept replaying itself in his imagination. From time to time he combed a grease-stained hand through his hair. I returned to my magazine and found another questionnaire, this one measuring self-esteem. After honestly answering all the questions, I tallied up my score, compared it to a chart, and found myself in the clinically depressed category. They advised me to immediately seek professional treatment. Apparently, 98 percent of the nation's populace possessed a brighter outlook on life than I did. That startled me. Wouldn't all those nuclear families living in their middle-class shoeboxes have to be more suicidal than I?

The Formica chair was pinching my ass and the rubbish in the magazines was aggravating my mood. I spotted a pay phone across the waiting room, got up, and dialed home for messages to brighten my outlook on life. A woman I had dated briefly months ago called to tell me her younger brother had just written a novel and she wondered if . . . fast-forward. Message number two was an unrecognizable voice speaking in an escalatingly threatening tone about one of my unusable credit cards (God! what an occupation!) . . . erase. Message three was a still-worried Victoria. This time she barraged me with apologies—her not having informed me that she'd remarried ("didn't want to set you off"), how she wished things had worked out between us—uh-huh—and a host of other mollifying assessments. Number four I didn't really pay attention to, mostly because Victoria's lengthy one was still reverberating in my head, but it was a friend whom I hadn't heard from in a while wondering if I was still alive. The last one was the creditor making a second, angrier, attempt to reach me, reciting an 800 number complete with name and extension. That was it. Nothing from my agent. Obviously, things were proceeding slowly at Conundrum, if at all. I slowly paced the linoleum back to my plastic seat, slumped down, and kept on waiting, the result of my self-esteem examination reaffirmed.

Jack emerged at last, clutching a sheaf of green-colored documents, his head bowed. He signed some forms at the registration desk, then came over to where I was sitting, avoiding my gaze.

"What is it?" I asked, rising to my feet.

He started walking toward the sunlit exit and I trailed. "Hairline fracture in one of the ribs," he said in a grim monotone over his shoulder.

"No golf today, I guess," I said, catching up with him.

"It's your fault, Homes."

"*My* fault?"

"You should be the one with the rib fracture," he said peevishly. "Not me."

"You're the one with health insurance," I reminded him.

"Maybe Hell does have a god," he said, loosening up a little.

I chuckled. "What'd they do for it?"

Jack came to a halt just outside the entrance to the ER, spun around and faced me. He unbuttoned his shirt and held it open, revealing a white body bandage swathed tightly around his torso.

"They've got you mummified, Jackson!"

"Don't piss me off, Homes."

"How long do you have to wear that?"

"Six weeks," he said dispiritedly. "Maybe longer." He rebuttoned his shirt and quickly covered himself up.

"*Six* weeks?"

He nodded and started walking toward the car.

"Can you have sex?"

He wheeled and crooked a finger at me. "Don't piss me off, Homes."

"What're you going to do on your honeymoon?"

"I'm not happy about this," Jack warbled in a warning tone.

"Maybe this'll be the oral sex icebreaker with Babs," I called out from behind him.

"That's it! That's *it!*" He stormed off.

I let him walk away so he could blow off some steam. The hot sun was beating down on me, so I got back in the 4Runner, turned on some music, and waited.

A good half hour later, I saw Jack angling toward the car. He went around to the passenger side and painfully hoisted himself in. Without a word, he slammed the door shut and stared miserably through the windshield, his face a block of granite. After a moment he barked, "Let's go."

"Where?"

"I don't care. Just move it."

I turned the engine over and let it idle. "Hearst Castle?" I ventured.

He turned slowly and glowered at me. "Are you kidding?" I shrugged. "You really want to see the Hearst Castle?"

"I'm tangentially interested in opulence, yeah. In the unlikely event my book becomes a bestseller."

"Doesn't it have to get published first?"

"Well, according to half the population of the Santa Ynez Valley, that's already a done deal."

Jack cracked a smile for the first time that morning, resigned, it seemed, to his injury. "All right," he said gruffly, "go call 'em."

"Let me use your cell."

"No. I've got to make some calls."

"All right," I said, opening the door, "I'll be back in a few."

On the emergency room pay phone that had insulted me earlier, I called information and got the Hearst Castle main number. After listening to a recorded message, I punched the appropriate numbers and was patched through to the tour reservations office. A cheerful female voice informed me that they had places available on one of their afternoon tours, and I booked space for two.

When I returned to the car, Jack was concluding a call, cradling his cell phone as if he didn't want to be overheard. He looked as though he was thinking about something important.

"Babs?"

He nodded.

"Tell her about the . . . mishap?"

He scrunched up his face and shook his head. "I don't want to worry her."

"How is she?"

"Weirdly distant."

"Are you worried that maybe *she's* having second thoughts?"

Jack pushed out his lips, then he faced me with a furrowed brow. "You didn't answer the phone and talk to her and not remember because you were looped, did you?"

"No," I said, aghast at the idea.

"And you don't remember what you said to Victoria?" he continued.

"I didn't say anything that would compromise you. When I'm drunk I say things that embarrass me, but I rarely, if ever, spread malicious gossip, especially when it's factual."

Jack turned slowly back to the window, captured by something in his mind. "Okay, let's go," he said, sounding unsatisfied with my explanation and still dismayed about whatever Babs had said.

We drove north on Highway 1 in the direction of Morro Bay. The first half of the drive featured towering eucalyptuses that flanked the road, making it feel like a wooded colonnade. A traveling sun, paralleling our movement on the opposite side of the trees, threw bolts of bright light in between their peeling trunks, dappling the asphalt. As the highway swung nearer the ocean, the wooded terrain broke up into smaller stands of trees and dense underbrush. It gradually opened into humped sand dunes dotted with hardy, windblown scrub huddled close to the ground. As we climbed above the dunes, the Pacific yawned into view. A strong wind marred the surface, churning up the endless ocean with ragged chop. I cracked my window open and a pungent fetor of seaweed stung my nostrils. The cold air invigorated me, but Jack made me close the window, faking a shiver.

In Morro Bay—a coastal retirement town pockmarked with cheap motels and bric-a-brac shops—we had an hour to kill, so we stopped for lunch in a marine-themed restaurant perched at the water's edge. Inside, the wall facing the ocean was broken by large, lightly tinted picture windows. It was the off-season and the restaurant was empty so we were led to a window table. Through a scrim of decorative fish nets sagging under the weight of old cork floats and rusted lures, we had a clear view of the famous Morro Rock, a gray skyscraper-sized, long-extinct volcano sitting in shallow waters, jutting up an impressive 576 feet.

"Should we get a bottle of wine?" I suggested

casually, glancing at my menu, checking to see if Jack remembered our morning's vow of abstinence for the day.

"No," Jack barked.

"Just kidding," I said.

"No, you weren't. You were testing me."

"How's the rib?" I asked with affected concern.

"What do you mean, '*How's the rib?*' "

"How's the rib?"

"The rib is the same as it was an hour ago," he answered, glaring at me over his menu.

"Does it hurt when you breathe?"

"No. It only hurts when I look at you."

I dropped my menu and met his gaze. "Look. I may be the reason we followed the boar hunter and you ended up hitting the deck in a valiant effort I'll never forget and will anecdotalize for years to come, but you're the reason I was pissed off enough to even get in that position in the first place. Just to set the record straight."

"What're you talking about?"

"I wasn't planning on drinking last night. But when I caught you and your small-town paramour in flagrante delicto, it just set me off," I said, raw annoyance throbbing in my voice.

Jack avoided my stare and pretended to look over the menu.

I raised my voice slightly to draw his attention. "I mean, what the fuck were you doing screwing her in my bed?"

"It just happened. I didn't have time to choose

beds. Fucking chick jumped me. Besides, what do you care? The maid puts new sheets on them every morning."

"Not at the Windmill they don't!"

"How do you know?"

"That's not the point."

"Oh, what *is* the point?" he asked sarcastically.

"I don't like witnessing sex. Except in movies. Even then, it usually embarrasses me."

Jack cocked his head to one side, perplexed. "I'm learning all kinds of shit about you, Homes."

"Check it out from my POV. There you are, my best friend, flagpole to the ceiling, your newfound lover flashing her dark luxuriant bush—which you know I have a fondness for—now, do I want to see this in my current eremitic state?"

"Current *what* state?" he demanded.

"Monastic. As in alone, without a bush of my own."

"Maybe we *should* get a bottle," Jack said half-heartedly. "You're starting to go Webster on me."

"Nope. We're staying sober today. It's the only way this nonsense will end."

A teenaged waitress wearing a pink short-sleeved dress finally approached, holding an order pad and a poised pen. She had a small turned-up nose, blond hair braided back in a ponytail, and eyes that sparkled with innocence. "Are you ready to order?" she asked in a high voice.

"I'll have the swordfish," I said.

"Don't get the swordfish," Jack reproved. "You're killing dolphins."

I pretended to give his eco-warning serious thought. "Then I'll have the dolphin," I said.

"We don't have dolphin on the menu, sir," the waitress replied ingenuously.

"Oh. Then I'll have the sea otter. Medium rare. Pelt on the side."

She raised her eyebrows and focused her gaze above my head. "Should I come back when you're ready to order?"

Jack tented his face in his hands and shook his head disgustedly.

"No, I'll have the halibut," I said in an apologetic tone, closing my menu and handing it to her. "It's been a long week."

She didn't care to hear me elaborate about my *long week* and wordlessly shifted her attention to Jack. Jack took his hands away from his haggard, unshaven face, manufactured a smile, and said politely, "I'll have the fish and chips."

The waitress, thoroughly uncharmed, turned and threaded her way through a jigsaw of empty tables in the direction of the kitchen.

"Okay. Let's get a bottle of Muscadet," I said. "Low in alcohol. Basically Kool-Aid."

"Kool-Aid. Give me a break. Let's just ride it out. Relax."

"Shouldn't have come into a restaurant. That's the problem." I picked up my glass of water and banged it down on the table. "I'm on vacation. I can't just drink fucking water. I feel like St. Francis of Assisi."

"I'm the one who should cave in because I'm the one with the cracked rib."

I pointed a finger at him. "A glass of wine will soothe that thing like you wouldn't believe."

"Do you really want to go to the Hearst Castle?"

"Sure, why not? What else are we going to do?"

"So, what do you know about William Randolph?" Jack asked. "Fill me in, Mr. Know-It-All."

"Well. He was a fat fuck involved with a beautiful woman who couldn't act her way out of a paper bag. Made millions with tabloid papers dishing daily drivel, bought a movie studio so his girlfriend could get parts without falling all over her face in auditions, fucked over our great national treasure, Orson Welles, by ordering *The Magnificent Ambersons* to be edited into an incomprehensible mess in retaliation for being skewered in *Citizen Kane*. Then he erected a monument to his ill-gotten wealth and bequeathed it to tourism so others could envy him in absentia for time immemorial. His sad, cynical legacy."

Jack sat back in his chair and folded his arms across his chest. "So, why do you want to go?"

"I've heard it's a pretty cool crib."

Jack suppressed a laugh, but a smile broke through.

"No, seriously, I'm interested in seeing the product of his demented hubris."

"Did your agent ever call back?" Jack asked.

"No."

"What do you think's happening?" he asked sincerely.

"No idea. Was supposed to have a decision some time this week. Obviously, the decision is not an easy one. Ergo, the book isn't being deemed commercial. Or they think it's a piece of shit, and I can just kiss off two years of my life."

Jack eyed me thoughtfully, but was at a loss for words.

"Obviously, a drink would help mask this rising tide of self-loathing."

Jack laughed. But the laughter quickly turned into a wince, as he clutched his side in pain.

"Obviously, I'm going to have to figure something out pretty soon."

"What about Maya?" Jack asked.

"What about her?"

"Woman's beautiful, man."

"I know," I admitted. "I just. . . ."

"What?"

"I don't want to talk about it," I said peevishly.

The waitress returned with our salads. "Would you like something to drink?" she asked innocently.

I banged my fist histrionically down on the table, clattering the cutlery. "No!"

"He's trying not to drink today," Jack explained.

"Oh," she replied as though it were an aspiration of trifling consequence. "How about you? Are you okay?"

"No, I'm not okay," Jack said, wincing in

response to another shooting pain from his cracked rib. "But I think it would be unfair to my good friend here if I ordered a glass."

"Okay," she replied, moving off.

We ate our lunches in a hurried silence, tipped outrageously to compensate the waitress, whose composure was admirable, then got back into the car and back onto Highway 1 bound for San Simeon. The road ribboned scenically along the Pacific, where large waves slapped against the black, seaweed-garlanded rocks, enveloping them with a brownish white foam. Stretching to the horizon, the ocean was a navy blue, still blistered by glistening whitecaps whipped up by a cold strengthening wind. Bordering us on the right, fields of tall emerald grass unfurled over gently rolling slopes that climbed steeply into craggy, gray spires that notched the bottom of the sky. Tenting the magnificent whole was an unstained, vast dome of infinite blue. Truly one of the most beautiful highways in the world.

In the seashore town of San Simeon we went into Hearst Castle's main office and picked up our tickets. After a long wait, we were herded into a bus with a gaggle of tourists. Most of them were elderly, potbellied, and wreathed with photographic gear. The bus roared to life, and an audiotape recording came on giving us some background information on the Hearst Castle. I tuned out. As we lurched slowly up the steep grade to The Enchanted Hill I felt less like Clark

Gable or Marion Davies or another luminary making an ascent to the fabled mansion, and more like some middle-aged loser marking time till I became an old fart sadly attired in worn sneakers and a San Simeon Hearst Castle baseball cap as my lone cherished memory.

When we reached the top of the hill, we pulled into a parking lot with a few other tour buses. Looking down from its great height, the view from the summit was heartstopping. The castle ruled over a sweep of unspoiled topography ending in a dramatic stretch of one of California's most pristine coastlines. I could probably see for sixty miles. The man who built this place clearly had godlike delusions of his corporeal worth. If money alone could buy an entry into heaven, he had tried his damnedest.

A middle-aged male guide, who wore an expression of worldly disillusionment and who spoke tonelessly as if he had recited his informational spiel thousands of times, led us on a perfunctory tour of the magnificently lavish grounds, eventually guiding us inside where additional treasures were to be found. Though the opulence of the castle was impressive—stately outdoor swimming pool, every surface carved or tiled—the place felt spectral, haunted by a history that seemed both unreal and unfathomable. As we paraded from one high-ceilinged room to another, walking over priceless Italian terra-cotta, floating past decadent Baroque artworks, our group finally ending up encircling the fabled, mosaic-inlaid indoor pool, I reached the prosaic conclusion that one could be unhappy anywhere. Or was I just projecting?

As the afternoon dragged on, our tour companions snapped pictures and filmed away, embalming the fantasy chateau into a complete state of lifelessness while the guide stuffed us with useless historical tidbits. All that mattered, I thought selfishly, irritated by my clearheadedness, was that I wasn't going to get to travel back in time and breaststroke through the rotunda pool in the wee hours of the morning and make underwater love to some sinuous starlet who mistook me for Montgomery Clift. Staring absently into the iridescent tiles on the pool's floor and trying to conjure the libidinous orgies that had supposedly occurred here years ago left me with the desolate feeling that sexual desire drove men to do some pretty ridiculous things. And, in the end, it was all an ephemeral, grand waste of time.

Jack, naturally, drew a different lesson from his visit to San Simeon. To him the place was magnificent, a sultan's majestic pleasure palace, an ultimate expression of one man's brilliantly hedonistic vision. Worth every penny if you could afford it.

"I don't deny the place is beautiful," I said as we bounced along in the bus heading down the hill back to the real world. "But is that how you would spend your millions if you had them?

What's its ultimate value except to impress others?"

"Exactly," Jack said. "The man was a lonely motherfucker. Probably didn't have a lot of friends. This was a way to meet people."

"What a hollow aspiration. All facade."

"No, it's not. The people came, didn't they?"

"They came the way people come if you bust open your wine cellar and uncork your finest Burgundies. That doesn't mean they're your friends. They probably laughed behind his back when he went to fetch more Beluga."

"And kissed his ass," Jack said.

"The guy was supposedly monogamous."

"So? Wouldn't you want to live there?"

"No," I insisted.

"No?"

"No."

"Why?" Jack asked.

"Because I have a sneaking suspicion I would go mad living the life of an eternal sybarite?"

"This from a guy who takes intense pleasure from good wine." Jack broke into laughter. "You'd live there."

"Yeah, but what would I write about?"

"What do you write about now?"

"Failure and redemption."

"Okay, so you would write about wealth and power. Something people might like to read about. Instead of your desperate little pathetic antiheroes."

"I think they ought to tear it down," I said, folding my arms petulantly across my chest.

"It's pure Americana," Jack countered.

"They've got hundreds of places like that in Europe. And more impressive."

"Exactly. But only one here."

"True. But it's just such a fucking eyesore."

Jack leapt to his feet, whirled around, and addressed the rest of the bus: "Does anyone on this ship have a cocktail? My friend here needs a drink."

The tourists stiffened with alarm and sat stony-faced, exchanging clouded looks with one another.

"Sit down, Jackson," I said, tugging at his shirt.

"Wine cooler?" Jack tried again, arms outstretched in supplication, the frustrated actor on his movable stage.

The bus driver, watching the scene in his rearview mirror, turned around and shot Jack an admonitory look. "Sit down," he said sharply.

Jack sank back into his seat, sagging in mock defeat. "Oh, well, I tried."

"I appreciate the effort," I said.

"You're welcome."

"Great improv."

"Thank you."

Back at sea level, the bus lurched to a halt with an earsplitting squeal of brakes. We filed off, tour-drugged and stiff. For a few minutes, we admired Hearst Castle one last time. In the high distance, shrouded in a light mist, it shimmered like one of those three-dimensional postcards, bewitched by wind and ocean smells. A replica of a monument to a forgotten civilization of shallow hedonists. Disgusting.

I glanced at my watch, hatching an idea. "We've still got time to make Babcock."

Jack stared at me for a delayed moment with a mock glower. He wagged a finger at me, then broke into a broad grin, clapped his hands together and said, "Let's hit it, brother."

We sped down Highway 1 in an ebullient mood and made it to Babcock Winery fifteen minutes before the tasting room closed. The affable pourer, a young man who told us he was studying to be a vintner, quickly broke us in on their Riesling, a dry Alsatian-style wine that was surprisingly complex. We continued on pro forma through the Sauvignon and Chardonnay, the less than impressive Pinot, until we arrived at the monster Black Label Cuvee. It was an inky, almost biblical, 100 percent Syrah with truckloads of ripe fruit and brambly tannins. I adored it, and so did Jack. We had abandoned the subtlety of Pinot for the pure unadulterated lust of Syrah.

When we'd finished the sampling, the glow had returned to our faces and we were once again, however ephemerally, elevated out of our individual morasses. Wanting to demonstrate his appreciation to the pourer for keeping the tasting room open past closing, Jack, at my urging, splurged on a case of the Black Label and a single bottle of chilled Riesling.

We drifted outside and parked ourselves on a lone picnic bench. Situated on a gentle rise, Babcock is at the western end of the Santa Ynez Valley in the midst of an extensive network of vineyards which seem to unfurl in every direction as far as the eye can see. I did the uncorking honors and filled us both up with the perfectly chilled Riesling. The knockout Syrah, though tempting, would have been too heavy in the warm, early evening air.

"This was an *excellent* idea," Jack said, the heaviness and pertubation lifed from his voice.

I held my glass of wine to the sun and examined the color. "Riesling's perfect right now."

"Babs would like this wine," he said, taking a sip.

"She likes fruity whites, huh?"

"Yeah." Jack's face clouded for a moment. "Something wrong with that?"

"No. Not at all. I used to think it was indicative of an unsophisticated palate, lack of taste, but not anymore."

Jack narrowed his eyes and examined me for sarcasm. "But for you it has to be Pinot?"

"I like all wines, but Pinot's my favorite, yeah."

"What's Victoria's grape preference?" Jack asked.

"Chardonnay," I said. For a moment I pictured us together around the dinner table—fragrant roast chicken, a cold Matanzas Creek Chard, talking about films and books and what we were going to do that weekend . . . but I shook the memory loose as quickly as it had surged up in me.

"Oh, that's right," Jack remembered. "Puligny-Montrachet."

"That's good, Jackson," I said condescendingly. "You're learning."

He made a gun with his hand, aimed it at me, and smiled. His face was ruddy from sun and wine. Looking at his rosy countenance, I was inclined to feel that he was, for the moment, content.

"In the beginning," I prattled on, "it was Californian. Massive oak-redolent fruit bombs, malolactic up the yin-yang, pure caramel candy and clotted cream. God, I got sick of those over-manipulated bottlings. I'm glad to hear she's crossed over to Bourgogne Blancs with a little more harmonic balance of acid and fruit and less ML."

"She'd never drink Pinot, huh?"

"Never. Not even *blanc de noir* champagnes once she found out they were made from red grapes," I said, shaking my head critically. I knew it was what Jack wanted to hear.

"You miss her badly, don't you?" Jack asked. He looked at me with real feeling and waited for a response.

I shrugged, not wanting to descend any deeper into that intimate labyrinth. Of course I missed her, but it didn't matter. If I confided to Jack that I didn't give a damn about drinking all those buttery Chardonnays and could just go back and replay the tape and somehow not be this sad mopey man, he would have chided me for not having the courage to move on. So I kept my feelings to myself.

"What's the real problem with Maya?" Jack probed.

I blinked him back into focus. "I don't want to get involved."

Jack sat back and scoffed, "You don't *have* to get involved."

I eyed the wine in my glass and drifted back into reflection. "Yeah, but I would. Because that's sort of how I am."

"If you slept with her, you mean?"

"Something like that. It changes things for me. The equation grows murkier."

"The equation grows murkier," Jack parodied. "What the hell does that mean?"

"I don't want someone to start caring about me and then be disappointed again. Not as if there's a reason anybody would."

"And you believe there aren't any people who care about you now?"

I looked away, embarrassed suddenly to meet Jack's eyes. "I don't want to bring any new ones into the equation," I said.

"Ohhh." Jack reached for the bottle and refreshed our glasses with just a splash. The afternoon sun was angling toward the ocean and the pale blue sky was streaked with tattered pennants of pink and mauve. The fall vineyards surrounding us were blooming with green-gold foliage. A sudden gust buffeted up the Lompoc Valley and clattered the leaves in the shade trees, freshening the air. For a moment, with the wine soothing my crabbiness, with the wind and the vineyard landscape imparting a sense of tranquility, I felt revived, emboldened to slam the door on the past. I looked up just as Jack was unfolding his cell phone and punching in a number he read off the back of a business card.

"Who're you calling?" I asked, my momentary state of calm evaporated.

Jack raised a finger to his lips to silence me. After a moment someone must have answered because Jack was suddenly sporting a flamboyant smile and belting out that hearty, infectious laugh of his. "Terra. Jack."

"Oh, Jesus." I rose from the bench, trying to avoid eavesdropping on the conversation.

"What're you up to, beautiful?" "Oh, goodie." "Is Maya working tonight?" I heard Jack say as I started to drift away. "Well, why don't we have dinner over at the Hitching Post, and then maybe afterward if you. . . ." His words faded as I sauntered off with the half-empty bottle of Riesling and gravitated down into the vineyard. Once out of earshot, I dawdled at one of the vines and inspected a greenish yellow cluster of ripe fruit. I picked a berry and sampled it. Couldn't make out the varietal so I spit out the tart skin. I wondered how the vineyardists and the winemakers could possibly determine, with their hydrometers and pH kits and simple olfactory senses, just what a grape will develop into two years hence.

I glanced up when I heard heavy footfalls in the dirt and saw Jack looming, strolling toward me along the shallow trench in between the rows of vines, the sun a halo behind him.

When Jack reached me he sheepishly extended his glass and I poured him a touch. We both sat down cross-legged on the dirt, concealed from view by the shoulder-high vines. "We've got to have dinner *somewhere* tonight," he reasoned.

"So, is this whole thing with Terra going to rev up again?" I leveled my eyes on his to let him know I was serious. "Because if it is, I'm splitting back to L.A."

Jack shook his head as if I were foolish even to let such a thing cross my mind.

"One last pop before you strap on the monkey suit?" I pressed.

"I don't know if the rib'll hold out," Jack joked, gingerly touching his torso, then wincing.

"She nice to you on the phone?"

Jack shrugged. "Chick digs me, I guess, I don't know. Girls just fall in love with me real easy," he said immodestly.

"You don't think you're playing fast and loose with her vulnerable femininity?"

Jack drank some of his wine, mulling my question. "No. She knows what the story is. Guys from out of town on a weeklong toot. What the hey, you know?"

"Because I really don't want your wedding to turn into a remake of *The Graduate*."

Jack laughed with gusto.

"What about Maya?" I asked.

"Well," Jack began thoughtfully. "She's apparently a little confused about you. But I explained to Terra that she wasn't alone in her . . . what's the word I'm looking for?"

"Ambivalence?"

Jack toasted me. "Thank you, Webster."

I toasted him back. "Glad to be of service."

Jack smacked his lips after another satisfying sip. "Damn, that's refreshing."

"Yeah, it's opening up a little as it warms."

Jack looked at me. "I'm not going to feel successful about this trip unless I hook you up with Maya. You know that, Homes." When I didn't say anything, Jack persisted. "Don't you want to get laid, man?" He made a fist with his free hand. "Feel her tight pussy grip down on you until you just cum molten lava?"

I cringed at the metaphor. "How do you know she wants to sleep with me?"

"Oh, come on, Miles. How many interesting men do you think they meet up here in *Buellton*? Huh?" He ruffled the hair on my head. "You're a handsome guy. You've still got all your hair. You're smart, funny, a little dark, but some chicks dig that. Besides, I hear you lick a mean pussy."

"Where'd you hear that? Babs?"

"Fuck you."

"You want me to sleep with her to justify your cheating on your fiancée." I looked up at him. His silence confirmed that my words had stabbed him in the heart.

Jack wrinkled his brow and squinted against the harsh sun. "I don't need any justification. What I'm doing here right now has no bearing on my relationship with Babs," he said in defense.

"Last night you were singing a different tune."

"Yeah, but that was right after I almost got offed and had a spiritual reawakening."

"Thank God for twisted boar hunters." I toasted the air.

Jack toasted me back. "Amen, brother. Amen."

"But you are going to spend the night with Terra?"

"I'll see how it goes. It's a last hurrah, Homes, before I park my equipment in one garage."

"Depends how much grape we get in us is what you're saying?"

"Depends how much grape we get in us. Absolutely. That's sort of how it always is with the two of us, isn't it, Homes?"

I smiled, finished off my glass, corked the bottle, and rose sluggishly to my feet. Jack hoisted himself up, too, and we started off. Shadows grew longer on the walk back to the car. I was glad that Jack was apparently coming to his senses about his marrying Babs, but I was growing tired of his pushing Maya on me. The plan for the rest of the trip was starting to come together though: I envisioned one last night with the Buellton girls, followed by a bacchanal at the Pinot festival, and then I would pack Jack off to the altar. Maybe he would turn out to be a good husband, who the hell knew? Maybe these last "hurrahs" would help him stay faithful once he was married. The one sure thing was that after the wedding, I wouldn't see much of him the way I had seen him this week. We both knew that, but were reticent in expressing it to each other. Babs was probably tolerating this pre-nuptial spree because she had accepted it as her man's last rite of passage, however portentous it might bode for their future. But she loved Jack desperately, and deep down he loved her, and despite his words and actions to the contrary, their relationship augured favorably for the near future. Or so I wanted to believe.

The sky had colored a darker shade of blue by the time we hiked out of the vineyard. The crickets had already started their nightly song. Jack draped an arm around my shoulder. He was demonstrative with others in an easy affectionate manner that usually made me uncomfortable. But, usually after a little vinous readjustment, I didn't mind.

Back at the Windmill Inn we took turns in the

bathroom, showering and shaving. We cracked wise, getting psyched up for the double date. Despite my reservations, I was genuinely looking forward to seeing Maya again.

Around eight, we piled into my 4Runner and motored over to the Hitching Post. We had vowed to go light on the grape, to pace ourselves for the evening ahead. "No more nuttiness" was our drive-over mantra.

The restaurant was hopping when we arrived. The smell of oak-grilled meat permeated the dark room. Terra was waiting for us at the bar, a glass of wine in front of her. She was wearing a form-fitting blue sweater and a pair of jet-black jeans that contrasted sharply with her blond hair, which had been restyled since we had last seen her. In my more sober state she appeared even prettier than I remembered, and I started to understand why Jack had flipped for her.

"Hey, guys," she called out as we approached.

Jack and I claimed empty stools on either side of Terra and gave her a hug. Reassured now that he wasn't going to blow off the wedding, I was more amiable toward her. I was also a little afraid for her when I caught that starry look she got in her eyes every time she gazed at Jack.

"Hi, Terra," I said, squeezing her shoulder. "You look beautiful."

"Thanks, Miles," she said, charmed by my compliment. Jack shot me a quick look that meant

I shouldn't even think about crossing *that* line. I shook my head and laughed; the last thing I would ever do is share a woman with Jack—at least not knowingly.

"What?" Terra asked, glancing back and forth between Jack and me.

"Nothing," I said. "We just haven't seen anyone as pretty as you all day and we're kind of giddy." Just then, as if on cue, Maya strode in from the dining room. "Until, that is. . . ." I said as our collective attention turned toward her.

"Hi, everyone," Maya greeted us. She was wearing a black cocktail dress featuring a (good for the gratuities) plunging neckline. Normally I'm not a breast man, but this voluptuous presentation was easy to get excited about—especially when she leaned forward over the bar and gently laid a hand on one of mine. "Hi, Miles, how was Hearst Castle?"

"It would have been much more entertaining if it had been Hearst Winery."

Maya laughed. Little dimples that I hadn't noticed before fissured her cheeks. "Glad you came," she said. "I was hoping you would."

I blushed. "Got a glass of Pinot for us back there?"

Maya threw her head back. "Charlie," she called out. "A couple of Highliners."

Charlie poured two generous glasses of the Highliner, the Hitching Post's high-end Pinot, barreled over, and placed them down in front of Jack and me. He winked at me over Maya's back.

I sipped my wine. "So, what do you recommend tonight, Maya?"

She smiled. "Ostrich."

"Oh, yeah? Don't think I've ever had it."

"Tastes like steak and pairs perfectly with the Pinot." She straightened her lanky figure and drew a few "oh wow" stares from a couple of guys at the other end of the bar. "I've got to get back to the restaurant. See you all in a bit." She pivoted, picked up a tray with a drinks order, and disappeared. An image of her mane of hair cascading over her half-naked back stayed with me after she was gone.

Terra excused herself to go to the ladies' room, but it was pretty clear that she was ducking out to confer with Maya about the evening's itinerary now that I had shown up to anchor the foursome.

Jack shifted over onto her stool and leaned into me. "Maya's got it going on tonight," he said.

"She looks pretty hot." I sipped the Highliner. "Too much woman for me," I added, just to get Jack's goat up.

"If you don't fuck her, Homes, I will."

"Why don't you just have a three-way and I'll go back to the motel," I shot back.

"Hey, Homes, what'd we talk about? Huh? Having fun, right? Let's not self-destruct, shall we? Leave that for your next novel."

"Woman intimidates me," I said, half-seriously.

"Oh, Christ. It's the kind of intimidation you need, brother. You probably intimidate *her*."

"Oh, bullshit," I said.

"Successful novelist. Hip movie business wine guy. Come on." He pinched my cheek. "Wipe that scowl off your face."

"Hey, let's not gild the lilted lily, shall we?"

"Are we talking about your pecker or your book?"

"Both."

Jack laughed boisterously, happy I had returned to form, and rewarded himself with a sip. I did the same. His voice dropped to a whisper. "It's the money thing, isn't it? That's what's got you worried, am I right? Finds out you're filching from poor ol' Mom, she'll. . . ."

"All right, Jackson," I chopped him off. "Can it."

"Can dish it out, but can't take it."

I sipped my wine.

"It's the money issue, isn't it?" Jack persisted.

"Yeah," I admitted. "The woman finds out how I'm living she's going to lose all interest. If you don't have money, especially at my age, you're not a breeder, you're a pasture animal waiting for your turn at the abattoir."

Jack eyed me thoughtfully. "I discussed this with Babs," he began haltingly, folding his hands and resting them on the bar. "We've decided to invest ten grand in your writing career."

I looked at him like he was mad. "What? I don't want you to."

"Why?" he said, looking genuinely surprised that I would reject his offer out of hand.

"Because I don't want to be indebted to you."

"Did you hear me? It's an investment, not a loan."

I frowned. "Investments are worse than loans because there's an expectation of repayment. Loans I don't repay, you know that."

He leaned in closer. "I'm telling you, Homes, we're going to give you ten Gs to get your life back on track, and you're telling me no deal? Our cash stinks?"

"That's right," I said flatly.

"Would it make a difference if I told you that Babs's parents are giving her a half a million the day we get married?"

I looked openmouthed at Jack. He nodded deliberately, a little ashamed, and I knew he wasn't making it up. "And you were about to run off with another woman?" I shook my head in complete bewilderment. "You're certifiable, Jackson."

"Did it occur to you that I might have doubts about entering the lap of luxury via the marriage route?"

"Well, I would certainly hope you're marrying her for more than just the fucking money."

"Look, Homes. She wants to marry me so *she* can get the money, too. Okay?" He turned away. He didn't want cynicism now; he wanted understanding. "And buy a house, and start a family. And all that other good stuff."

"Well, I'm flabbergasted, Jackson. I didn't realize it was a white-picket-fence kind of package."

Jack ignored my remark. "So, ten grand ain't shit. And if your book sells—which it will—you can pay us back. If it doesn't, fuck it, we'll write it off." He raised the glass of Highliner to his lips.

"You're going to have children?" I asked, envisioning suddenly this long friendship closing a chapter and slipping into the past.

"Might pop a couple out," Jack said.

I was floored. I gestured to the imaginary figures of Maya and Terra conferring in the ladies' room, or wherever the hell women convened to finalize the booty call. "So, what's this? Practice?"

"No, it ain't *practice*. It's about knowing there's still life left in these limbs, and that this face"—he tapped his cheekbone—"has still got the goods to rope 'em in."

"So, you're going to invest ten large ones in my writing career, without any guarantee of remuneration?"

"I believe that's what I said. And I ain't drunk either. *Yet!*"

I chuckled. I was getting a fuzzy wonderful feeling envisioning all my money problems being resolved for the next few months. No creditors hounding me. No ambushes from my landlord. "And Babs approved this?"

"Absolutely. Without hesitation." He laid a hand on my neck and squeezed it. "I care about you, man. So does Babs. She still asks about you all the time."

A sick feeling crept up on me that he was trying to buy my trust with money, but it seemed churlish to accuse him of it. Besides, I needed the cash badly, and if that meant tomcatting another night away, then so be it.

Terra suddenly appeared and Jack hopped off the bar stool with a grand flourish, shepherding her back between us. A great weight had been lifted from my mind knowing that I'd be able to replace the two grand I had heisted from my mother. I'd be able to stop worrying about the rent and dive headlong into my next book. I even felt better about my agent not calling back.

I leaned over to hear Terra saying, "How would you guys like to go to the Cedar Spa? It's up in the mountains." She turned to me with that peach-pretty face of hers. "They have these incredible outdoor hot tubs where you can see the stars like you wouldn't believe." She glanced back and forth between Jack and me expectantly, waiting for the answer she was sure would be coming. "What do you think, Miles? Sound like fun?" Over her shoulder, I could make out Jack nodding up and down, face plastered with that affected Cheshire-cat smile of his.

"Sure, Terra," I said, all of a sudden finding myself factoring in the ten grand that might have been hanging in the balance. But Maya half-naked in a bathing suit, and glasses of Pinot to savor under the stars, made it a no-brainer.

"Great," Terra said. Jack closed his eyes with the nirvanic look of a Buddha and held his nod prayerfully on the downstroke.

We killed time waiting for Maya, miraculously pacing ourselves for the hot-tub bacchanal with two glasses of Highliner each and oak-grilled ostrich filets from the kitchen, compliments of the house. Terra was a free spirit, and her wonderfully crude sense of humor delighted Jack and me. Under different circumstances, I might have found her endearing and cultivated a long-distance friendship.

From time to time, Maya came in to pick up drink orders and check in on us, and each time she made an appearance she seemed to grow ever more beautiful. Every pair of male eyes at the bar followed her movements wolfishly. I relished their attentions, thinking how truly envious they would be if they knew I was taking her to a hot tub spa after closing time.

Around nine, Maya broke off work early and we all piled into Terra's red Jeep Cherokee. We stopped briefly at the Windmill so Jack and I could get our bathing suits, and then drove east toward the San Rafael Mountains. The two women sat up front bouncing up and down and singing along to Ivy's CD, *Long Distance*, while the two of us lounged in the back, reveling in being whisked away by two spirited beauties.

Halfway to the Cedar Spa, Maya turned around and wordlessly handed me a bottle of wine. She switched on the interior light so I could examine it. I read the lettering on the simple white label: '85 LA TÂCHE. "Holy Christ," I said. "Wow."

"I thought we'd open it when we get up there," she said. "I know it's one for the auction house, but it's time to be drunk, and I'd hate to see some rich asshole cellar it till it turned into vinegar."

"I agree," I said, practically breathless with excitement.

Everyone laughed. Maya turned away, leaving the bottle cradled in my lap. I kept staring at the label, mesmerized. I had sampled some fine wines over the years, courtesy of film industry connections, larcenous wine store employees I'd befriended, prospective dates who understood that the way to this man's heart was not through his stomach but through his liver, and the odd high-end tastings I managed to crash. But an '85 La Tâche? This was an uncharted plateau, a cloud drifting heavenward, Robert Parker's world, but not mine. Jack was right. Maya *must've* been trying to impress me! I thought, flattered that she would think of me in connection with this great Burgundian producer.

I passed the bottle as gently as if it were a slumbering infant over to Jack. He studied the label for a minute, knowing that it must have been a pretty special bottle to ratchet up my attention.

He leaned into me, put his mouth close to my ear, and whispered, "I bet this makes your little man stand up."

I laughed. "Yeah, fucking A it does, bubba."

Jack laughed so hard, tears watered his eyes. Maya and Terra turned to us, smiles on their faces, everyone excited and feeling a little silly about the prospect of rare Bourgogne Rouges and beckoning hot tubs under starry skies.

The drive east darkened and the terrain turned mountainous, a piney redolence scenting the air. We were climbing now on twisting roads, guided expertly by Terra who knew the route well—past lovers? I wondered to myself. I was sitting directly behind Maya and with each inhalation of her perfume, memories of old romances disinterred. As we climbed higher into the mountains, Jack jabbed me in the ribs and bumped his shoulder against mine, smiled insinuatingly, and winked suggestively, and all but announced that we were going to have the orgy of a lifetime. Late in the ride, he leaned over and whispered into my ear, "I'm worried about you, Homes."

I turned to him with a smirk.

"I *am*," he said loudly.

"Should we tell them about the boar hunt?"

"Don't go there, Homes. Don't go there." And he pointed a finger at me for emphasis. Then, dropping his voice so that it was barely audible: "This is one of my last nights. I want to go out with a bang, not a whimper."

"Literally *and* figuratively," I said.

Jack grinned.

The Cedar Spa was perched on a ledge in the side of a mountain. Despite being nestled in the deep woods, it commanded a panoramic view of the Santa Ynez Valley. Soft yellow lights mounted low to the ground marked the way up the narrow gravel road to the main office.

The moment we climbed out of the Cherokee, we were assaulted by the ringing chirr of legions of crickets. In the sky, when I arched my neck back for a view, stars riddled the blackness, the really dense clusters forming opalescent rivers of luminescence.

Terra and Jack, eager to get a jumpstart on the festivities, disappeared into the office to make the arrangements for the hot tubs while Maya and I remained out front admiring the empyrean in all its amplitude.

"There's your comet," I said, pointing out a spot just above the horizon.

"Yeah, you can really see it from up here, can't you?" she said warmly.

"Beautiful out here," I added, lowering my head. "Be a good place to write. If you didn't go mad."

She lowered her head, smiling. Our faces were close. We shifted awkwardly in place, our shoes crunching on the gravel.

Jack and Terra reeled out of the office, arm in arm, laughing and leaning into each other.

"All right, guys, follow us," Terra said.

Maya, carrying a canvas tote bag with the La Tâche and who knows what other accoutrements of indulgence, and I followed Jack and Terra down a gently winding gravel path, the two of them giggling like horny teenagers all the way. We came to a small wood-framed cabana and went inside. The tiny, square room contained a twin bed, a working fireplace already lit and crackling romantically, plushy towels and terrycloth robes, and not much else.

Jack and I waited outside to give Terra and Maya privacy to change into their bathing suits. Under the patchwork of stars, next to the steaming hot tub, we quickly peeled off our clothes and slipped into our trunks. Galvanized by the chilly mountain air, we lowered ourselves into the scorching water, our skin tingling as we sank down. I noticed that Jack had removed his bandage, obviously not wanting to call attention to his injury; and, also quite obviously, not wanting to diminish his chances of one last circumnavigational exploration of a willing woman's every soft fleshy curve, and warm wet orificial vent of sin. "Ahh," he sighed, settling down until his chin rested on the surface of the water, dreaming of sucking and fucking in his quest for the nadir of perdition. "Ahh, this is life."

A few minutes later, our dream dates joined us. They paused for a moment, striking poses like models on a fashion runway so we could admire their transformation. Maya had changed into a black one-piece suit that elongated her already statuesque figure and celebrated her sinuous curves. Terra sported a red, skimpy bikini, the bottom shaped like a little fig leaf and the top barely concealing her perky breasts. I had to admit, she possessed all the components of one hot, indefatigable, soul-enlightening fuck.

On a small deck table, Maya carefully uncorked the La Tâche and distributed generous dollops of the regal wine into four Riedel Sommeliers glasses she probably reserved for special occasions, while a goosefleshed Terra eased into the hot tub next to Jack. I had an unwelcome image of a Sunday wedding tuxedo waiting in a garment bag a scant ninety miles north. *Jesus, get me through this one last night,* I thought.

Maya handed us each a glass, then slipped slowly into the hot water next to me. I put my nose into the glass. When I looked around everyone was absorbed in the wine, sniffing and swirling and admiring its pale garnet color. Then, simultaneously, meeting one another's eyes over the Riedel rims, we all tasted.

Jack was the first to weigh in. "Mm. *Damn,*" he said, smacking his lips, at a loss apparently for an adjectival appraisal.

Then, Terra chimed in: "Yummy." I liked her response. "So supple and well balanced," she added, taking some more into her mouth.

Maya turned to me for my assessment. The wine had three distinct acts, like any well-written story.

288

Act one revealed a tart, almost perfumed fruit unlike any Pinot Noir I'd ever tasted. Then, somewhere in the middle, I could detect black truffles and rose petals, almost impossibly harmonized. And, then, act three, it kept calling out caressingly as it went down, like a voice echoing plaintively in a tunnel, while we lamented its absence. In that single glass, the storied *terroir* of the famous Vosne-Romanée demonstrated why it's one of the greatest regions for Pinot Noir in all the world.

The wine was so ridiculously ethereal that all I managed was: "It's really come together beautifully, hasn't it?"

"Mm hm," Maya murmured, teasing the La Tâche around in her mouth. "Very little tannin. Good acidic backbone. Still opulent fruit. It's almost like being in Burgundy." She looked so lovely rhapsodizing like that. Jack was simply smiling. I was growing rapidly enamored. Here, at the final frontier of impecuniousness and artistic failure, I was drinking one of the finest wines ever made with a woman I could fall deeply for.

The steam rising off the hot water enveloped us in a chlorinated mist. We sipped the Burgundy, exulting in every sip, taking our time and savoring it. Jack had his arm draped around Terra's naked shoulder and she was looking up at him, practically in a swoon. He nuzzled her cheek and started exploring her body with unrepentant hands. Terra surrendered to his advances, believing—it was in her eyes and her body language—that they were truly in love. It wasn't long before their faces were clamped together and they had abandoned their stemware. As extraordinary as the wine was, their ardor for each other outweighed its rarity and allusive charms and rendered it for the moment irrelevant. Maya and I exchanged embarrassed glances and tried to keep our eyes off Jack and Terra, who were now basically going at it as if they were completely alone.

Mercifully, they excused themselves, clambered out of the water, and disappeared inside the cabana. I breaststroked over to the opposite side of the hot tub, rolled over on my back in the languid manner of a seal, and faced Maya through the steam. I felt more comfortable looking directly at her than being shoulder-to-shoulder with her. "It was really incredibly generous of you to open this bottle," I said.

She smiled. "My pleasure. I wanted to drink it with someone I knew would appreciate it."

"I'll put you on my '82 Latour list."

"Thank you." She splashed some water at me. "When're you going to drink it? I'm serious. I heard it's past its prime."

"Soon. When the moment's really right." I stared into the dark tunnels of her eyes and she stared back.

From the cabana we heard Terra shriek, then break into convulsive laughter, closely followed by Jack's heavy guffawing. From the sounds that escaped out of there, I had a pornographic picture in my head of Terra bent over and Jack crimsoning her bottom with lusty spanks. Or maybe it was the reverse: a guilty Jack, prostrate, receiving private absolution for his wicked duplicity.

I realized I'd been staring toward the cabana as though I could actually see the carnal scene inside. When I looked back at the hot tub all I found was Maya's empty wineglass on the deck. A moment later, she rose up out of the water in between my legs, her wet hair clinging to her face, and her eyes looming unnaturally large and luminous with desire. Before I could get my bearings she brought her lips to mine in an assertive shift of her abundant body and kissed me passionately, her tongue plunged deeply into my mouth as if seeking a toehold on a crumbling precipice. She must have sensed a moment of hesitation—God knows I had so many reservations, what with Jack rewiring some poor woman's heart to self-immolate and my being complicit in the act—because she brushed her lips across my ear and whispered, "Don't you want me?"

"Yeah," I said through my ambivalence, wondering if I should tell her everything before things went any further.

"Because I want *you*," she said, kissing my ear, then my cheek, then my mouth.

I didn't say anything in response. A joke about wine and failed erections came to mind—though funny, it seemed inappropriate. A whispered endearment didn't seem right either, so I just stayed quiet and let her have her way with me. She was a forceful woman who clearly knew what she wanted and even if I had wanted to play coy I'm not sure it would have stopped her.

After a few minutes of sensual kissing, she slid a hand down into my trunks. My cock quickly stiffened in her exploratory grasp, and my heart hammered wildly when she murmured, "Get up on the edge."

She coaxed me up out of the water. I leveraged myself on the sunken step with both feet and perched on the lip of the deck. She shimmied off my trunks and my cock flipped out and angled skyward—borne aloft by a year of abstinence. She looked up at me for a moment, then drew my erection into her warm, generous mouth. Looking into the heavens, I clamped my hands to her head and stroked her hair. The comet was flaring in the distance, and I locked my gaze on it. It occurred to me at that moment that this was the only time in my life that spirit and flesh had merged in a transcendent oneness.

"God," I cried out loud as her mouth lingered on me.

After a while, Maya abandoned my cock and slithered slowly up my body, tracing her tongue along my sternum, until she reached my face. We kissed a little bit longer until she announced, "We need a room of our own, baby."

I waited, powerless, still erect, and possibly falling in love, while Maya—now swaddled in a white terrycloth robe—walked over to the main office, vanishing wraithlike into the darkness. When she came back, she simply and silently took me by the hand and led me a short way down a gravel path to another, identical, cabana.

Inside, there was a fire hissing and spitting. The '90 Jayer Richebourg she had tempted me with at Terra's three nights before stood uncorked on the table.

"Maya," I said. "This is just all so incredible."

"Shh," she said, putting an index finger to her lips. "It's my treat."

She deftly uncorked the Richebourg, poured two glasses, and handed one to me. We sat down next to each other on the small bed and tasted. It was another remarkable expression of Burgundy's viniferous splendors, different in subtle ways from the La Tâche, perhaps more powerful and explosive, definitely more voluptuous.

We shared tasting notes for a moment, but our passions quickly flared up again, heightened now by the wine and the romantic ambiance. Maya took my glass away and placed it with hers on the end table. She turned and smiled. The upward light of the fire made her look even more beautiful, if that was possible. I smiled back and she moved toward me, falling on me and pushing me down to the mattress. She maneuvered herself on

293

top of me and with deft hands quickly removed her bathing suit. All the while her mouth was firmly planted on mine in a tight, heart-stopping kiss. Her warm skin felt sumptuous against mine and I let myself completely go.

"Are you clean?" she whispered, pulling away far enough to look into my eyes.

"Yeah. Long periods of abstinence have their virtues."

She chuckled. "I'm not on the pill, so don't climax inside me, okay?"

"Okay," I said.

She kissed me some more, then reached over to the end table, took one of the unfinished glasses of Richebourg, and lay on her back. She took a sip of the wine, closed her eyes, and sighed. With her eyes still closed, she held out the glass and instructed, "I want you to christen me with some of this, and then do what I was doing to you outside."

I accepted the wineglass from her and braced myself with a sip. I shifted to the region in between her legs. Hovering over her, I teasingly tipped the wineglass and trickled a little of Burgundy's finest on her bellybutton. She giggled. I moved lower and poured a few more nectarous dribbles on her pubis and dyed it ruby red. She moaned audibly when I parted her legs and gently fingered her open and sampled the Richebourg sans Riedel. Palate properly whetted, I spelunked for her clitoris, tasting Bourgogne Rouge and Maya's body. I flicked lightly at the nipplelike appendage with the tip of my tongue. Her legs tensed as I applied more pressure and went faster. In the midst of my ardor, I glanced up and saw her with a forearm swept across her eyes and a hand clamped to her mouth to muffle her moans, as if in a world of her own creation. Her lower body started moving rhythmically and her moans rose proportionately in volume. After a delicious interlude of ardent licking she finally said, "Stop. That's enough. Oh, my God," in a breathless voice. Her body instantly untensed and she was still. I lingered in her wine-soaked crotch as she regained her composure, lapping the spilled remains of the Richebourg.

After years of mostly frustrating experimentation I had finally discovered the perfect Pinot pairing.

It was after midnight when we finally packed up, left the Cedar Spa, and drove down out of the mountains. Jack sat shotgun, while Maya and I nestled in each other's arms in the backseat. Periodically, Jack would throw us a backward glance, flashing a smile that was both happy and sad—thinking perhaps of these times that we would never share again and how that was something already to be mourned.

Terra dropped Maya and me off at the Hitching Post and then she and Jack continued on to her place. Maya and I shifted over to her car and she ferried me back to the Windmill Inn. I wasn't sure if she wanted to spend the night, but we still had a half bottle of the Richebourg, so I invited her in for a nightcap.

Inside the room, the red message light on the phone wasn't blinking, which completely surprised me. Maya eased onto the edge of one of the beds while I rinsed out the Riedels in the bathroom sink. I poured off the remainder of the bottle into our two glasses, handed one to her, then sat down on the edge of the other bed, facing her. Our knees touched and we rubbed them together slowly. I wanted to kiss her, but when her gaze shifted to take inventory of the room, I realized, with nauseating unease, that I may have made a mistake inviting her in.

"What's that?" Maya asked, gesturing to Brad's Remington still propped up against the wall next to the cases of wine. "You guys hunting?"

"No." I tried to laugh it off. "It's a long story."

"Tell me," she said. "I want to hear it."

So, reluctantly, I told her the story of the aborted boar hunt that almost ended up in homicide. She laughed so hard I thought I saw tears pool in her large, flashing eyes.

"You guys *are* nuts!"

"How were we supposed to know he was going to shoot at us?" I said.

Maya shook her head, still laughing. She sipped the last of her wine and asked, "What do you think of this Richebourg?"

"Beautiful," I said, bending my head back and

savoring the last of a wine I probably wouldn't experience again for some time.

"Compared to the La Tâche?" She stifled a yawn.

"They were just both literally transporting," I said. "I think if I could die now, I would. What do you think?"

"Two vineyards so close and yet producing wines so remarkably different. That's what makes wine so fascinating."

Our eyes melted into each other's. I set my glass down, stood and turned and sat next to her so that our bodies were touching. I bumped my shoulder against hers. She set her glass aside and then fell into my arms with a womanly warmth. We began a long, truly ardent kiss, as though there was something more than physical attraction at work between us. This time, when we made love it was more personal than at the Cedar Spa and, for me, as powerful as any lovemaking had ever been.

In the dark, sated and resting under the covers, Maya lit an American Spirit cigarette she had rummaged out of her purse. I bummed one from her and we lay in the quiet of the room, blowing smoke up at the ceiling, each engrossed in our own thoughts. Mine were simply: I'm in love.

"How's your book coming?" I asked.

"Good," she said. "About halfway through."

"I'd love to read it."

She turned and smiled at me and I smiled back,

our faces illuminated by the pale light of the parking lot seeping through the curtain.

After painful consideration, I cleared my throat, the weight of our little world descending on me. "I have a confession," I said haltingly.

"You're married."

"No," I said. "That part's true."

"You're having trouble getting over your ex-wife and are wary of pursuing a new relationship."

"Why? Did I talk about my ex the other night when I was drunk?"

"Well, you called her from the restaurant," she reminded me, taking a drag of her cigarette and exhaling dramatically. "You must still be very attached to her."

I blew smoke in a sigh. "I suppose in a way I am and always will be." She bent her head and looked at me in the dark but didn't say anything. "But that isn't what I wanted to confess." Her cigarette sizzled next to my ear, as she waited for me to continue. I took a deep breath and came clean: "Jack . . . is getting married this Sunday."

Her hand with the cigarette froze in front of her lips as she bore the full nuclear winter of my words.

I barreled headlong into the details, fully aware I was ruining a perfect night. "I'm the best man. We're having kind of a last blowout before he becomes domesticated. I just thought I should say something because I understand Terra is kind of stuck on him."

Maya slowly brought the cigarette to her lips, dragged deeply, and exhaled two columns of smoke through flared nostrils. "Well, that's great. Fucking great." Her anger was palpable and her words throbbed with raw emotion.

"It's why I didn't want to join you the other night. I didn't want to encourage the whole thing. Point of fact, I tried to talk him out of it."

Maya stiffened next to me, partitioning the space between us. "Do you know what your asshole friend said to Terra?"

"He's an actor," I said with disdain. "I can only imagine."

"She's going to be beyond hurt when she realizes how used she's been," Maya said, folding her arms across her naked chest, a chest I would probably now never see again.

"Well, I guess that's part of the reason why I'm finally telling you this," I said, hoping against hope that she could distance me from Jack and his outlandish behavior.

"I wish you would have said something earlier," she said harshly. "I think maybe you had a moral responsibility."

I sat up in bed. "First of all, Maya, I was a little drunk, and when I'm drunk, surprisingly I'm careful about what I say, and at the time I didn't want to risk alienating my friend. And I thought that maybe for Terra it was just a fling, I didn't know."

"She's been completely lied to," Maya said without meeting my eyes.

I didn't say anything. There was nothing *to* say. My words rang hollow and anything I said would have dug a deeper hole.

Maya squashed her cigarette in a glass ashtray on the nightstand, then lay back down. She breathed in short bursts through her nostrils. "I don't blame you, I guess," she said, less critical. "But whether you like it or not I'm going to have to tell Terra, just so she doesn't get massively hurt when she finds out a couple of weeks from now that your asshole friend is blowing her off and driving her *fucking insane!*" Her words echoed in the room.

I finished my cigarette and put it out. "What kind of things did Jack say to her?"

"Oh. That he loved her. That she was the only woman in ages who had rocked his world, how he was considering moving up here, getting a place with her, commuting back and forth to L.A. Other than that, I'm sure he was pretty fucking honest."

I squeezed my eyes closed; I wanted Maya to see me wince in disgust. I could easily picture Jack, liquored up, whispering those disingenuous endearments until Terra melted, until her knees weakened and she knelt before him and unzipped him because he was the one. "I think he believed every word," I said to Maya. "Shockingly."

"But he's getting married."

"I have no answer for that," I said weakly.

"Why do men say such outrageous things to women, knowing it's going to hurt them?"

"I'm afraid the majority of men are pathological liars. They'll do anything, say anything, to get a woman's clothes off. It's in their DNA. Some have more of the bad genetic stuff than others. As cynical as it sounds, if I didn't associate with them, I probably would have no male friends." I turned to her. "I apologize on behalf of our sex."

Maya laughed sardonically, but her laugh quickly faded.

"If it makes Terra feel any better, a couple of days ago Jack was actually considering calling off the wedding. I think he really is taken with her, however ludicrous that might seem."

"That's crazy," Maya said.

"He's an actor. They're inveterate liars, and they're *all* fucking kooky."

"What's his fiancée like, if I might ask?"

"Gorgeous. Comes from a wealthy family. Everything a man could dream for."

"Figures," she snorted. "What would she think if she knew what was going on?"

"I guess 'if she doesn't find out then it doesn't matter' is probably Jack's dumb-ass rationalization."

"And you support that philosophy?" she asked uneasily.

"No. I said I didn't. I was pissed off. But what was I going to do?"

"Are you like that, too?" she asked, gentler now. "You did say all men are like that."

"I probably used to be. But I've reformed. I

believe in fidelity. Hard as that may be to accept."

She raised her head from my shoulder and regarded me with an expression of misgiving. "Is that why you got divorced? You cheated on her?"

My eyes strayed away from hers to the wall, fantasizing about another cigarette and rewinding the tape to that Edenic moment just before my confession. "There were a whole bunch of complicated reasons," I replied evasively.

Maya apparently couldn't wait another moment, because she lunged for the phone. "I should call Terra right now and tell her all this."

"Maya?" I grabbed her wrist and gently held her back. "We're leaving Saturday. Just wait. He's going to blame me, and you're going to destroy a long-standing friendship. Remember, I didn't *have* to tell you. Not that that makes me a saint or anything."

Maya hesitated, then slowly replaced the receiver on its base. The annoying dial tone stopped. Sighing, she lay back down on the bed. I started to kiss her, but she didn't want to be kissed and turned her face away coldly.

"Look, I'm sorry. I guess we're just a couple of fucked-up guys."

"Yeah, *hello*," Maya singsonged, not intending it to be funny. The way she said it made me feel pitiful and I rolled over and sank into my own self-loathing.

We lay in the dark without speaking for a long time. I could feel her anger and disapproval, palpable as the crappy sheets that scratched my naked body. The heater came on and warm air started blowing into the room, momentarily drowning out the crickets and the sound of Maya's breathing next to me. I wanted to gather her in my arms and hold her—it had been a long night and so much had happened and I was drained and desired the comfort of her body— but I sensed her affections had long since been withdrawn. Like all writers, I hate rejection, so I remained on my side, wretchedly alone, not needing her to verbally affirm our sudden disconnection. Eventually, we both drifted into an uneasy slumber.

Sometime in the early hours of the morning I felt a painful stab of yearning as I heard Maya slip out of bed and disappear into the bathroom. A moment later, the shower started running. I rubbed my eyes. Early dawnlight produced a salmon-hued corona around the edges of the curtains. We couldn't have slept more than a few restless hours.

She came out of the bathroom, toweling off her hair, and dressed hurriedly. I didn't get out of bed or say anything; I just followed her movements in the murky light and waited, letting her leave without saying good-bye if that's what she wanted.

After Maya had finished dressing, she sat down heavily on the edge of the bed with her back turned to me and sighed. She bowed her head, unsnapped her purse, and removed her wallet. I could hear the rustling of bills being counted and I sat up in bed. She laid a raft of fifties on the covers as if she were a blackjack dealer spreading out a deck of cards.

"Maya?" I asked, puzzled.

"Now, *I* have something to confess," she started.

I looked from her to the bills on the bed and back to her.

Her eyes strayed to the wall for a moment, as if she were wrestling with a dark confession. She sucked in her breath and said quickly but deliberately, "Jack gave me a thousand dollars if I would bust out my best bottles and essentially seduce you."

I could feel my eyes blinking, struggling to bring *this* picture into focus. "What?" I said, staggered.

She combed a hand through her long, bed-tangled hair, visibly ill-at-ease. Her face looked sad and tired. "Of course I wouldn't have done it if I didn't want to, if I didn't feel anything for you," she continued. "Jack said you hadn't been intimate with anyone since your divorce and encouraged me to coax you out of your shell." Then she stiffened and her voice trembled with rage. "But your friend is such a manipulating fucking pig. Tell him to take his thousand lousy dollars and shove them up his ass!"

I stared at her, speechless. It was all a little too much to absorb.

"I'm sorry." She rose implacably from the bed. "I hope you don't hate me." She looked at me one last time. "And I did think there was something between us last night besides just sex. It's too bad it had to all shake out like this." She picked up her purse and fled, slamming the door behind her.

"Maya?" I called out after her.

The room plunged back into darkness. I tried to swallow what I was feeling, but I couldn't. I crawled off the bed and staggered jackknifed over at the waist into the bathroom. I collapsed to my knees in front of the toilet and threw up over a thousand dollars' worth of Burgundy's finest.

THURSDAY: REVELATIONS

Around ten thirty that morning the door opened and Jack swaggered in. I rose swiftly from the chair I'd been parked in for four hours, stepped forward, and slugged him right in the face. He staggered back a few feet, then sat down hard on the carpet, clutching his nose. I shook my hand, which hurt like hell.

"What the fuck was that for?" Jack yelled, sprawled on the floor.

"You know what the fuck that was for!"

Jack stared at his bloodstained hand in shock. "I'm bleeding."

"Get up, motherfucker," I said, standing astride him.

Jack remained anchored to the floor. I could see that he wasn't getting up right away, that there was no retaliatory fight in him, so I found a hand towel in the bathroom and tossed it to him. "I hate the sight of blood," I said.

He wadded up the towel and pressed it to his nose. "What'd you hit me for?" he said crossly.

I scooped up the fifties and flung them at him wildly. The bills fragmented in the air and rained down on him like large feathers. "You actually gave Maya a grand to have sex with me? What the fuck is up with that?"

Jack heaved himself to his feet, still woozy from my haymaker. He plodded over to a chair and planted himself heavily in it. "So what's the big deal?" he said feebly.

"What's the big deal? You turned the woman into a fucking hooker. That's what the big *deal* is." I spread my arms in disbelief. "And just when I was beginning to have feelings for her."

"It wasn't my idea. It was Terra's."

"Oh, right. *She* put you up to it? Is that what you're telling me?" I telescoped my head forward, daring him to explain himself.

"That's right." He glanced at the towel, saw that he was still bleeding badly, then returned it to his face.

"Come on, give me a fucking break."

His voice rose a little as his argument started to take form. "I told Terra that you had a problem sleeping with someone just for the hell of it, and *she* was the one who suggested I give Maya some money and set the stage, so to speak."

"It was really Terra's idea?" I said.

Jack nodded.

"Jesus. I thought I'd hit rock bottom. But I guess I've got a few more floors to go!" I sat on the edge of the bed and buried my face in my hands. "I just don't fucking believe this." I lifted my face

307

up out of my hands. "How do you think this is supposed to make *me* feel?"

"Well, she wasn't supposed to tell you for Christ's sake!"

"But she did! Now, among the other indignities in my life, I'm left with the ignomiy of a woman having fucked me because she was paid to."

"Don't go Webster on me."

"I need an explanation here before I head for the nearest overpass."

"She wanted to sleep with you, Homes. She digs the shit out of you. You wanted to sleep with her. She was waiting for you to make your move. I just orchestrated it, lubed the chassis."

"Did it ever occur to you that maybe there was a *reason* I wasn't making my move?"

"Yeah, what?"

I didn't say anything in response. It was all just too absurd.

"I just wanted to get you laid, man," Jack said remorsefully.

I looked over at him gloomily. A malignant silence fell over the room. I was a hair's breadth from packing my bags and abandoning him on the spot, but in my anger I still possessed the requisite forbearance to realize that this rash move, no matter how warranted by his traitorous actions, would severely compromise him. Besides, I had resolved in my paradoxically moral way to somehow make sure that he made it to the goddamn altar. If for no other reason now than that I could jettison him from my fucking life.

"How was she?" he asked sheepishly.

"Fuck you."

"She gave the money back." He gestured to the bills scattered on the carpet. "That means she likes you."

"Did it ever occur to you when you were dreaming up this nuttiness that if I did like her and found out that you had paid her to seduce me I would never be able to get involved with her? Huh?"

"Oh, come on, don't be like that."

"I can't believe you did it."

"I just wanted to give her a nudge."

"A thousand-dollar nudge?"

"That was way over a thousand dollars' worth of wine, you fucking grape geek. It was our birthday gift to you."

I shook my head over and over again. I couldn't decide if we'd just been drinking too much and had momentarily lost our grip on reality, or if there actually was a justifiable foundation to his madness.

"I didn't say, 'Here's a thousand dollars, sugar, go fuck my friend,' " Jack said. "It didn't go down like that. I did not pay her to seduce you. I just told her that you liked assertive women."

He kept his eyes welded on mine to prove his sincerity. His defense, at first unconvincing, slowly began to gain some merit in its unfolding, and I felt myself, against my will, beginning to soften.

"How was the wine?" he asked meekly.

"Rapturous," I grudgingly admitted. "Beyond words."

"See. It all worked out."

I straightened my bone-weary body from the bed, drifted over to the window, and parted the curtains. Sunlight streamed into the room; another chamber-of-commerce morning in Buellton. I squinted against the glaring light. Then I gave a backward glance to Brad's Remington and wondered mordantly if it was still loaded.

Jack rose cumbrously from the chair. He still had the blood-soaked towel pressed to his nose and it occurred to me that he might be seriously hurt. "I think you broke it, man." He grimaced.

"Sorry," I murmured. "Sorry."

He hobbled into the bathroom with heavy foot-falls. A moment later I heard the shower hiss to life. I lay down on the bed and waited for him to finish up so we could figure out what to do with the long day stretching ahead of us. Maya's fragrance lingered on the pillow and I inhaled it over and over, hoping it would sear itself indelibly in my memory.

When Jack finished his shower and had dressed, his nose was still bleeding. Against his objections, I chauffeured him back to Lompoc Hospital. We didn't talk a whole lot—hangovers, betrayals, hurt feelings—on the short trip west down 246. As we approached Lompoc, a dense marine layer had trundled in off the cold ocean and dimmed the sun, transforming the surrounding topography into a featureless gray.

"Any messages from last night?" Jack finally spoke.

I shook my head.

"That's weird."

"What?"

"That means Babs hasn't called in over twenty-four hours."

"Maybe she's backing off. Letting you have your little last *hurrah*."

He frowned and shook his head.

"Are you worried?"

Jack shrugged. But I could tell by his expression that he was.

In Lompoc, a mostly cheerless town sprinkled with cheap Mexican restaurants and minimalls with American franchises, ad nauseum, I remembered the way to the hospital without needing directions. Inside the emergency room, the same young intern who had treated Jack's fractured rib the previous morning greeted us after admittance forms were signed.

"You guys are becoming frequent flyers," he joked.

I chuckled, but Jack didn't crack a smile.

"So, what happened to your nose?" the doctor asked, pointing at Jack's swollen schnoz.

"I ran into a door," Jack lied. "Think I might have broken it."

The doctor narrowed his eyes skeptically and gave Jack's nose a cursory look. Then he reached a hand up and pressed it gently with his index finger. Evidently not gently enough because Jack leapt back, yelping in pain. "Hey, come on, Doc."

"I think you're right. It may be broken. Let's get you down to radiology and get a CT Scan."

The intern led a reluctant, shambling Jack down a drab green corridor. I retreated into the same fluorescent-lit waiting room I had haunted two days before and found a seat. Directly across from me, a young couple was sitting together gripping and regripping each other's hands. The girl was sniffling and the boy was attempting to console her by imploring her to pray with him. I bent forward and rooted around in the out-of-date magazines on the coffee table, searching for the issue that had featured the self-esteem test I had taken on our previous visit. After a night with Maya I was eager to see if I had gone up—or fallen down—a notch. I couldn't find it, but I did happen across my horoscope for the month. It read: "Remember those times when you looked and felt like a million dollars—and had the self-assurance to know it? Although this year has been turbulent, Venus and Mars (the passion planets) are supporting you—and your glory days are about to make a big comeback!"

I decided this was an auspicious time to check for messages, so I crossed the waiting room to the pay phone, praying my glory days were about to begin.

"You—have—no—new—messages," intoned the electronic voice. I hung up, wondering if I was projecting mournfulness into the uninflected voice or if Panasonic deliberately made him sound that way. And why not a charming female voice? Have her reply cheerily: "No messages, but I'm sure there are some on the way. Hang in there, Miles, your glory days are coming!"

An hour later, Jack came back to the waiting room wearing thick surgical tape over his nose and his nostrils packed with gauze. He wouldn't have looked so comical were it not for the fact that the tape was crosshatched to his face. The discoloration of his eyes only added to the comical effect. His look dared me to laugh at him. I brought a hand to my mouth to muzzle myself. Then, finally unable to maintain my composure, I started snickering through my nose. Jack turned his back on me and marched toward the exit.

Back in the 4Runner I turned over the engine and let it idle for a moment. I turned to Jack, who was staring morosely into space. "Two X-rays in two days. You've got to be radioactive, Jackson."

After a few minutes, he turned his head slowly toward me. Close up, he looked monstrous. "Drive," he ordered.

"So, what's the verdict?"

"Deviated septum," he answered sullenly.

I pointed to the tape. "And that . . . is going to

fix it?" Laughter engulfed me and I lost it for a moment and I had to bend over the steering wheel for support.

"No," Jack said calmly. "It's precautionary."

"I'm not going to punch you again," I blurted through snorts of laughter.

"I appreciate that, Miles," Jack noted. "I appreciate that."

I shifted the 4Runner into reverse and started to back out of the parking lot. "So, what are they planning to do?"

Jack, unable to contain himself any longer, slammed his fist on the dash and thundered: "After the wedding I'm going to have to see an ENT and have it set! Either that or end up with a nose like fucking Gérard Depardieu!" His face was tomato red, his eyes apocalyptically wide, and the hair on his head spiked skyward.

I steered onto the main drag and headed out of town, suppressing retorts like *"Vive le France"* and "What about Jimmy Durante?" Jack attempted to don his sunglasses but he had difficulty getting the frame to rest on the bridge of his now-colossal nose. He finally got them settled, the shades protruding from his face so he resembled some kind of human arachnid. After a moment, his gaze swung slowly over to me. I returned his look. There was a slight delay, then the floodgates opened and I lost myself in another paroxysm of eye-watering laughter. Jack, maintaining his cool, flipped the visor down and studied himself in the makeup mirror. Then—slowly at first—he, too, began laughing. It was really all there was left to do.

We needed some way to kill the afternoon, but Jack didn't feel like hitting more wineries with his grotesque nose bandage, so we decided to head over to La Purisima for a friendly round of golf— "No bets this time," Jack announced—since we were more likely to be on our own out there. Jack wasn't sure his fractured rib could tolerate his savage swing, but he wanted to give it a try.

We pulled into La Purisima and lugged our bags out. While I paid the green fees and cart rental— the least I could do—Jack loaded up on beverages at the snack bar, desperately in search of an attitude adjustment.

Hindered by his injury, Jack's normally ferocious swing became the flailing of a caveman clubbing his dinner to death. After four painful holes and a succession of worm burners that deflated his spirits, Jack decided his rib was hurting too much to continue. He retired to the cart, happily resigned to chugging Firestone Ales and watching me finish out the round. The wind was up, the marine layer had retreated under the hot sun, and the sky was once again bright and azure. One didn't need to be playing to appreciate the scenery.

"I'm sorry I punched you," I said sincerely as we carted down the humpbacked sixth fairway.

"I didn't think you had it in you," Jack said, two

Firestones into recovery and beginning to regain his sense of humor.

"I think the last time I actually hit someone was in fourth grade," I said. "I was really steaming mad, I have to admit."

"I understand," Jack said conciliatorily, "but I just can't believe that chick told you and gave you the money back. Doesn't make sense." He shook his head, bewildered. Then, as if a light had popped on in his foggy brain, he peered intently at me. "Did you say anything to her?"

"No," I lied. Under the circumstances, I didn't think it was the right moment to disclose that I'd spilled the beans about the wedding.

"Well, something must have ticked her off that she would give you the thousand back," he said suspiciously.

"Maybe she thought the sex was so dynamite she didn't require compensation," I said, braking the cart by my ball. I climbed out, unquivered my 3-wood, and took a few lazy practice swings.

"Now I *know* you're lying," Jack said, twisting the cap off his third beer and taking a long pull.

"Maybe she gave me the money because you told her I was broke and needed it."

"Fuck, Homes, why would I say that, huh?"

"Well, you told her I hadn't been laid since my divorce. Which isn't true, by the way."

Jack hung his head guiltily. He brooded for a moment, then reached for his beer and took a healthy swig.

I checked my yardage book out of habit, but I wasn't really thinking about the distance to the green. "I mean, why would you say such a thing to a woman you barely know? That pisses me off more than your giving her a grand to open a couple of great bottles and seduce me."

Jack remained frozen in silence.

"Because you wanted her to feel sorry for me, right? Isn't that it?"

"Hit your shot," Jack barked.

"So, she gave me a mercy pop, but her conscience got the better of her. How would you feel, apprised of such a thing? Huh?"

"She likes you, man," Jack said halfheartedly. "*That's* why she returned the money. She realized it was going to come out eventually, so she gave the money up because it didn't feel right."

"Why wouldn't she just give it back to you and keep the whole thing quiet? If she genuinely cared about me, she might have spared my feelings." Jack didn't respond. Of course he wasn't privy to the true source of Maya's wrath. "And you wonder why your nose is broken!"

Suddenly, a ball thudded against the grass directly behind us, kangarooed forward, landed inside the cart, and ricocheted around inside it, making several sharp reports like gunshots.

"What the fuck?" Jack said, leaping out of the cart.

I whirled around. Back on the tee box, a foursome of two couples could be made out. One of the men in the foursome was waving his driver over his head and shouting in our direction: "Get the lead out, would you?"

"Fucker hit into us," I said to Jack in disbelief.

Jack cupped his hands around his mouth and yelled, "Hey, asshole, that wasn't cool!"

"Throw me his ball," I said to Jack.

Jack retrieved the trespasser's ball and tossed it over the cart to where I was standing. I pushed it around with the head of my club until it was teed up nicely on a tuft of grass. Then, without a practice swing, I took a beastly cut at it with my 3-wood, aiming straight in their direction. I flushed it, and the ball took off low and stayed low with the flat deadly trajectory of a cruse missile.

"Great shot, Homes!" Jack exclaimed, applauding.

The foursome, hearing the *thwock* of metal on Surlyn, took cover behind their carts as the ball whistled over their heads. Jack slapped his knee and laughed. The two men, irate, jumped into one of the carts and sped in our direction to exact revenge.

Jack, quickly rising to the challenge, jerked an iron from his bag and started slashing the air with it like a swashbuckler. "Oh, this is going to be fun," he sang. "This is going to be fun."

The cart slowed some fifty yards from us. Jack started to advance on it, brandishing the iron with the fury of a bouncer wielding a baseball bat on a bad night. After getting an eyeful of the big-headed, burly man with the bandaged nose, cut-off shorts, beer-stained T-shirt, and ill-fitting Ray-Bans charging toward them with a raised two-iron, the men fishtailed their cart around and sped back to the tee.

Jack sprinted after the retreating cart in a crazy zigzag course, shaking the iron at them like an enraged shepherd with his crook. "Hit into us again, motherfucker, and I'll rape your wife!"

Jack returned to our cart. He was feeling good about his success in chasing the two guys off. Neither one of us could stop laughing. Maybe we'd be able to move beyond the whole Maya and Terra mess after all, I thought.

Jack got into the beers on the back nine. I wasn't playing particularly well, but I didn't really care. Jack seemed to have completely forgiven me for punching him that morning. I think he had reached the conclusion that he had more or less deserved it, even if, as he pointed out, a more prudent target would have been his jaw.

"I wasn't aiming for your nose," I said, as we putted up the fifteenth fairway, the sun lowering in a churning fog bank ahead of us. "It was just one of those wild punches born of anger and lack of sleep."

"I understand," he said, his speech slightly garbled by the ales. "I'm not blaming you. In fact, I think it's brought us closer together in some strange fucked-up way."

319

Although I tended to laugh at his beer-blurred observations, I reined myself in for once. Underneath his words some honest emotion resonated. So, when he held up his hand and said, "Give me five, brother," I clasped it in mine and let him grip it tightly, pull me toward him, and shake our hands close to our faces as if he were forging a blood pact. "I'm sorry," he said.

"You deserved it," I said, pointing at his broken nose.

"I know," he said mournfully. "I fucked up."

"Forget about it."

He smiled and let go of my hand.

We finished out the round, loaded up our clubs, and headed back to Buellton. The sun now had been swallowed by the fog bank and the highway was cloaked in a fine gray mist. We debated the night's plan. Terra and Maya were obviously out, the movies seemed like a boring compromise, so we decided, at Jack's suggestion, to spend a quiet evening at a new, pricey restaurant in Santa Ynez and uncork the '82 Latour: Jack's idea of burying the hatchet.

"Are you sure you want to pop it?" I asked. "You don't have to."

"Absolutely. Fuck it. It's the last chance I'm going to have to drink it with you for a while and you're the one who said it was . . . what?"

"On the declivity."

"Right. Losing its fruit," he mocked.

"It is my duty as someone semi-knowledgeable

about wine to inform you that you can probably get over a grand for that bottle."

Jack swiped the air with his hand. "I don't give a shit. Besides, I like Cabs better than Pinots." I turned and he met my look. "We're not the same," he said.

"Amen."

We were laughing about the crazy bachelor week when I arced into the parking lot at the Windmill Inn. As we rounded the corner leading to the rear of the motel, Jack suddenly tensed. He bent forward and stared out the window, horrified. "Oh, fuck!" he said. "Go. Just go."

"What?"

"Go! Just fucking go!" he said in a frantic voice, both hands pushing against the dash as if he were trying to force the car along.

I pushed my foot down hard on the accelerator. Jack kept his gaze fixed on our room as we sped past it. I steered around to the opposite side of the motel, found a parking spot in front of the Clubhouse, and killed the engine. Jack was breathing heavily; he looked almost frantic. "What's up? What was that all about?"

He turned slowly toward me, his eyes filled with foreboding. "That's Terra's fucking red Cherokee parked in front of our room."

"What?"

"She's in the fucking room, man!"

"So? Maybe she's lying naked in bed, waiting for you."

Jack weighed this possibility for a brief moment. "Did you say anything to Maya last night?"

"No," I lied again.

"What's she doing in the fucking room, then?"

"How do you know it's her car?"

"It's her car. Who else has a 'Got Wine?' bumper sticker?"

"Oh." I pretended to consider for a moment. "Remember the first night we got up here, we told Charlie at the Hitching Post that you were getting married? Maybe *he* blew your cover."

"That's right," Jack recalled. "Fuck." He turned to me for advice. "What're we going to do?"

"Just go over there," I suggested as though it were no big deal.

"That's easy for you to say."

"In that case, I'll say it again: Just go over there. Take your medicine like a man."

Jack pointed angrily at his nose bandage. "I've been taking my medicine for the last two days, nimrod!" I laughed in spite of his predicament. "How'd she get in the fucking room?" Jack spoke to himself more than to me.

"You probably gave her a key, Jason."

He jerked his head and glared. "No, I didn't." He pointed a finger at me. "And don't start calling me Jason or I'm going to use that Latour for fucking mouthwash."

"It'd be easy to get into the room," I reasoned. "Everybody knows everybody around here."

Jack drew a deep breath and heaved a sigh.

"Fuck, man." He drummed his hands nervously on his thighs. "Fuck."

"I need a shower," I grumbled to push him along.

"I'm thinking. I'm thinking." He flipped down the visor and regarded himself in the mirror. It was obvious he didn't like what stared back at him. "Fuck, man, I can't let her see me like this." With one swift move, he stripped off the bandage, screaming, "Ow. *Jesus*. Shit. *Shit*." He examined himself again. His nose and the area surrounding it had turned a hideous yellowish purple.

"Do you want me to tag along, or do you want to handle this solo?" I asked.

"No, come with me."

"All right, let's get this over with."

We climbed out of the 4Runner and walked toward our room. Jack was moving haltingly, and I kept bumping into him from behind.

"She misses you, man," I teased, as we approached the stairs.

"Yeah, right," Jack said. "Something is definitely weird."

We mounted the stairs and started cautiously upward, not particularly eager to reach our destination. "You probably told her to meet you here and were so drunk you forgot all about it," I said.

Jack threw me a dismissive backward glance. "I don't think so, Homes. This isn't funny, so cut the play-by-play already."

We ascended the stairs and then skulked down the outdoor corridor toward our room bent at the waist like two grade-school boys trying to elude the teacher. One room away from ours, I stopped. Jack turned and looked at me and I gave him a little wave to signal that I had gone far enough. He nodded understandingly, then moved grimly ahead to meet his fate.

He continued down the corridor, stepping cautiously, as if it were booby-trapped. When he finally reached the door to our room, Jack knocked instead of using his key and just going in, which I thought was a little odd—maybe *he* knew something *I* didn't.

"Hello? Terra? It's me, Jack. Are you in there?" he called out. There was no answer from inside. Jack turned and shrugged at me.

I made a little pushing motion with my right hand as though it held an imaginary electronic card and gestured with my head toward the inside, pressuring him to go in.

Jack dug a hand into his back pocket and found his card. He inserted it into the lock, pulled it out, then pushed down on the handle. He cracked the door open circumspectly and barely poked his head in. "Terra? Are you in there?" he said.

The initial absence of a response made me optimistic, and I closed the distance to take a position behind Jack as he pushed the door open wider and risked a step inside.

It all happened with lightning speed. I got a quick glimpse of a fully-dressed Terra leaping up from the bed. The next thing I remember was a large object being raised aloft and the almost simultaneous blinding muzzle flash and earsplitting explosion of a gun shot. The whole room seemed to tremble, and blown plaster rained down from the ceiling as if a grenade had detonated.

Jack was glued to my tail as we spun around with a flurry of *Oh shit! Oh shit!* and hauled ass back down the corridor. When we reached the top of the stairs we skidded to a stop to reconnoiter what we were up against. What we saw terrified us down to our scrotums. Terra was standing out in the corridor in front of our room, which she had commandeered, aiming Brad's Remington directly at our cowering, cowardly selves. Her blond hair was in a tangle and her eyes were wild with rage.

"You fucking bastard," Terra screamed. "Liar! Motherfucker! Liar!"

"Terra," Jack said, lifting his hands up slowly in apparent surrender. "Put the gun down. Someone could get killed."

"You better fucking believe it, Loverboy." She angled the rifle just above our heads and discharged another round into the twilight sky. The firearm bucked against her tiny frame and she staggered in place briefly before recovering her balance.

From my inadequate cover, I started to back away, but Jack brazenly began inching slowly toward her, a step at a time. "Come on, Terra," he pleaded, putting a brave face on. "Put the gun down. Please."

"Why didn't you tell me you were getting married?" Terra shrieked, becoming more enraged the closer he got to her.

"I'm sorry," Jack said lamely, continuing to advance one tentative step at a time. "I'm really sorry."

"So, it's true? You *are* getting married this Sunday?"

Jack, now less then ten paces from her, stopped and hung his head in ostensible shame, instinctively adopting the protective posture of a sympathetic character and ventriloquizing through him. "I'm sorry," Jack repeated, attempting to soft-soap her. "I'm really sorry."

Terra jutted her head forward. "You're *sorry?* What was all that shit you said to me? You fucking bastard." Her voice became a frenzied scream. "You motherfucking liar!"

"Okay, okay," Jack tried to calm her. "I lied to you. I apologize. Now, put the gun down. Please, Terra, don't do something stupid."

Terra slowly leveled Brad's boar annihilator at Jack and sighted down the barrel, a modern-day Annie Oakley. A couple of curious motel guests peeked around the curtains of their nearby rooms to see what all the commotion was about, their expressions suggesting they were too petrified to come out for a better view. I suspected the cops weren't too far away.

For a protracted moment I truly feared for Jack's life. Then, with the two of us frozen in place, waiting for Terra's next move, tears suddenly sprang to her eyes and flooded her cheeks. Her arms collapsed to her sides and the gun clattered to the cement. Terra's hands rushed to her face and she wept openly.

Jack, seizing the opportunity, moved toward her cautiously, much as one might approach a wounded animal. "Come on, Terra, it's all right." He closed the gap between them, moving stealthily. Still wary, he sidled even closer, all the while extending a tentative hand like an insect's antenna. When he reached her, he quickly clutched her by the forearms and attempted to pull her hands away from her eyes. "Terra, listen to me," Jack said firmly. "Listen to me!"

"No," she wailed in a new adrenalin-rush of fury. "You're a liar! A motherfucking dirtbag liar!"

With difficulty, Jack managed to pry her hands from her eyes. They were puffy with raw emotion and smeared mascara. "Listen to me," Jack beseeched, not making headway, but merely holding the situation in check.

"No!" she screamed. She tore her hands out of Jack's grasp. Then, in a blazing moment of ferocity, she windmilled her right hand and slashed at Jack's face like a frantic animal.

Jack brought a hand to his face and cried out in pain. "Ow! Jesus!" His knees buckled a little and he quailed to protect himself from further blows.

Terra scuttled backward, jackknifed at the waist,

her pretty face contorted with rage. "I thought you loved me. You're getting *married* on Sunday?" She cackled like a movie witch. "You fuck! I hope you die!" She straightened up, pivoted, and stormed down the opposite end of the corridor, then surged down the stairs. I heard the door of her red Cherokee slam shut and the car gun to life. Squealing tires marked her swerving, swearing, smoking exclamation point of an exit.

I hurried over to where Jack was slumped against the doorjamb, still clutching the right side of his face. When he moved it away, I got my first glimpse at the rake job Terra had delivered, and it wasn't an improvement on an already woeful-looking mug. "Fuck," he groaned.

"Man, that's deep," I said.

"It's fucking bleeding," Jack said, staring in consternation at his hands.

"She swiped you pretty good," I concurred. "Don't look in a mirror for a while. Maybe a month."

"Fuck, that chick's nuts."

"Aren't you glad you didn't move up here and marry her?"

"Shut up, Homes," Jack snapped.

"You should have told her," I said in Terra's defense.

"Told her what?"

"The truth. Instead of feeding her all that lovey-dovey hornswoggling nonsense. She might have gone to bed with you anyway."

"I don't need a lecture from you. I'm hurtin' here."

I was ready to launch into an argument when I heard the wail of a police siren, rising in volume. We both stiffened.

With a surprising presence of mind, Jack commanded, "Get the gun. Take it to the car. Get the fuck out of here."

I squatted down, grabbed the rifle lying at my feet, and sprinted off. I got a quick glimpse of the elderly couple who had probably placed the call to the cops, their heads fused together like Siamese twins, gawking through their narrowly parted curtains.

I made it back to the 4Runner just as a sheriff's dispatcher was rounding the parking lot into the rear of the motel, its overhead warning lights alternately pulsing blue and red. I stowed Brad's rifle in the car and then walked back. Several guests, hearing the siren, had ventured out of their rooms and had congregated on the balcony and down in the parking lot, whispering and pointing, trying to reconstruct what had happened.

I climbed the stairs and went back to the room to check on Jack, acting like I was coming back from the Clubhouse with a couple of drinks in me—a role I could easily handle. When I got there, Jack was standing just outside our room, flanked by two Santa Barbara County sheriffs about our age. The one in charge was tall, with a stomach that ballooned over his belt. His partner was six inches shorter and had the twitchy mannerisms of a bird. Both had identical drooping, bushy moustaches that made them appear as though they were missing their upper lips. Scanners pinned to their jacket collars squawked obnoxiously.

"It was just a fight with my girlfriend," Jack was explaining, trying to paint a harmless domestic picture.

"What's going on, Jack?" I asked ingenuously. "What happened to your face?"

"Oh, Michelle and I got into a little fight," Jack replied, playing the faux-naïf to perfection.

"Who are you?" the big one asked suspiciously.

"He's my friend," Jack answered.

The sheriff pointed a warning finger at me. "Stay there." Then he turned his attention back to Jack. In the dim light Jack's injury didn't look quite as horrifying as it really was. "Where's your girlfriend now?" the sheriff asked.

"Ex-girlfriend," Jack corrected. "Fuck if I care. I hope I never see her again. I mean, look what she did to me." He pointed at his face, seeking their sympathy.

The little one stepped toward Jack to get a closer view. "Looks pretty bad. Do you want to go to the emergency room?"

"No," Jack said, clearly alarmed at the prospect of a third visit. "No, I'll live."

"Someone reported shots," the taller one continued. "Do you have a weapon in your possession,"—he glanced at Jack's driver's license—". . . Mr. Cole?"

"No, absolutely not. I support gun control," Jack said, by way of explanation. He spread open his arms as if a light had snapped on in his head. "It was probably her car backfiring. Bitch hasn't had a tune-up in ages."

"Why was she so angry with you that she would do something like that?" the little one followed up.

Jack let his chin settle on his chest, dredging deep for some Stanislavsky. "It's kind of embarrassing," Jack began sheepishly, shifting uneasily in place.

"Just tell us," the bigger sheriff said.

"She claimed I gave her herpes," Jack said in a low voice. He looked away in credible disbelief.

The short sheriff looked up at him and said challengingly, as if to humiliate him, "Well, did you?"

Their rapport was deteriorating and I was sure Jack was about to say, *Fuck you, midget,* but he reined himself in, recovering his composure just in time to answer in unctuous politeness, "No, sir."

The two sheriffs looked at each other like a Mutt and Jeff combo. "Check out the room," the tall one said, obviously in charge.

The little one disappeared inside. Jack gestured subtly to me.

"I got to rinse a kidney badly," I said to the taller one.

"All right," he said, excusing me to go to the bathroom.

I went inside, walked past the one-not-in-charge,

and quickly emptied my bladder. When I came back out, the short sheriff had his attention focused on all the cases of wine stacked against the wall.

"What's with all the wine?" he said with an air of suspicion, lifting the lids on some of the boxes and poking his nose inside.

"I'm a wine writer," I said. "I'm doing an article on Santa Barbara County wineries for *Wine Spectator*."

He nodded briefly, as if my fabrication had satisfied him. Then he looked up at the ceiling where Terra's shot had blasted a small hole. His head panned down to the plaster on the bedspread. It wasn't as noticeable as I had imagined it would be. "What's that?" he said, gesturing to the ceiling, suspicions rekindled.

"Champagne cork from a vintage '90 Krug," I answered. "Fuckers get tight when they've been in that long. A guy was killed by one of them once."

"Oh, yeah," he replied, unimpressed. He narrowed his eyes, gave the room a second quick once-over, then went outside to report to his superior. I followed him out and dawdled in the doorway.

"Didn't see anything," he said. "Except a lot of cases of wine." He jerked his thumb back over his shoulder at me. "Claims he writes for wine magazines."

The one in charge didn't seem interested. He turned his attention back to Jack's face. In addition to the four bleeding slash marks, my punch that morning had severely swollen his nose and given him raccoon eyes. "Looks like your girlfriend really got the better of you," he said to Jack in a belittling tone.

The two sheriffs shared a snicker at Jack's expense. Then they got back to business and copied down information off our driver's licenses.

As they returned our IDs, the taller one warned, "There better not be any more ruckus around here, because if we have to come back, we're going to haul you in."

"Don't worry," Jack assured them. "She's long gone."

The tall sheriff laid an avuncular hand on Jack's shoulder as if he sympathized with his plight. "Next girlfriend you manage to land, may I suggest it be someone *you* can beat up."

The sheriffs marched off, chuckling, their scanners directing them to another small-town crime of no doubt equal hilarity.

Jack and I retreated into the room and closed the door, completely exhausted. I went into the bathroom and took my long-awaited shower. When I came out, clean and somewhat refreshed, Jack was lying on the bed, holding a makeshift ice pack to his scarred face, staring sullenly at a baseball game on TV.

"I guess the Latour dinner is out," I said wistfully.

Jack didn't say anything, his expression downcast. At a commercial break, he shuttled impatiently through the limited selection of channels, skipping past them over and over, as if trying to obliterate all thought and all feeling.

I pulled on my pants and shirt and sat down on my queen, hungry, tired, and in need of a glass of wine. "So, what do you want to do?" I asked.

Jack didn't answer. He crawled wordlessly off the bed and lumbered slowly over to the dresser mirror. He withdrew the ice pack from his cheek and examined his face. "What's it look like to you?"

I took a long thoughtful look at my friend. "Looks like you were in a car accident."

He nodded, weighing the positives and negatives of the bogus story that he was beginning to script.

"Except for the scratches," I added.

He shot me a forbidding look in the mirror.

"Unless. . . ." I snapped my fingers. "There was a cat in the car!"

Jack wagged a reproving finger at me. "I'm warning you, Homes."

"Sorry." I straightened from the bed. "Come on, let's go get something to eat."

Outside, the weather had deteriorated and only a few patches of starlit sky peeked through the ragged clouds. We drove a short distance east on a rain-slicked 246 to A. J. Spurs, a tacky tourist barbecue joint that served huge portions to mostly huge diners.

Inside, the décor was all timber and resinated-wood tables and hard pine chairs under raftered ceilings. The upper part of the walls was festooned with taxidermic heads of trophy game of all sizes and species who gazed down on the diners out of blank glass eyes, while classic rock assaulted them over the stereo system.

We were gratefully tucked away in a crescent-shaped booth that faced away from most of the other diners. I had elected to go light on the grape, not only because their wine list was appalling, but because I was saving myself for the Pinot festival the following day. Jack was in a somber mood and not into drinking either. All things considered, I could hardly criticize his lack of enthusiasm. We both had a glass of the house red, an oaky, Raid-rancid Merlot that was a far cry from the '82 Latour we had planned on earlier.

Walking out to the car after dinner in a drizzly rain, Jack insisted on driving. He had the keys and wouldn't take no for an answer.

We got in the car and Jack fired it to life. Out of the parking lot he turned east on 246 and pointed the 4Runner in the direction of Solvang.

"Where're we going?" I asked, exhausted, wanting to get back to the room and hunker down.

"I don't want to go back to the motel. In case that bitch comes back. Let's get a glass at that bar in Los Olivos where you said they have a good wine list," he proposed, desperate, it appeared, to keep the night—and the whole bachelor trip—alive.

"Okay," I said reluctantly. "But I'm driving back."

An impish look—the first I had seen in a while—glinted in his eyes, and he depressed the accelerator.

We cruised through a deserted, shuttered Solvang waiting in hibernation for the next schlocky tourist Christmas, then hung a left on Alamo Pintado Road and headed north toward Los Olivos. Without streetlights, the surrounding topography was pitch-black, illuminated only by our headlights. A peaceful feeling came over me suddenly as we drove silently along. We were closing in on the Sunday wedding and I really was ready to cut the big guy loose. It had been an eventful, emotional week, and I was relieved to see the end in sight.

About a mile from the turnoff leading into Los Olivos, Jack pulled over onto the gravel shoulder of the road directly in front of a massive, gnarled old oak. As the car idled, he turned to me and instructed, "Buckle up."

"What?"

"Put your damn seat belt on." He raised his voice. "I don't want to get pulled over. Okay?"

"Okay, okay. Jesus."

I pulled the shoulder harness across my chest and clicked it securely into the fastener. "Okay, let's go," I said.

Without hesitation, Jack slammed his foot on the accelerator and smashed head-on into the oak tree. I heard a loud crash, and at the same moment I lurched violently forward. But the seat belt prevented me—thank God!—from hurtling through the windshield and somersaulting over the hood.

"What the *fuck!*" I cried.

"Don't worry," Jack said calmly, "I'll pay for it."

"What the fuck are you doing?"

He pointed at his ravaged face. "How am I going to explain this? Huh? Got in a fight with some chick and she beat the shit out of me because she found out I was getting married and she wasn't the bride?" His voice steepened an octave. "Visited the zoo and fell into the bear's den and went one-on-one with Smokey?" He jammed the shift lever into reverse, backed the 4Runner up about twenty paces, the tires spinning in an attempt to grip the gravely shoulder. Then, before I could protest, he dropped his foot on the accelerator and slammed into the oak a second time. Again, I lurched forward and whiplashed back like a crash dummy.

"Who the fuck do you think you are?" I shrieked.

Jack spun the tires in reverse again, ground the shift lever into drive, and fishtailed onto Alamo Pintado Road before anyone could report us to the cops.

I sat with my arms folded across my chest, staring out the windshield, seething.

"It still runs," Jack said to break the tension.

"What a consolation."

"How come the air bags didn't deploy?"

"Fuck if I know."

"I'll pay for it, Homes."

"I've got to drive this fucking thing!"

"I'll get you a rental when we get to Paso Robles. We'll get your car fixed up there. I'll drive it back to L.A. after the wedding."

I shook my head in disgust. "You're fucking nuts. God, I can't wait until you get married and get out of my fucking life!"

Jack did a double take, but didn't say a word.

We rode the rest of the way in a pin-dropping silence. In Los Olivos, Jack nosed into a parking space in front of Skorpios, a quaint Greek café. I climbed out wearily and circled around to the front of my car to assess the damage. The hood and grille were crumpled in like a gigantic wad of tin foil. The left headlight had sprung and drooped forward on a tangled mess of twisted metal and wires. And the front fender was bent inward into a v and dangled comically from its mounts.

"That's going to be a couple of grand at least," I estimated dismally as Jack came around from the driver's side for a look.

"Fuck it, I don't care," Jack said cavalierly. He placed a mollifying hand on my shoulder and nudged me toward the café. "Come on, I'll buy you a bottle of anything you want."

We went into the café. It was a dark, casual open-air restaurant with a Greek-costumed staff. It wasn't crowded and we easily found stools at the long, wood-planked bar. I scanned the wine list with revenge in mind and, after some internal debate, decided on the '97 Silver Oak Napa Cab,

$175 a bottle. Jack didn't flinch. I wanted to hold off on Pinots and save my palate for the upcoming festival. Cabs can be rich and powerful and exalting, but they usually seem prosaic to me for some reason. But the Silver Oak was satiny and full-throttle, almost geological. *Mm. Mm mm*, I exulted, drinking not just to experience the pleasures of the wine but to cushion the image of my damaged 4Runner.

As the evening wore on, I started to forgive and forget the deliberate destruction of my car. And Jack, in high spirits, his hearty laugh back in full force, was somewhat shockingly making progress with the porcine-featured bartender. She had dishwater blond hair with corkscrew curls and a zaftig figure that bulged her anachronistic dirndl blouse. Massive breasts threatened to explode her laced black vest and a silly red beret completed the outfit, crowning a face so heavily made up it looked like she had done a face-plant into a bowl of flour. More abhorrently, she was one of those risible women who laugh at everything, no matter how moronic. Her laughter rose and surged and built to high-pitched crescendos at every single thing Jack said. In the murky light, I don't think she registered the full extent of Jack's disfigurement. Or maybe she was charmed by the U.S. Grants he kept magnanimously laying on the bar, letting her know that he might have looked like damaged goods, but he had bank.

Returning from the bathroom, I almost couldn't

believe what I heard—Jack leaning across the bar, callously forgetful of me, closing the deal to meet her back at her apartment in Solvang. How had flirtatious banter and a profligate waste of high denominations so quickly spiraled into the makings of a one-night stand? I wondered.

When Zaftig trundled off to take care of some of the customers she had been ignoring, he turned to me and whispered, "You're going to take me into Solvang and drop me off. Pick me up in the morning."

"You're joking?"

"Homes, I just sprang for a bottle of Silver Oak Cab."

"She's a fucking porker. Bottom of the barrel for you, Jackson. You slip out of the saddle and I'm warning you, you're going to end up with your cock in a cast."

"The girl's a load of laughs. And right now I need some giggles, Homes." There was something sad about the way he said it and I turned away, almost feeling sorry for him.

Too tired to protest—not that it would have done any good—I drove into Solvang, following the directions Zaftig had scrawled on the back of a cocktail napkin.

We located her place easily enough. As we waited for her to arrive, I turned to Jack and asked, "Are you sure you want to do this? She doesn't seem your type."

"Look," Jack started, slurry from all the drinks,

"I know you think I'm going for Miss Last Call. And I know you disapprove. That's cool. But I've got something to get out of my system. I'm not sure you understand. You understand wine and literature and movies, but you don't understand my plight."

"Okay. I guess I'm at a loss in that department."

The headlights of a beat-up Ford Escort rounded the corner into view, interrupting our conversation. Zaftig tooted her horn when she spotted my idling car, then she shoehorned her compact into a parking space on the street, killed her headlights, and bounded out, waving excitedly as though she hadn't seen a naked man in ages.

"She doesn't look too bad," Jack said. "Besides, I like 'em a little Rubenesque," he rationalized, flashing me a leer.

"Are you going to make the Pinot festival tomorrow?"

"Absolutely. Wouldn't miss Brad chauffeuring us around for anything." He reached for the door handle. "Even a girl."

"Have fun," I said dully. "Got your banana peels?"

"Got my banana peels." He slapped his wallet in his shirt pocket.

"Don't want to give Babs herpes."

"I hear you, brother, I hear you."

Jack climbed out of the car and skipped across the street to greet Zaftig. They came together in a rush like long-separated lovers in a sappy romance. Jack wrapped her up in a bear hug and lifted her off the ground. Her tittering cascaded all the way over to my open window. Given the motif of the trip, I worried for a moment about Jack rupturing a disk.

I watched as they disappeared arm and arm into her apartment complex. Then I rolled up my window, put Hope Sandoval in the CD player, and cranked the volume. I made a U-turn and headed back toward Buellton, Hope's smoky music-to-slit-your-wrists-by the perfect accompaniment to the depressing end to my night.

FRIDAY: COME HELL OR HIGH ALTAR

Sometime early in the morning I was awakened from a vivid dream to the din of pounding on the door. I sat bolt upright in bed, thinking for a moment that our friends the sheriffs had returned for a second look at the room. As my brain struggled to consciousness, I heard a familiar voice.

"Open the door," a frantic Jack called out. "It's me, Homes. Wake up. Open the door."

"Just a sec," I said groggily.

"Hurry *up*."

I slipped out of bed, crossed the room, and unlocked the door. I found Jack, looming shadowed against a penumbra of raw dawnlight, wearing only his boxer shorts, his arms crossed against his naked torso, shivering. Droplets of sweat pockmarked his forehead and he was breathing heavily, his exhalations visible in the cold morning air. "Jesus fucking Christ. Let me in, it's freezing." He pushed past me into the room.

"What's going on?" I asked, closing the door, still half asleep. I wiped a hand across my eyes to get the sleep out, hoping the image would change. It didn't; on a second look, it was even more disconcerting. "What are you doing in boxers, man?"

Jack pulled on a coat, slumped on the edge of the bed, and tented his forehead shamefacedly. He looked up at me after a long moment. "Fucking chick's married."

"What?" I said, closing the door, starting to come into consciousness.

"Her husband pulls a night shift or something and he comes in at like six and I'm sprawled out on the floor eating his wife's pussy."

"Jesus, Jack! Jesus."

"I just bolted. Had no choice."

"In your underwear?"

"I was lucky to get those!" He shuddered, attempting to shake off the memory of his narrow escape.

"And you ran all the way from Solvang?"

"Damn tootin'."

"That's five klicks, Jackson."

"Fucking A it's five klicks. And without shoes!"

"You're lucky someone didn't see you. Jesus."

"Yeah," Jack said. "Like Mr. Rodent Sheriff, for instance."

"You'd be in a fucking loony bin."

"I hear you, Homes. Trust me, it was not a fun trek. I cut through an ostrich farm and one of those fucking pterodactyls chased me. Fucking mean son of a bitch. I thought he was going to bite my dick off!"

"Might have done you a world of good."

Jack laughed caustically. "I felt like Cornell Wilde in *The Naked Prey*."

"Well, you made it back in one piece," I said. "I hope you at least got out of there with your wallet."

Jack shook his head.

"Oh, fuck man. What're you going to do?"

He raised his large, unshaven, scratched, and bruised face and glued his purple-and-black ringed eyes on mine. "We've got to go back."

"No. No. Nuts is nuts, but I ain't going Planters." I stalked to the other side of the room.

"It's got all my credit cards, the thousand bucks, fucking ID, everything," Jack appealed.

I spun around angrily. "How do you propose we're going to retrieve it?"

Jack reached under the bed and rooted out Brad's Remington and held it up at an angle across his chest. "They're probably in there arguing or something. We'll just go up, knock on the door, stick this in his face, and tell him I want my wallet back."

"That's lunacy! Just blow it off. You lost your wallet. Pretend you left it at some fucking bar." I subsided into the room's only chair to punctuate my point.

A silence fell. "Homes," Jack began appeasingly after a while. "The fucking wedding bands are in my wallet."

"What?"

"You heard me."

"Buy some new ones. Who fucking cares about some lousy wedding bands?"

"Babs picked 'em out. They've got this special little design on them with our names engraved and shit. We've got to go back. She'll fucking crucify me if I don't show up with them."

A bad feeling suffused me. "Oh, fuck, you have *got* to be kidding me."

"I am not shitting you, man."

In the pale light of dawn I drove east on 246 in the wreckage of my 4Runner, feeling like Rommel rumbling across the Sahara in his final campaign. Jack sat shotgun with Brad's Remington sticking up in between his legs like a giant steel erection. He stared grim-faced but determined through the filthy windshield.

"She tell you she was married?" I asked.

"Yeah," Jack said sheepishly.

"What the fuck were you thinking? I would have gotten out of there as soon as she told me."

"She claimed he wouldn't be back until nine. Fucker rolls in at six."

"Cutting it a little close, weren't you, Romeo?"

Jack ignored my criticism. "I just want to get my fucking wallet back."

"How was she?" I said, out of habit.

"Horny as shit. Flopping around like a landed trout. Said her husband hadn't fucked her in years."

"Great! A guy getting off a night shift who hasn't been laid in years finds his wife in flagrante with some hamburger-faced guy who hightails it out the front door in his underwear. We're walking into a hornet's nest, Jackson."

Jack clutched the rifle and raised it at an angle with the ramrod air of a new recruit. "That's why we're going in prepared."

"Fuck, man, let's reconsider this."

"I'm getting those bands!" he shrieked. "They're irreplaceable."

"So're our lives." I slammed my foot on the brakes, jerked the car over to the shoulder, and skidded to a stop. "I'm going back to the motel and checking out. I'm not spending the rest of my life in prison over a couple of sentimental trinkets."

Jack turned to me. I couldn't have been more shocked to find his ravaged face in tears. "I've got to get those rings, Miles. I've got to make it to this wedding." He wiped his eyes with the back of his hand. I couldn't tell if it was an act, but if it was, it was Academy Award-worthy. "I fucked up, okay?" He wept. He touched my shoulder. "I need your help. I can't do this alone. I've *got* to get my wallet. *Please.*" His hands were trembling. "Please. This one last thing."

Wordlessly, I shifted into drive and merged back onto 246, disgust locked in combat with understanding, and losing. We rumbled on.

Since we were approaching Solvang from

347

Buellton instead of from Los Olivos, I had to intuit my way to where Zaftig was bunkered with her cuckolded husband. After a few false turns I managed to orient myself, find her apartment complex, and slip into a parking space across the street. In the daylight, the neighborhood came into focus. Clusters of two- and three-story, candy-colored stucco apartment complexes stood in shadow framed by a cold, cobalt sky. It was the perfect setting for a phalanx of squad cars with SWAT teams, and a circling flock of TV news copters.

"We're not going in with the Remington," I said, summoning our last collective scrap of sanity.

"We have to," Jack argued. "The fucker's big."

"That's a B&E, Jackson, with an armed weapon. We could do serious time for that." I looked him straight in the eye. "I'm not going over there with you carrying that thing."

"I've got to get my wallet," he said, whining like a child.

"Okay, stop your bellyaching, will you?" I reproached him.

A flare went off in his head, and his face brightened. "Why don't *you* go?"

"Me?"

"He won't recognize you. Explain the situation."

"Uh, excuse me, sir, my friend was balling your wife a couple of hours ago and he accidentally left his wallet here, and I was hoping. . . ." I cut my little speech short.

"Yeah. Sounds good."

"Oh, so I can get a broken nose like yours? Fuck that, Jackson. I did not get us into this mess."

"I'm giving you ten grand, man. I mean, can't you just go up there and try to reason with the guy?"

"Oh, now the ten grand's got conditions! Fuck your ten grand. I'd rather be destitute."

Jack angrily slammed his hand down on the door handle and started to awkwardly climb out with the rifle.

I grabbed him by the shirt and hauled him back. "Where're you going, Rambo?"

"I'll get it myself, fucking pussy."

"Wait a minute. Wait a minute."

Jack got back into his seat and turned away from me.

I reached across his chest and pulled the door closed. "You go charging in there with a rifle looking the way you do and the only vows you're going to be taking this Sunday will be behind bars with a felon twice your size for a roommate."

"I have to get my wallet back."

"Fucking stop whining about your goddamned wallet! Jesus Christ!" I drew a deep breath and leaned back in my seat. A minute or so crawled by as I considered the repercussions. "What building is it?" I asked, resigned to my part in the scheme.

Jack pointed over at the most prominent one: a pink-and-white stucco monstrosity with the ironic name EDEN GARDENS hung in verdigris metal lettering across the facade.

"What's the apartment number?"

"Thirteen."

"Thirteen? You're joking? There's not supposed to be a thirteen."

"No, I know, that's why I remember it."

"Fuck. Fuck me. Fuck *you*. I don't believe I'm in this situation." I banged both hands on the steering wheel so many times that they hurt. "All right. If I'm not back here in ten minutes, fuck, I don't know, call my agent and tell her to rewrite my bio. 'Was stomped to death by irate husband while retrieving worthless wedding bands for psychotic friend before he could see publication of his first novel.'" I looked at him angrily. "And leave that fucking gun in here, whatever you do!"

I leapt out of my car and strode across the street. Fury at Jack—and the raw nerves that came with it—propelled me forward. What's the worst that could happen? I asked myself as I mounted the narrow concrete walkway that led into the complex. And what right did I have to the wallet? Surely, contributing unknowingly to adultery wasn't a crime, I reasoned, as if working out an argument. In truth, I was scared out of my fucking mind.

Apartment 13 was on the first level tucked away in a corner. Over a weed-fissured concrete deck, I skirted a pathetic, algae-discolored swimming pool that looked as if it hadn't been used in years.

Instead of walking straight up to the door, I approached it from the side, skulking, my whole body tensed for impending violence. Thinking of the single punch I'd decked Jack with, I had resolved on the walk into the complex to give Cuckold one chance to be reasonable, then deck him, too, and quickly claim the wallet before he had a chance to figure out what hit him. I was in a bellicose mood and, crude as it was, that was my plan.

At the front porch, I pressed my ear to the door, but didn't hear anything. A few feet down the corridor I noticed a sliding glass door, partially opened. That must have been Jack's escape route, I realized. I tiptoed over and cocked my ear toward the interior, listening. Nothing. I carefully pulled back one parcel of the curtains with the back of my hand and peered inside. The living room was a riot of strewn clothes, overturned furniture, and broken dishes. Draped over a puke-yellow bean bag I spotted what were probably Jack's faded Levi's. I started for it, then froze when I thought I heard something. It sounded faintly like someone was crying, but I couldn't be certain. No, on second thought, as I listened more closely, it sounded like someone was crying and another voice was moaning. The moans were rhythmical, as if sound effects for some form of bizarre sex.

I felt sick to my stomach as I slipped through the curtains into the living room, pushing the sliding glass door all the way open for an easy retreat. The bizarre sounds seemed to be coming from a bedroom at the end of a short hallway. I determined that the crying was definitely female while the moaning was male. An odious image leapt into my mind, unbidden but fully formed. I shook it off and crossed the room to claim Jack's Levi's. I rapidly rooted around in all the pockets, but the wallet wasn't anywhere to be found. *Shit!*

As the moaning and crying rose both in force and volume, I frantically foraged through the mess in the living room in search of the wallet, but I couldn't come up with it. Desperate now, knowing that losing both the wallet and the bands—not to mention Jack's broken nose and my smashed car—would be the *coup de grâce* for Babs to call off the wedding, I clambered down on all fours and began crawling along the carpeted hall toward the back bedroom like an infantryman in a DMZ. My heart thudded in my chest.

I bellied past a trail of discarded shoes and clothes, moving with the twisting motion of a sidewinder, carpet-burning my elbows. The apparel appeared in the traditional order one might expect of people disrobing for sex: shirts, pants, and finally undergarments. I recognized Jack's leather jacket, and I felt around in it as the twin moans of sexual activity and crying grew louder and closer, more heated and more strange. No wallet. *Goddamn it.* For a brief moment I wondered what my literary agent would think if she could see me now.

As I neared the bedroom, I began hearing not just moaning but voices to accompany it. Cuckold was berating Zaftig, haranguing her, "You don't think I fuck you, bitch? I'll fuck you."

When I reached the open door, I got my first appalling eyeful of what was underway. There's something violent about witnessing other people making love, no matter who they are and what the circumstances. Cuckold, a beer-bellied, barrel-chested, balding man with a disturbingly hairy ass, was on top of Zaftig, slamming away with a lobster-faced urgency, a jackhammer run amok. Zaftig was splayed out underneath, her hands tethered with scarves to the faux brass headboard. She was swinging her head back and forth as if swooning to some Baptist snake ritual as Cuckold slapped her face hard on both cheeks.

"You picked him up and fucked him, didn't you, bitch?"

"Yeah, I picked him up and fucked him," Zaftig said defiantly. "I'm a bad girl. I'm a *bad* girl."

Cuckold slapped her face hard without losing stride. "And was his cock as big as mine?"

"No, Daryl. Your cock is bigger. It's the biggest, I swear to God."

He slapped her again, grunting. "But you liked *fucking* him, didn't you, you fat little whore?"

"I liked seeing you catching me fucking him."
Whoa!

"I bet you did, bitch," was Cuckold's reply. "You're just a horny little fucking slut who likes

353

to be bad so she can be spanked, aren't you, huh?"

They fucked and bantered like that, taunting each other with mounting accusations of faithlessness. I took it all in from my low vantage point as my eyes roamed the bedroom searching frantically for Jack's wallet.

I was about to throw in the towel when suddenly I spotted it on the opposite side of the room, lying open on the dresser, ten forbidding paces away. Jack must have unpocketed it and brought it in when it was time to go for his condoms—at least the man had some semblance of sanity, given that Zaftig's vagina must have been a petri dish of every imaginable STD.

I hung my head, thinking what to do, breathing hard. The screwing continued unabated, their dirty talk bordering on the burlesque. Zaftig wasn't going to be a problem for me, obviously, because she was secured to the bed. Cuckold was the problem. Not only was he a big man, he was an enraged man—a potentially violent, pugilistic lunatic with an angry erection. Desperate for a quick resolution to the crisis, I hatched a risky plan.

The years without sex—probably a lie, I thought—must have numbed him because it took the son of a bitch a good fifteen minutes more before he finally gave it his Hail Mary shot. As his thrusts and running monologue sped up, indicating he was reaching the end of his sordid mission, I scrambled to my feet, dashed across the room, grabbed the wallet, and tore back down the hallway. Behind me, I heard Cuckold shouting, "What? What the fuck?" followed by Zaftig shrieking, "He got the thousand bucks! Get him! *Get* him!"

Cuckold came hurtling, massive and buck naked, out of the sliding glass door and tackled me on the dead run just as I was making what I thought was a triumphant escape around the pool. We plunged into the cold fetid water together. His weight dragged me down, holding me underwater. I flailed helplessly, hitting the bottom of the pool, as he relentlessly pushed down on my head. Precious seconds passed and my lungs started to surrender the last of their oxygen. In that suspended moment, as the final images of life passed through my brain, I saw Victoria and a succession of snapshots of our normal, loving life, and thought regretfully how stupid I was to have so royally fucked it up.

I pushed and struggled, feeling close to blacking out. Then I heard a sustained scream followed by a crash. All at once the weight that was holding me underwater was released and I popped to the surface as light as a cork, gasping for air. When my eyes finally focused, I saw Jack in the pool. He had Cuckold in a headlock and was towing him out into the deep end. Cuckold thrashed in Jack's strong, demented grasp, cursing and sputtering and trying to get his arms above water.

"Fucking stop it, man. Or I'll break your fucking neck!" Jack was screaming.

I clambered out of the pool, coughing up water and sputtering for air. Out of breath, I knelt down on the deck and inhaled deeply over and over in an effort to get my wind.

"Did you get my wallet?" Jack hollered.

Still in a daze, I shot up my right hand, wallet triumphantly aloft, Aeneas with the Golden Bough.

"Good job, Homes!" Jack let go of Cuckold and shoved him roughly away. Then he swiftly breast-stroked to the shallow end and climbed backward up the sunken steps out of the pool, wringing wet.

"You fuckers! I'll kill you if I ever see you again," Cuckold shouted from the pool where he was treading water. A number of people had poked their heads from their units to see what was going on, and I think Cuckold wasn't too eager to get out in his undressed state and chase after us.

Jack helped me to my feet, harnessed an arm around my torso, and said, "Let's boogie."

We half trotted, half stumbled back to my 4Runner like contestants in a three-legged potato sack race. Safely inside, Jack rooted through the sopping wet wallet until he found the wedding bands. They were in a small, square, blue felt jewelry sack. He emptied out the sack and cupped the rings in his hand to display them to me. I took my eyes off the road briefly and met his. Tears were actually streaming down the ravines of his scabbed face. You would have thought we'd won the state championship at the buzzer or summited Everest in a blizzard the way he was carrying on.

"You got the rings, man," he said through hysterical laughter and tears. "Fucking amazing. I want to hear all about it."

I regaled Jack with all the details on our drive back to Buellton. We were bedraggled and weary, but still keyed up and laughing, as we pulled into familiar territory.

"But you got the rings, man," Jack kept repeating as if he couldn't believe it, as if their existence alone was an epiphany. "I'm proud of you. I did not think you had it in you, Shorthorn."

"You owe me, Jackson. You owe me."

Back at the Windmill Inn, we showered and changed into dry clothes and then headed over to Ellen's Pancake House for a fortifying, celebratory breakfast. It was the day of the big Pinot festival and I wanted to load up on protein. Over breakfast, we continued to congratulate each other on the morning's successful raid. Jack was in stitches as I described the surreal bedroom scene at Zaftig's. We were both positively giddy, bonding again over our latest trial and triumph.

"So," I said as I dug into my five-egg Denver omelet, "today we have a glass—or five—of exquisite Pinot, a quiet dinner somewhere afterward, get you up to Paso Robles tomorrow in time for the rehearsal. Sound like a plan?"

"I do think it's time to settle down," Jack said. "One woman. One house. One piece of snatch. I'm looking forward to it." He smiled, and for a moment I believed him.

"Amen, brother," I concurred. "Amen."

Jack laughed again. "I still can't believe you went in there, Homes. Fucking outstanding."

"You were crying, man. I haven't seen a grown man cry since those reviews of our film hit the newsstands."

"I picked that up from Babs," Jack said, wanting me to believe he had seduced me with an act. "When she wants something, she cries."

"Yeah, right. I think for once in your life you were scared shitless."

Jack smiled wryly.

After a sip of coffee, I added: "You think Babs is going to buy the car accident?"

"I hope so." Jack gazed out the window at my damaged 4Runner. "Looks pretty much like she's been in a smashup to me."

"So does your face. You might want to reschedule the wedding photos. Wait until that mug of yours heals. You're going to do some serious camera damage."

"No," he said, proud. "I want to remember this face."

We settled the bill and then lumbered out. The storm had blown through and washed the skies clean. Everything glistened.

When we got back to the Windmill Inn, to our

utter astonishment we found Brad, the repentant boar hunter, perched on the hood of his Ford pickup thumbing through a *Soldier of Fortune* magazine. He jumped down when he saw us and greeted us affably.

"Jeeves!" Jack said, spreading out his arms to welcome our designated driver—seemingly forgetful of the fact that the man he was preparing to hug had only recently tried to shoot him. "Look at you, man."

Brad was spiffed up in a white cotton button-up shirt, dark pants, and a pair of dress shoes that were newly polished. Brad grinned. "Sorry if I'm a little early," he said diffidently. "I wanted to make sure I got here on time." His smile vanished when he got a closer look at Jack's face. "What happened to you?"

Jack gestured to the front of the 4Runner. "Got in a little fender bender," he said, trying his story out for the first time.

"How'd you get the scratches?"

Jack turned to me and shrugged. "Sorry, Homes, but I think we're going to have to do a number on the windshield to seal the deal."

"Whatever," I said wearily. "Get it on."

Jack turned his attention back to Brad. "Well, actually, Bradley, there've been a *couple* of incidents. When you get older, you'll understand." Brad nodded dubiously. Jack clapped him on the shoulder, and raised his voice as if emoting from a stage. "We didn't think you were going to make it, Bradley."

Brad shifted in place and looked down at his feet. Was this shyness I detected? Whatever it was, it was a complete transformation from the beer-drinking hillbilly who had fired a couple of shots at us for kicks. "Well, I would kind of like to get my gun and wallet back," he said.

"Well," Jack said in an exaggerated drawl. "We'll start with the wallet and put you on a point system with regard to the firearm."

"Okay," Brad agreed.

"I'm a little apprehensive about giving you the gun back just yet—all things considered." Jack slapped Brad on the shoulder again. "But I have a lot of sympathy this morning for guys without their wallets." Jack and I shared a confidential chuckle.

"That's cool," Brad said. "I like totally understand."

"I'm going to check for messages," I said, breaking up Jack's and Brad's pseudo-bonding moment. "Then, let's hit it. I've got a mean thirst for the grape."

In the room, I dialed home for messages. There were two. The first one was the now-familiar stentorian voice of the debt collector threatening all kinds of heinous future credit consequences. I was about to hang up, assuming the second message was destined to be an echo of the first, but I hung in there, fingers crossed.

The second call was from my agent. My heart quickened. Evelyn's message was brief, just saying call her. She also reminded me that she left the office early on Fridays. I glanced at my watch. It was 2:00 in New York; she'd probably be gone already. Or was I just afraid to call and learn the verdict? I slowly replaced the receiver in the cradle and stood up. I paced back and forth along the wall stacked with the cases of wine we had amassed on the trip, trying to interpret the tone in Evelyn's voice. If it had been good news, wouldn't she have said something? Maybe it was qualified good news and she didn't want to raise my hopes.

I went back outside, lost in my thoughts.

"What's up, Homes?" Jack asked. "Any news?"

"Agent called," I said tonelessly.

"Did you call her back?"

"She's out of the office."

"Got her home number?"

I nodded, thinking.

"Call her."

"I'll wait."

"What'd she say?"

I shrugged. "Nothing, specifically. Maybe it's gone to committee and a final decision has yet to be made."

"Well, you can call her from Fess Parker's."

"After I get a couple of tastes in me," I said, smiling uneasily.

"After you get a few tastes in you, absolutely." Jack peered at me over his blotched nose. "But not too many." Then, in high spirits, he clapped his hands together. "Okay, gentlemen, let's rock and roll."

We all piled into the 4Runner. Jack and I took places in the backseat while our designated driver settled in behind the wheel and fired up the engine. The dangling front bumper started rattling like crazy, but it didn't seem to bother anyone except me. Brad shifted into reverse and slowly backed up.

"Do you know where Foxen Canyon Road is, Bradley?" Jack asked.

"Yeah," he replied. "I live here. Remember?"

Jack flung an arm jauntily in the air. "Head that way, Jeeves! And tarry not."

Brad circled around the Windmill Inn and turned onto 246. Jack had surreptitiously slipped a bottle of sparkling wine into an ice bucket before breakfast and now he was handing me the dripping wet Byron for the uncorking duties. I did the honors with alacrity as Jack held out two plastic cups and nodded for me to fill them up. "It's our last day. Let's go out in style."

I filled the cups to overflowing, recorked the bottle, and dunked it back in the bucket. Jack handed me a cup and we toasted.

"Here's to good news from your agent," Jack said, broadening into a smile.

"Here's to your getting my car fixed."

"Here's to your getting my wallet back. Fucking awesome, dude."

I raised my glass for another toast. "Here's to your finally coming to your senses."

He toasted me back. "Here's to your ex-wife and her new husband. May they lose all their money in the stock market and have to take jobs at Starbucks."

I laughed. "Here's to your lovely fiancée, Babs. May she never learn what went down in this valley of sin."

Jack howled with delight. "Amen, brother. Amen. I escaped the wrath of God and lived to tell the tale!" He turned his attention to Brad, who was driving responsibly—staying below the speed limit, overusing the turn signals—making me wonder if his driver's license might still have a little probation time left on it.

"Bradley, what do you do for a living?" Jack asked. "Besides poaching wild boar and taking potshots at strangers, of course?"

"Construction," Brad answered, as he cautiously merged onto the 101 and headed north. "What do *you* do?"

"Work in the film business," Jack said matter-of-factly.

Brad turned around, startled and maybe a little impressed. "No shit. Are you a producer?"

"No, I'm an actor and a director."

Brad turned back to the road and the streaming flow of speeding cars. "No shit? I once worked on a commercial up here."

"What'd you do on it?" Jack asked. "Security?"

"No. Rigging," Brad answered, adjusting the rearview mirror so he could frame us in it. He

363

spoke earnestly into the mirror: "Can you get me a job in Hollywood?"

"I don't know, Bradley. But I've got some advice for you."

Brad swiveled his head around and said eagerly, "What?"

Jack bent forward. "Don't go shooting at prospective employers. Bad first impression."

Brad laughed nervously, or possibly dementedly, depending on how one interpreted his strange, stuttering snicker.

"That's all right, Bradley," Jack said, slapping him on the shoulder reassuringly. "You're a little nutty. But you're in luck, because we're the kind of guys who understand nuttiness."

Brad cackled again. In the mirror I could see his eyes pinched shut and his acne-stippled cheeks coloring red. Jack and I fell into a laughing jag. Somehow Brad's was bizarrely infectious. The Byron was beginning to sandpaper the edges and once again I felt myself dissolving into its delicious emollience. There was so much to think about: the fate of my manuscript, my tenuous life as a writer in L.A., and Maya. I wondered now if there was any way in hell that something could be salvaged from the wreckage of our last encounter. The champagne coalesced all my worries into one amorphous blur, distancing them with each palate-puckering sip.

I rolled down the window and let some warm air buffet my face. Jack was chatting up Brad, inquiring about his sex life of all things, but I tuned out and let the rushing wind mute their voices. I couldn't remember if I was so sex-obsessed before *my* marriage, but I also thought this particular rite of passage did something to a man. Maybe marriage isn't natural, I philosophized. Sure, bonding, coupling, that's in the genes, but perhaps marriage is just too inadequate an institution, faultily designed to curb our primitive instincts and preserve the family unit. Is that why men go nuts before taking the vows and women make such ceremonial pageantry of the whole thing? I suddenly tuned back into Jack, who was eliciting a confession from Brad that he'd surrendered his virginity on the high school football field when he was seventeen. I rolled the window up and rejoined the conversation.

"Homes, what was your first sexual encounter?" Jack asked, turning his florid face to mine, elated to be off on one last adventure.

"A car," I said laconically.

"Brad fucked a cheerleader on the football field," Jack roared.

"She *tried* out for cheerleader," Brad corrected, making an important distinction.

"Oh, a *failed* cheerleader," Jack teased. "Is that when you went off the beam?"

Brad cackled again. It sounded like an automatic weapon with a jammed trigger. He liked Jack. So did most who made his acquaintance.

Brad took the 154 exit and headed east toward

Foxen Canyon. Vineyards started to come into view as the terrain turned bucolically agricultural.

"You want to know where *I* first had sex?" Jack asked.

"We don't want to know, do we Brad?" I said.

"All right, I'll tell you," Jack said. "High school play. Her name was Nicoletta. I was her leading man."

"How fucking trite," I commented, with a smile.

"No, listen to this, Homes. After rehearsal, we used to hang out backstage and do it in our costumes. She had a thing about my costume."

"What was the play, *Come Blow Your Horn?*"

Jack laughed so hard I thought his nose bandage was going to come unmoored from his face. Brad cackled, too, even though it seemed unlikely he was up on his repertory theater.

"And guess what, Bradley?" I added. "He's *marrying* a costume designer."

Brad gave us another round of his rat-a-tat-tat laugh.

Jack, growing quickly tipsy on the bubbly, turned to me and sputtered, "God, that first snatch is something, isn't it, Homes?"

I looked at him and smiled. I had a vague memory of six months of heavy petting, ending one clumsy night in the parking lot of a Presbyterian church in five minutes of frenetic, soul-emptying penetration. I remember Lisa looked stunned, like, *Is that all it is?* Three months later I was holding her hand in a fluorescent-lit office listening to a gynecologist sympathetic to teenage mistakes, a thousand bucks lighter in the wallet, and scared shitless I had almost become a teenaged father.

"Jeeves! Did that cheerleader scream 'touchdown' when she came?" Jack asked, jerking me out of my reverie.

Brad wrinkled his nose up like a bunny and laughed his peculiar laugh all over again. It was beginning to grow on us.

Jack elbowed me in the ribs. "This cracker's cool." Then, louder, toward the front seat. "Critterman, you're cool, you know that? Just stay off the brewskis and you'll get through this journey."

Brad blinked and concentrated on the narrow, winding Foxen Canyon Road, feeling happily like he was now one of the gang. Jack, despite his facial injuries and fractured rib and bruised ego, was in the best mood he'd been in since the beginning of the trip. The prospect of losing those wedding bands must have weighed more heavily on him than I realized. Perhaps the early-morning tears had not been hyperbole after all. Okay, so he had fallen for Terra, but we both knew it was an unrealistic pairing, and that as the big day approached, reason and the comforts of marriage would prevail. As I watched him yuk it up with Brad, his face growing rosier and rosier from the champagne and the boisterous repartee, I felt just a trace of jealousy that he had finally found happiness with a woman and I had not.

Jack must have sensed my pensive mood because he suddenly called out to Brad to stop the car.

"We're not there yet," Brad said.

"I know. Just do what I tell you and pull over."

Brad steered the 4Runner onto the dirt shoulder of Foxen Canyon at the edge of a vineyard. The harvest here had already come and gone and the leaves on the vines had turned gold and ochre, foreshadowing winter.

"Get out, Homes," Jack instructed.

"Where're we going?"

He reached an arm across me and pushed open the door. "Come on," he urged, gently shoving me out. He turned to Brad. "We'll just be a few minutes, Bradley. Don't boost the car."

"Don't worry," Brad replied, shutting off the engine.

Jack and I clambered out. He hooked an arm around my neck and drew me into the leafy, neatly rowed vineyard. Billowy gray-white clouds mushroomed in slow motion in the creamy blue sky. Insects buzzed in the balmy air. A crow chattered territorially on a fence post when he heard our footfalls in the crusty dirt.

"So, what's the call mean?" he asked.

"I don't know," I said sourly. "All I know is a Friday-leaving-the-office call is not the same as a Monday-morning-I'm-dying-to-dial-those-digits call. All the scripts I ever sold, my agent was on the phone to me early." I looked down at the ground, which was appropriately crawling with ants feasting on a large insect.

"You've got to put it out of your mind. We're going to have a good time. You've been looking forward to this Pinot festival for a while."

I gazed off at the horizon. "I'm also a little apprehensive about seeing Maya there," I confided. "Thus, my less than enthusiastic mood."

"Let me handle it."

"I've *been* letting you handle it, and it's gotten seriously out of control."

"I appreciate your going into that chick's apartment and getting my wallet back. I will never forget that."

I nodded facetiously. "Yeah, yeah, yeah."

"And I appreciate your helping me put Terra in perspective. Had it been me and someone else up here, it might have been a different story."

"It's just the grape, man," I said. "It's just the grape."

"No, it's *not* just the grape," he protested. "Okay, so the grape liberates some shit, I'll grant you that. But that doesn't mean that shit isn't brewing down there, that it's some illusory nothing thing."

"Oh, *illusory*. Big word for you."

"Don't make fun of me, Homes." For a moment, he looked fragile.

"What's the point then?"

"The *point*? We had to descend, you and I. We had to go down. *In vino veritas* and all that shit you talk about."

"Okay, we had to descend," I said sarcastically. "To find what?"

Jack swatted one of the grapevines violently, annoyed that I wasn't getting the message. "Fuck, man, you know what I'm talking about."

Maybe I did but didn't want to acknowledge it openly just then. I'd always had trouble with men who wanted to bond, to get emotional, to slit our thumbs with Boy Scout knives and make a blood pact. I just never wanted to get that close. Not to Jack, not to anyone, and at that moment in the vineyard I realized that I was the lesser for it. And that Jack, despite his carelessness and amorality, genuinely possessed a depth of feeling that served him well and endeared him to others.

"You're not still sore at me?" he asked.

I shook my head, my mind on something that had been gnawing at me too long and needed to surface. Drawing a deep breath, I dropped the bombshell: "Here's the reason I'm being pissy," I started. Jack waited with his hands on his hips. "I'm not going to be able to make the wedding."

Jack's head sagged forward, his brows knit together, and his mouth hung open in stupefaction.

"You're going to have to press Peter into service. I'm sure it won't be a problem. Rent me a car here. Drive mine back when you get it repaired."

"Homes?" he said, a little plaintive.

"I don't want to see Victoria up there with her

370

new husband." I lowered my head. "Surely, you can understand that much."

"Oh, fuck, Homes! How are you ever going to get over the fact that you're divorced and she's no longer in your life unless you *do* see them together, in the flesh and blood?"

"That's your solution, not mine," I countered.

"You see them. You see they're just another couple, and I'm telling you it's all going to be fine. Trust me." Jack remained motionless, waiting for a change of heart.

I turned away. "Can't do it," I said.

Jack jerked around and shadowboxed one of the rootstocks. Then he turned to me, a little desperate. "I need you up there, man. It's important to me. It's the end of the cycle. The curtain call. Without you, it's incomplete."

I shook my head no in response.

Jack planted both hands on my shoulders and jerked me toward him like a coach chiding a player. "Why?"

"Because you lied to me," I said in a rising tone. "Victoria has a new husband and they're going to be there together. That's why Babs didn't want me to be the best man. Because *Victoria* didn't want me up there." I was hot in the face now. "You could have told me so at least I would have had the option. Now, I look like some fucking party-crashing loser."

"They've accepted your coming."

"Yeah. Under duress."

"Okay, so I wasn't on the up-and-up with you," Jack acknowledged, reaching deep into his arsenal. "But, we wouldn't have had this wonderful week if I had been."

"*Wonderful?*" I coughed out a laugh.

"Yeah, wonderful. The best."

I conceded that the week had had its moments, but it didn't change my resolve not to participate in Jack's wedding.

Suddenly, it was as if a light snapped on in his face. "Why don't you invite Maya?"

"Are you *kidding?*" I snorted at the suggestion. "Half a bottle of champagne and you're fucking stinko."

"She's got it all over Victoria, man. She is such a fucking babe. You walk in with her on your arm and you're going to be the story, dude, not me and Babs, and surely not Victoria and what's his name."

"Forget it."

"You want me to ask her?"

"What are you? A blockhead? You think she's even going to *talk* to either one of us after what happened with Terra? Not to mention the thousand-dollar hay roll. Forget it. Not interested."

"What if I get her to come?"

"That's not the issue, man," I said irascibly.

"What's the issue? Huh? Tell me?"

I faced him squarely. "The issue is: I'm going to be in the monkey suit on the sidelines while you and Babs and Victoria and Mr. New Hubby are whooping it up, celebrating the joy of matrimony. That's not a happening thing for me. Surely, you can sympathize."

"I understand," Jack said. "But I still want you up there. For me."

I fell silent, unreachable.

"Well, this is a fucking bummer," Jack said. "You've got me on a bummer now."

"Tell Babs and the family I had to go to the hospital because of the car accident. I'm sure she and Victoria will be delighted to hear I'm in traction and won't be around."

"You're *really* not coming?" Jack said as if it were finally dawning on him.

"No," I said stubbornly. "Weddings depress me. Especially ones where my ex-wife and her new husband are going to be present, fresh off their own honeymoon!"

"I don't believe this," Jack said.

"You don't get it. That woman was my Rock of Gibraltar for eight fucking years. She supported me through some tough times and believed in me. And I *fucked* her over. I've been wanting to find atonement ever since, but I can't find it." I paused. "And now, knowing there's no chance of any reconciliation is just more than I can bear."

"You can't keep running from your failures, Miles."

His words pissed me off precisely because they were true. "Can't do it."

Jack came forward and wrapped his arms around

me and put his mouth close to my ear. "It's going to be all right, man." I let my arms dangle at my sides, unable to reciprocate. He tried to hug me tighter.

I pushed him away and stared off. "Sorry," I mumbled.

Jack looked at me, crimson with anger. Then he spun in place and started stalking back toward the car. He got ten paces away, wheeled around and yelled, "Then I'm not fucking getting married!" He turned and cupped his hands around his mouth. "Hey, Brad! Let's get nutty and go boar hunting. I feel like shooting something!" He stormed off, slapping at grape leaves and leaving a wake of dust clouds where he'd stepped.

Jack wasn't taking off anywhere without me. That I knew. I felt guilty that I had waited so long to spring my resentment on him, not to mention my reason for not wanting to attend the wedding. Then, too, he shouldn't have hoodwinked me into coming to the wedding knowing that Victoria and her new husband were going to be there. I vacillated between my peevish feelings about the whole affair and Jack's big moment in the sun and what it meant to him to have me there at his side. After a long debate, I reluctantly came down on the side that Jack was right: I was being unreasonable in pulling the plug at the penultimate moment, and whether Victoria was remarried or not wasn't the crucial issue.

I let a few protracted minutes pass. The clouds

didn't seem to have drifted much and the crow hadn't stopped chattering the entire time. His anguished cawing was making me sick. I clapped my hands loudly and the crow rose with a furious clattering of wings and flew off at a low trajectory over the vineyard.

I turned and trudged slowly up the vineyard furrow back to the car. When I got there, Brad was sitting on the hood puffing a cigarette, looking bored. I climbed into the back and shut the door quietly. Jack had his arms folded morosely across his chest.

"All right, I'll go," I said, less than enthusiastically.

Jack slowly turned his head and gave me a glower.

"And try to have a good time," I reassured him, manufacturing a smile.

A smile dawned slowly on his ravaged face, and he appeared victorious for a moment. "It's going to be all right, Homes," he said consolingly.

I shrugged. "Yeah, I know."

Jack, relieved, raised his right arm and snapped his fingers sharply three times. "Jeeves! Tally ho!"

Brad flicked his cigarette away and leapt off the hood and returned to the driver's seat. He looked back at Jack, awaiting his marching orders.

"Fess Parker. On the double. We've got some Pinots waiting."

"Yes, sir," Brad said, springing into action and firing up the rattletrap.

"So, who's the guy Victoria married?" I asked as Brad started off.

"David somebody," Jack answered reluctantly.

"David who?"

"O'Keefe," Jack mumbled.

I turned and looked at Jack for a long moment. "Guy who directed *Lessons in Reality*?"

"Yeah," Jack admitted. "That's the guy."

"One goes up, the other comes down," I muttered, musing about my ex-wife married to a high-profile Hollywood director whose debut feature had been a critical and box-office success, assuring him of a solid future in the business.

"She wasn't right for you, Homes," Jack said, hoping to assuage any feelings of diminished self-esteem—not that I could sink any lower.

"Is there any woman really totally right for anybody?" I declared cynically.

"You find the best you can," Jack philosophized. "Then hang on for dear life."

I turned to him, taken aback. "That may be the most intelligent thing you've uttered all week."

"I may be dumb, but I'm not stupid."

"I think it's the other way around."

We both laughed.

Fess Parker Winery is a monument to kitsch: a large, wood building nestled amidst manicured lawns and manicured vineyards and gravel paths bounded by blooming flowers. My idea of a winery tasting room is a small, clapboard tool-shed with open windows, buzzing flies, stinky cheeses, and serious wines. Fess Parker's was designed to look like the lobby of a resort golf club, complete with wine pourers wearing identical monogrammed Izod golf shirts and flashing trained smiles.

At the entrance, Jack and I checked in for the Pinot festival and were each handed a tasting glass and a pamphlet detailing the representative wineries and the barrel samples they would be pouring.

As soon as we entered the festival setting I was disappointed. An hour after the noon starting time, the place was suffocatingly jam-packed with wine aficionados from all over California jockeying for position at the numerous booths. Clearly, the Santa Barbara County Vintners' Association had oversold the event.

All the local big Pinot guns were in attendance: Au Bon Climat, Calera, Brewer-Clifton, Sanford, Byron, and some lesser-known wineries like Tantara, Whitcraft, Longoria, Melville, Clos Pepe, and Ojai. Despite the obnoxious noise level and the elbowing necessary to get to the wines, I settled down and began to feel a tingle of excitement. Maybe we really would discover something new and breathtaking.

We threaded our way through the crowd, wine-glasses clutched to our chests, toward Au Bon Climat, a consistently solid producer of Pinots.

I noticed some of the regulars from Epicurus—Eekoo, with his own Riedel Sommeliers glass, and Carl, with a cheap-looking woman in tow—and it seemed like months since I had last seen them.

At Au Bon Climat it was four-deep to get a taste. After a frustrating, jostling wait, we finally managed to make our way to the front. We sampled through four single-vineyard Pinots, but the pourers, swamped by all the arms extending empty wineglasses and clamoring for more, were slow and we were constantly getting pushed and shoved. I quickly grew irritable.

At one point, Jack nudged me in the ribs and gestured with a nod of his head. I glanced in the direction he wanted me to look. Over the shifting room of oenophiles, I spotted Maya at the Brewer-Clifton station engaged in conversation with an older, sandy-haired man. I don't know if she had seen me first and was looking to see if I had noticed her, but she glanced over at me and, I thought, managed a smile.

I turned back to Jack. "She moves fast."

"I'm sure it's not a boyfriend," Jack said, making a face. "Guy's not her type."

"Depends how stocked his cellar is," I quipped, reaching my glass out for another taste of the Rosemary Talley single-vineyard. "Fuck, it's crowded in here. I can't get settled in."

"Call your agent, would you?" he urged. "Then you can relax."

"I've got to get some wine in me."

I went back through the Climats. They were uniformly fine, if not transcendent. But then what could compare to the rarefied Bourgogne Rouges that Maya had uncorked? I had new standards now and they were pretty exalted benchmarks to meet. I couldn't help looking over at Maya from time to time. She occasionally shot back a glance that I had trouble deciphering. Finally, bored with the glacial pace of the pourings, I broke away and went off to make *the call.*

Outside, I found a pay phone anchored to the side of the building. In the distance, motionless swells of Fess's immaculately tended vines spread in every direction. I had a buzz, but I wasn't drunk when I dialed Evelyn's home phone, reading the number off the back of an old business card. I decided I was in the perfect frame of mind for good *or* bad news.

"Hello, Evelyn?" I said, enunciating carefully in an effort not to slur.

"Speaking," I heard her familiar husky voice reply.

"It's Miles Raymond, your roustabout client, returning."

She chuckled a little. "Miles. How's your trip?"

"Pretty adventurous," I said. "Might be a book in it."

"Oh, yeah? Well, I hope you're drinking some fabulous wines."

"Oh, yeah, that I am. So, what's happening?"

She cleared her throat. "Conundrum passed," she said, getting right to the point.

"I see," I said, not sure what I was supposed to say.

"They really liked it, they really wanted to do it, but they had trouble figuring out how to market it. It was a tough call." She labored in an effort to find some consoling words.

"I see," I said blankly.

"I'm sorry."

I didn't say anything else. I was trying to figure out who exactly had punched me in the solar plexus.

"So, I don't know where that leaves us," she said, measuring her words. "I'm not sure there's any more mileage I can get out of continuing to submit it," she said, hammering in the final nail. "I think it's one of those unfortunate things that happens in this business, Miles. A terrific book with no home."

I was nodding, but again couldn't think of anything to say. I could tell this was difficult for her, too.

"Are you there? Miles?"

"Yeah, still breathing."

"I'm really sorry. We tried."

"So, I guess that's it," I said, unable to summon anything else.

"These things are so subjective. So many deserving books go unpublished. You're not the first."

Platitudes rushed in to fill the breaching chasm.

"I thank you, Evelyn. You've been great. Really. You believed in me when no one else did and you tried your heart out. What more can a writer ask?"

She didn't reply for a long moment. Her silence and her obvious discomfort with the call was her way of demonstrating just how awful she felt. She attempted to diminish the disappointment the only way she knew how. "Are you enjoying your trip?"

"I was," I said.

She laughed uneasily. "Well, write that book," she encouraged, trying desperately to conclude the conversation on an optimistic note.

"Right," I decrescendoed.

"I've got another call coming in, Miles. Don't be a stranger."

"I promise."

She hung up. And that was that. I stood there holding the receiver in my hand as though it were a dead bird. Slowly, I replaced it on the hook, then turned and stared at the vineyards. Everything was imploding, blurred by the despair that had rushed in over me. The landscape started heaving, the sky purpled, clouds raced across it at high velocity, the buzzing of insects rose dramatically in volume. I thought I might be going mad, or at least having a breakdown, and that this was how it happened. It began with visual hallucinations, a sudden retreat into a paranormal world where everything was heightened. Colors were vivid to the point of luridness. Sounds had strange timbres and loud, dissonant crosscurrents. I felt my heart racing. I unpocketed my vial of Xanax and swallowed two as quickly as I could. I planted one hand against the side of the building to steady myself. Shutting my eyes and closing off the world seemed to help. The bitter-tasting Xanax dissolving under my tongue reassured me a little. After a few moments, I mustered up my courage and went back inside, my future no longer hanging in the balance, but foundering instead with every shambolic step.

Inside Fess Parker's, the business and conviviality of wine sampling was fully underway. The white table-clothed stations were now all three- and four-deep. As the wine flowed and the participants grew increasingly inebriated, the noise level climbed until eventually it was difficult to hear the person next to you. I had suddenly lost all my love for Pinot Noir as the *ne plus ultra* of varietals and now viewed it coarsely as a vehicle to get sideways. With that purpose in mind, I bullied my way to the Brewer-Clifton station, stemware brandished. Out of the din, I vaguely heard some muttering—"Hey, watch out," "There's no rush," "Jerk!"—but I ignored it. My glass was given the usual one-ounce dollop. I jacked it home and belligerently held it out again for the second Pinot.

"Do you want to rinse your glass?" the Brewer-Clifton rep asked me. He had one of those supercilious goateed faces you see in audiences at cello recitals.

"No," I said crossly. "Hit me again."

I was poured another dismally tiny amount, and I practically inhaled it.

I thrust out my glass again. "Pour me a full glass," I demanded. "I'll pay for it."

He looked at me aghast. "This is a tasting, sir, not a bar."

I fished out one of the U.S. Grants Jack had given me and slapped it down on the tablecloth. "Give me a full pour," I insisted.

He sneered at my money, then turned brusquely away to serve another party.

Panic seized me. I scoured the tasting room and spotted Jack chatting up Maya. I could tell by the way Jack was gesticulating and the laughing responses that blossomed in Maya's pretty face that he was, indeed, trying his damnedest to make amends and charm her into coming to his wedding. I couldn't believe she would even talk to him after what had happened. But Jack possessed an uncanny ability to mend fences, smooth acrimonies, and come out on the other side unscathed.

Maya caught me looking and lifted her wineglass in a conciliatory little wave. She shot me a forlorn smile over the heads of the oenophiles and tilted her head to one side. I interpreted it to mean that she thought it was too bad things had gotten so fucked up.

I turned away, unable to bear the thought of actually talking to Maya now. The Xanax had begun to go to work on my central nervous system, dulling my senses. Combined with the wine, it was making me slightly disoriented. I returned my attention to the table. The rep was at the far end, pouring barrel samples and taking in the idiotic purple prose winespeak that filled the room. I picked up one of the bottles and brazenly poured myself a glass.

The rep darted over with daggers in his eyes and snatched the bottle away from me.

"What do you think you're doing?" he yelled.

"I need a drink. I'm not getting enough. I paid good money for this event and I intend to get my fill!"

"Buy a bottle and go somewhere else." He reached for the glass in my hand and managed to get a hold of my wrist. The wine sloshed out of the glass, Rorschaching my shirt.

"Oh, that's lovely," I said. "Thank you."

Out of the corner of my eye, I saw Jack hurrying over, zigzagging through the crowd. The Brewer-Clifton rep was snapping his fingers above his head, desperate to get the attention of a security person roaming the room.

"So, you're not going to pour me a full glass?" I persisted, knowing exactly how obnoxious I was being.

"You're going to have to leave, sir," he said officiously.

"Fuck you!" I shouted. Then, in juvenile defiance of his authority, I reached for the spit bucket—nearly full from a few hours of avid tasting—raised it aloft with both hands, and swilled from it. Pinot Noir—and God knows what else!—streamed down the sides of my face, but I kept guzzling, chugging it like a frat boy upending a pitcher of beer. Moments later I felt strong hands gripping my arms, but I maintained my hold on the bucket. When I had emptied it to its last, I calmly set it down and looked around. All attention was centered on me. I shouted: "Notes of burnt raspberries and truffles comingled with fresh dingleberries."

Jack broke into the circle to take charge of the situation. "It's all right, everyone. His mother just died."

Jack roughhoused me through a bewildered knot of oenophiles who had stopped to see what the commotion was and hustled me outside. My head was swimming from the staggering amount of wine I had consumed. My legs were rubbery and I thought for a moment that I was going to die.

"What's the matter with you, Homes?" Jack said as he led me toward the parking lot.

"Novel's dead," I slurred, barely able to stand.

"What?" Jack said, as if he were voicing from underwater.

"Dead matter. Waste of a forest."

"Oh, shit, man," Jack replied.

Brad clambered out of the 4Runner and hurried toward us.

"Help me get him in the car," Jack said to Brad. "He's had a little too much."

Jack and Brad each took an arm, helped me to my feet, and towed me back to the 4Runner. My legs dragged limply behind me, and my feet hoed the dirt all the way. To passersby I must have looked like a passed-out lush being hauled to the curbside. I remember Jack saying, "Where do you want to go?" All I could think of was fresh air and wide open expanses of sky, so I urged them to take me to the ocean, anywhere not claustrophobic.

I don't remember the ride out to Jalama Beach. Snatches of conversation, but that's about all. According to Jack's account later, I was babbling some pretty weird shit, as if I had fallen under the spell of some powerful force surging up out of the recesses of my unconscious. I vaguely remember him trying to cheer me up by claiming he had scored Maya as my date for the wedding, but of course that would have been before I poured a bucket of Brewer-Clifton's finest barrel samples of mass expectorations down my gullet.

The ocean at Jalama was wild, a vast washing machine of changing whitecaps churned up by a strong afternoon wind. The sky had been bleached of its blue and was the color of desiccated skeletal remains. The campground was too cold for camping, so the parking lot was deserted. The gusting wind blew sand from the beach across the asphalt in whispery drifts.

I remember staggering across the sand, angled

in the direction of the water. Jack kept pulling me back by the arm, then letting me go when I started screaming, then running to catch up with me.

"Homes? Where're you going, huh?" he implored, frightened.

"Hawaii," I shouted back in my drunken delirium. "I'm going to surf Waimea!" I plunged tangle-footed into the water. It was fucking frigid, but I didn't care. I saw the sun setting in the distance, hurtling a spear of infinite light directly at me and I thought that it was calling me, that it was where I was meant to go.

"Come back, man," Jack pleaded from the shore.

But I had seen the light, I had seen my path to heaven unfolding before me, and there was nowhere else for me in the universe.

When I was in waist-high water, I looked back and saw Jack pulling off his clunky shoes. A wave loomed and broke before I could react and I was sucked under. A moment later, I shot back up, spitting briny water and trying to regain my footing. I dived forward and began a flailing Australian crawl toward what I deliriously thought was the Promised Land. But I seemed to be moving backward. A muscular forearm hooked under my chin and pressed against my Adam's apple, and I felt myself being towed across the surface of the water like floating driftwood. I thrashed wildly about, but Jack wouldn't let go of me.

After a few minutes of struggling, waves bashing us and helping propel us shoreward, we finally managed to slog our way to the water's edge, soaked to the bone and shivering. The fight was out of me, the St. Vitus's dance had all but abated, and I lay there on the cold, cement-firm sand, powerless, broken, a dismal failure at both writing and suicide.

"You scared me, Homes," I heard Jack say over the roar of crashing waves. "You scared me, man."

I opened my eyes and saw a cloud-mottled sky. It seemed to be pitching back and forth, as if it were a two-dimensional backdrop mounted on gimbals and manipulated by a lunatic god. I sat up, turned onto all fours, and puked hard once. Jack had a hand on my neck, I remember, and was massaging it. After I had finished heaving, I lay back down on the sand, enervated. The vomiting had done some good and the cold swim had restored my circulation and I was slowly starting to emerge from my insensible state. I started to think about all the great writers who had ended their lives: Hemingway sucking on the barrel of a shotgun; Plath putting out her lights in an oven; Fitzgerald drinking himself to an early heart attack; Virginia Woolf drowning herself in a cold river; Anne Sexton gassing herself in her garage; Delmore Schwartz; Randall Jarrell; Malcolm Lowry; Yukio Mishima; on and on. I started laughing out loud. I can't kill myself, I thought. I'm too insignificant. I'm nothing. I'm a thumbprint on the first-floor window of a skyscraper, a smudge of excrement on a tissue surging out to sea along with millions of tons of raw sewage, a squirrel eating a nut as a car bore down on him. I started laughing.

"What's so funny?" Jack asked.

"I'm too insignificant to kill myself," I voiced my epiphany with a laugh.

"It's not the end of the world," Jack consoled.

"I know," I said. "Expectations were just so high, you know?"

"I know, man. Just fucking write another one."

The sky seemed to settle a little. Clouds came back into focus. Suddenly, a flock of pelicans flew low just in front of us, obscuring the sun and briefly shadowing us. Tears overwhelmed me.

"What's wrong?" Jack asked.

"Pelicans," I said, pointing feebly. "That's beautiful, man. That's beautiful."

There was a half minute of silence and then Jack started to laugh. His laughter, as always, was infectious and I started to laugh, too, through my tears.

"I wonder what Bradley's thinking?" I finally said.

Jack just laughed again in response.

"And we thought *he* was nuts."

Jack's laughter doubled and the ground shook from his convulsions.

Neither of us said anything for a while. It seemed pacific just to lie in the sand, facing nothing but ocean and sky, the real world blissfully at our backs.

"Maya said she might come to the wedding?" I asked weakly.

"Yeah, man. That's what I've been trying to tell you. You've got to call her. She wants to talk about it."

"Of course now when she finds out my book's not going to be published," I started, then faltered, my occupational cynicism momentarily failing me.

"I already told her you didn't have a publishing deal sewed up," Jack confessed.

"You told her?" I asked, horrified.

"Yeah. I figure why keep fucking lying."

"So, now I'm the loser divorcé who drank from the spit bucket whose novel was turned down by every publisher in New York?"

"That's one way of phrasing it," Jack conceded. "Except that you've got a lot of soul, brother."

"Oh, yeah?" I said wearily.

Jack sat up on his elbows in the sand. "Fuck, why do you think you're my friend? Why do you think I want you to be my best man?"

"Can't imagine. No takers?"

"No takers! Fuck. Give me a break, Homes. Give—me—a—break." Jack shifted into a sitting position and crossed his legs. "You understand me, man. You understand me better than Babs."

I didn't say anything. I clambered to a sitting position, my legs stretched straight out in front of me. Another flock of pelicans winged into view, gliding inches above the surface of the water, their lives simplified to foraging for food and procreating. Envy would be an understatement.

"How're you feeling?" Jack asked.

"Coming around," I said somberly.

He hesitated for a moment, then said, "You *are* coming to the wedding, I hope?"

I nodded slowly several times. "Yeah." I kept my eyes on the horizon. The sinking sun was glowing yellow-orange and losing its shape in the mist. The sea was colored a darker shade of blue, and the wind was letting up, quieting its cold, god-forsaken surface.

Jack climbed to his feet and brushed sand off his clothes. He hooked both of his meaty hands in my armpits and hoisted me up. I was still a little unsteady and shivery cold, so Jack wrapped his arms around me and clenched me tightly to his chest. He patted my back and kept saying, "It's going to be okay." This time I allowed my arms to raise up and reach around his torso in reciprocation. He pulled me even tighter toward him. "Come on, Homes. Let's go get some rest and then drink that Latour, what do you say?"

"Yeah," I said, giving the sun and sea one last admiring look over Jack's shoulder. "Let's do something."

We released each other, then trudged across the beach, stepping over driftwood and zigzagging around piles of seaweed, back to the 4Runner.

A dismayed Brad chauffeured us back to the Windmill Inn, our earlier camaraderie replaced by a downcast silence. Jack was no longer the life of the party, Brad was eager to reclaim his Remington for a job well done and get home, and certainly no one expected me to add anything to the somber atmosphere. My depression over the novel's failure was magnified by the tacit understanding that our friendship was coming to an end. Neither of us was in the mood for conversation.

When we arrived, it was night, and we were all bone-weary. Jack retrieved Brad's rifle from the room and ceremoniously presented it to him. Hands were shaken all around. Jack exchanged phone numbers with Brad and invited him to call him if he decided to move to L.A. Brad, in turn, implored Jack to get in touch with him if Jack heard about any grip or driver work. Then, Brad climbed into his truck and chugged off, waving a last good-bye out the window, redeemed.

Back in the room, I took a long, hot soak in the bath while Jack spoke quietly to his Babs. I assumed they were talking about things couples about to be married talk about, and I was relieved that the tension between them had finally ebbed.

After a fitful nap, we cleaned up and drove over to Brothers Restaurant in Los Olivos. Two sibling chefs had taken over Mattei's Tavern, a local landmark, and had transformed it into an unpretentious gourmet restaurant. We got a table in the greenhouse where we were afforded a view of the lighted gardens. We ordered the prime rib, one of their specialties, then I uncorked the '82 and poured it off into a decanter. Jack wondered if it should breathe a while before we drank it, but I explained to him that old wines often radically change in the first hour they're opened and that it's important to track their deterioration, their fading glory.

There wasn't a problem with the '82 fading, however. The wine was so powerfully built at bottling that it still possessed all the necessary components to hold it together. The twenty years had softened it and rounded it and tamed its furred tannins, transforming it into a supple, satiny wine.

We were drinking a memory, one that would be forever associated with the memory of this trip. When I poured the last of the '82 into my glass, it left me gloomy. Maybe it was the moment. Maybe I wanted to tell Jack something I couldn't; whatever it was, it remained forever inchoate, imparting a sadness that even more wine couldn't assuage.

When we left Brother's I noticed that Jack was limping badly.

On the drive back to Buellton I asked him, "What's wrong with your leg?"

"I think I fucked up my ankle when I went into the ocean. Stepped on a rock or something." He grimaced. "It's killing me."

SATURDAY: DRESS REHEARSAL

The next morning I awoke to find Jack sitting on the edge of the bed, his left leg crossed over his right thigh, gently fingering his ankle, which had swollen overnight to twice its normal size. Jack looked at me with a pained expression and I just shrugged.

We packed up our luggage and cases of wine and checked out of the Windmill Inn. Then we rode back out to Lompoc Hospital for the third time that week. Our friend, the insolent young intern, reared back when he saw us and jestingly made a crude cross with both arms in front of his face like a nun shielding her eyes from an image of sin. Shaking his head, he recommended that we clear out of the area for a while, joking that the next time he saw us, Jack was sure to be in a body bag.

Jack was required to make yet another trip down to radiology. His hobbling was so pathetic that this time I went with him, offering my arm for support. The X-rays revealed a fractured ankle. The intern said it would have to be set or Jack could risk permanent injury.

While Jack was helped onto a gurney and wheeled into the OR to get his ankle set, I repaired to the waiting room.

At Jack's request, I called Babs at her parents' place. Her mother answered.

"Is Barbara in?" I asked.

"Who's calling, please?"

"Miles Raymond. Jack's best man."

"Just a moment," was her brisk reply.

Babs came quickly to the phone. There was a frostiness in her voice, so instead of glad-handing her, I got right down to the business at hand.

"Hi, Barbara, it's Miles. Jack and I had a minor car accident."

"What?" she shrieked.

"It's nothing to worry about. Jack's a little banged up, but we're going to be up there in a few hours, so don't worry."

I could sense her unease on the other end. "What is it? What's wrong?"

"He broke his ankle." I paused. "And his nose. And fractured a rib. Plus, one side of his face is a little mangled where. . . ."—I glanced up at the ceiling, hoping the good Lord wouldn't cast a lightning bolt down at me—". . . he hit the windshield."

"Is he all right?" she asked, practically frantic with concern.

"He's fine," I said coolly.

"Is he there? Put him on."

"He's in the OR getting his ankle set. He doesn't want you to worry."

"Miles?"

"Look," I chopped her off. "I've got to get going. We'll see you soon." I hung up, leaving Babs stranded with a gallery of lurid images.

Jack was pretty doped up when they brought him out of the OR an hour later, his face sad and droopy from painkillers and lack of sleep. Equipped with a pair of crutches, he hitched along in a stutter step back out to the car, a cumbersome plastic- and foam-ankle support weighing down his left foot. I helped Jack in, took his crutches from him, and tossed them into the back. Then I started up my rattletrap and we lurched off.

The sun was high in the sky as we rode 246 back to Buellton, where we swung onto the 101 and headed northbound toward Paso Robles and the wedding. Jack was in a suitably somber mood as I negotiated the drive with its pleasant rural scenery and intermittent ocean views. There wasn't a whole lot to say. Besides, Jack, zonked on Vicodin, kept dozing in and out, his head lolling from side to side.

Just before the turnoff to Paso Robles, I woke Jack up and said, "We're almost there. Do you want to go over our story one last time?"

He forced his eyes open and came half-awake. "No. Pull over," he said, remembering something.

"What?"

"Pull over," he snapped.

I steered to the shoulder and braked to a stop. Jack groped around in the back until he found an empty bottle of champagne under the seat. He climbed painfully out of the 4Runner and hobbled around to the driver's side window. Using the butt of the bottle, he starred the front windshield directly in my line of vision with one swift blow. Then he slowly limped his way back around the front of the car and climbed back into the passenger seat, sweating from the exertion.

"Sorry," he said.

I sat for a minute and stared expressionlessly through my spiderwebbed windshield. The way it altered the landscape in front of me seemed to mirror my fractured life appropriately. I bowed my head, dropped the shift lever into drive, and headed off.

We arrived late in the afternoon. Jack's future in-laws lived in a Mediterranean-style house perched on a sloping grass-covered knoll. The rising semi-circular driveway was gridlocked with cars, so I pulled up to the curb and braked to a halt. Seeing us approach, Babs and her extended family rushed from the house and fanned out over the massive lawn with the ragtag appearance of an unsupervised tour group. They surrounded the car, gasping and uttering *Oh my*s and *You poor thing*s. I helped Jack out, handed him his crutches, and turned him over to the care of his future bride. She and the others were grouped around the front of my 4Runner, examining its sorry condition. Coupled with Jack's scary appearance, it was determined then and there that the rehearsal would be a run-through without Jack and me. They seemed to accept our lame, but well-rehearsed, explanation for the accident, focusing more on all the planning and money that had been poured into the wedding. I got the impression they were desperate to prevent it from being postponed.

I didn't hang around long enough to find out if my presence was needed or desired. Wanting to get settled, I climbed back into my car and wandered out to the freeway, where I found a Motel 6 and checked in. The room bore all the traditional features of any depersonalized budget-motel. After an hour of staring at the white walls and reflecting on the past week, I got up and rattled off in my car to find a restaurant.

I ate alone at a franchise steak house in a relaxing silence. Tapering off, I had two glasses of a good local Zinfandel and called it a night.

Back in the motel room I tried to watch television, but quickly grew restless. I called Jack and gave him the number where I was staying. He told me that Babs's dad had arranged to have a rental car at the house that I could drive back to L.A. after the reception. Paranoid that he was possibly being eavesdropped on, he cut our conversation short.

After I hung up, the silence in the tiny room grew oppressive. I drifted out to the concrete balcony and watched the traffic hurtle past on the 101. Red lights astream one way, white the opposite. With the exception of an occasional 18-wheeler laboring up the grade and grinding its gears, the noise was an unremitting drone.

Back inside the room, I fiddled around with the business card that Maya had scribbled her phone number on earlier in the week. Screwing up my courage, I dialed it. Her voice mail answered.

"Maya, it's Miles. Hey, I'm up here in Paso Robles. The big wedding's tomorrow. I understand you and Jack talked about your maybe coming and, anyway, I'm holed up here at the Motel 6, give me a call if you feel like it, um, maybe you'd be interested in breaking some plates with me, I don't know. Hope to hear from you."

I gently replaced the receiver on the cradle and switched the lights off and lay in the dark fully clothed.

The next thing I remember was the phone ringing. It was Jack. He spoke in sober, confidentially lowered tones from his cell phone. "Hey, Homes, are you okay?"

"I was sleeping," I said groggily.

"I think they bought the car accident."

"Congratulations."

"You're coming tomorrow, aren't you?"

"Yeah, I'm up here, aren't I?"

"Did you call Maya?"

"Yeah. Left a message. She didn't call back."

"Do you want me to call her?"

"No. Don't. Please."

There was a belated pause. Finally, he said, "I had a great time."

I didn't say anything.

"Do me a favor tomorrow, will you?"

"What's that?"

"Dance with Babs. I'm out of commission. I want to see you dance with her."

"You're going maudlin."

"Fuck, I'm not going maudlin."

"Okay, I'll dance with her," I said to shut him up.

"I love you, man."

"Jesus! Cork that bottle. Good night, Jackson." And I dropped the phone on the cradle.

A few minutes later, just as I was dozing off, the phone rang again. Thinking it was Jack with some more paternalistic counsel, I answered crossly, "What?"

"Is this Miles?" Maya's voice woke me.

"Yeah. Maya?"

"Yeah."

"Hi."

"How are you?"

"A little worn out."

"I can imagine." She laughed uneasily. Then, after an awkward silence: "You called?"

"Do you want to come to Jack's wedding reception tomorrow? I realize it's pretty last-minute. Of course I would have invited you earlier in the week, but, you know." I hoped making light of the Jack/Terra fiasco was the right way to go.

She didn't laugh. "I can't," she said. "I'm working."

"Oh."

There was another silence. Sentences formed and then broke apart unspoken before I finally said, "Maybe I'll stop by in Buellton after the reception and say hello."

"What do you want, Miles?" she said plaintively, rather than coldly, tired of bullshit.

"I'd like to see you."

"Why?"

"Because I enjoy your company."

There was a pause on her end. I pictured her puzzled face and pretended it was different. "I don't think that's a good idea," she said.

"Oh," I replied, pierced by the rejection. "Okay, so I won't, I guess."

"You live three hours away, Miles. That's not going to work for me."

"I understand."

Neither of us said anything for a minute. I heard traffic, but that was it.

"I don't think a relationship is what you're looking for anyway," Maya finally said.

"How'd you reach that assessment?"

She cleared her throat. "I think you're still hung up on your ex-wife and all women are but pale reminders of her and will never be enough."

I didn't say anything, frozen in place.

"Am I wrong?" she asked, after my silence had grown excruciating.

402

I looked up at the ceiling. "Perhaps not. But I'm trying to let her go. It hasn't been easy."

After a pause, she said, "Is that why you're drinking yourself to death?"

I didn't like having my face pushed into my own shit and my voice sharpened: "I don't know. I thought you admired that ability of mine."

She collected herself. "I like the Miles in between sober and drunk, when he's still comparatively happy and believes there's hope for life."

It was like a second curare dart and I hung my head and stared at my feet. If I were capable of tears, they would have come then. "That's an elusive Miles," I finally said.

"I would like to think not," Maya said, her voice flat.

"Sorry I called. I didn't mean to presume there was still anything between us." I tried to bite down on my addendum, but couldn't: "Or ever was."

Neither of us said anything, but neither made the move to hang up. I could hear her breathing on the other end, waiting for something.

"I'm sorry," I said.

"Your friend's wedding must depress you, huh?" she asked perceptively, shifting to a softer tone.

"I guess, yeah."

There was another awkward silence. Traffic roared on the other side of the wall as if closing in on me. The beginnings of an anxiety attack started to gather momentum as my bleak feelings snowballed. I hoped she would keep talking, would say anything at all.

"You really want me to come to this thing?" she finally asked.

Relief briefly washed over me, and I brightened. "You wouldn't be any more unwelcome than I am."

She rasped a chuckle. "Give me the details."

I gave her the details.

"All right, I'll think about it," she replied, more as if she wanted to conclude the call on a ceasefire note than as if she were really considering coming.

SUNDAY: THE BLESSED EVENT

The wedding was held in a large Mission-style church in the heart of old Paso Robles. It was one of those high-ceilinged places with dark wood crossbeams, painted frescoes, stained-glass windows, pilastered walls, burnished pews, and baroque religious iconography decorating the apse. As the two hundred or so guests filed in, Pachelbel's "Canon" thundered from an upper-level organ. Sunlight rayed through the colored windows, painting the church in an iridescent splendor.

In an effort to diminish the magnitude of his various infirmities, Jack stutter-stepped in discreetly from the wings and took his place at the base of the altar next to me, he in his formal black tuxedo and me in my Burgundy-colored, velvet eyesore. We stood shoulder to shoulder, but he refused to look at me. I knew he was afraid I was going to start cracking up, and then that would make *him* start cracking up. With his ankle cast, raked face, and broken nose, it was a surprise to me that the entire congregation wasn't already in hysterics. It was fitting, however, that he had landed in a house of worship. What he needed more than a priest to administer his wedding vows was a spiritual cleansing of his depraved soul.

When the wedding party was all in place and Pachelbel's "Canon" had ended, the priest intoned a few words, then music filled the church again, signaling the beginning of the wedding processional. Sensing something momentous in the ceremony, Jack and I both turned and watched Babs in her traditional white gown, complete with beaded veil and flowing train trailing over the tile, glide to the altar escorted by her proud, imperious-looking father. I glanced furtively at Jack; the big lug was wiping away tears with the back of his hand. Tears of relief, I assumed.

Then, the sacramental rite turned serious. The priest solemnly read the vows, the *I do*s were iterated without hesitation, and the newlywed couple briefly kissed. Throughout it all I reflected on my own wedding, sentimentalizing it in my fractured memory. When Jack and Babs exchanged rings I had to look down and bite my lip to keep from bursting out laughing. All I could think of was where those personalized bands were a scant 48 hours ago. Oh, well I thought. Though he was damaged goods, I had delivered Jack to the altar in virtually one piece. Mission accomplished.

As they paraded back down the aisle, passing beneath the nave and atrium with colored light spilling over them and Jack hobbling awkwardly on his crutches in an effort to keep pace, I caught a glimpse of Victoria with her new husband. I hadn't seen her in months, but she looked sensational in a dark blue designer dress that I'm sure had cost her a fortune. Her husband was a stocky guy with a head of thick wavy hair and a chiseled face that exuded quiet self-confidence.

When the wedding ceremony had concluded and the organ music had faded and the rice had been tossed, I walked alone out to the parking lot. A marine layer had come in while we were in the church and closed off the sky, dulling the grounds and appropriately reflecting my glum mood. A chilly mist came with it and I hugged my chest and shivered.

As I climbed into my wreck of a car and fired it up, I spotted Victoria being helped up into a mammoth black SUV. She had obviously traded me in for a security blanket—although the armored vehicle seemed like overkill. Her new husband closed the door gently on her, making her disappear behind the dark-tinted windows, then strode around to the driver's side, climbed up into the cockpit, and roared off. I closed my eyes and leaned back, debating whether I should just make the exchange for the rental and blow off the reception, which was likely to be more depressing than I could tolerate. No, I remembered, I had promised Jack I would dance with Babs.

The reception was held in the backyard of the bride's family's house, and it must have cost close to six figures because there were Japanese lanterns and a live band and numerous food stations overflowing with platters upon platters of shrimp and prime rib and, of course, all the champagne and wine that Jack and I had picked up in the course of our Dionysian week, and then some.

Once I started drinking I knew it was going to be difficult to stop—under nerve-racking circumstances it always was—so I concentrated hard on pacing myself. I poured a glass of champagne and then worked my way over to where Jack was schmoozing the relatives. In their company he was a changed person. Charming, decorously so, even if it was all a role he was destined to play. We exchanged a few nods, confidential winks, and wry smiles, but that was the extent of our interaction. Jack was heading off into another world, one I could only be a peripheral part of now.

The jazz ensemble started up and Babs came over to where Jack and I were making small talk. Jack elbowed me, so I turned to his wife and said: "Do I get a dance with the bride?"

"Sure, Miles," she said, swept up in the emotion of the moment. She held out her hand and I took it and we walked out to the middle of the yard where a parquet dance floor had been laid down. We danced to that treacly wedding standard, "The Way You Look Tonight." It was a slow number so I held her lightly in my arms close to my body. She was a slender, beautiful woman with medium-long hair that was pulled into an upsweep of waves for the once-in-a-lifetime (she hoped!) event. Her silk Dior wedding gown felt quietly luxurious, further emphasizing the gulf that was opening up between Jack and me.

"So, did you two have a good time?" she slyly asked as we stepped to the melodic rhythms.

"Up until the car accident," I skirted the question.

She laughed and threw back her head and looked at me with the benevolent expression of a gently scolding mother. "How'd that *really* happen?"

I narrowed my eyes, trying to read her. "Jack told you, didn't he?"

"I'd love to hear your version."

"His is better."

Surprisingly, she threw back her head and laughed again. Then, she brought her red-lipsticked mouth close to my ear and whispered, in a nastier tone, "Did he fuck anybody?"

"Barbara," I said, holding her away from me, feigning shock. "Would I allow that to happen?"

She gave me a skeptical look, then erased it with a smile like she didn't really care. We resumed our cheek-to-cheek dancing position and she brushed her mouth against my ear and said, her voice roughened, "Well, if he did, tell him we're even."

Touché.

The band finished the number and I thanked Babs for the dance, kissed her on the cheek, and wished her good fortune.

I strolled over to the drinks table and poured a second glass of champagne. When I turned around, Victoria was standing in front of me. Her black hair was cut shoulder-length and she was wearing a little more makeup than she used to, but otherwise she looked exactly as she had the day I married her, and I had trouble meeting her large hazel eyes.

"Hi, Miles," she greeted me—somewhat formally, I thought.

"Hi, Vicki."

We awkwardly kissed cheeks like Hollywood phonies.

"How're you doing?" she asked.

"Could be better. Could be worse," I said evasively.

"What's happening with your book?"

"Was universally rejected." I held up my glass of champagne. *"C'est la vie."*

"That's too bad," she said inadequately. "So, what're you going to do? Get a job?"

"I don't know. I just found out. Write another one, I guess."

Possibly afraid that the topic was going to shift to money and I was going to hit her up for a loan, she scanned me from head to toe and scoffed lightly, "What is this you're wearing?"

"My tux," I said. Jack and I had not had time to swap my unconventional outfit for something more traditional.

Her face twisted into a good-natured smirk.

"You don't like it?"

"That color, what is it?"

"Pinot Noir. I would have rented the Chardonnay, but they were all out."

She shook her head, laughing. I always could make her laugh. I think she liked the humor part more than the reality part.

"I didn't realize this was going to be such a formal affair," I excused myself. "You're looking terrific. Still working for what's his name?"

"Yeah. We've got a big film in preproduction. A terrific script that I found. I'm a full-fledged producer now."

"That's great," I said, not interested in her elaborating and making me feel smaller than I already felt.

"Are you dating anyone these days?" she asked, an embarrassed giggle trailing her words.

"No. I'm undatable."

She frowned for a brief moment, then she broke into a smile and said, "So, I'm remarried."

"Yeah. That's great. Congratulations." I swept my champagne glass across the gala reception. "Everybody's getting married. A year ago it was all divorces, now it's all marriages. I'm sure it's cyclical."

She looked at me reprovingly, bristling a little at my cynicism. Please, I could sense her thinking, not here at this party, where everybody was celebrating the promise of the newlyweds' future together.

I sipped my champagne, sensing the shift. Then I drained the glass. I reached around and fished a chilled bottle out of a large tub of ice water and refreshed it. I poured a second glass for Victoria and offered it to her.

"No, I can't," she said, holding up a hand to halt me.

"Quit drinking?"

"No." She paused for effect, then said: "I'm pregnant."

I drained half my glass and refilled it to overflowing, then returned the bottle back to its icy waters. "Congratulations again."

"Thank you," she said.

In that moment I realized that not only had we stopped growing together but that I no longer really knew her. The eight years we had spent together were now buried in our separate memories, passionlessly chronicled by photos and other now-meaningless memorabilia. Touching, talking intimately on a daily basis, sleeping together, were now so much confetti fluttering into the void. Someone once said that you only loved once in your life, and perhaps, instead of other women, I had filled the emptiness of Victoria's leaving with the more constant pleasure of wine. She could be a cruel mistress in the morning, but by evening she would always rise and greet me with a welcoming embrace. Bushwhacking my way through life companionless, and often rudderless, it was a relief to know that I, too, could feel desired by someone or something.

Victoria's new husband materialized out of the crowd to reclaim her. They wrapped their arms around each other to demonstrate the solidarity of their recent marriage. His head looked even bigger and his features more chiseled than they had from afar.

"This is David," Victoria introduced. "David, this is Miles."

"I've heard a lot about you," he said diplomatically, extending his hand.

We clasped hands and he tested mine with a bone-crushing grip. "Likewise," I said collegially, the champagne having begun to deaden any feelings of envy.

In the end, I guess Jack was right. It *was* a good idea to see Victoria in the flesh with her new husband, instead of allowing them to float around in my imagination where I could spend my life in speculation.

"Take care of yourself," Victoria said, somewhat wistfully. "And stay in touch."

"I will."

David winked at me, a practiced affectation that seemed to serve him well in awkward social situations. They wheeled around and strolled arm-in-arm toward the dance floor. I looked away. Across the yard I could make out Jack still ingratiating himself with Babs's father. He was laughing hard, but I couldn't hear him over the noise of the party. He was drifting away now like a boat heading out to sea and dwindling to a dot on the horizon. All his body movements and laughter appeared in pantomime to me. He had retreated into a silent movie of his own making and I was watching from the anonymous remove of a theater seat. He was flickering, growing distant, fading like the '82 Latour.

I could tell Jack was making Babs's old man laugh, no doubt fabricating colorful stories about the origin of his various injuries. Then, in a fleeting instant, Jack turned and caught my eye. He held up a glass of red wine high in the cool night air and toasted me over the festive crowd. It was as if those opposing lanes of freeway lights were streaming between us now and we were slowly withdrawing into our separate universes. *Good-bye, my friend,* I mouthed silently. *Good luck.*

I turned my attention back to the tub of champagne. The bobbing bottles of Byron and Veuve were waiting for me like meowing cats. I started to pluck one out when I heard a familiar voice at my flank. "Hey, you."

I turned and found Maya. She was wearing a mauve sleeveless summer evening dress that stopped just above her knees. Her brunette hair fell over her bare shoulders and trellised her arms. She tilted her head slightly and smiled gently. I was stunned she had showed.

"Champagne?" I offered, feeling a smile creasing my face.

She pursed her lips and shook her head. "Do you still have that '82 Latour?"

"Sorry. I drank it with Jack. I didn't think I would see you again."

"How was it?"

I shrugged. "Still prefer chasing Pinots."

She smiled, then shifted her head toward where the party was in full swing. "I'm not really into wedding receptions, are you?"

"No," I agreed. "They're so damn obligatory."

"Plus, I don't know anybody here, other than you and Jack."

"We make up for the rest."

Her smile broadened into a grin. "Do you want to go somewhere private and talk? I know a couple of places here in Paso Robles."

"Sure," I said. "That'd be nice."

Maya came forward and kissed me lightly on the mouth, seeking reassurance that it was okay she had come. She withdrew a few inches, but no more, and her voice dropped into a lower register. "Hi."

"Hi. I'm glad you made it. Really glad."

Her eyes penetrated mine meaningfully. "Yeah, I am, too."

"Before we bolt, do you want to meet my ex-wife?"

"Not particularly."

"How about Jack's bride?"

She shook her head again. "They're going to be divorced in a year anyway."

I laughed hard. "I forgot how amusing you are."

"I have my moments." Her eyes sank into mine. "Besides, I only came to see you."

I nodded. "Do you want to go now?" I asked.

"I'd prefer, yeah. Unless you need to hang out."

I glanced at my watch. Then I looked up. From the dance floor I could make out Victoria looking over at me with a questioning expression. I turned and faced Maya. "Is that comet still up there?"

Maya threw back her head and searched the night sky for a moment. "No, I think it's gone."

"Kaput?"

"With all the clouds we wouldn't be able to see it anyway. Besides, it happened millions of years ago." She lowered her gaze and smiled at me again. "All that matters is what's happening now."

I nodded a few times, staring inward. I gave one more long look at the wedding festivities. Victoria and her new husband had been swallowed up by the crowd and I couldn't see them anymore. Jack and Babs and the relatives, compelled by the twin forces of propriety and sentimentality, had been rounded up and herded into an illuminated gazebo in the rear of the backyard where wedding photos were being taken. As the photographer leapt around snapping pictures from various angles, one of the flashes left an afterimage on my retinas, and I knew that moment—which captured Babs and Jack smiling and laughing—like the comet, would be forever fixed in place and time. Tears came to my eyes and the party scene went blurry. I turned to Maya.

"What's the matter?" she sweetly inquired.

"Oh," I faltered, blinking her lovely face back into focus. I tilted my head toward the starless sky and murmured, "I think for once He listened."

I bowed my head and looked down. Maya had her lips pressed together, sensing a private thought inadvertently uttered out loud, and let it hang in the air for a moment. Then she offered me her arm to take and said softly, "Come on, Miles. We don't belong here."

I accepted her waiting arm.

ACKNOWLEDGMENTS

I want to thank profusely my erstwhile agent, Jess Taylor, for resurrecting me from the dead. Without him, I would not have written the book, nor would it have found its way into the hands of the gifted filmmaker Alexander Payne. Bottomless gratitude to Alexander who, with his talented writing partner, Jim Taylor, faithfully adapted it for the screen, and gave me the experience of a lifetime. Scattered, but equally profuse, thanks to my brother Hack, Bobbie and George Kohrt, Scott and Wendy Paulin, Amy Hobby, and Brian Lifson; all of whom helped me in a variety of ways when times were grim. I want to single out: Shiri Hoshen for her unflagging friendship; Robert Roth for introducing me to Jess; Julian Davies, for educating me on wine free of charge; Roy Gittens for unwittingly providing the inspiration for one of the characters; and, after the die was cast, Krista Carlson for her love, support, and numerous, mind-numbing copyedits. Thanks to my current agents, Marti Blumenthal (Los Angeles) and Dan Strone (Trident Media Group, New York), and to my producing partner,

Michael London, for tirelessly championing me. A special thank you to Elizabeth Beier, my editor at St. Martin's, for her diligent work on the book. And last, but not least, for Barbara Schock for too many reasons to enumerate; without her and her family's support I would never have made it this far.